Island
of the
Doomed

Island
of the
Doomed

STIG DAGERMAN

Foreword by J. M. G. LE CLÉZIO
Translated by LAURIE THOMPSON

University of Minnesota Press
Minneapolis

Originally published in Swedish as *De dömdas ö* by Norstedts,
Sweden, in 1946; copyright 1946 Stig Dagerman.

First published in English in Great Britain by Quartet Books
Limited, 1991

First U.S. edition published by the University of Minnesota Press,
2012, by agreement with Norstedts Agency

English translation copyright 1991 by Laurie Thompson

Foreword copyright 2012 by J. M. G. Le Clézio

Published by the University of Minnesota Press
111 Third Avenue South, Suite 290
Minneapolis, MN 55401-2520
http://www.upress.umn.edu

LIBRARY OF CONGRESS CATALOGING-IN-PUBLICATION DATA
Dagerman, Stig, 1923–1954.
[De dömdas ö. English]
Island of the doomed / Stig Dagerman ; foreword by
J. M. G. Le Clézio ; translated by Laurie Thompson. — 1st U.S.
ed.
Translation from Swedish to English.
ISBN 978-0-8166-7798-6 (pb : alk. paper)
I. Thompson, Laurie. II. Title.
PT9875.D1213 2012
839.73'72—dc23   2011044458

Printed in the United States of America on acid-free paper

The University of Minnesota is an equal-opportunity educator and
employer.

20 19 18 17 16 15 14 13 12   10 9 8 7 6 5 4 3 2 1

Contents

Foreword: The Star of Myself

J. M. G. Le Clézio

Here is undoubtedly one of the strangest novels of
the twentieth century, written in haste and with passion, and which irresistibly evokes another book (not
a novel, but where to draw the line?) published in
the middle of the preceding century by a young man
(of the same age, in fact) under the title *Les Chants
de Maldoror*. In reality, very different books, one produced by the unbearable exile of a young Uruguayan
in the most typically intellectual city of his time, the
other by a militant in the anarchist movement that
culminates in the rise of fascism and war. Yet, what
one reads in these books is similar, even if Dagerman
never mentions the writing of Isidore Ducasse: one
finds in them the same resurgence, the same iconoclas-
tic and torrential, uncontrolled, darkly jubilant will,
the same self-destructive humor. What links these
two books is the period, the extreme conformism of
the bourgeoisie of the Second Empire for Ducasse,
for Stig Dagerman the loathing of the right-thinking
politically involved people, the self-satisfied militance
during clashes between classes, and the birth of great

humanitarian undertakings—all of which was negated by the cowardice of abandon in the Spanish civil war and by the obscenity of the dictatorships in the Soviet Union and Latin America. Another literary example of the spirit of the times would be the pessimistic and suicidal Juan Rulfo, author of one of the key novels of the twentieth century, *Pedro Páramo,* conceived in the violence of the counterrevolution in Mexico in the 1930s.

But is Stig Dagerman only the product of an era? *Island of the Doomed* is his second novel, following closely on the heels of the literary success of *The Snake,* and it places him on the path of intellectual and moral solitude. It is—as will be all his novels—a text loaded with his own experiences, his rebellions, his failures, but (more than any of the others) consisting of curses and despair, articulating his rejection of all humanistic comfort. A purely anarchist novel? No doubt, since it denies all progress achieved through violence and shuts itself up in the closed universe of a small island, at once stalag, military camp, penal colony, and insane asylum. A piece lost in the imaginary republic of Velamesia, where there are no laws, no money, no armed police—in short, an anarchist paradise, except that "you kow-tow with the same unwilling willingness, let yourself be subjugated, feel this fatal sensation of impotent inferiority."

Like the exile of Montevideo, Stig Dagerman is led to a rediscovery of all the elements that have obsessed his life—the crushing image of the father, Cronos, who tortures and devours his children, and the tyranny of the Boss, wielding an absurd and flexible authority in his reign over a servile population locked into a nightmarish décor on this island surrounded by a poisonous lagoon where—supreme punishment—prowls a great invisible exterminating fish. The only heroes on this island are the romantic Lucas Egmont from another century; Loel (who reminds of Falmer in *Les Chants de Maldoror*), angelic, devoted to sacrifice; the giant Tim Solider; or the lost aviator Boy Larus, who finds consolation only next to an erratic young Englishwoman. The hero is all those at the same time, obsessed by an invisible wound that eats at his body, like the fox in the Spartan fable. Stig Dagerman's imaginary is close to the Surrealists, except (and here again he reminds of Lautréamont) that chaos emerges from within the narrator, and no longer in his gaze on the external world. We are far removed from the absurd: on the contrary, for Egmont, war, organized crime, and treason are consequences of the unconsciousness of victims. "Living meant obeying and obeying meant never wanting anything, obeying meant receiving and passing on whatever couldn't be kept and letting whatever couldn't be passed on stay and form new wounds."

Dead end. As is usually said, on an island there are no thieves, because where would they hide? In the end, the captain is condemned to death, and the hero to live as a living dead person in his dream world where pure cruelty (the free lions, the sawfish of the depths) triumphs.

What we find astonishing and upsetting in Stig Dagerman's novel is the perfection of the destiny he portrays in the absolute ardor and sarcasm of youth, this destiny that is so short-lived. This tumultuous novel, a whirlwind of sensations and images, in a way contains Dagerman's entire oeuvre—his novels, his poems, his political essays. He holds them not like a matrix but rather like a fatal vortex in which everything is slowly carried along and broken down. For that reason, reading a book like *Island of the Doomed* does not leave us undamaged, and makes us question today our illusory certitudes. On the one hand, as the captain says, "the boundless solitude of the world, it's greater than anyone dares to imagine apart from a few ecstatic moments when there's nothing you can do about them, but even so, you can feel it in every nerve-end." And, on the other hand, like the trick stone hidden in the hand of the bettor Lucas Egmont, this superior force of existence (without which there is no existence), lucidity: "the open eyes which fearlessly scrutinize their dangerous position must be the stars of our ego, our only compass, the compass which decides which direction we take, because if there is no compass, there can be no direction."

In humble recognition to Stig Dagerman, who burned himself up to show us the way.

April 2010
Translated by David Thorstad

THE CASTAWAYS

Two things fill me with horror: the Executioner within me and the axe over my head.

The Thirst of Dawn

Mind you, gin with a touch of meltwater from a cascading mountain stream, a few half-chewed young holly leaves, a pinch of roasted cardamom soaked in gallic acid, hastily swallowed at dawn as the car door slams shut on the last peal of laughter – ah, well –

Lucas Egmont's right hand crept a little way in his sleep over the rough, glittering, salt-encrusted sand, dragged by his finger tips. Was it caressing a cheek? A long worm, white, but with thread-like, closely-packed joint rings in deepest black, suddenly seemed to emerge from the lapping surf and come wriggling over the gently sloping beach, menacing, terrifying. Was it real, or was it just a figment of his fear?

Lucas Egmont lay prostrate with his uninjured leg pressed close to the ground, a position not as comforting as it seemed, since quite soon after sunset the sand began to transmit a sharp, aggressive chill which enveloped his limbs in an inflexible film, hard as armour-plate, becoming ever more unyielding as this island fell further and further through the night.

Yes, fell. Was he alone in noticing that the nights no longer wafted down from some roof up above, or that daylight no longer surged in like white gas filling the black balloon? No, the shifts were violent and unexpected: candles lit to produce an apparently reliable flame, and then suddenly snuffed out – but the hand doing the snuffing was never glimpsed. Was he alone on this hurtling planet, this sand-strewn marble plunging down into the cosmic well? Transparent strata of air green at the edges, mauve streaks, deep-red flames flashing past and driving wedges like elephant tusks into one's own trembling being, which itself was constantly changing colour, chameleon-like, in the constant flux. Blue bands broken brutally asunder by exploding formations of violently yellow swallows' wings. Fathomless darkness, the same air, but the colour itself must have a consistency enabling it to check the speed of descent. The fall through the night was no less terrifying, but now the pace was slower. Swarms of sparks rose slowly in the form of stars encircling the island and were visible far below in a grey, milky layer where white rivulets trickled in as if from some hidden giant udder.

Dawn. Lucas Egmont, lying prostrate in the sand, his wounded leg with its pierced calf raised in a slight curve like a long bridge, sloping gently down on each side, was woken slowly by the grey, bitter-sharp streaks brushing his eyelids. His eyes cowered in terror under their trembling lids as he watched his hand coming crawling towards him over the sand. A swollen, toad-like creature with bleeding limbs. 'Go away!' he wanted to scream, 'Leave me alone!' – but the creature merely dug holes in the ground, from which dazzling white strands of smoke, as thin as copper wire, rose skywards.

Note his predicament: he wanted to scream but found

it impossible: his swollen tongue lay like a large, quivering, clenched fist in his mouth. When they'd run aground, the metal kegs of fresh water had been hurled overboard and split open against the sharp reef. Now they were lying there like seals halfway out of the water on the seaward side of the reef, and the slow swell, detaching itself from the horizon in an endless series of blue pulses, drummed all day long with its soft knuckles on their gleaming metal shoulders.

At least they had some music, then. The muffled, hollow roll of funeral drums droned on relentlessly, penetrating the swishing sighs of the surf, and as the island plunged through the scorching expanses of fiery yellow, Lucas Egmont could feel fine, live electric wires linking his auditory nerves to the restless throbbing from the reef. He tried to tear himself away from the agonizing noise by fleeing to the interior of the island, but the wires trailed behind him over grinding, bone-dry sand, squelching shallows, sharp-toothed pinnacles of rock, in whose shadows huge brown lizards, iguanas, lurked. Their noisy thudding pursued him through the dense, green, hissing scrub, pregnant with mysterious silence, into shoulder-high grass crowned with large, frightening panicles and filled with mysterious little sounds; from snakes, perhaps, or some of those little rabbits hungry Tim Solider claimed to have glimpsed at the edge of the island's undergrowth.

The run set his heart pounding, the wound in his calf opened up, and at last, exhausted by the loss of blood and the terror ripping him apart, he came up on to the open, weather-worn rocks looming high above the thin strip of sand which encircled the island like a frieze. There was usually one of the others wandering about up there, peering down into the lagoon for edible fish, gazing into the distance in the all too vain hope of seeing another, more amenable and more communicative island bobbing up and down against the horizon. 'Mr Egmont, Mr Egmont!' they would cry those first few days when the meat was still appetizing and healthily red in the red provision boxes that had floated ashore. 'Mr Egmont, let me help you! Your leg . . .'

Couldn't they hear the incessant drumming from the reef, throbbing away in his head through these fiendishly designed, elastic wires, no matter where he went?

Ah well! As he lay here, he wondered if it might be a dream after all. Could it really be true that these almost paralysed legs he couldn't prevent from trembling, their flesh swelling up and gradually turning blue – God, if only he had a knife – had carried him over the steep slope of the island, past these people wandering about without understanding the seriousness of his predicament, never mind their own? He'd have loved to prise open their jaws and convince himself once and for all that their tongues were just as much like grotesque, bloated, slimy lumps of sand as his own. Right to the very end, indeed, as long as there was one last drop of water left, if their legs would still carry them, they'd be scuttling around on the high ground as carefree as butterfly-hunters, sleeping through the dawn even though every change of light brought them ever closer to the bottom of the world.

Aaah! Without his being able to move a limb to prevent it, a whole series of groans, cadences with neither beginning nor end, suddenly started shooting through him, thumping at his diaphragm, rasping against his chest, burning into his throat, forcing their way like daggers past his tongue. Where were they going? Suddenly a noise spilled out all around him, seeming to transport him, to raise him up, to envelop him on all sides like water, running into his ears, hot and stimulating like steam from a bath; undercurrents carried him slowly through widening channels, and his body rotated slowly in response to their slightest movements, as if on a swivel; all the time, his skin could feel the gentle, gloved pressure from the noise, which was now becoming more intense; persistent, groping fingers stretched his skin until it shimmered like a transparent membrane in the penetrating green light of the water, his nerves coiled themselves painfully around three of those cruel fingers, and then sank down into fast-flowing, bitingly cold water: it was like being skinned alive until nothing remained but the sensitive core of his being – and then he woke up and found himself on the usual little meadow of his thirst-dream:

Grass, the grass of childhood with its soft, seed-laden tips, his pony Pontiac loping over the meadow, the grass whispering past its haunches; the saddle had come loose and was thumping, thumping against its shoe-polished black flanks. Racing over the long, green grass and flinging his arms round the neck of the dancing animal with a shriek of suddenly felt pain and incipient happiness. A damp muzzle imprinting itself on his nape, his bare neck, his hot brow, being forced gently down into the warm grass of summer. For it's always summer in this dream, with its big, white butterfly fluttering hither and thither around his summery head. Up in the saddle now, kicking against Pontiac's belly, the trees in the park dripping sun-drops, and look! That cricket ball Uncle Jim hit into the mists the other evening, there it is by the roots of that oak tree – but why not, let it stay there! Pontiac's panting now, its black hide's stretching tighter and tighter over its heart, lungs, nerves, but the boy in the red cap on its back is still urging it on with the heels of his shoes. Now Pontiac's galloping down the middle of the path in the big park, dust rising around its hooves; the tracks made by the calèche meander first one way, then the other, and as they career round a bend, it suddenly collapses on to its knees and its head thuds dully into the sand.

The gardener's children appear immediately from their hiding place behind the oak tree; they stand looking in silence, just looking in silence, at the horse and rider. A boy and a girl, their incongruously long arms hanging down like unemployed pendulum cords; their four eyes are like membranes stretched over their hatred, their clothes are scruffy and too often washed and, with some difficulty, Lucas Egmont recognizes them from the distant past as having once been his own. Neither of them steps forward, they just stand there in silence, looking at the rider and the dead horse; the four legs of the dead horse are still now, no longer twitching, and the dust slowly settles, forming a powdery film on the horse's hindquarters, which are still glowing with the sweat it exuded when it was still alive. Everything is still now, and the shadows cast by the oak suddenly become sharp black cavities chiselled into the road; the soughing of the leaves fades away, and beyond the park, the windmill with the damaged sail that can always be heard precisely because it's damaged, falls silent; the narrow, white path is behind him and in front of him, and beside him is Pontiac, the dead horse. The breathing of the gardener's children has overshadowed the world, the great park is veiled in lace and the clouds of the summery blue sky, even the twittering of the birds filter through as Lucas Egmont stands there beside the dead horse.

So as not to be overshadowed himself, or for some other reason he may not even know about until quite long afterwards, he takes out his silk handkerchief, bends down and polishes his brown shoes, made of the very best patent leather. He does it very slowly and carefully and methodically: first the long, rather pointed toes, till they sparkle like a halberd in the sun, and then the rest as far as the nicely rounded heels. All the time, he keeps glancing surreptitiously at the bare feet of the gardener's children; he wants to see them trembling, digging their toes into the sand, quivering with impatience before running off into the park. He simply wants to defeat their breathing. Then, with the same preposterous care, he brushes the dust from his riding breeches, all the time glancing guardedly at the gardener's children's bare legs: he wants to see them start dancing, shattering the strained silence – but nothing of the sort happens. Their legs are as still as Pontiac's dead ones. The dust from off his clothes just falls slowly down on to the dead horse's body, on which the sweat has now dried, and the slime from its very last panting is already being invaded by flies.

For quite a while, in fact, nothing at all happens. The gamekeeper's dogs, whose chains can usually be heard all over the district, don't seem to be stirring from their kennels, and there's no sound of hammering from the castle smithy, either. He takes off his short, red velvet jacket in bewilderment, and flaps it around a few times over the horse; in eerie silence, masses of insects are now sinking their stings into its soft flesh, and an army of red ants marches out from the grass, crosses over the path like an open vein, up the horse's tail, which has

9

suddenly lost its sheen, and spreads out over its back and belly in fan formation. The long arms of the jacket have been embroidered by his grandmother: a man reading books suspended in mid-air, white roses over naked sabre-blades, the family coat-of-arms. In order to delay the life-or-death decision, for that is what it could easily be, and in order to gain control of the gardener's children's breathing, his hands dwell for an eternity on each rose and each sabre. Is there still no sound to be heard in the silence of the park? The splash of an oar in the pond, subdued whispers from the lads cutting the hedges? No, only the breathing. Its hands, sticky with low desire, are now approaching Lucas from all sides. He looks at the pendulum-cord arms of the gardener's children, more motionless than ever; the slightest little movement – they could bend down with respectful expressions on their faces and stroke the horse, on its hindquarters, for instance – anything could yet come to his rescue; but silence and being rooted to the spot are still equally unbearable. And then, it being the only respite he has left, he takes off his red hat extremely slowly and beats it over his knee, at the same time keeping an eye on the gardener's children's hair, which seems to have been pulled together and held in place at the top by a dull copper ring; but they're still as marble statues, leaning against the horse in silence. And then all is lost; cap in hand, he suddenly has no option but to react to their brutal breathing and, beside himself with sorrow, fear, regret – indeed, everything, Lucas looks into the eyes of the gardener's children, one after the other. Implacable flames of hatred, like the flames from a welding gun, shoot back at his own eyes, and with a shudder he acknowledges the triumph with which they're celebrating his fall and the dead horse, and he's possessed by feelings he's had to learn to suppress from the very start in connection with cricket, riding, hunting with his falcon Ajax, and perhaps also all those shy detours to avoid confronting the local poor children: it's very much like what he knows as guilt feelings.

For a moment, nothing but motionless pain; like a brook of bitter wine, the red ants are now streaming over the road, and the dead horse's belly and hindquarters are soaked in ants; flies and other winged insects take fright and fly silently up into the treetops. And then, without meaning to do it quite so violently perhaps, he delivers a kick right into the horse's side, so vicious that one of its hooves rises up a little, killing several ants underneath it.

Now the boy's running as if he means never to return, as if he wants to place light years between himself and the park, down the white summery path, where the wheel tracks of the calèche and the hoof-marks from its four horses are imprinted in the dust like an endless trail of silver coins between two parallel lines. – And the man who's dreaming knows full well why the boy's running and why he kicked the horse as well, but the little boy on the white path with the red velvet jacket over his shoulder knows nothing, except that the hedge is suddenly closing in on him and the frog he's so afraid of is lying there green, smelly and disgusting at his feet; he runs between looming carriage wheels, big carthorses, ploughs lying on the ground and white hens fluttering in all directions, he reaches the castle garden, runs over flower beds, past groups of lilies and his mother's elegant society lady-friends, sleeping on the lawn with handkerchiefs over their faces, runs through the little door and up to the library and only now bursts into tears as he dives on to the fur rug and burrows his whole self into its aroma of bear's blood and cigars.

Now the years go by, and he slowly learns to understand. He avoids the park; filled with a strange sort of despair, as the evenings wear on he often stands at the french windows in the tower, staring down into the darkness between the trees; if he sees a raven dive down among some blue trunks in the direction of the windmill, whose halting sails are the only thing unchanged, he immediately imagines the horse is still lying there on the path, old carrion with deep cavities in its flesh, marks made by beaks and teeth, and in a state of confusion and despair, he wants to race down the tower staircase and dig a grave for his old friend, but darkness is falling fast and he always collapses into somebody's arms and is carried unconscious through the cold, damp halls, stinking of dust and rotting portraits, back to his room in the green shadow of the wing wall.

Sick, they whisper in the castle. Barmy, out in the village. Indeed, psychologists, psychiatrists, psychotherapists and psychoanalysts, all those concertina-tuners of the soul, come rolling up by train, motor cycle, car, bus and aeroplane to his bed, like suitors in old marriage sagas: schemes are drawn up, diagrams multiply, ink is always having to be ordered from the town, armouries and store-rooms for the family mummies are now adapted to make libraries and laboratories, questions are placed before him from left, right and centre, with the greatest solemnity, all requiring answers; throw paper aeroplanes from the roof, the oscillations of the soul must be investigated thoroughly; a steady stream of equipment looking like small fountains or dish-washers keeps turning up, and everything is very interesting and very confusing.

But the terror remains, and the guilt, all the other flotsam as well; somebody wants to lead him down to the park like a bull, they show him samples of gravel from the park path and from entirely different ones and tell him, quite correctly, that there's next to no difference between them. Certificates with all kinds of warranties state, quite correctly, that pony Pontiac was given away as food to a starving family dependent on the estate, people who'd never been dissatisfied with their lot and become involved with those agitating for better food. But in order to understand for himself – that's what's being denied him, after all – how to sort out the dark secrets of the events, he runs away early one morning, as the servants are approaching with ropes and a palanquin to take him out into the park, races up the blue spiral staircase and out on to the roof behind the old defences, the haunts of jackdaws and the place urchins would love to visit. Dark points gather among the statues in the courtyard below, drawing-pin-small faces suddenly open out like buds from their black calyxes.

'Enough of your ropes and silly questions,' he calls down to them, balancing on a pinnacle, standing on one leg and leaning out over the silent abyss. 'Enough of your doctors, medicines and silly machines, X-ray machines, the whole lot!' His father is no doubt down there somewhere as well, the old officer with his mad circus dreams. Yes, there he is, he's running now, a two-legged ant scuttling across the courtyard, no doubt that's his spurs glinting in the sun. Then there's life and movement everywhere: coaches are harnessed, cars come creeping up like ugly beetles, boxes are loaded on board, people climb in and out, horns are sounding non-stop, and the sound flies up towards him like large mosquitoes, and at last the column of vehicles starts flowing out towards the main road, sluggish as pitch – and Lucas runs downstairs in order to solve the mystery of the pony Pontiac and the gardener's children in peace and quiet.

But instead, his father grabs him roughly by the arm and drags him off through the deserted state-rooms where the smell of dying portraits is becoming more and more unbearable – people in various stages of decomposition even when alive start to smell like portraits after a certain number of years. Into the library, where father bolts the door, draws the curtains, lights the candles in the candelabra, and takes down from the wall the whip with the twelve-foot lash. The old man ran away and joined a circus in his youth, combed the prima donna's hair, assisted the lion-tamer, was brought back home, and locked in the cellar for a period of four months. There, among the rats, mould and dungeon-dampness he learnt how to use a whip; the ringmaster of his own longings could eventually, at the height of his career, kill a fleeing rat, or a squirrel in the top of a birch tree, and soon he forgot about lions and tigers and concentrated on rats and young squirrels. Generally liked for his stupidity, generally admired for his cruelty, generally respected for his wealth, he gradually acquired the biggest collection of whips in the country.

'Get undressed,' his father now ordered the boy, 'take everything off, put your clothes on the fur rug, bend over like the miserable wretch you are, legs slightly apart, back towards the door, head as near the ground as you can, your mane should be hanging down, so that you look like a lion.'

He unwinds the endlessly long whip, turns the key

one more time in the lock; the terrified footsteps of the servants can be heard tip-tapping on the floor outside. Then a minute's silence, and suddenly the carts start rumbling through the archway, horses neigh, a coachman is singing some song or other, the thong creeps slowly over the floor like a snake as it approaches the terrified boy, whose body is as white as ivory. Then the thong rises in response to its owner's command, wraps itself gracefully round a silver candelabra, and hurls it violently across the room.

'Stand still now, hands on knees, stretch your back so that I can get in better lashes.'

Now the whip swishes across the room again, and suddenly, from the boy's shoulder diagonally across his back and down towards his left hip, it has dug a red canal across the expanse of white desert.

'One for your damned worrying. Worrying is an unclean occupation, best suited to monks, paupers, swine and subalterns. But when you have plenty of wine, whips and horses, it's a sin to worry. Think about how well your wine's tickling your palate – if it doesn't, choose another wine. Feel how comfortably the whip fits into your hand – if it doesn't, get a carpenter to make a new handle which suits you better. Horses run fast, if one falls it's his own fault, there are plenty more. Never have pity, it only makes you look foolish and takes up valuable time; kick the horse up its backside and make yourself respected.

'One for all your damned prattle about feeling guilty. Guilt is just for the weak, that's what they're there for. Sit comfortably in the dress circle and watch how they go about their puppet-lives, they generally act for money, the director might well be a brother-in-law. Don't join in the play-acting, just sit and watch for as long as you find it amusing. People don't expect you to do anything in this big farce of a life, and if they do, then disappoint them.

'One for your damned youth, but you'll get over that.

'One in the hope you'll get over it as soon as possible.

'One for every horse you'll ride till it drops in the big wild boar hunt next October, and laugh at like all the rest of us.'

Then the boy slowly collapses, the network of canals across his back is slowly filling up, the whole world is a bowl of whip-lashes joined together, the fur rug closes around him, its smell of bear's blood has breathed its last after all the years, now it smells of cigars, spilled whisky, mistresses' perfumes. Minutes pass and the boy doesn't wake up, hours pass and the boy doesn't wake up, years pass: there's still no sign of him. Then he suddenly finds himself, time has rushed by, he's a boy no more, his back feels a little sore when his jacket rubs against it, when he puts his shirt on or takes it off, but apart from that he's no doubt completely restored. His father's got older, shrunk somewhat, and leans forward at a frightening angle when he walks; his mother, whom he hardly noticed before, is always at the stove nowadays with red peppery eyes, or lying on the sofa in the hall with some secret pains. Yes, it's true: the castle disappeared as well; according to his father speculators and profiteers were in league, their finances collapsed, first all the horses were sold, land followed a bit at a time, the servants were sent packing, but nothing helped.

Now all three walk these grey streets, bowed under the yoke of dreams and hopeless expectations. Take the old man, for example: every evening when it's sufficiently dark, he sneaks up into the attic of the old block of flats, and all alone with a length of strong cord and a broken fishing rod he revives his old whip-dreams. Otherwise, he's broken with the past: now he hangs around one of the four pubs in the area for half the day, grumbles away about politics in rather a loud voice, frequently writes letters to newspapers about the local dogs, and apart from that there's most probably no one who knows how he feels.

His mother's in a pitiful state. No doubt it irritates her to find the only thing she has to throw at the rampant cats copulating in the back yard in March are bundles of old correspondence from the castle.

And Lucas himself? As noted, the scars from the lashes get a little bit sore, but who can say why the park still keeps cropping up in his nasty dreams? When he's working at his desk in the suburban bank, he often sees its contours in bits of the wall where the paint is flaking off, and the pony often emerges from some crack or other. Is the guilt still there, will it go on for ever? The circumstances change; if you're sitting on a log making music and somebody's lying trapped underneath it, practically unable to hear, it might seem a simple matter to do your duty, get up and roll the log away. But if the one on the log's young, he's often told by the others who are used to sitting up there that the slightest little movement can cause the whole building – symbolically speaking, it's true, but even so – to collapse. Better to tune your instrument and blow hard so that his moans are drowned; perhaps the poor creature trapped under the log and supporting the whole system can get some pleasure out of the concert. Poking around a bit in one of his ears, so that the music can get through more easily, is the best you can do to help without risking your own skull being smashed in.

If you're young, then, and rather soft-centred, as

Lucas was at the time, for instance, you think you're duty-bound to stay on the log; if you move slightly the whole world trembles ominously, the baying of the instrument and the red, puffed-out cheeks of the player arouse both disgust and despair, the feeling of helpless guilt is almost overpowering. Then you may get lucky, somebody presses a recorder into your hands, soon you learn which holes to cover and how to blow, and soon you find your own spiral staircase in oblivion's mansion of notes, and soon you're sitting of your own free will on that fatal log, conjuring up the little temple of symbolism and adding on ornamentations of your own. You hang up your guilt on the highest point of the gable end like a silly little tin souvenir of your childhood. But it was a bit different for Lucas, that initial period when the child had stopped jumping about on the log without realizing it, the time of inhibitions and guilt: fear of the park, the death of the horse and the gardener's children, it all held him in a vice-like grip – but the whip came and set him free after all; the little flute flourished for a while in his hands, but it didn't sound quite right even so, the undertone of fear, guilt and bitterness was rather shrill and was noticed by the family. Just when his father had been practising with his whip enough to drive the last remains of his disobedience out of his body, however, came the crash, the log rolled slowly over, and now they were lying underneath it them-selves, gasping in terror for breath. But Lucas – did it happen as one has a right to expect, did his silent conscience do an about-turn and start protesting bitterly against those who were grinding his body down into the dust? Before, he'd felt guilty; surely he now felt vindicated? But it's remarkable how lonely Lucas always seemed to be! His new friends who sweated away in the same room as him ten hours a day and snatched a hurried meal of warmed-up potatoes and soya beans at their desks, afraid that if they didn't they'd have to stay behind and not get home in time to do the overtime they had to do in order to be able to afford to pay for the room where they did the overtime when they weren't sleeping and in order to be able to buy more soya beans so that they'd have enough strength to work both at home and at the bank; these new friends with bent backs and short laughs who gave off a vague aroma of lard and not excessively clean socks had no sensation of being squashed by logs and being slowly serenaded to death by people who were using the logs as benches.

'Never mind, old chap, it's to do with the air pressure, it'll soon pass,' they would say patronizingly to Lucas when he tried to spell out how things were. 'Look, some headache tablets might help.' They were a friendly bunch, albeit a bit forced in the way they displayed their sympathy; they had to save time and strength for their work, and tablets always help, of course. Lucas was confused and swallowed a handful of the evil-smelling oval pills, they irritated his throat like pepper, and they didn't help at first; but after a few weeks the pressure of the log was no more than that of a pair of over-short braces against his chest. Well, what good did it do for the guilt to keep on coming back? It was absurd to feel guilty when no one was being oppressed by him any longer, why should the one lying under the log feel guilt on behalf of the one sitting up above playing the recorder? He read theology at the library, but that didn't get him anywhere. The Chinese in China were starving to death in rather large numbers nowadays, and in a Velamese newspaper he read how people in a previously undiscovered country were being tortured by bandits, people with unusually grey eyes had them gouged out, for instance, at the whim of their cruel masters. Lucas couldn't do anything about that, communications alone made any suggestion of intervening out of the question: journeys cost money for a start, though of course he might be able to steal money from the bank – but was it right to put yourself in debt in order to be able to help somebody else pay his debts? It's a hell of a world when somebody gets kicked every time you raise your foot, and someone is crushed every time you put it down again.

Lucas worried, and was painfully aware that for every hour that passed, more and more poor people in the Velamesian Republic had their eyes gouged out. He explained his dilemma to all his friends and acquaintances, but they read different newspapers and hence didn't believe him. And so he took upon himself their guilt as well, for somebody had to bear it after all, and his back became bowed because of the weight on his shoulders, so that people naturally advised him to do gymnastic exercises. One day, however, a very perceptive man who used to prey on schoolmasters' widows, full of cynicism, the only form of wisdom he could still accept, took Lucas by the arm and explained a few facts: for instance, was Lucas in the best position to save those people's eyes? Those best placed were surely the Velamese themselves, and then, if one thought of Velamesia as the middle point of an enormous circle with Lucas wandering about on its periphery, between him and all its horrors were gigantic segments of guilt-laden silence, and between Lucas's world and the Velamesian crimes was a wall of people as high as the skies, like a fire break, and it was the same no matter which way he turned. Of course, the whole business was messy – but if that's how things were? Moreover, something had happened at the bank: worried by the deterioration in his performance at work, or as they preferred to put it: his excessively pallid appearance, possibly due to a change of air, he was called before the management of the bank and requested in clear enough terms to sort out the reasons for his indisposition, or face dismissal.

Pressed between the cardboard partition of guilt and the iron wall of existence, therefore, he chose remarkably enough to push back the former in order to create room for his body. As if by coincidence, the wounds he thought had healed long ago opened up again, and he was obliged to walk carefully and avoid exposing himself to any kind of risk. Fire breaks shot up around him, in fact, enclosing the world. Together with a friend from the bank, he would go out on certain Sundays and public holidays to a beck on the outskirts of the town and fish for a species of tiny trout, which were barely big enough for a single breakfast. There on the boggy banks of the fast-flowing beck, Lucas appreciated for the first time the meaning of a life without guilt. Lucky enough to be born with fire breaks in most directions, he felt himself obliged to enjoy his situation for as long as it lasted. Incidents like the gouging out of eyes in Velamesia were bad enough, it's true, but they were no doubt only made worse by irrelevant lamentations; and obvious injustices nearer home were just as little to do with him, for wasn't it also unjust fundamentally to let one's attitudes be governed by geographical considerations? Being doubly careful to take into account all parties concerned as well as himself, and to ensure that no injustice befell those who craved sympathy, there was clearly no better way than leaving everything well alone, including those who were suffering, because if you really had to spell it out, wasn't guilt merely another word for a lack of concentration? If you acted in response to your guilt, well, how many people would get kicked over every time you moved your foot, and how many people were going to feel delighted when your guilt picked out some objects and not others? Wasn't it best, not least out of consideration for others, to avoid having any views at all on the vices of the age?

His work output began to increase slowly, and note how he adopted a delightful handwriting style, artistically ornamented; no more than a glance at his lace-like S was needed to convince the management at the bank that he'd be a faithful servant until he died of consumption due to unsatisfactory ventilation at his workplace. Something of himself, it might even have been most of him, flowed from his nib as he wrote the most trivial things, and he acquired a remarkable urge to draw diagrams: he'd portray Sunday's trout and his everyday walk to the bank in the form of delicate curves on graph paper; in his own way he was no doubt typical of an age which stole its own agony: you'd stand in the midst of the black throng like a pickpocket, slipping your hand into your own pocket and grabbing the evil thing. Then it was time to play the double role of the person robbed, and you always tried to let your torment slink into another pocket, another person's pocket. But all too often your lack of dexterity led to your choosing the wrong pocket, and it was annoying when you came back home with a hip pocket swollen up like an enormous abscess, and the thief-victim was nearly exposed as a result of his mistake; finger exercises were the only hope, in fact.

But one day the letter comes even so. It's standing on the shelf over the stove when he comes home one evening, like a white, menacing shadow. He sees it immediately, no doubt, but first he has something to eat and pretends he's not seen it; he builds tunnels of prawn shells on his plate, and covers the openings with potato peel, not that it helps. With his knife of fear and his sharp conscience-fork, he presses hard and scrapes the grey china, and the gilded layer of duty slowly starts flaking off; he looks into his mother's eyes and they are festering, the skin is stretched tightly across the bones of her face, the little triangular room seems to be compressing all their thoughts, hopes, imaginings and desires into disgusting triangles. Ah, now he feels he wants to emerge from this prawn-shell and potato-peel tunnel which is set to enclose him for ever. He begs of his knife: cut through my woollen layer, the gilded surface of my nakedness; and of his fork: pierce my contentment and my unscrupulous diagram-poisoning with your silver claws.

Hurriedly, he picks up the letter, opens it, reads it and shouts: 'I have to leave!'

But his mother has realized that and she's already packed; he picks up his suitcase without even deigning to give her one last look, echoing up the staircase he can hear his father's whip, newly bought with money intended for food, clicking its tongue down in the vaulted cellar. He starts running, and his ear is almost torn off by a lash from the whip.

'Father!' he shouts, 'I have to leave.'

The whip falls silent.

'Why?'

23

'I've had a letter. It says I have to go to a certain meeting-place.'

'Something to do with the bank?'

'No, I have to leave everything behind. It's time something I failed to do ages ago is finally put right.'

'Stay where you are and don't move.'

'Yes, Father.'

And it's the same moment as once before, the whip seems to be the same in any case, no, not quite, maybe even more savage and bloodthirsty. Lucas collapses now on to the cellar passageway, all the walls between then and now have crumbled, the concrete cellar floor fades away and in its place, the soft pelt of a bear rises up, he burrows down into the fur rug and knows he will stay after all.

He gets up and wanders back up the stairs, and behind him the whip suddenly bursts out laughing as it comes into sudden contact with a cellar wall, his mother unpacks again, he sees how she hides the only suitcase under a pile of bank journals in a wall cupboard. They go on eating in silence, and everything is just as it has been for a long time: family happiness, and the greasy smell of cooking and mixed perfumes from mouldy wallpaper waft once more through the room.

Now time passes quickly once more, columns and trout intertwine to form fences round his life; to be sure, he notices the black car following him as he walks home in the afternoon, it keeps flashing its lights, and the man who bundles him in through the back door is somehow familiar. They drive out into the desolate countryside, and by a bridge with a single silvery lamp is an old man playing his fiddle in the middle of the night, his instrument case lying open to receive contributions; suddenly the car skids and crushes the case under a front wheel. They hear the shouts behind them, but gaze down into the darkness under the bridge where the lights on a barge are threading their soft strands through the mists over the water. Lucas is sitting in the back seat squashed between two hefty men with testy voices; they don't need to guard him so keenly, no one needs to worry about Lucas making a run for it; his firmly laced-up will can be moulded gently by any hand that cares to try, any move from his side will only make an even bigger mess of things, he knows that.

Where are they going? He's completely calm and has no expectations – what is there for him to hope for any more? – and he listens to the big car roaring into the silence of the night; sometimes farm carts stand sleepily at crossroads, their shafts bowed; terrified cows woken up by the car's engine scramble in vain to get up on their knees as the headlights catch them; rather less noisily they purr on to a bumpy, crooked side-road where the headlights crash repeatedly into oak trunks or bob over little black, scared ponds. Grass is growing right down to the edge of the road and sways gently as if the headlights were a breeze, and now he recognizes where he is, but without any great feelings of fear or surprise: the path and the oak forest of his childhood have found him again, and the pony also appears as they round a bend, as if emerging from a dream; it still hasn't moved since it fell, and in the sharp beams before the car brakes to a halt, the bodies of millions of ants glisten like a network of neon lights stretched over the body of the pony, which is still not quite dead.

'Get out,' says the gardener's son, one of those sitting at his side throughout the long journey and smelling of cigars, a podgy man approaching middle age with flabby folds in his face; the woman sitting beside the driver is his sister, the one who's been hunched over a local map all the time and wearing a transparent mourning veil; she glances up and then gets out on to the path. Lucas walks quickly past her, and can hear her breathing behind the veil.

'That's enough,' she whispers. 'Get down on your knees.'

He sinks slowly down in front of the dead horse, his legs telescope together as if pressed by an unseen hand, the car lights go out, it suddenly swivels round on the path with a snarl and is sucked into the darkness under the trees. Is the woman still there? His ears grope around helplessly and return empty-handed, and with a sob of loneliness he stretches himself out beside the horse and reaches out his arms to draw it towards him. But by then it's disappeared, as you might expect, and there's just a hollow lying by his side, a grave with the outline of a horse five times blacker than the darkness; that's what he's trying to caress in all his isolation, and something sucks his body slowly over the edge, his head is pulled gently like a barge falling slowly down into the depths, indeed, the fall is incredibly slow. Doubled up like a foetus, his body sinks downwards, his hands, those white feelers, are quivering in expectation of touching the rough skin, but instead, the white wave rises up from the bottom and wafts over him like a light breeze. Protecting himself, flapping around like a swimmer is of no avail, he's preparing to choke and opens himself up completely so that the wave can engulf him, when he realizes that nothing can happen, not a single drop has flowed into his mouth, no, the wave wraps itself around his body like a silken sheet and although his body suddenly turns into a gigantic tongue wriggling like a snake in an attempt to capture a little dampness, the result is ill-fated. Meanwhile he goes on sinking, and tempting smells rise up towards him from the distant depths: ambergris and gin, the scent of birdsong over a bubbling spring, the broken clinking of a wine cellar's chill, the hard smell of metal and poverty from a brass water tap, nothing will be missed, everything pierces his heavy body like sharpened drills, and when he's endured everything, the dead horse is still lying there dumbly at the bottom, and even the ants can be seen through the water: he's possessed once again by rage; now he understands the horse's cruel role as an agent of torture, it's lying on the bottom of the well of his thirst, and all the scents of pain are rising from its skin. His fingers are hooked voraciously as he hurls himself upon the horse and digs his sharp nails into its soft flesh like needles, his caresses are long since forgotten, now all he wants is bitter revenge.

With his hands buried deep down in the sand, he slowly emerged from the gigantic parcel of his dream with the seventy seals, a worthless little kernel in the last and smallest box of the hundred boxes that are his dream; he rolled over on his back, groaning, his mouth wide open and desperate to catch the insubstantial rain.

But like balloons in spring, the grey tufts of dawn wrenched themselves loose from the fold of the sea, the emerging contours of the island and the wreck's shattered masts, the liana-like confusion of rigging and the explosion of anchor cables, rose directly into the skies, whose loosely draped silken screen was suddenly flung aside and stretched tightly as ice; it was inadequate to cover the whole space, and from some of the gaps light oozed forth like apple juice and poured into the sea, which was consumed in turn as darts of golden flame licked the shiny black expanse like the tongue of a hungry dog. The green silk of dawn was now snipped away at the edges by the scissors of new light, slits appeared, and pieces of grey mist were set ablaze as light came plunging down; a bloodshot gigantic eye blinked momentarily, then the whole sea burst into flames and bobbed against the eastern horizon like a fisherman's float in the early morning.

To Lucas Egmont it was all one long fall; still yawning wide, he tried scrambling to his feet, but couldn't manage it until his speed of fall diminished. Swaying to and fro, pains shooting through his legs and his throat still twitching in response to the water of his dream, he stood there in the sand; his canvas shoes squeaked every time he moved a muscle and the rubbing of sand under his finger-nails made him feel sick. Intoxicated by the certainty of his fate, he staggered forward to the water, sunk to his knees by the lagoon, and thrust his fingers violently into the cooling water; someone was hanging like a dead weight round his shoulders, someone was pressing down on the back of his neck, the urge to dive in became almost irresistible, his lips were drawn to the water like a magnet, his face came nearer and nearer to the surface and his jerky reflection rose from the bottom of the lagoon.

Fragments of his dream were bobbing about on the water, he sank to his knees and relived everything that had happened in his dream. Meanwhile the red float – splashed with the blood of the giant fish – gradually rose up from the sea with meticulous care, as if the invisible fisherman were trying to do all he could not to scare his prey. Thirst, thought Lucas Egmont, all is thirst. Guilt, fear, all aspects of guilty conscience, cruelty and lies, it's all thirst; flight and degradation, desires and social aspirations, everything is merely thirst.

Forced slowly on to his back by all his certainties, he watched as the sea was suddenly stretched like a fire blanket and formed a vast blue stillness under the balancing act of the sun, which was still standing on the ground, red and bulky, gazing at the ladder and the rope. Thirst, he thought, around which everything revolves, the only firm point in a slack universe: where would we be without thirst – like a helpless guest invited to a dinner for the first time, not knowing what to do with his hands in an overwhelmingly big hall?

Because, he thought, because thirst is the only certainty, I can live a little longer: but not in order to slake it, no, to keep it going since if I lose my thirst – then what?

And between dawn and morning, the dreamer within us, the greatest cynic of them all, helped him to mount fast horses and run away from everything which had been chasing him up to now: his guilt from the castle and the bank, his fear of everything which might force him to act, guilt feelings about his flight into the world of diagrams and bewitched trout. What else can you do, he thought, but maintain your thirst? If you want irrelevancies to tear you to pieces, go ahead and drink!

White clouds of the only birds on the island, like seagulls but with bare necks and red bills made for hacking, dumb, and silent in flight, rose up from the interior of the island; transfixed by *angst*, he recalled those hectic minutes round the buried water keg, the shoving, the sharpness of the foot which always kicked him, the supreme moment of satisfaction as his palate was flooded, and the long agony afterwards when everything had to be investigated: why had he deceived the bank, shamelessly tricked his employers and fled with the money he'd kept hidden so long? It was like masturbation: an hour of blissful self-abuse, a moment when everything dissolved into blissful agony, a day of regret and furtive reproach.

But he was the one who could see most clearly what was going to happen, knew the ship coming to rescue them was still in Melbourne or Casablanca: he'd better be spared the shameful period of brooding that followed once he'd slaked his thirst. Trembling in every limb, not just from the cold, but also from *angst*, he scrambled to his feet and tried to suppress the crackling noise coming from the pieces of canvas round his feet as he walked. Was everyone asleep now? Gazing down greedily – yes, looks like that must be from greed, what else? – the birds circled around some fifteen feet up, their rubber necks stretched out before them. Yes, all six seemed to be asleep: the three men under a sheet of canvas between the fire and the white rock, with the mad captain furthest away, his shoulders hunched contemptuously even in his sleep, turned impatiently away from the nervous airman, whose heavy frame seemed to be lying at attention even as he slept; next to him the giant Tim Solider, calm and impassive under canvas as if relaxing on the *chaise-longue* at home with his wife beside him; closely intertwined by the fire under a bale of cotton they had managed to salvage lay the young English girl, her buttocks constantly quivering, and the sturdy red-haired woman, enclosed in a secret no one yet knew about; on his own near the water keg the crippled boxer, on his back, motionless, like a champion counted out for ever.

Unaware of committing any sort of crime, driven only by the force which always drove him: the urge to avoid normal guilt feelings, the only thing which for him could ever justify an action, Lucas Egmont took a plank from one of the wooden boxes and started digging in the sand until he heard the dull clang. His terror and triumph combined to fling him to the ground and his fingers sped like sand torpedoes over the cool metal of the keg, digging out a hollow for the water under the tap, and he was shaking as he unscrewed the tap, forcing every muscle in his body to keep his head still under the axe of *angst* and prevent himself from rolling over and simply drinking. But sand drinks quickly, one enormous gulp and it had imbibed all the water from the last keg they'd all helped to roll from the boat that first day when it was still an adventure, over the whole length of the half-moon-shaped reef, crooking its finger along the distant beach. When he lifted up the keg in his dirty hands, it was light and silent, and he buried it along with all their hopes of rescue just as the sun placed its foot on the first rung of the ladder and the sea seemed to fill its chest with its first breath of morning, the birds were swooping down into the forest in eerie silence, and he could hear the thud of an early-bird iguana.

He went down to the lagoon with his wooden plank and hurled it out over the water, which welcomed it with a tender embrace; and then suddenly something remarkable happened: the bottom of the lagoon was smooth and yellow and seemed almost to be floating just beneath the painfully clear water, but now a clutch of white bubbles floated up towards the plank like balloons, the sand became agitated, a fish slowly wriggled free from its grip, and with one lightning-fast twitch of its tail it launched itself from its hiding place, three feet at least it was from its tail to its shark-like mouth, its back covered in horrifyingly sharp, six-inch spikes, and with a sickening shudder it crashed into the plank, then circled round the lagoon in silence, slicing

31

up the surface with its spikes, before sinking down slowly, burrowing into the loose sand, and disappearing once more. For a few seconds, the bottom was murky, a few clouds of froth floated on the water, then suddenly, everything was exactly as before.

Pale with emotion, as if he had seen a ghost, Lucas Egmont staggered backwards – was he afraid of being stabbed from behind otherwise? – then raced back to the smouldering fire and threw another branch on to it, adjusted the cotton over the English girl's back as she muttered away non-stop in her sleep, then, feeling a little calmer, returned to the keg in order to go back to sleep under the boxer's canvas. As he lifted the edge, the crippled boxer said without opening his eyes and barely parting his lips: 'I saw what you did all right.'

Lucas Egmont bent over him till he raised his eyelids and allowed his hatred to seep out through the gaps. Then Lucas smiled down at the boxer as he untied the laces of his makeshift canvas shoes, since it was morning now, and warm. Still bent over him, he dangled the red laces like a pendulum in front of his eyes. Then the boxer closed his eyes like a man slamming a door, a shudder crept through him like a snake, and he seemed to be sinking although he was still lying there.

'Enjoy your thirst,' said Lucas Egmont, still smiling.

The Paralysis of Morning

For a moment Jimmie Baaz thought his paralysis had loosened its grip, his hips became supple and the dull pain abated, his legs bent once more after years of stiffness, he wanted to run away, and he could do so once again. He flung back the canvas and then thought he could hear the stimulating reveille of a drum as his feet thudded quickly and regularly on the hard morning-sand. My God but he felt jubilant! The air was mild and cool at the same time, still hard after the chill of night, and closed in like leaves around his heat. The sun was like a newly painted red croquet ball, resting for a moment almost motionless on the black line, and the silent clouds of birds, splashed from below by the red glitter of morning on the sea, hovered over the world like white palm leaves. The path over the cliffs came racing towards him and made merry little leaps into the midst of the newly awakened greenery, discarded iguana skins on some of the green stones glittered like stiff lamé, and in the high grass where he had never been before he would find a depression between some hidden stones into which he could force down his body and then abandon himself to eternal tranquillity. He would have reached the terminus of his long flight, and then it could be closed down as there weren't going to be any more travellers. None of the other survivors would find him, they'd run around in the thickets shouting eagerly that he must come out, they just couldn't live without him.

'Couldn't live' – oh, he knew full well they only wanted to share their own dread of soon having to die with the cripple who couldn't look after himself. They'd sit there for endlessly long days on end, inquiring over and over again in their frightened voices, glancing furtively at each other, if he was in pain and if he still wanted to go on living, they were all so very keen for him to be there the day the rescue ship dropped anchor in the bay.

They'd lift off the canvas sheet, and with meticulous dignity unwind the rags from both his legs, shattered between the rocks on the reef and a water keg the night of the shipwreck, and they'd nod at him, their faces distorted by optimism and false cheerfulness. They'd raise his hand and pretend to take his pulse, although the only heartbeats they could hear would be their own. They'd place their hands on his blood-stained shirt in order to feel his heart beating, that is, they wanted to confirm that they were still alive themselves. They'd talk to him about the excellent attention he'd receive on board the ship they were expecting, but only to convince themselves it would come. They'd remind him of his times of glory as a boxer, such as that occasion when he felled three bulls with punches on the piazza at Gadenia and was honoured with the Empire Medal, speeches by three lord mayors, short films and radio broadcasts, and a maternity home had also been named after him – but they didn't do this to ease his pain, only to remind themselves that they weren't abandoned after all; they could pretend they were runaway children who are the only ones who think they're hidden, and any minute now their big brothers will be arriving to take them home.

They'd carefully dip their hands into the drinking water and let him suck their fingers like a calf, and would stick hard crusts of bread or chunks of pineapple between his lips because they thought: our charity will save us, injustice can't possibly be so harsh that all this charity will go unrewarded. They were watching him die, of course, and as the days passed they became less and less willing to uncover his injured legs; the smell of death noticed by everyone but himself oozed out of the dirty bandages, and their charity became increasingly in the mind, but no less consoling for that. Drowning themselves, they'd watch him sinking slowly like a rotten lifebuoy, but still they were cowardly enough to cling on to him, thinking: he's sinking because he's rotten, but we who are unsullied will float thanks to our clothes and our own will-power, until someone throws us a real lifebuoy. They didn't need to keep pretending the crippled boxer was in fact the one keeping their heads above water, it was just a case of speaking the words of consolation so loudly and so frequently that the cynic inside them could never be heard whispering: where would we be without our dying, what would be the point of our health without our sick, our happiness without the unhappiness of others, our courage without our cowards?

'Let go of me!' he longed to cry. 'What are you doing here, you hypocrites and water snakes! My misfortune is my own, let me die in peace like the rest of you. Why should I be the one to bear all your fear, all your stifled

35

certainty that the rescue ship, as you call it, will in fact never come!' But he never shouted any such thing, for he was paralysed after all; he'd lain stiffly under the water keg, pressed against the naked rocks of the reef like a beaten wrestler while the long, broken waves lashed his body, stamping in the agony; afraid of being sucked back down into the precipitous depths, he'd tried to cling fast to the rocks with his free hand, and as blood gushed out of his tattered fingers he could feel his life coming and going, sliding out of him and shuffling away over the slippery rocks before having second thoughts and creeping back again. He remembered defending himself desperately every time their octopus-like grip tugged at him anew. He'd tried to kick his rescuers with his useless legs when they rolled the keg aside and dragged him over the rocks by his shoulder, but although he aimed blows at them and struggled with all his body to wrench himself away, his attempts to flee were in vain. He hung in their voracious hands like a morally indignant, stolen parcel, and allowed himself to be rescued on to this cruel island which had surreptitiously clamped its gentle jaws round all their necks like the strands of a man-eating plant.

Full of agonized longing, he'd gazed down like a bird into the overturned well that was the world, with the horizon as the dividing line between the wall of the sea and the sky. If the ship had appeared after all, everything would have been lost and yet saved, his flight would have failed even more pitifully than ever, and as good an opportunity as this would never come again. But his paralysis had betrayed him, it told him he would never be able to flee unless his legs could carry him away to the deep hole under the grass and away from the people roving about on the shore, the ones who were sucking out his own pain, Death, he sometimes thought; but death, said his paralysis, death isn't the same as running away, death isn't really running away, just a continuation of the ultimate *angst*. Everything would have to be cured if he were to be able to flee. But they all had claws, everybody's nails were growing and no one thought of ripping them off now, and they were keeping watch on him, obsessed with the hope of rescue, obsessed with the hope that he would soon die; we're healthy and therefore we'll survive, we're alive because we're healthy and have enough strength to wait for the rescue boat.

Are there no cracks in their compact dream? Oh, how he tried to grope his way around those white sepulchral walls in search of secret cavities, but he was too weak, too crippled, too isolated in himself. Then one morning, when they'd all gathered round him again with their commiserations and their chilly *angst*, he bit hard into the hand of the artillery captain, Wilson, who was feeding him crumbs of ship's biscuits with the cynical patience of an animal trainer. He remembers how the hand, already on its journey to death, with ragged blue fingers where the flesh was glowing hard and red in deep hollows, hovered temptingly above his eagerly open mouth, whose lips always curled to form a ring without his being able to prevent them. The sea below them was like the giant black wall of a gasometer and the sand seemed to be crunching under the feet of some unseen rambler, while the sky itself was as blue as metal, seemingly bowed under the weight of some unknown force: only the powerful columns of their will kept them up. Then, just before he bit, clouds of birds as white as snow seemed to emerge from the captain's shoulders, their cruel beaks, with small drops of congealed blood seeming to hang from their vicious, pincer-like tips, were pointing steadily down; it was painful enough to feel, as it were, the pecking which would sever the ailing flesh from his bones, skilfully and triumphantly. Then he shuddered with horror as he noticed the self-satisfied red spot on the end of the captain's nose acquiring a life of its own, just as vicious and ruthless as the beaks in the air above, and when he looked slowly round, he saw that all the people encircling him had identical spikes of blood pointing directly at him. Scared, but also determined to break down once and for all the secret door behind which their secret hopes were hiding, he first closed his eyes in readiness for the preposterous happening; he suddenly found himself shut in a blood-red cave dotted with stalactites, filled with forgotten, hushed, primitive music; the stalactites dug their long fingers into his soft being and seemed to resound with furious whispering. Then, in order to free himself at last from this horrific company, he tensed himself like a catapult, oblivious to his paralysis, but all he could manage was a weak thrust with his upper body; even so, it was so high and so unexpected that he was able to dig his teeth into the captain's hand, just under the knuckle of his thumb. He bit as hard as he could, dragging the hand with him as he fell back on to the sand.

Now he expected a violent outburst, a powerful, spiteful blow across his cheek which would have released him from any form of obligation to suppress the truth – but the captain's face and his nose with the fierce red spot merely sank down towards him, and the circle of the doomed closed in on him. Smiling confidently the captain slowly coaxed his hand out of his grip, slowly straightened his back and, half turning towards the circle of onlookers, raised his hand towards his heart, as if it had been a medal. All that happened was a regretful shrug of the shoulders; then the circle dissolved and he tried to flee and flee, but in vain, as they always came back and kept him paralysed with their watchful charity. The fear of death, now growing by the hour, seemed to envelop them all as they sat beside him wearing their cosmetic masks of clay; they hardened in the hot sun, and every quick, fearful smile left behind a battery of creases and furrows; these faces looked like a ghastly ruined landscape in what had once been beautiful countryside as they bent over his: curious, frowning uncomfortably, inquiring anxiously, half triumphant in advance or merely riddled with terror, whenever they thought he was asleep or had fallen into terminal unconsciousness. Worst of all was the young English girl who lay down beside him, slender and gazelle-like, her thin birch-leaf fingers frequently fluttering about his face; eyes increasingly as fixed as frozen lakes in the snowy landscapes surrounding her pupils examined him meticulously, and interpreted every change of expression with remarkable rapidity.

'You want something to drink now,' she would say immediately – or, 'Now you'd like to get rid of this canvas sheet for a while.'

She spoke his language, slowly, darkly, with strange palatizations, almost like a tropical negress. It would have been touching and loveable in normal circumstances, but now he found it extremely distasteful, another stage in the process of stifling imprisonment. The girl's peculiarities forced their way under his hard shell of resistance and scratched like a grain of sand, more irritating than the others' easily exposed charity

39

born of fear, since he detected a comical genuineness about the girl as she lay beside him; at first it seemed boundlessly ridiculous, but soon it became painfully intolerable as it immediately made everything so complicated, even more so than the hypocrisy of the others hindering his flight. Aha, a'Florence Nightingale, he thought contemptuously, and made himself extra heavy when she came with her thin hands and tried to change the rags wrapped round his filthy lower body, He could see point in annoying her as she didn't possess the honourable falsehood characteristic of all her shipwrecked companions. She was genuine, that is, she considered herself to be genuine, and so her lies were all the greater.

She would lie down beside him, and they often watched the velvet ships of the clouds gliding majestically over the sea. The new line running from the blood-red corner of her mouth grew severe and deep, and the fine, blue bow of her temples was ready to snap at any moment; her frozen gaze suddenly thawed, she seemed to reach out for him even though she was lying there without moving.

'Can you see it?' she said in his language, trembling away in the parcel of cloth her body was encased in, 'There goes the good ship *Tong*, with its masts lost in the mists. Can you see the captain, the one standing smoking by the rail: the mists come from his pipe. A sailor is just emptying a bucket of mist overboard, you see, the *Tong* would go too fast otherwise. A lady from Shetland in her phantom fur-coat is evidently not feeling too well, can't you see how sinister she looks as she stands on deck, waving her white letter of credit? The schoolboy who's run away from my smoke-infested homeland has just whistled a shrill greeting to freedom, you can see that white column shooting up from the ship and you probably think it's the steam whistle, but it's the boy, I can assure you: his jubilation is so boundless that it has to look just like that.'

With meaningless prattle of that kind in the air, she'd go for a little walk on her own, but Jimmie refused to let himself get carried away; silent and compressed by his longing to run away from it all, his hunger, his thirst and his contempt, he wanted to cry out: 'You're lying, you're making up that rescue ship in the clouds, you're emptying your heavy box of fear on to a bank of clouds, but keep out of the way when it falls, the floor isn't very steady. Just wait till my legs have got better and my paralysis has eased, there'll be nothing to hold me back; I know your fear and your plans for me, but I'll run away to where nothing can get at me.'

But then one day he came to with a start, it may even have been the same day everything else happened, for periods of consciousness in between the darkness of his oblivion were deplorably short. There was a new nuance in her way of talking; it's possible it had been there all the time, knocking away at his window, but now it suddenly struck him: words that she palatized with the same noble energy as before took on a new tenor, and the blue quaking of her thin nostrils also had some message to impart. He lay there with his eyes almost closed and seemed to hear or see nothing, but in fact he was observing everything she did with intense concentration; at first he was put out, but increasingly he was filled with disgust and despair as he saw the love for himself that glinted like SOS signals behind her every movement and every word. She turned bravely away from him, but even so he could see her face muscles twitching with a desire to turn and face him, and tear down all the curtains of modesty.

41

'Now I'm standing there on the upper deck with my white suitcase. I've been sailing on board the *Tong* for a long time, just wandering all over the boat like a lost soul, waiting eagerly and nervously for my friend. I was wandering about like that when we nudged the Antilles, and almost touched the Hebridean Isles; it's been foggy all the time, you see, and we've only been able to follow the route on our maps. So there I am on the upper deck, with no idea of what I'm going to do. We keep coming across other boats, little round dinghies in the mist, wrapped in a froth of cigar smoke, but also whalers still engulfed in the remains of the smoke from the phantom whale that's now dead. I wave sadly at them, but they don't notice me because I'm so alone. Then you suddenly come along. Can you see yourself up there under the golden crown? You've been looking for me, no doubt, and like a Cassandra, I run towards you to tell you all the things that are going to happen to us. And then the accident happens, you can see up there what's happened, can't you? I'm so eager I simply drop my suitcase, the one I've been lugging around with me all the time since we left port, the whole voyage; it slides away over the deck, which is very slippery, and as it's not locked, it comes open and everything falls into the sea before we know where we are. You can see the contents streaming down into the sea, can't you? That haze of fiery smoke floating slowly down towards us, that was the contents of my suitcase. – You can be really awful.'

Oh, what wouldn't he have given for healthy, mobile legs so that he could run away from this deceitful but, to make matters worse, quite honourably intended gush of words entangling his desire to flee in the blind threads of the drifting mist! But he was crippled, albeit

42

only temporarily, and as the pain kept on growing in his chest, his ankles, his pulse and his temples, he was confronted by his paralysis every time he tried to turn over in the dry sand, which merely wailed plaintively by way of reply under the canvas sheet. He had to stay where he was, but flee even so – the cripple's dilemma. He must get rid of her, the only one who, thanks to her lack of calculation, her unselfish desire to see him remain alive, was still able to make him want to stay instead of running away – and he didn't want to be convinced that running away never does any good, or that there can ever be anything to justify staying behind. To call off a flight that's already begun is a horrifying undertaking; the moment when the brakes are applied is always a millstone round one's neck, and everything pitches into the person trying to run away like a pack of heavy, savage dogs, trampling over one's belly and tearing at one's body until one's guts are exposed.

'If you think I can love you, you're sadly mistaken,' he whispered softly to her, so that no one else could hear. 'I'm lying here rotting away, as you well know. It's sheer torture for you to choose me to fawn on, a man who can't move from the spot, who can't even attend to his bodily needs without disgusting himself and everybody else. Why don't you go straight to the captain, that hunk of muscle: he should be potent enough to keep you happy. But keep me away from everybody's gaze, especially yours; wrap me up in the canvas as you would somebody who's dead already, and then pound away at my hidden body as hard as you can, I won't put up any resistance any more, I'm not going to live as you know full well.'

Involuntarily, he then looked up quickly, past the

large, dense, all-too-bright surface of the sea, and his eyes settled on the cheeky white yachts of the midday clouds scudding towards the horizon. Her gaze sank down, and he could see how the ice in her eyes slowly engulfed the island that was her pupil, an icy wind seemed to blow over her features which suddenly stiffened like rifts in a tundra. Then she slowly rose up from the sand, wrapped up like a mummy in the thick cotton, and just then a shriek rang out from the interior of the island, quite loud and shrill, but extremely short – was it from some lonely human, or some animal? – but the English girl heard nothing of this, she struck him with the back of her right hand, brown and pitted by the sand, struck him four times over his cheek-bone and his nose, casually and absent-mindedly, and all the while she was frozen in her pain; it was like a dead body raising its hand by mistake, a statue that comes to life – and that's all.

Stiff-legged, strangely statuesque, she then walked over the sand towards the fire; the cloth round her injured right foot slowly worked loose and trailed behind her like a split-open snake with blood running out; she noticed nothing, and spiralled down in front of the fire. They were alone on the beach just then, it was as if the world had forsaken them; a lone bird swooped down over the smoke and seemed to drop something from its beak into the fire. The dull thudding of iguanas drifted over from the rocks, and someone was shouting stubbornly from the trees on the highest part of the island; they were evidently still looking for the shriek.

How the blows helped him to overcome his inner paralysis! The world was once again clearly defined in its pure malevolence, and remarkably: the hollow in the high grass, which he could hear snorting up above them, seemed to be moving nearer all the time. His muscles were softened up by the merry hands of invisible masseuses, and all he was waiting for now was the last rush of malevolence which would pluck him up from out of his trance and fling his body the last few remaining paces. He lay there abandoned all night long, just as he had done in the afternoon; no one pretended to see him any more, it was now evidently part of their plans to let him die in tranquillity, and part of his plans as well – their profound malevolence increased his chances of fleeing enormously.

Night had fallen, suddenly, black and starless; the white wings of the birds flashed occasionally like signal lights over the sea, which seemed to be smacking its gigantic lips, clicking its huge tongue. The dumb birds suddenly acquired voices in the darkness, or was it just his imagination? A gruff, gutteral sound forced out with great difficulty, occasionally broke through their silence; they didn't seem to be talking to each other, but to themselves. Then the sand suddenly became damp, as if someone had been licking it hurriedly; the cold closed in like a suit of armour, and the stars lit up as well, horribly high and no longer twinkling, like the pupils of a fresh corpse.

And at dawn, something wonderful happened: Lucas Egmont, his bedfellow, rose to his feet with a groan and drowned his false charity in the stream of water under the water keg. Jimmie was so grateful for that: another mooring rope had been cut, and now he could rise up like a balloon into silence and solitude. His limbs were filled with painful desire; as noted, he thought his paralysis had eased and suddenly found himself running. He felt as if he were swishing through the morning, his feet were like typewriter keys striking the unwritten sand, which had so often been rinsed by the waves; soon he felt the sun on his back, but the sea was not yet melting in the heat, its vast blue expanse still quivered after the night like the back of an impatient racehorse; the dolphins glistened like flashes of lightning into the horizon, the lagoon was as smooth as a millpond as it reflected his flight; the ship lay on the belly of the reef, apparently still whimpering over its broken back, and the masses of seaweed pouring out of the ship's gaping side glistened with moisture; a porthole whose glass was still only half smashed seemed to be weeping darkness down into the blond water. Once again the birds rose out of the grass above him; in close formation with only a wing's breadth between them, the whole flock soared over the lagoon in near silence, only their wing beats rustling gently like the leaves of a book being read to oneself, their reflection skimming improbably lightly over the lagoon, and they headed for the ship where they suddenly swooped down. The birds waddled unsteadily over the stern deck, and disappeared one by one into the hull through some hole or other. It would have been very easy now to run halfway round the island and block the way out for the flock with planks or a piece of canvas, then lie in wait by the portholes where they might be expected to creep out, stun them as they tried to take off – and there would have been enough food for some considerable time to come.

But Jimmie immediately chose the higher path, and flushed with the thrill of his escape, he raced over the rocks, iguana skins exploding loudly under his feet; now he was supreme and refused to be surprised when he found that the path over the rocks, covered in sharp stones, caused him no pain at all; the iguanas scuttled quickly out of his way, beating their long tails against the stones with sharp cracks.

Why was he running away? Well, why does one run away? Jimmie Baaz had a painful memory he always ran away from. He had been chased up long ladders and dreamt of being rescued on the last rung, but in his dream the ladder had always fallen over pitifully and the swamp had once more wrapped its sticky arms around him. In other dreams he was running down the long road leading away from there, but just like at a fairground, the pavements were rolling in the opposite direction and so he was drawn inexorably back again. He would tense his body in readiness for an enormous thrust which would free him from the iron grip of the road, but everything just seized up. A helpless bundle lashed together with the red threads of his own terror, he would wake up in a cold sweat, and it was hours before he could straighten his twisted limbs properly again. His muscles ached for a long time afterwards, his punches became dull and half-hearted, especially the left one which bounced back ineffectively before it had reached its target. For fear of tightening up in his dream, he would take strong injections the night before every important bout, and sink quickly down into the depths of unconsciousness. But although he was rescued temporarily from his dream, he would be hounded all the more relentlessly while awake by his pursuer; a certain type of person passing him by in the street would give rise to remarkable feelings of alarm inside him, certain streets exuded a certain type of smell which affected him just as badly, and if he therefore chose the wide, pearl-studded boulevards where people hurrying past thrust visiting cards into his famous fists, he might come across some annoying vehicle or an unattended dog which would jump up at him, panting – and the ground would give way under his feet as he sank back once more into this bottomless well.

At the peak of his career, the supreme pinnacle, he was always being exposed just as painfully to his pursuer's arrogance; he had conquered almost everything: the nation had presented him with a house by a lake teeming with salmon, a dazzling white villa surmounted by a cupola bearing the national coat of arms, and moreover surrounded by just as many yards of barbed-wire fencing when the top men of his country came to visit him; but what was the point of it all when he ended up by barely daring to set foot outside the front door? Every little breeze blowing over the great lake carried with it his merciless pursuer. The first time he tried out his new boat, he was whipped up into a state of fury, ran aground and sank. It might well have been easy to die, but even so he allowed himself to be rescued because during the few seconds he'd been fighting against death he realized that for someone who's running away, it's just as pointless to die as it is to live, and his desperation held him up like a giant float.

Then came the period when he was evidently so great that no one expected anything of him any more; like a star, he was firmly fixed in the firmament and he no longer needed to box – indeed, to do so could be harmful to his fame; he was only allowed to perform at big events staged for the imperial family, fighting against famous, but not too famous boxers, young bulls who had been prepared before the match like noblemen's shields that are to be broken at a funeral, and suddenly they would collapse under his punches after the stipulated time, But as he crouched in the cave into which his long flight had banished him, he realized he was in fact less protected than ever and this would be the end of his flight even so; in the innermost of the eighteen caves forming his escape route, he beat like a madman against the stone walls in an attempt to pass further, but in vain; and when he tried to withdraw he found the entrance door to the final cave had closed as well. Locked in the vault where the nation kept its heroes, he ran around ceaselessly like a squirrel in a wheel, while the applause from the stalls and the dress circle bored its way like drills into his brain, heart, kidneys. Now he longed for the trapdoor to open, and then the rapid fall to the source of his agony, the green swamp of his memories, oh, let the sticky wave of decay break over him, flow into his throat and lap around his lungs, rock him like a swollen corpse in all eternity; even the harshest of possibilities now seemed to him almost like paradise – anything but the torture he was now subjected to. Salvation through ignominy was the only possibility, but how could he humiliate himself when even the slightest error on his part was immediately excused with reference to his greatness?

Then he made a terrible attempt to prise open the trapdoor himself. During a gala performance, as the imperial family were scattering flakes of silver over the stage from their box, he suddenly fell headlong and stayed down with his head in his hands; indeed, he was almost holding it in his hands like a fruit. Pale with emotion, the young boxer who had felled him staggered over to the ropes, all the time staring wide-eyed at his hands as if they were splashed with the blood of an unknown person. The red lamp over the stage was suddenly extinguished, and subdued grey-green light filtered down on to the sacrifice that had been accomplished. As he waited for the furious yells of disappointed hope to ensue, Jimmie lay prone, although the back of his neck probably trembled a moment in expectation of the sharp blade; but otherwise he awaited the trapdoor with the calm only extreme desperation can give. There was a subdued rustling like the sound of thousands of sweet-bags falling, then nothing but a transparent, crystal-clear membrane of silence as the man in the white coat emerged from the wings and announced quietly, like a priest at a funeral: he's ill, he had a sudden attack; I suggest we rise to our feet and give the unfortunate man an indication of our appreciation. The orchestra struck up a patriotic tune, and men picked him up carefully by his limbs, made sure his head was still attached, and then carried him off the stage in time with the music.

He lay there helplessly in their arms, more cut off than ever before from any possibility of running away from flight. Then just as the curtains were closing behind him, he heard them giving three cheers for him, the eternal victor who can win everything but defeat. Oh, how he would have loved to tear himself loose from those sixteen sticky hands and run out on to the stage, screaming out his agony, spraying his *angst* like an untamed fountain until it swamped the whole world; but all he was still capable of was to twitch a little, a pitiful death-throe which merely served to make his bearers tighten their firm grip.

Ah well, as he was ill he was at least allowed to go away on holiday. He loved wandering around oriental harbours where nobody recognized him, and loved accepting the feelings of contempt and disgust directed towards him. Of course, he was never really alone; the nation had invisible spies keeping watch on his every move from a distance, but even so, even this form of solitude helped him considerably. He could sink down behind the raffia basket of the snake charmer, close his eyes tightly and shut out all other noises apart from the soft, velvety rustling from inside the basket and think: now I'm only a Tartar lying here in the heat, far away from home, to which only a chain of broken horses links him. Or lie in the bottom of a river-barge hung with brocade, like those used by the sailors from Belize, just drifting around in the little harbour; longboats weighed down with small fruits sparkling silver, smelling strangely of caraway and despair, their oarsmen shouting merrily, wend their way among rafts bearing drowned sacrificial animals; masses of dead horses were also floating around in the becalmed waters, and on the shore clay gods peered from the ape-laden trees; occasional music, the lavender beat of a drum spreading slowly from the brown, summery huts half-buried in gorse, many of them desolated in the latest revolution. From the bottom of the boat, however, the only view was the silken tent of the bright day, and the many desiccated wisps of grey smoke puffing out from the clearings among the cedars. Then he thought: what am I but a drowned man, rescued too late among the horses, floating here for ever without even knowing whose body I am? He was stupefied by the pleasure the thought gave him; the swell rolling in from the sea brought tranquillity in every wave, and the gentle thuds each time the boat hit a drowned animal spread a feeling of warm well-being throughout his body; life was merely a sleepy stretch of water into which he'd fallen like a raindrop from a cloud. Oh, what bliss to surrender oneself to a lake!

Then the monsoons came, smoke columns fluttered wildly and aggressively like battle standards, and natives in the huts were preparing for slaughter. The animals not yet sacrificed and kept tethered in the cedar forests wailed as they were led home, and small, nearly naked boys hung on to the bulls' horns, shouting away and trying to recall the joys of summer, but in vain. Soon a blood-stained column of terrified bellowing rose up from every hut, a bitter stench gathered beneath the trees, and the natives, rarely visible, clamped their hands over their ears at the sight of the stranger, screeching as they disappeared from view.

It was time to go, that was clear. In a stabilized paddle boat he made his way through rough, blue-black weather up the coast, with its frightening white sand bars extending between land and sea like hyphens. The voyage took three days; the nights were the most difficult, when he was possessed by extreme anxiety and frequently thought he'd been swallowed by a monster in whose belly he was now floundering about. The oarsmen he'd hired were deathly silent, and their white arms swinging to and fro in the darkness hardly proved they weren't in fact dead. He flung himself down and trailed his hands over the side of the boat, filling them with water from the silent sea, and drank until his tongue swelled with fire. At peace once more, he collapsed into the bottom of the boat; but his old dreams of being rocked into silence, unknown to anyone including himself, were finished even so.

In Ronton, the capital, he embarked as a sick passenger on a little vessel which was just about to depart on a pleasure trip to a little archipelago far away, in among the Bridge Islands. The ship's doctor soon had him on his feet again, it only needed a little blood-letting, and protected by the false identity he had acquired temporarily, he thought he'd soon be able to recover the peace of mind he'd found during his stay in Belize. He borrowed a mirror the last day he was alone in the cramped sick bay, stinking of veronal, and examined his face closely in the green light from the porthole. Was it not new, was it not the face of another man, a face which hadn't existed previously but had been born painfully on the bottom of the long, narrow boat, cruising among the dead animals in the harbour? What? Was it possible after all to become a completely new person, to shake off the odious personality one could no longer bear? How he longed for a miracle of transformation!

In a mood of superior gaiety, he noted how the other passengers observed him with sober indifference, evidently no one suspected anything; the experience of boundless beauty, the sea a well of light and blueness, the horizon a hair-fine thread stretched like elastic by the billowing waves, the yellow, pearl-like balloon of the sky, everything combined to make each individual a solitary and removed for the moment any desire to find out more about them. He lay on the after deck in the shadow of a lifeboat, listening to people talking, an infectious laugh, or the cook prattling with his parrot: but none of this affected him, he was possessed once more by blissful tranquillity. Not even over dinner did he need to return to the past; when they talked at all, they only discussed new sensations provided by another day of their voyage: a new kind of fish had leapt up over the surface from the depths beneath, a reddish star had been following them all day and seemed to reflect something in the sea, or a ship had passed uncomfortably close to their own.

They gradually approached their destination; the brave little steamer chugged away merrily, quite unlike the big greyhounds they'd passed at the beginning of the trip which didn't dare venture so far out to sea, but a little work-horse plodding away gamely, straining its every sinew up the hill.

Then he was lying down one day and could feel when he pressed his hands to his eyes that someone was watching him from the side. He looked up quickly: it was only the English miss, slim, always cool no matter how hot the weather, leaning back against the rail and watching him with a remarkable intensity which stabbed into his own eyes. He met her gaze, although he was already starting to tremble as he realized with acute certainty that all was lost. Eventually, she became unsure of herself as well, looked down, kicked a piece of rope end towards him, then walked slowly over the hot deck towards the bridge.

He closed his eyes again and pretended calmly to untwist the little rope and wrap it hard around his wrists. He lay there all afternoon and the thumping of the engines seeped into his excessively fast pulse and every time the pain came on he would tighten the rope as hard as he could, as if he could strangle what was going to come anyway. At dinner he sat there trembling, waiting, could hardly eat a thing, replying sullenly and monosyllabically to all the sympathetic questions, and it wasn't until the dessert, as she sat there crumbling a rusk over her cream, that she slowly looked up at him and said quickly, through clenched lips, stiff and austere like the daughter of a colonel in the colonial army she may well have been: 'You're the boxer Jimmie Baaz, aren't you?'

Oh, what could he say to that? He pushed his chair back and jumped to his feet, and tried to deny the claimed acquaintance; but inexorably, it all took possession of him, he was forced down cruelly but slowly by a merciless force which affected all parts of his body, he was doubled up by a slow cramp, not even his throat was spared. He wanted to deny it with all the vocal resources he could muster, but everything except a whimper was brutally restrained; exposed to everyone's gaze like a dartboard, he slumped back on to his chair.

'Yes,' he whispered, trying to eat. 'Yes, yes.'

All was lost now, once and for all. The voyage had lost all its meaning and the destination had never had any meaning, he was the kind of traveller who sets off on a journey in the secret hope of never arriving, just travelling for the sake of travelling, we all know the type. Now the others had him in an octopus-like embrace, it seemed to him, and there was no point in running away. They were crowding round him all the time on deck now; in their way they respected his incognito, and would sit silently for ages in his company, as if just enjoying his presence, sucking out his silence with their voluptuous lips. All he wanted now in his nocturnal frenzy was to get back to Ronton; he was tortured by the slow beat of the pistons which kept him awake all night, and when he did occasionally doze off, he dreamt he was a tall giant wading through the sea alongside the boat in rubber boots; the boat was always a paddle steamer in his dreams, and he was spinning the paddles round at a tremendous speed with his little finger. Filled with despair, he would then be woken up again by the noise of the engines and the nocturnal seas slapping against his porthole. The last night before the shipwreck, he jumped out of his berth and raced upstairs on to the deck into the cold dawn, just when the moon was speeding up. Everywhere the sea was speckled with white foam, the horizons seemed to be raised above the water and hovering loosely between the sea and the sky before moving in on him, drawn by some unseen hand, and the pressure was already beginning to grow around his head. He flung himself down in his usual place by the lifeboat and his fingers started fiddling absent-mindedly with the little piece of rope the girl had kicked over to him. Without realizing it, he lay there freezing in the wind at first, listening to the orchestra playing; an iron rod was clanging down in the engine room, and the parrot seemed to be fluttering around the cook's cabin.

Then he suddenly felt the rough rope around his fingers and pulled it slowly over his chest and up towards his chin. He held his right arm stiffly in the air, watching the rope in horror; some gruesome quality he had only just seen in it put him in a frenzy, he rolled over on to his stomach and pounded the deck like a man possessed. The rope coiled itself before his very eyes, no, he couldn't avoid the rope's red colour, a red which stabbed him from pulse to pulse with a thousand concealed spikes, and howling inwardly, he was flung backwards like a bullet through space, and with a merciless sucking noise the green wave enveloped him once more. He ran from bows to stern, no one was allowed near him; the English girl sometimes stood in his way, gazing at him pleadingly. The artillery captain with the big boxer dog, which later drowned, was running around the after deck in his clattering boots, playfully setting the dog on him while pretending not to notice they existed.

When the storm broke, they could see it rising suddenly from the western horizon like a giant bird, then setting course for their ship, faster and faster, spreading its pearl-grey wings wider and wider; a leaden cloud hung down from its claws like a stolen lamb as it swooped down over them, howling, apparently intent on hacking them to pieces; just before they were smothered, they could see how one of its wings dropped stone-like towards the water, and as if it had been hit by a shot, blood in the form of a blood-red glow was running down its white feathers and all over them. Then everything was compressed into a pitiful mass under the bird, fears and fantasies, happiness, pain, malice and all the other special things; they huddled together in the shuddering lounge as the panelling bulged, and yelled at each other confidential things they would normally only be able to whisper while the captain's boxer and Madame's senile little boy lay terrified in a crumpled heap at the top of a staircase, trembling together. Only Jimmie, filled with a disgust which drowned everything else, was on his own, rolling about on the floor of his cabin.

The catastrophe saved him, indeed, here was no place for hypocrisy, and the shipwreck actually saved him from the worst – and now, as he races through the island's blond morning only a few rocks away from the longed-for hollow which will swallow him up, everything is childishly simple, like a croquet lawn where every hoop has learnt to obey the swishing of the balls. The sun released its cluster of balloons as it detached itself from the sea and lay there shivering half an inch over the horizon, metallically yellow but still chilled by the night frost; as he approached rapidly, the bushes stirred slightly in the gentle, still-cool breeze the sea was blowing nonchalantly at them, and even before he could see it, the grass was rustling sleepily in front of them. His feet now launched him upwards in a series of little bounces, and ignoring the iguanas slithering over the rocks, he breasted the tape triumphantly as he entered the thicket, thrusting the branches effortlessly aside as if he were diving into water, and suddenly he found himself in the long grass.

He felt dizzy and stood absolutely still, everything was so fantastically different and his sense of liberation enveloped him like a breeze, laden with his own warmth and filled with mysterious scents. Seen through the latticed tips of the grass which was much taller than a man, the light flowed past like cool, silent streams, the warm shadow of the cathedral pressed gently down upon him and he sank slowly to the ground, overcome by events. It was windier now, but he felt nothing of it, merely saw it in the grass high above him as the expanse of panicles straining towards the sun swayed violently, and white butterflies with thin red markings on their left wings bobbed up and down like distressed boats on the elevated ocean. He felt he was lying on the sea bottom, no pain touched him any more, no chill cut through him, no heat attempted to embrace him, no hatred flowed over him, no love seemed to scratch him, no longing to carve him up.

He was dragging his fingers over the ground, flat, hard, still slightly damp after the night, then suddenly cried out in alarm as he came up against an obstacle, and when he looked down and round about him he realized to his indifferent surprise he was already lying in a hollow in the ground. The sides were like polished crystal, but the bottom was soft and fluffy, a clump of low grass was waving like a cloud at his feet, weak puffs of invisible warmth were blowing down regularly between the blades of grass and the peaceful church-light was reflected in the oystered edges; yes, this was a hollow for all eternity. He lay there on his back for a long time without attempting to move any part of his body, not even in his mind, as butterflies fluttered lazily like listless sailing boats in the grassy swell above and small, green insects and small, spherical blobs of sticky fluid sprayed down, urged on by the wind to sink beneath the surface like drifting mines.

Then something ominous glinted high above in the slowly swaying tips of eternity; he saw it straight away of course, but tried to forget it, clenched his fists to form a cushion under his neck, and kept his eyes firmly shut. But he knew nevertheless, indeed, he could see behind his eyelids that the spider was getting closer and closer, the yellow thread swung gently between the downy stalks of the grass; in a vain attempt to embrace the whole world with its graceful claws, the big, red body expanded and throbbed menacingly, filled with animal desire, animal agony, and a kind of human despair. Jimmie suddenly cried out, but when he attempted to leap out of the deep hollow, a shudder passed through his body like a swollen vein and he lay paralysed as the spider's body hovered large and lazy, indeed, it was the laziness that scared him most, just a hand's breadth above his face. Powerless and at the mercy of the insect, his face distorted by his terrified muscles, more helplessly naked than ever before, deprived of any vestige of hard-won dignity, he waited for the spider to fall. The wait seemed endless, and the very delay was the high point of his torture; only a moment more and the disgusting contact would be his liberation.

Suddenly a gust of wind dispersed the suffocating atmosphere, the spider glided over him, lacerating Jimmie's left cheek with a hastily lowered claw on its way past, and landed on the left-hand edge of the hollow with a soundless thump, throbbing against the silence. Then the spider lay there, crouched diagonally above him, motionless as it lay in wait for some motionless victim, its colour shifting with awe-inspiring speed from grape-green to deep blue and back again; shadows dancing in the grass seemed to gasp in horror when they settled here, and a butterfly which had gone astray and wandered into the darkness was pulled down irresistibly as if it had wings of iron.

Suddenly, the spider darted out from the edge and swung quickly past him, a thread trembled just above his mouth and then, before he knew what was happening, the red web was secured above his face, and the spider lay there, fat and self-assured; it swung lightly to and fro so that the whole web dipped down towards him, as if its mere existence were not torture enough. Oh, if only it would break and embrace him stickily, he would prefer slow suffocation despite everything. But the spider kept on swinging tantalizingly back and forth, as if trying to imprint its image upon its prey; he had been blind thus far, it seemed, but now he was overwhelmed by certainty; the red peril invaded his eyes and in the midst of his agony he cried out for help, pinioned by his fear. His words stretched the mesh in desperation, but eventually they fell back into his mouth, as cold and flaccid as coins. He could no longer count on the feelings of fellowship he had so laboriously dismantled, but would have to remain in the web for ever, always alone.

Then he felt as if the bottom of the hollow were giving way, he was sinking slowly, the spider shrunk into a tiny grape as the web suddenly came loose and drifted slowly down towards him. Deeper, deeper, he cried out in desperation and fell faster and faster; the ferocious outline of the web imprinted itself as a shadow against the icy grey mouth of his grave, and with a final, pitiful gesture of self-defence, after years of agony, he reached its blind bottom.

Once more he was on his knees outside the stone base of the barracks, in one of those years when all was indescribable confusion. Hulks of merchant vessels floated in the harbour where they lived, pillaged and plundered by the locals; no coachman dared direct his horses into the harbour district any more, horses had been slaughtered in broad daylight by the starving masses, grass had already overrun the harbour railway lines, the harbour rats were thin and easily provoked, the cannonades from the sea grew more intense by the day, and on certain mornings he could never forget, the local children followed their mothers with empty baskets to the barracks at the top of the hill. They lay alongside the long, cold, perimeter wall, shivering vacantly, without a word, without a smile, without a glance at their neighbour, and they had long since given up trying to interpret the wild laughter and terrified shrieks which engulfed the barracks. 'Did they hit you, Mum?' he yelled the first time she came out on to the steps, holding on to the wall so as not to fall, and he snatched eagerly at the basket full of whatever the soldiers did not want.

'They didn't hit, just fondled.'

His childhood was full of dreary games. Deadly serious, they would smash the windows in the cockpit of the crane with pebbles from the forgotten store, and for hours on end would crouch – crouching was their constant characteristic – on the girders of the crane and pretend they were being besieged by rats; one morning, next to the first of the cranes where his father moored the boat he used for smuggling, they found a tall, oblong bundle tied firmly to a pole. They crowded round the canvas parcel like a flock of jackdaws, clambered up the pole, fiddled with the red string, danced around it like Red Indians. The July heat pressed down heavily on all their heads, and next day they were met by an unknown smell lurking around the bundle; strangely subdued, they sat down on the quay frowning like old men until the harbour patrol arrived in their armoured car, cut the red string, slit open the white sack and flung the naked corpse on to the wharf. Then they all ran off home, shouting, taking pieces of string with them as souvenirs.

There was a distinct atmosphere of *angst* in Jimmie's kitchen; his father was lying on the floor pretending to be asleep although he was only drunk, his naked chest was covered in scratches, a newly washed shirt was hanging by a piece of string over the stove. *A newly washed shirt was hanging by a piece of string over the stove –* Jimmie didn't need to look more closely at the string over the stove and compare it with the piece he had in his pocket; as he ran up the steep hill towards the barracks, everything was excruciatingly clear, everything was finished and hopeless, his never-ending flight had begun. Huddled under the years of his childhood, he allowed everything to flow over him: the brutality of the barracks, the brutal hatred of the starving masses when the streets had to be cleared, the contempt of those who had eaten to satiety, oh yes, he knew all about running away from humiliation. The red string always wrapped itself round his legs at critical moments, new ways of running away had always to be found, panic softened his back and hollowed out his will; success, a

62

career established in doubtful circumstances were the new ways of running away he hit upon, but over and over again he was cast back into the mire of memory. Why was everything so cruel, oh, that he would never understand! How could he understand that when he was always running away?

But now the bottom on which he lay was rising like the floor of a lift, the red spider was already embracing its prey as it swayed in the shadows under the grass. All was lost, all had gone to waste, all the years ignoring what was right propelled him ruthlessly towards the web. And then those cruel claws, the hairy body engulfing him like a wave, and everything dissolving into a blood-red haze. Then just sinking, sinking, and oblivion.

The Hunger of Day

How did day come to the island? Ah, there is plenty to
say about that. First of all a bow looked as if it were
rising from the eastern horizon, horseshoe-like, coated
with silver on its outer edge; it pressed up gently against
the sun, framing it for a moment like a bucolic
triumphal arch, then shot off at reckless speed in well-
practised loops across the sky, over everyone's head, as
far as the opposite horizon, and then seemed to give way
to some unknown pressure and fall towards the sea.
Eddies appeared here and there in the morning-blue
water, and before it was hit by the broken bow, you
could sense a degree of understandable nervousness
clinging to the surface which until recently had been so
hysterically tense; suddenly the nerves of the sea were
exposed so nakedly that an enormous outbreak of
despair seemed about to occur at any moment; the
gigantic fish whose spears used to pierce the bare flesh
of the blue expanse nevertheless seemed blissfully
unaware of their role as executioners. Then the crash
came; still pliant despite its broken back, the bow sank
down into the sea, its long, supple lines outlined for one
brief moment on the surface itself before being pulled

rapidly down by an invisible hand, and all at once a remarkable colour change took place: the bright silvery gleam disappeared without warning, leaving only a stinging blueness which spread rapidly under the surface of the sea from the pitiful remains of the bow, only to be hauled up into the day like nets being winched into a boat. The blue of day made its entrance and the white morning horses of the clouds galloped wearily towards the horizon, in rolled the round sheep, grazing lazily in the very hot sun which was now a lonely ball of fire swelling slowly from its own heat.

A remarkable period of great, confused optimism now followed on the island. Once again, they all realized with a shudder that they were still alive; the chill of death which had clung to them throughout the night was thawed yet again as the heat caressed their limbs, gently, gently. If anyone thought he suddenly heard birdsong, they would all stand up apprehensively without a word and stare at each other in bewilderment; it was like diving into unknown waters – but nothing happened as yet. They were just sucked down into the greenery, but nothing happened yet, only those floating corals that were always pushed aside by their foreheads. The fire was burning on the beach, the wet branches they broke off and threw down from the cliff top gave off unwavering, tearful smoke which always rose vertically and produced little heat; and now there was nothing to roast or boil over it. It just went on burning, like a hope rising to the heavens, unstoppable.

In silence, but filled with joy which was perhaps not obvious but nevertheless for most of them felt like the glow that used to emanate from their nursery window the first Sunday in Advent, they gathered round the fire, pushed the dark leaves closer to the flames, poked at a charred branch and steered their gaze along the column of smoke right to the top, where it broadened to form a blue plateau. Occasionally they would also glance out to sea, surreptitiously or quite openly like the English girl: she would shade her eyes with her hand and watch the banks of clouds sailing like convoys across the horizon. She was still calm, unspoilt by all the temptations which hopelessness entails willy-nilly; but her gentleness, in her face, body, movements and thoughts, sank slowly down, fell off her like the soft clay clinging to a shell, leaving it glistening and hard as enamel.

It was still not very warm, not as hot as it would become when the heat flung itself upon them almost with a roar, and they would collapse panting in somebody's shadow. If one wanted, one could now close one's eyes and be strolling along the holiday beach in the quiet summer bay some years previously. The water slowly fell asleep and, suddenly, the white edging of froth bordering the beach started gleaming red as tens of thousands of shells were caressed out of the calm. The English girl waded slowly out into the water in her bare feet, while the captain sat in the sand rubbing away at his only jackboot with a stone; and invariably, never varying her familiar posture – leaning far forward in front of the fire, a dirty length of cloth wrapped around her and her hair hanging loose around her head like that of a madwoman, one hand stubbornly shielding her forehead, eyes, nose, and her left arm dangling nonchalantly as if it were out of joint – Madame. Boy Larus, the airman, was still standing timidly by the fire, just gazing down at it, occasionally stamping on the ashes at its edge, occasionally glancing sadly at the crouching woman. Lucas Egmont seemed to be still trying to sleep, lying on his back with arms outstretched like those of a swimmer floating on a lake; the boxer was completely hidden by his canvas sheet and lay there rather more motionless than his paralysis would seem to dictate.

This was the time when hunger would make its presence felt. Not the whimpering kind; hunger would slowly take possession of them as silently as a float in the morning pond, nudging all thoughts gently aside, its sharp, spool-like form relieving some of them just for a moment from the disgusting green slime, and their longing became solid and indivisible. As if in a painful, dream-like trance, for their brief hunger had already tired them out, they felt the lure of the hollow beside the crippled boxer, where the remains of their food supplies were buried in a box: ship's rusks, a few tins of sardines, green half-rotten pineapples. They'd do anything to secure that hollow for themselves, or so they thought; but they knew they'd never do it in fact. As they felt themselves fading, their hunger seemed to be a kind of promise: I am hungry, therefore I am – and just now, as the merciful sun caressed them so soothingly, this promise was all they needed.

The water had risen over the English girl's ankles, but she kept on wading out to sea as shells floated up and gathered round her calves like a ring of coral. She looked down, and found she could still base dreams on this red ring. It was that time in the lounge at Beavershill; cousin Charles, the one everyone called Caruso because his voice had broken, had also come for Christmas. '*Ah ma chère,*' he said in affected French, he was only fifteen after all, '*comme vous êtes belle, comme vous êtes belle.*' Blushing, he sank to his knees before where she was sitting on the carpet in front of the fire, it was that Christmas she'd twisted her ankle when she fell off a sledge and she still had difficulty in walking.

Quick as a flash, he tied two rattles round her thin calves, and how she shook as he helped her to her feet, how the wainscot seemed to bulge, and how endlessly long and uneven the carpet seemed to be because she had to support herself on him as she walked!

Yes, everyone seemed to be dreaming, hoping for a happy end, or just out of despair: there are so many reasons for dreaming. – One of them was not dreaming, though; he'd disappeared an hour earlier. He was still roaming through the jungle, indeed, as it was not until these last six months of his life that he'd ever seen so many trees, such high grass, such marvellous plants, everything was jungle; every step he took, he bent cautiously to avoid being hit in the forehead by the pinacles of the grass; he was no doubt a little afraid as well. Sometimes he stepped into little holes concealed by moss and spiders' webs, and then he would shake so much with fear that he even had to laugh himself. If only his mates from the dredger could see him now, the giant, the Giant, the Giant Tim Solider.

Now he was scared by every unknown noise that pierced the air, his legs were so tired they might give way any moment, him, the man who'd never been scared of anything. Well, once something awful had happened, a preliminary to what was happening to him now, imprinted on his very being by the claws of the ravens. The dredger had run aground in the fog, they suddenly found themselves stuck in the sand, five hundred yards south of the stone quay of Nosara. It was quiet and still and damp and the fog surrounded them like four walls, seagulls rose and fell all around them, and the tug was half a cable's length ahead, its engines thudding softly. He was alone, and could hear clattering and shouting from the boat, and then all of a sudden something remarkable happened and what happened was so terrible that he had to rub his eyes to see if he was dreaming – but it was true even so. Wide open mouthed, he watched his own eyes come floating towards him through the fog, inflated like little balloons but his even so, the enlargement was incredible and horrific: he could see all the terrible details of those drumskin-tight globes; the red lines over the whites looked like whiplash wounds, and what a pitiful little membrane it was holding back his pupils and their green globes from falling out and dropping down into the sea! Then the eyes were hoisted up by a sudden gust of wind and extinguished by the fog, boats immediately started bellowing, near and far, but even so he'd never been as isolated as he was on that occasion.

I'm blind, he thought, I've gone blind, for now it had dawned on him how ghastly his eyes were, it no longer seemed possible for him to see. He could never shake off the memory of that stretched membrane, and the enormous red edges. You can't possibly see with eyes like that, he thought, groping for the rail like a blind man. At that point the dredger must have refloated itself and gradually started moving again; as the cables tightened the water started singing, but the fog only got thicker, and the hull of a white passenger ship loomed up in ghostly slow motion to starboard, only to sink back again like a mirage as a seagull's cry tore open a chalk-white rip in the veil. Otherwise there was nothing to suggest he wasn't blind: once you've seen your eyes you don't dare to see. You close your eyes in panic, terrified they'll cease to work just as suddenly as a clock stops; you can see nothing but your own inadequate eyes.

Oh, how did he get over it? It took months of

harrowing attempts to forget before he regained control, before the machinery was working perfectly once more. And now the same thing was happening all over again – what can you do with a machine that has sprouted eyes and is filled with distrust as it watches itself functioning? He was ground down by misgivings, he could see the idiotic pointlessness of all his finely formed joints, his big muscles, all the bones in his body, his movements – and he stepped to one side with his doubts and his fears and watched himself surreptitiously, and look: his body was no longer alive, it only moved with difficulty. He was so scared when he thought of the day when everything would come to a standstill, when everything would become entangled in one monumental fit of cramp. As always, he relied on his strength, protected himself with his speed, thought that the key was to wake up, feel his muscles longing to be tensed, feel normal, healthy hunger, healthy because he knew it would soon be satisfied; he could already see himself stretched out at the water's edge, loosely stretched like a broken cable, whimpering faintly from the effects of this fire whose greedy tongue was poking into all the channels of his body. In his delirium he would get it into his head that the sun was a ripe apple, just one thrust of his body, a lunge with his teeth, and there it was in his mouth, crunching as he bit into it, the juice trickling down his chin like blood, the soft flesh being forced violently down his throat, the more vehemently the better. Or fish would start creeping up the beach, their red eyes blinking, wriggling towards him on their bellies; he only had to open wide and they would creep into his mouth, then just bite, and bite again.

Right from the start, of course, his position was so

exposed, so hopelessly confused; unfortunate, but it couldn't be helped. As he was the only member of the crew to survive, he was their leader, with responsibility for his passengers even after the catastrophe, and hence to some extent he ought to impose his will on them; he was also a subordinate, their servant, someone they could still shout at in frustration: carry that box over here, give me your canvas sheet, I want to rest, we're hungry, bring in the food.

Why should I be the one to survive, he often moaned to himself during those long nights of hunger when his kitchen at home in Dunbari embraced him with its green walls (oh, the eternal frying pan, always the frying pan on the gas stove complete with lid, white steam spurting out of the cracks, and the smell of that steam, the smell of all the butchers' shops, all the bars, pubs, grocery stores, restaurants and galleys he had ever been in throughout his life; and his wife, his blonde wife with the bun in her hair secured by a rubber band: she had the same smell in her hair, the same smell in her hair as she stood with arms painfully outstretched in front of the stove, her pure white arms, stopping him from eating, always stopping him from eating, shouting, My child, my child!). Why was I the one who survived, he thought, why not the captain, for instance?

But the truth was, the captain had been drunk when the catastrophe happened. He often used to sense omens three days in advance, and asked to be locked in his cabin with the whole supply of whisky; the first mate had kept him company that last day, and Tim was the one who swung the wheel round after the fatal change of course; just when everything happened, Tim saw him hurled to the deck by a huge wave and then, painfully and almost disgustingly slowly, float a little way aft before changing direction and being washed just as slowly out through the smashed rail, disappearing for ever without the slightest sign of resistance nor even a word of farewell. Not a sound came from the crew in the engine room, not the slightest whisper; they'd just stayed put, anonymous as always; and then there were some people the lifeboat had fallen on to, it seemed that somebody heavy had suddenly hung on to its side, and it overturned in a flash and sank beneath the waves with awesome speed. All those who had sought refuge in it were lost without trace.

But Tim Solider had escaped, more or less miraculously. He'd been flung overboard like the mate, but they weren't all that far from land in fact; he felt full of water and seemed to be sinking, getting as heavy as lead with the whole of the ocean pressing down on his chest like a stone cross. But to his amazement, his back had suddenly scraped against sharp rocks, he lay there, still, apathetic, limp, and a grey-green membrane of boundless majesty spread itself over his whole world; as if trapped in a soap bubble, he could see the blurred outline of the ship on the other side of the membrane, the shriek staggered through to him and the membrane vibrated slightly, then it exploded in a puff of foam and he found himself kneeling in the path of the sea as it raced towards him like an express train. Oh, how he struggled that morning to remain alive, he was possessed by a raging fury and nothing, be it the slippery stones under everyone's feet, this cyclone determined to suck everyone into the air only to fling them down again on their backs, or these frenzied people wrestling with him in desperation on the reef, for fear of not being rescued or fear of being rescued – nothing could stop him. Together with some of the few sensible survivors – the airman, the otherwise unpleasant artillery captain – he carried ashore first the women, green and shaking and moaning away doggedly as if they were in labour. Then, some days after everyone had come to their senses without yet realizing their plight, they established their heroes.

'Don't mention it,' said the captain modestly to the English girl, although he was the one who started it off, with his I know about organization, I'm a soldier you see. These catastrophes will happen, you know, and so I naturally take over, organize things, get a grip on things, if you like. It's just our duty, you see, duty, my dear lady; my young friend the airman and I know best when it comes to that sort of thing – isn't that right? Take my boot, will you, and buff it up as well as you can, it's the twelfth of May today, if I'm not mistaken. No, don't mention it, my young friend and I are no heroes, it's just that we've learnt how to organize things.

What about Tim, then? Oh no, nobody said a word about him. He would have liked to shout out in disgust: organization! Come off it, panic more like! But something held him back. Every time one of the survivors turned to him, he felt as if a stream of cold air was flowing towards him; it only happened when there was something that needed doing, something dirty, something that had broken, something that hurt, something involving a risk. You're so big and strong, etc., you've been coping so well, you're in better shape than any of us, and so on, but their voices were hard and superficial. It was all orders, no requests, no warmth, they just wanted him to do as he was told. Even so, at first he was proud of the way they appealed to his body; he didn't see through their brutal cunning until his hunger became so strong he realized it would never be satisfied. His body refused to obey him, it became extremely difficult to move a single limb because, all the time, he could see the dead bones moving underneath his skin, his cranium was gruesomely bare under skin and sinews, his heart compressed and opened with a rhythm that was worryingly unsteady.

Now nothing was quite so easy any more, he built up his mental barricades in the hope that he might one day be able to fight on them; he lay there at night, calm on the surface but all the time hunted down ruthlessly by his ego, along the beach, up the cliffs, through the jungle, and down again along a vertical crevice with few holds for his hands and feet.

Who am I, he would think, who am I? Why should I? Why should I sacrifice myself for all these people, when none of them is prepared to sacrifice himself for me? Aren't we all castaways? I was a crewman on the boat, that's true, but does it matter any more what any of us was? Haven't we changed our lives fundamentally, hasn't some of what we were been destroyed? Aren't we all equally naked, aren't all our fingers equally greedy when the food is shared out, aren't all our fingernails equally sharp when we gather round the water tank? Is there anything here apart from skeletons, our skin and our guts to indicate that anybody should have power over anybody else? It may well have been the case on board the boat that somebody could shout to somebody else: listen here, slave, I'm hungry; but surely that right, if indeed it was a right, must have lapsed now that we're all living in the same conditions, where money, social position and background have been stripped away from us all? Haven't we been resurrected from the cruel sea, or are the memories of how things used to be going to dictate the way we treat each other for ever? Shouldn't whoever is strongest, who does most to ensure we can live a bit longer, be the one in authority, the one who gets most credit, the one who earns everybody's respect, the one who glows in the warmth others bestow upon him? And if not? Well, if that isn't the case, why not stop delivering the goods, why not just lie down on the sands and listen to the cradle-song of the sea, get up when you feel hungry and go hunting on your own account, for it isn't necessary, nor even possible, to take responsibility for people who have nothing but contempt for your services and yourself.

But a new day dawned, and when everybody had woken up and gone for their usual walk round the white rock and come back again, he could feel the instinct to obey taking possession of him once again, and it was terrible. Although nobody said a word to him, although nobody shouted at him, they only needed to gesture towards him and he found himself helplessly subordinate to these people; jump like a fish, wriggle like a snake – no, nothing was any good. It was his fire burning on the beach; the others might well lie watching its cool blue flames or throw a twig on when the mood took them, but he was the one who had to keep it going, he was the one who had to break off spiky branches from the bushes although he disliked doing it because they seemed to conceal so much that was unknown, he was the one who had to keep a constant check on the height of the smoke column over the beach and the intensity of the flames, and he was the one everybody would set upon if the fire should go out, complaining, accusing, passing judgement, sentencing and banishing.

Oh, what was it that held him captive? Was there

75

some special quality present in the others which made them so superior to him? He observed them all in turn, weighed their every word, analysed their every movement, scrutinized their every action, and eventually concluded that even the softest of them, the gentlest, the most sensitive of them treated him with a kind of self-evident brutality nobody but he seemed to notice, precisely because it was primarily directed at him. The English girl would wade out into the water, in exactly the same way day after day; her brown calves were attractively taut, just for one rare moment the cloth she had wrapped round her would glide down from her right shoulder, which glowed a dark white colour, stimulating but chastely repulsing his gaze; the beautifully tense curve of her neck would resist all efforts to bend it down, and no, there was no trace of subservience, everything seemed to belong to her with a kind of mystical naturalness, although she herself didn't raise a finger to acquire it. The women he'd known before he was sentenced to death here on the island were different, and didn't even dare to own what they'd acquired. Everything had to be asked about over and over again: are we allowed to sit here on the grass, just think if somebody comes, are we allowed on this road, isn't it private, am I allowed to like you, don't you belong to somebody else? He'd never owned himself either, and he was just like the women he'd had. Always being aware; nothing is mine, least of all my body; all those movements I make under the tap when I get home from the smithy, they're just on loan; all those thoughts buzzing around in my head are just tourists stopping there for the night, homeless pairs who have rented somewhere where they can make love; the noise from the dredger's crane will always be heard, the moments of sweet unrest in my heart are stolen from the shipping company that employs me.

What cure is there, what should a desperate man do when he becomes aware of his own impotence? One day he's a little drunk and merry and has a bit more money than usual, takes his old lady to a little pub away from their usual blue-grey haunts, an upper-class pub. Let's have a bit of fun shall we, and let the dredger go to hell, and that stink of sewers and rotten fish we have to put up with every day, poisoning the atmosphere in our gloomy flat. Now they can forget all that, the wine is sparkling just like it does in the adverts, laughter is bubbling away, everything round about them will smell nice for once, of wine and flowers, clean glasses, big soft carpets and the musicians all dressed in white – but why does everybody stare at them when they come in, it cuts him to the bone, pierces right through the effects of the drink he's already had, and his wife Sally by his side, why is she whispering: oh, it's so posh, do we dare go in? But why does everybody stare at you when you're carving the joint so that you get all nervous and your knife slips, why does everybody hold their breath and listen in such a provocative way when you laugh, why does Sally go on all evening about the price of the food, the quality of the tablecloth, the age of the musicians, instead of turning her back on all that, like some people can? No, they all stare at you all the time: do you still smell of sewers even though you have clean clothes on and have had several baths during the course of the afternoon? Yes, that's it exactly, you always smell of sewers, there's an invisible cloud around you giving off a smell which always prevents you from assuming the handsome mien of supremacy which certain other people can, you can never move about in complete freedom, you always have to ask yourself: am I allowed to do this, who's in charge of this, how much does all this cost, will it break if I touch it? How do you think anyone can escape from it all? You are sitting there as securely as anybody can, but secure in your own filth, secure in your own poverty, secure in your own impotence.

If anybody comes along and says it will all get better, or some of it at least, if you don't believe him, send the idiot packing. Should you make a scene? What should you make a scene about – about those people who stare at you when you enter forbidden territory wanting a good time? Oh, yes. But what is it you're risking, and that little hideaway you've got on the dredger, well, if they find that – what have you gained? No, you're on your own, people are on their own, just get used to that and show your teeth if anybody approaches. Good God, you carry your slave nature around with you wherever you go, drag him round all the parks and gardens where the police are on patrol: that's Tim Solider, the taller they are the further they fall.

Why not run away then? Yes, you could go out in a boat even though you've never done it before, and sail away from it all, Brisbane and Mogadishu, Muscat, Trincomali, Petsamo and Jacksonville, yes, you could sail round and round the map for ever and ever and still not get away from what you want to get away from, still be identified as a servant even so, someone anybody can make use of whenever they like. And then one day you come to an unknown country, a little country, well, to be really accurate, an island, where they have no laws, no currency restrictions, no armed police, none of the things you've always complained about – and even so, you kow-tow with the same unwilling willingness, let yourself be subjugated, feel this fatal sensation of impotent inferiority which you first came across that time in the restaurant and then keep coming across wherever you go, whatever you do, wherever you try to escape.

The night of the thirteenth of May was probably the worst. Everybody seemed to go to bed early, though it is not clear if they were already so exhausted or whether it was illusory; in any case, the captain snored in self-satisfaction, and in the weak glow from the fire you could see his hands creeping back and forth over the canvas, like a wolf stalking some prey. The airman's delicate little head seemed to tremble when touched by the shadows, and his breathing was almost inaudible. The fire crackled discreetly, the occasional iguana still awake rattled away up in the cliffs, and the two women lay closely intertwined, even in their sleep continuing to radiate the usual touch-me-not contempt should anyone look at them uninvited. The light from the fire glowed on red-headed Madame's forehead, and at frequent intervals, convulsed by some limitless agony, she would repeat a few half-choked words sounding like: glisso-loo-emm-glisso-loo-emm.

The cold descended, the sea seemed to be turned to stone, even the soughing sounded frozen and was left hanging from the stiff waves; but Tim Solider didn't feel cold, he felt no cold because his hunger was a fire burning right through him; his hunger was an awl sticking into him wherever it could cause pain; his hunger was a bird roasting over the fire, being turned round and round on a little stick; his hunger was a woman whispering out of the darkness: of course you can eat, but kiss me first; his hunger was a memory from the kitchen back at home where the frying pan was

79

always on the gas stove; his hunger was another memory, enclosed by a sea-grey membrane, enthusiastically and yet coolly rising and falling like the indicator on an unsteady thermometer inside him, the memory of a path along the beach, up the cliffs, through the jungle and back down along a vertical crevice with few holds for his hands and feet.

That's where he was heading for now, unsteadily and frequently stumbling, and already the hot day had arrived. The first mild warmth had pushed its little joke as far as it could, and now the real heat zoomed in like a rocket and exploded in the sea, where the breakers seemed to be writhing in agony, and in one's own body and in everything round about. The iguanas slid off their rocks, fell four or five feet, landed on their backs and lay there motionless, their yellow bellies arched towards the sun. Tim Solider suddenly fell flat on his face as if hit in the neck by a rabbit punch, cut his arm on a sharp grass stalk and lay there panting in the grass, sucking voraciously at his wound. Sweat poured off him, only his mouth was dry as a desert; he made a heroic effort and rose to his knees, groped for support, then fell down again. Then he crawled slowly through the grass, feeling as if he were being grilled over embers; it grew hotter and hotter as time went by. His sweat dried up, the whole of his body was now painfully dry, all his fluids seemed to have been sucked away and every time he crawled over some unevenness in the ground, he was convinced he would be reduced to crumbs. Now and then giant lizards rattled past in front of him, horrifyingly slowly, and from some angles looked like snakes; something with a cold, rasping belly crawled agonizingly slowly over both his legs, but he didn't have the strength, nor the courage, to turn round and see what it was.

Hours passed by, and still he was crawling along with exasperated energy; thousands of shooting pains plagued his body, his nerves were exposed to every agony homing in on him, smoke was rising from the ground, acrid and bitter, until in the end he could hardly breathe. This plain was endless; even when he raised his head as far as he could manage, he could see no end to it, only this tall, scorched grass with panicles swinging to and fro like hanged corpses high above his head. In an infinite vision of terror, he experienced eternity, all time ceased to exist, space ceased to exist, he was no longer a human being, he had no human qualities left, what did action mean? Colours faded away, sound was muted, thoughts were no longer thought, words lost their meaning, surfaces lost their edges, everything ossified, leaving only himself an anonymous being, crawling like a snake indefatigably over this horrific expanse without moving forwards or backwards, since all directions and all points of the compass were no more. Immersed in a hazy dream, he remembered his happy childhood when there was a five-minute run through what was now eternity.

He lay there for quite a long time with his face pressed hard into the ground, his hands outstretched, palms upwards as if he were expecting it to rain, senseless, apparently lifeless; but all the time something inside him was working intensively towards a particular goal, indeed, he was there already even though he couldn't move because of the intense heat and his own exhaustion. Gradually, however, the heat of the sun eased somewhat, he slowly recovered consciousness,

81

and after many pitiful attempts to get to his feet, he eventually managed it.

Still dizzy and weak after his loss of consciousness, he staggered through the grass once again, not really in a position to see anything at all, but nevertheless aiming stubbornly in a particular direction. The ground was no longer smoking now, a very large iguana at least a couple of feet long lay asleep in the grass: he stumbled over it and whipped round, ready to defend himself if it should attack. But the iguana had not moved, and somewhat surprised, he bent down over it and poked it cautiously with his foot; but still it didn't stir. Then he turned it over quickly, so that it was lying on its back: it was dead, of course, its belly split open by a stone; somebody had crushed the iguana with a stone, and turned it upright before running away. Tim lifted the heavy corpse and hurled it into the undergrowth.

Perplexed, he looked back in the direction he'd come from, and saw the white column of smoke rising above the trees, vertical, like a rope hanging down from the sky. The sky was unbearably blue and empty, and out of the void, as if emerging from a magician's hat, a flock of birds appeared, then descended upon him in deathly silence, dragging their wings over the grass, apparently without seeing him even though the nearest one swooped past only a hand's breath above his head; he had ducked involuntarily, and only now did he realize how unusually large the birds were.

He continued wandering through the grass, guided by his memory, and emerged on to a stony plateau, with black, volcanic rocks splashed with bird droppings. Cliffs rose steeply on either side of the plateau, naked and scarred, but at one point the cliff was pierced, and a v-shaped crack big enough to take a human body presented a hazardous route down to the beach. He paused and listened to the sea crashing on to the rocks down below: it sounded like a percussionist's first tentative beats on his drum. His heart started pounding as he strode towards the crevice, excited without knowing why; or rather: without wanting to know why.

Then he paused again, gripped by a strong feeling of being watched by someone he couldn't see as yet. The penny dropped immediately, and he stepped back in irritation. It was the birds that were observing him as they sat clamped to the cliff, apparently guarding the way down to the beach, motionless and silent, without so much as a twitching of their wings; he could see now that they weren't in fact as big as he'd thought when they swooped down a short while ago. They were dangerous because of their numbers rather than their size, and their beaks were as sharp as talons; he couldn't make out their eyes, which seemed to be directed at him and yet failed to follow him when he backed off; they were grey as well, as if covered by a film. Without a sound, he broke off a blade of grass and moved stealthily towards the crevice, letting the grass blade swing to and fro all the way along the row of birds: but their eyes just kept on staring vacantly in the same direction.

No doubt about it: the birds were blind, and that was why they brushed along the grass before landing. Dumb and blind, they led their lives on this island, and one could well ask why. Were they waiting for something? Were they intending to take advantage of a certain shipwreck? Was their sole purpose to wait for these seven people condemned to die? Tim dropped his blade of grass, then stood motionless to see if they'd noticed anything yet, but everything was as before. Then he tentatively took hold of a rocky pinnacle, crouched down and crawled along through the crevice, emerging unharmed on the other side. Stunned by the vastness of the panorama, he almost fell but flung himself backwards against the cliff and hung on as the vista impressed itself upon him. The sea was in a state of perpetual motion, surging in over the horizon; the tension between sea and sky was almost unbearable, everything was clear and large, no dirty smoke rose from ships to smudge the brilliant colours, not a sliver of land was to be seen, the sun was already starting its descent and the heat was growing less intense; a few red stars rose slowly up from the depths, everything was so classically beautiful, and yet so completely indifferent.

All the time his gaze was drawn irresistibly towards the island, towards the thin strip of beach, covered in sand and stones at this point. For the second time in his life on the island, he saw the green box lying down below like a little die wedged between two large stones, dangerously tempting, aiming an invisible beam of heat straight up at the cliff. Hot and eager, he decided on the spot to begin the risky descent. He forgot the birds and all the rest of it, his hunger clamped him firmly to the cliff face, his hunger selected the best footholds and the best projections for his hands. But when he was about halfway down and still had not got round to thinking about being afraid, a little stone right next to the one supporting his right foot suddenly came loose and tumbled down the cliff in a series of sharp thuds. His foot began to twitch in ridiculous fashion, and he had to take a firm grip on himself and calm down again; then he heard a fluttering sound above his head, and when he bent his head back to see what was happening, he saw one of the birds on its way down towards him, hopping from ledge to ledge, its eyes staring indifferently out into space; but its feet were as sensitive as a blind man's fingers and unerring in their choice of secure grips.

At first, he didn't realize what might happen, but when he eventually caught on, he forced himself back, trembling, against the cliff face, rubbed his body against it as if that would help him to achieve a firmer hold. It only needed the bird to touch one of his hands, brush against his shoulder, bump into his foot – and he would hurtle down to his death, would die with the green box only a couple of miserable yards away from him, would die just when salvation was so desperately near. But the bird came closer and closer, worst of all was the assured way in which it was progressing, oh, if only it had screeched, had flapped its wings madly, tried to peck him with its beak; but no: only this silence waiting to be shattered by violent action, whose terrible nature he couldn't yet conceive.

Then it made one final lunge towards him, down towards his right hand, and in desperation he let go, groping in thin air, rasping his nails against the cliff, and for one agonizing second he could feel himself slipping, the whole cliff seemed to collapse and spin round with him, blood seeped out from under his shredded finger-nails, then everything calmed down again gradually and he regained his grip with his right hand, hugging the cliff as tightly as he could.

The bird was now still again just a couple of feet above his head, waiting motionlessly, ruthlessly calm and staring vacantly at the horizon; its red-tipped beak was pointing downwards all the time as if it could see, as if it took pleasure in observing his fear. Was the bird already suspicious, did it know he was there, was he merely being given the moment of grace by his executioner? Oh, he didn't dare breathe although his chest was fit to burst from the terrible pressure; he slowly let go again with his right hand, stood up on his toes, grasped a spike of rock with his left hand so tightly that he was in pain, and stretched his right hand out towards the bird, fingers outstretched; he grabbed it by the neck, and then like lightning, with a jerk more violent than he thought himself capable of, he hurled its heavy body into space. He could hear the swishing noise as it fell, and heard it flop into the water. Sweat was pouring off him, he was shaking in every sinew and he suddenly forgot where he was, was about to take a step backwards, and had already raised one foot in the air before he came back to his senses. With eyes closed, he clambered slowly down the cliff face like a big, grey caterpillar, and it was only when he reached the safety of the last few feet and he saw the green box lying between the stones like a green die that he once again became aware of his hunger.

As frenzied as a hound following a scent, he let go much too soon and crashed down on to the sands, the sea filled his ears with a deafening roar and its spray splattered all over the sand and the pebbles, a rainbow quivered back and forth before his startled eyes and the smooth, empty, half-buried iguana skins glistened in the wavy sands. His body came alive again, it was like waking up from a dream of a dream, he was no longer watching himself, his movements were no longer skeleton-like; even his hunger was transformed into delicious pain, but it didn't hurt, merely warmed him. Oh, how he wanted to wallow in his salvation, enjoy it, taste it, lick it with his voluptuous tongue.

Agonizingly slowly, he crawled over the sand to the box; with eyes closed, he extracted every ounce of pleasure from the rare perfumes flowing into him, opened his mouth and tasted pineapples melting on his tongue, bread from Myra and Lendarsis, long white loaves with green seeds and an aroma of cherry blossom, the smell of winter apples stored in the attic in old houses in the country, the spiced scent of meat and sawdust that filled the quayside warehouses also emanated from the box, this box was indeed infinite in what it had to offer, bottomless, it had everything: the fresh bread his brother the baker sometimes used to bake on winter mornings and sent home with little Christine, the smells from the frying pan at home and the big bag of sweets his mother always kept in a cupboard as a bribe to make him tell lies when his father used to ask if anything had been happening at home that week when he was working nights. In the end he embraced the box as if it had been a woman, pressed his ear against it and heard all the dishes in the world boiling, frying, bubbling away on the stove, being poured out, being carved up, sliced, ground, clinking of knives and forks, quick gulps and little belches, chairs being pushed back from the table and the muffled sizzling of soups in soup kitchens, the turgid slurping of greasy soups, a magnificent rumble as gigantic cauldrons were emptied, then nothing but the roar of the ocean cascading over him with its vast choir of voices, and then those voices, one of which, rancorous and obstinate, took possession of him, accused him with acid urgency, forcing him on the defensive.

Stupefied, but still inspired by all that had happened to him, he just lay there, clutching the box tightly to him and watching the dead bird bobbing up and down over towards the headland. If he turned over, he could see the big, silent flock of birds clinging high up on the cliffs, motionless, and the smoke from the little camp on the other side of the island, spiralling devoutly heavenwards; he was disturbed to note how it gradually changed direction and started wafting right across the island in a gigantic arc, straight towards him; was that someone running up there in the dry grass, maybe whoever it was who had killed the iguana, or perhaps it was just some animal trying to scare him? Was someone standing up there now in that narrow exit, guarded by the birds, staring at him frenziedly? It would be very easy to loosen a little stone and throw it down at him. Scared in advance, uncertain in advance, already rocked back on his pedestal, he huddled in the tiny shadow of the box: such a big man and such a little shadow. The dialogue between Tim and the sea, so long prepared for, could begin at last:

'So, you've found something good, have you?'

'Yes, I saw this box the very first day. It was in exactly the same place as it is now, only a bit closer to the sea. I noticed a fish jumping out of the water just behind it.'

'But you didn't climb down and fetch it then, did you?'

'No, I wasn't hungry then, I thought like everybody else that our rescuers were just round the corner. We'd got plenty of meat come to that, and pineapples, and biscuits, and somebody thought they'd seen hares in the undergrowth near the camp. Somebody suggested we could go fishing and get by in that way.'

'You didn't tell anybody you'd seen a box of provisions on the beach, did you?'

'No. Nobody was hungry, but even so the mood was edgy and I thought my discovery would only make everything even worse. They might start arguing about how to divide the spoils, for instance, especially as somebody had already suggested the women and the injured man should be on reduced rations.'

'Ah, so you kept it quiet out of consideration for the others, not for yourself. It didn't occur to you that you'd pretty soon start running short of food, especially when the meat started stinking and had to be buried. You weren't thinking of keeping the box for your own use later on? You weren't reckoning quite ruthlessly on getting to the point where your own hunger would crave everything you could lay your hands on?'

'No, a hungry man doesn't rationalize things, a hungry man is passionate and ruthless, a hungry man has to do anything he can in order to satisfy his hunger, and everything else goes by the board. Being considerate is just something you do when you're mixing with people who aren't hungry.'

'But you weren't hungry when you first saw the box. And you weren't all that hungry when you started spreading the rumour about hares being seen in the undergrowth – it was you who started that one – and you weren't hungry even when you started suggesting to the others that they could catch fish, although you knew full well it wasn't possible. Why did you spread rumours you knew full well weren't true? Was it to distract them from the possibility of maybe finding things washed up on the beach? Or were you just being nice and preventing them from getting over-excited?'

'What consideration do I owe to these people who call themselves my comrades? I've saved several of them – isn't that enough? What consideration have they shown me, what comradeship, what warmth, what respect, what faith? All the time they've made it clear that I'm the servant and they're the masters, and what does a slave owe his master apart from actually serving him?'

'Yet again a pitiful failure to face the truth. What is comradeship but living together in the same circumstances? If the provision merchant loses all he owns and comes to beg a share of your wretched lot, do you send him packing like a stranger, or do you try and win him round instead, because you know you two have the most fundamental things in common: hunger which must be satisfied, and the affront of need which must be washed away?'

'Didn't I do everything I could to win them round? I did everything they asked me to do, opened those boxes, fed the injured, kept that fire going, went without sleep, all for their sake.'

'Since when has it been so praiseworthy to have a slave mentality? You didn't need to obey once all the symbols of power had been shipwrecked, but you kept on doing so all the same. What kind of mysterious quality made you click your heels and bow your head as soon as these people, who are just as ragged and naked as you are, gave you an order? You were too cowardly to see whether you could act in the same way yourself, whether you could say to the captain: fetch me a branch, I want to warm myself by the fire. No, you found another way round it all; while you were still well-fed you reckoned in cold blood that a time would come eventually when your hunger would be greater than anybody else's. Then you thought: soon I'll be hungry, I'll be wild and ruthless, that's when I'll rebel against these terrorists, not openly, but in a roundabout way. You sat there coolly and worked out how you could take advantage of your state of intoxication, that was what was so contemptible. Just how much is a man's lust for rebellion worth if it stays in hiding when he has plenty to eat? Now you're lying here beside your box, your big secret, and you think you're rebelling; but all you're managing to do is to run away from your rebellion, you're hiding away like a coward behind the most noble of pretexts.

'Ah well, it wasn't the first time; it's something you're used to, my friend. Fair enough, William was bleeding something awful when the police had finished with him on the strike-breaker boat's foredeck, once it had become known he was the one trying to organize the underground campaign on behalf of the strikers. Fair enough, it's quite understandable: you had no desire to bleed like that. Your liver, kidneys, spleen, lungs – they're all pretty sensitive organs, and if you get thoroughly beaten up like that any one of then could easily burst. And what's more, it's understandable that you wanted to avoid other kinds of unpleasantness, we all know how vulnerable some people's nerves and some people's marriages are. Most of all: you were afraid all kinds of injustice would become unavoidable if you faced the consequences of organizing the disturbances. No doubt there are problem children and orphans even among the ones who were regarded as oppressors. On those grounds alone there was no obvious duty to rebel like you'd heard somebody going on about, despite the fact that the old lady who'd been sleeping in the stairway the last four nights died coughing and obviously in great pain in a loony-bin bed a week or two later.

'Come on now, there were probably all kinds of things you could have done but didn't, and now it's too late. You can't stir up trouble when you're in among comrades, that's not rebellion any longer, it's treachery.'

91

'Then all I ask is: let me live a little bit longer. I can drop all my excuses, I can drop all my masks; look, I'm standing here naked, indecently naked before myself, and I'm begging myself: let me live a little bit longer. I do so want to breathe, I do so want to smell the sea as it breaks again and again over the reef till it goes down on its knees and begs for mercy, and I'm so scared my body will start observing itself again, that my eye will stare at my naked eye and hence won't be able to see a thing. I want to live a little bit longer, no matter how wretched a state I'm in.'

'Then all you have to do is attack that box, split it open, laths and all, grab all the contents and gobble up the whole lot, lie there for days on end, and lick the wood clean when there's nothing else left. Then just feel how much alive you are, how easily your legs carry you up the steep slopes and over to the camp, and how eagerly your nose registers the smell of an abandoned camp, burnt-out fire, and dead bodies; how keen your hands will be when you seek out a suitably big branch that'll serve as a spade, and fill the whole of that beautiful beach with seven graves. Don't forget yourself, you'll have gained yourself a week or so, and during that time you can stroll around the island like one of those iguanas. Maybe you'll get a hard shell in the end, just like them. Learn their habits, take up their way of life, and then you won't have to die for another three hundred years yet! You'll avoid all those relationships in time and space with other people, all those obligations, all those invisible contacts and mutual dependencies which make human life worth living. But before you turn into an iguana, before you go numb, before you lose the ability to speak, cry out into the silence: my last action as a human being was treachery.'

Seven seas erupted over him, one after another they poured in over the horizon, no, they came from the box, the boundless box; the swell rose and fell, then suddenly it was only falling. Now cauldrons were being emptied in a million kitchens, water was running over all the floorboards, rippling over polished pine, seeping through cracks and swishing in stringy strands out of his dream. Suddenly the box fell silent, something in it died once and for all, and wakened by this silence, scared by it, Tim sat up quickly. The sight that confronted him was fantastic, and he grew first stiff, then limp with terror. The high, black cliff he had clambered down now seemed much higher, its black streaks projected spitefully and brutally like swollen veins; the sun was sinking rapidly into the sea and seemed not to be able to find a foothold on the cliff, but it glistened on the red beaks of the birds as they trooped down the cliff face, spread out in a vast formation, hopping slowly from ledge to ledge, with just a wing's breadth between them. That was a net he could never penetrate.

If I run, he thought, it's because I'm running away from the birds. If I take the box with me, it's so that the blind birds can't plunder it. Oh, how he ran over the uneven beach, stumbling over stones, splashing into treacherous pools, clawing his way up rocks, sliding down the other side, wading across little inlets where slender rays lived their hermit-lives, half-swimming in deep water around cliffs where there was no beach, all the time clinging on to that heavy box, carrying it on his head, on one shoulder or the other, clutched to his thigh or hanging down his back. Once he saw the bird he had killed: it had floated round a headland and was now just lying there in a pool of still water. At last, the ship came into view on its reef, the sun was playing gently on its skeleton, the fire was burning on the beach, and someone was walking up and down, wringing his hands.

He yelled out in a whisper: here I am, I've got food for you, you bastards; and he fell in a heap, gasping. They turned the box the right way up, saw it was marked C.O. (Captain's Office), and ripped open the lid. Madame, for once enticed out of her agony, suddenly burst into laughter, squirting it out like a whale, as she groped around with her savage fingers among the multicoloured glass beads the box was full of, the pearls for which the Eslamite natives sold their hides and themselves to anyone with enough boats, charts and stars to find their way there.

The Sorrow of Sunset

It was at sunset one day when Madame killed an iguana. She had a stone in one hand, and when she heard the rustling in the grass, she stopped and waited, without a sound. When the animal emerged out of the gloom, she was frightened at first by its size: she hadn't intended to kill such a big iguana, but with the aid of the stone she soon had it over on its back before it could bite her or run away. Once she'd killed the iguana with the stone, she turned it over on to its belly again, so that it would look as if it were still alive, sleeping in the grass, or on its way somewhere extremely slowly. She threw the sticky stone a long way away, and heard it crash into another one on the beach.

On her way back, she nearly fell over a big iguana sleeping in the grass, whipped it over on its back with her bare hands, and discovered it was dead. On her way back to camp, she'd been going round in circles and returned to the exact spot where she'd killed the iguana. The third time it happened, she decided to scream. She gave a short, piercing scream and, immediately, someone came rushing through the grass; she could tell from the crackling of the canvas and the squeaking of the jackboot that it was the captain.

She stood in front of the iguana so that he couldn't see it, wrapped her cloth sheet tightly around her as if she were cold, and when he arrived, said to him in a plaintive voice: 'Captain, help me down again, please. I suddenly feel unwell.'

Without saying a word, they crossed over the grassy plateau, where the horizontal light of the setting sun was lighting up the grass panicles from underneath, so that they looked like lips, blood-red lips pursing to meet other lips. They emerged on to the cliff top, and Madame paused to enjoy the view down the path, over the beach, the ship, the sea, the horizon, which now seemed to be bulging under the weight of the sun. The rocks below them were gleaming red with a modest brick-like colour very familiar to her; large expanses of sea as still as water in a glass had assumed the same soothing hue, and the wavy columns of smoke coming from the fire on the beach also looked red. As usual, the thin English girl was at the boxer's side, more interested in herself than in him. The captain's arm was resting gently on Madame's shoulder; she could feel its wretched inertness through the cloth, and put off by this sensation of coldness, she started on her way down in order to be alone at last.

The small iguanas were scuttling around agilely at her feet, but she no longer had any feelings when it came to iguanas. Ignoring everybody's gaze, she made her way to her place by the fire, which was marked out by four thin lines she drew in the sand with her forefinger every morning in order to be alone. In order to be even more alone, she curled herself into a ball so that her face was hidden by her hands and her hands by her knees and her knees by the cloth. Thus ensured of her privacy, she felt as if she were sinking down from the world as if in a lift, confused and cluttered up with inessentials, sinking down into a necessary sorrow.

The sorrow took possession of her, cleansing, vehement, untarnished now that the iguana had been killed, and precise and cruel in such a natural way that there was no room for any other thoughts. Pure sorrow is majestic in its ferocity, and for these brief moments in the sunset, she experienced all its necessary stages: the brief, stupefying paralysis when you think you've gasped the truth, although you know next to nothing about the truth as yet; something protests inside you and your heart suddenly feels staggeringly strong, as if it were beating outside your body somehow or other. Then the first tears come to your eyes, even though you're not actually crying and don't even want to cry. They are unusually big and hot as tears go, and if you tried tasting them, they'd probably be much saltier than your usual cut-price tears. You dry these tears, and all is well again for the moment; but well in a kind of tense, glass-like way. It's as if you might put your foot through it at any moment, and fall at breakneck speed.

But you haven't started falling yet, and the glass gets thicker and thicker, as if you were drifting further and further away from your sorrow, and you feel furious but helpless as the distance between you and your sorrow grows, a dull despair fills you in large, thick lumps. But then you find something in time or space which helps to bring you down again, an open door through which you can fall, and on a purely physical level it comes as a relief after all the hard tension you've been through. Something gives way inside you, tears come to your eyes and lie there like radiators until they

97

dissolve. Then one thing leads to another in an unending chain, and soon there's nothing more you can see, hear or feel which isn't directly connected with the object of your sorrow, and every time something new emerges, there's an explosion inside you, violent at first, giving rise to tears and a strange soporific pain which starts in your diaphragm and then moves upwards, the explosions grow weaker, but there is no pause. Now you're sobbing quietly and constantly and copiously, you gave up drying your tears ages ago, but your sobbing gives you a strangely fresh and pure feeling in your nose, as if you'd been sucking certain throat tablets.

Time passes, and gradually, everything closes around your sorrow like a flower closing for the night; it's not like being encased in armour, just a cool, flower-like envelope through which you can hear it pulsating, you're still partaking of it, it's alive and well inside you and you can moisten your lips with it whenever you wish, like sipping from a fresh, clear stream; but even now you can choose yourself, to some extent, exactly when you want to associate with it. The danger, however, is that you leave it in peace for too long: fresh sorrow has to be tended assiduously, taken out occasionally like the dearest of treasures and polished like a mirror, or else it will all too soon acquire that hard shell, and the armour plating becomes a fact, something which cannot be prevented in the long run, of course.

And once the armour plating is there, you're in a way back where you started from, once again there's this distance in time and space, but now it feels more hopeless than it used to do because you know there's nothing to expect. Instead of the dull, insistent despair which filled every cavity within you the first time, a horrible period of apathy now takes over, of restless waiting, waiting for nothing to happen. Nothing matters any more, everything round about you takes on a hardness, you want to take hold of something, but all you can grasp is dead, you want to look but your gaze is rejected by the hardness of the object, you want to make love but you realize you can't, for you yourself are also encased in the same hard film, all your feelings seem to have frozen stiff, you're dried up and shrivelled, and not even your own unbearable loneliness can make you tremble.

Of course, not even this lasts for ever, at first you notice little currents working away industriously under the armour and under the ice, and one day it all breaks apart and for one last time you are reunited with your sorrow. But you don't feel numb this time, your body doesn't partake as heavy-handedly as it did before, it's as if your muscles, your blood vessels and your joints which used to become tense with sorrow can no longer manage it. Everything shifts now to the level of memory, you keep returning over and over again to the site of the fire, search through the devastated ruins and find twisted bits of a life lying coiled up like snakes under soot and girders. Now your memory drags these remnants like a crowbar, a useful yoke or a copper bucket out into the street, into its merciless cold light, and identifies them slowly and in a state of quiet agony, also called melancholy, under a street lamp. On the anvil of memory, with the aid of memory's hammer and tongs, you beat these bits and pieces until they're straight, then meticulously reconstruct their position in time and space and emotions, and this ruin is inexhaustible, this site devastated by fire conceals under the ashes things you'd thought lost long ago, hands not yet quite dead reach out towards you from the bonfires, and everywhere are those foreheads whose white domes can never be completely covered by charcoal and ashes.

These periods of sorrow usually take months, even years to pass through, but Madame endures all of them during the brief sunset, the shock, the first painful surprise, the fateful tension, the fall, the dissolution and the temporary hardening, and then this chase through memory which, to the accompaniment of horses' hooves, led her into the deepest recesses of solitude.

Now the sun was sinking so very, painfully slowly, as if for the last time; a red spring seemed to gush forth from under the sea, and the gigantic grey clouds, spurting upwards as if from a kettle behind a spiky headland crowned by gigantic fingers, climbed vertically upwards like factory chimneys, gradually turning brick-red, into a sky where pink shadows were still darting around, uncertain of what to do next. And all those birds, creeping out of the ship's innards one by one, and waddling over the sloping deck before taking off. They were flying unusually high, and for a while circled around the column of smoke rising tirelessly from the beach. Everything was so silent, the rattling of the iguanas had ceased, and the breezes were no longer penetrating Tim Solider's jungle. There was a moment when life seemed to shrink, and the pulse of time, already beating weakly enough in this island environment, seemed to have stopped altogether; now anything could happen, everything could be compressed and drawn-out events foreshortened as in a drama, and everything could be experienced in the time it took to draw breath.

Madame had had a lot of men, but none of them was quite like him. Several of them had racing cars and drove them slowly along the boulevards: she still hadn't seen any of them driving fast, and soon saw through their petty wiles. They loved to give the impression of something they called 'latent power'. Just as the long, throbbing bonnets of their cars were supposed to suggest speeds of a hundred miles an hour, they wanted women to caress their leather jackets and feel them bristling with enormous power which they were only able to hold back with the greatest difficulty. They wore long leather gloves with thick fingers, and would gesture eagerly at the steering wheel during intimate conversations, as if involved in a continual boxing match. But bereft of their gloves and leather jackets and riding breeches with green bindings, they were insecure and hesitant, almost shy in fact. How touching it was to keep hearing them whisper when they'd stopped the car among the willows in some luxuriant park, and embraced you, roughly and brutally, with hands that had only too reluctantly let go of the steering wheel and gear lever, preoccupied despite their apparent frenzy, and with bodies which, even when they seemed brimming over with latent power and at the most tender of moments, longed to feel the throbbing of the engine: I expect I'm your first, aren't I; or when they discover you're already married: I expect I'm the first man you've been unfaithful with.

Oh yes, she thought she knew these vain, ridiculous people who claimed to despise passion and affection, because they themselves were too cowardly to dare to feel anything but frigidity. Even so, they could be passionate enough when they thought no one was looking, and the warmth they were too cowardly to show their women they squandered on the gleaming cylinders of their racing cars. You sometimes caught them alone in their cars with an expression in their eyes and around their lips which would have been natural and desirable when they were together with a woman, but was perverse precisely because they were alone. Then they would sit up with a start, they would be terrified and look as guilty as if you'd caught them in a compromising situation with their friend's wife.

Oh yes, she knew all of them. The makes of their cars varied, as did the colour of their jackets and the way they sipped their cognac, but they all shared that cowardice dressed up as strength, they always started their seduction in the same, brutal way which was so funny because it seemed to leave so little room for variations, it was like reading the same syndicalized leader in the same newspaper day out and day in, and the result was always just as uninteresting and clumsily offensive. They thought they were skilful and knew all there was to know about women, and you could put up with observing ironically their ridiculous self-confidence as long as it remained within the bounds of moderation and harmless self-deception; but when they started being insolent and, because of their imagined skills, insisted shamelessly on complete surrender to all their peculiar whims, then she had to call a halt.

And my God, it was so easy; the slightest little obstacle in the way of the programme they'd planned which boded no awkward surprises, and they immediately became irritable and their strength drained away as if a plug had been pulled out of their pounding chests. After all, their programme was intended to run for all eternity, and there was no room for anybody tampering with it: after a few phrases about the weather, the moonlight, the latest news from the racing circuits, the splendid qualities of the car, her own mouth and her own hair, fate had decreed that the next step was to kiss, and so the car came to a halt half a mile short of the little side road. Five minutes later it was time to turn down it and stop at the little sloping glade fate always seems to have planted alongside minor roads suitably far from inhabited areas. In the same old deathly silence, one would return to the car, cold and wet from the grass, and the journey home would soon pass, the only replies one received were inaudible mutterings, and one would be dropped off with the necessary degree of rudeness outside one's front door, if one was lucky and the garage wasn't situated in some other part of town.

Faces flicker past like stills from a film as she gazes into the darkness of her cupped hands. Percival, the one with the yellow car, the insufferable bore who always whistled as they got to their feet afterwards; Charles, who died later in some accident involving gas and was one of the most inoffensive; Lucien, one of the few who drove just as fast on the way out as he did on the way back; Henri, who could not help crying like a spoilt child when he was not allowed to be as brutal as he needed to be if he were to make it; Jean, the gentleman who had already achieved middle age and was so afraid of his reputation that he forbade her to walk past the house he lived in, not far from hers; Jacques, young Jacques, who was so young he thought he knew all there was to know, and was about to be enlightened where women were concerned. That's why she was so keen to conquer him. All right, he was so sweet when a quiff of hair fell down over his forehead and he was too preoccupied with something to notice; his eyes were never still for a second, not even when he was kissing her, but he was so sure of her, despite the difference in their age, or because of it perhaps, that he demanded she should submit herself without reservation to his tyrannical programme.

They'd come to a little headland, quite high up and in the middle of the night; water had been flowing down below on both sides, the air was warm and yet fresh at the same time, the peace was so immense that she hardly dared breathe as they got out of the car. Then he got it into his head that the engine should be running all the time, and she protested, gently at first but increasingly energetically. It offended his vanity that she refused to submit immediately, and so he revved up the engine until it was roaring like a bull into the night. Then he grabbed her roughly by the arm and pushed her in front of him to the tip of the headland, but when he tried to force her down, she just started laughing. She realized of course it was the car he really wanted to make love to, not her: her gasps and whispered words of passion would be drowned by the roaring of the car.

'What are you laughing at?' he asked; she could feel the tight grip he had on her arm slackening off, and noticed with satisfaction the acrimonious insecurity in his voice.

Of course, she didn't answer, just carried on laughing as before, demolishing his great self-confidence bit by bit, and when she was finally convinced he was conquered once and for all, she pulled him to her urgently and they sank down together. Everything had gone as she knew it would; he plucked nervously at her clothes, and afterwards he jerked himself violently away from her and lay in the grass, abandoned to his own sobs.

She went back and sat in the car, and when he'd finished crying he returned and started the car with a tremendous jolt, then hurtled off through the darkness and silence at a hysterical speed, brushing against tree trunks and buckling the right wing and losing a headlight; but Jacques kept on driving like a madman until they came to the turning from the side road on to the main road when he lost control for a split second and they crashed into a milk lorry which skidded into a ditch. The smash ripped the door off one of its hinges, but that only made him drive even faster. Strangely enough she was quite calm, and it was not until some days later she grew scared when she thought of what might have happened. She realized of course he was only seeking revenge for his defeat, but that he would never be able to achieve it. She was just enjoying herself instead of being scared, enjoying the wind whistling past their ears and the black road which seemed to be spinning away beneath them. She remembered that night for the rest of her life, and the more frigid she became, the brighter the halo grew over her night with Jacques; she adorned the memory with flowers and garlands, built a triumphal arch around it, and the more frigid she became, the higher the arch grew.

But when she remembered it now on the island, it was not for the sake of her triumph – sorrow comes with great humility – but because it marked the end of something and the beginning of something else, the beginning of something which would finally force her into a solitude which was greater than most other people's, the beginning of something which eventually, one day at sunset, made her crush an innocent iguana with a heavy, round stone.

No more cars screeched to a halt outside her front door, no horns sounded to bring her running to the window. Apart from a few walks in the immediate vicinity together with her housekeeper Mlle Claire, she would spend all her time in an armchair in her room, sorting out Paul's stamp collection or pasting her amateurish photographs into blue albums, something she'd put off for far too long.

She'd been standing in Paul's room with her back towards him the day after the interlude with Jacques. She had tensed her back as hard as she could in order to withstand everything that was now engulfing her, but in the end, she was unable to resist any more. It was as if her back caved in, she fell to her knees and ground her head red against the windowsill, pressed her burning face against the wall in order to avoid the temptation of looking at the cripple in the bed.

'You must think I'm deaf and dumb, but that's not true as you may be aware, what I am is crippled. You think I can't hear your laughter echoing throughout the flat, you think I can't hear the sweet nothings at the front door, and the young boys in their cars queueing up outside.'

'Don't be silly, I've never made any secret of the fact that I sometimes go out for a bit of fun. I can't wander about in this big house on my own all the time.'

Paul started rapping the bed end with his knuckles; he'd found an infernal way of grating on her nerves by a rhythmical succession of words, rapping and silence.

'Have your fun, then. But when are we going to stop receiving these anonymous letters from people who take pleasure in tormenting me, and the signed letters from types who think they might get a reward for exposing the spicy situations they've seen you in? Or the anonymous telephone calls, those kind of telephone calls are always anonymous, which torment Mlle Claire day in, day out? I didn't marry a whore, but it's a funny thing: you don't marry whores, but one fine day you discover you've got them in the house never-theless.'

More rapping. Then silence.

'Why don't you answer? Why don't you say what you're thinking: I didn't marry a cripple. No, but you married an old man, because your father had been cooking the books. Shame and disgrace were looming, and you were his only chance of salvation, by marrying a rich man.'

'Oh, why do you keep on tormenting me with the same old thing?'

'I'm not the one who ought to be tormented, you are. And anyway, you're not going to be tormented, just punished. You'll get just punishment this time, but look out: next time it might be unjust. And you shouldn't keep going on about blackmail, not even to yourself; I can read your thoughts, you see.'

More rapping. Then silence.

'You know full well it's not blackmail. Of course, it is true I won't let you go without withdrawing all financial support for your father and his family; but once you're caught, you're caught – and that applies to both parties. And then there was some talk about punishment. It isn't even a question of punishment, come to that; it's just a simple penance for an unfaithful wife. You see, my charity is almost boundless, I'm ready to forgive almost anything. I expect you know the old penance for unfaithful wives: they have to go on their knees all round a church, carrying a candle. Well, you can choose your own day and your own time as long as it's this month, that's how charitable I am. For instance, you could do penance on a rainy day when not many people are around, and so there won't be many who see you. Mlle Claire will go with you as a witness. I've also bought a couple of dogs to keep you company so that you won't get lonely in future, and a new caretaker's due to start work any day now: he's ugly and has only got one eye, so you won't be tempted to seduce him. As you can see, I've only got your best interests at heart. But I really do insist you do your penance, not least in view of your father's financial state.'

That day she slunk out of Paul's room with a broken back, and it took a very long time to heal, especially as, nowadays, she wasted far too much time hunched up over postage stamps and photographs. Her skin grew grey and dirty, and the ageing process was rapid and ruthless. She rarely looked in the mirror any more, but when she sat in with Paul for a while every morning and every afternoon, her decline was reflected in his satisfied eyes.

'The penance did you good,' he said, 'you ought to go to church more often. You don't need to crawl on your knees any more.'

More rapping. Then silence.

She planned so many things now, but her knees were still sore after her penance, and her back was far from well again. She thought about the long German bayonet hanging on the wall over his bed as she was polishing her tarnished memories. But she was on friendly terms with the new caretaker until, one day, she noticed how eagerly he was watching her with his good eye, how intimately, more so with each day that passed. He went up to her room whenever Mlle Claire wasn't at home, and one evening he tried to kiss her in the Euridyce niche upstairs. She complained to Paul, and he said, 'That's right, you fight for your virtue.'

This period was weighed down by shadows and insidious premonitions, darkness held sway behind the pillars of this vast house, and Claire kept the blinds down in several rooms. She complained that the dust coming in from the street was so awful. Eventually all contact with the outside world was lost, and the house stood there like a memorial stone raised over a small number of living creatures who were barely alive: only the inscription was missing. No one went out of the dead house any more, and messenger boys came round with goods which they handed over to Claire or the caretaker on the doorstep; she herself would stand high up on the landing, watching wild-eyed as a thin white beam of light filtered into the hall through the crack in the door. She had an enormous desire to scream, not because she was afraid, but she thought there were far too many silent rooms in this house. She wandered about imagining which instruments could transform them with music: the cello room, the grand piano room, a little niche for the xylophone. She imagined what kind of screams would suit some rooms but be out of place in others; she imagined for instance what a scream would sound like in Paul's room or her own or Claire's or the porter's cubby-hole.

One night when everything was quiet in the house and outside in the street, and as usual she was lying wide awake in her big oak bed, she got the urge to try just a little scream, to see how it went. She opened her mouth, and it was amazing how easily it slipped out. It was a little bit louder than she'd expected, and she was so frightened when it echoed back at her that she soon fell silent and waited in fear in case somebody had heard it and would come racing up to investigate. But everything was so quiet. So she calmed down again and lay there, trying to remember what it had sounded like. She couldn't quite remember, but she thought it had probably been a little bit too highly pitched for this dignified room; but as she didn't really have more than one scream as yet, she had to find another room where it might be more suitable. So she crept quietly along the corridor, opening all the doors. She started with the lounge overlooking the street, then passed slowly through the five rooms, screaming in all of them. She paused for a while and pondered when she'd finished, and decided she'd have to lower her voice at least an octave before the scream was anywhere near appropriate for the sobriety and solid good taste characteristic of the furniture. She went back through the rooms in reverse order, just screaming and listening at the same time to hear whether they would do.

It still wasn't quite right. The screams had a vulgarity of style that must have been due to her opening her mouth too wide, so she'd have to close it slightly when she tried for a third time. But there was no third time. Mlle Claire and the grim-faced porter came rushing in from opposite directions, obviously as arranged in advance, knocked her to the ground, stuffed rags into her mouth and pinioned her arms. She twisted about and tried to spit out the gag so that she could explain it was all just a refurnishing exercise, but they were too strong for her, they managed to drug her somehow or other, and she woke up one day exhausted and terribly hot, and found them standing beside her bed, keeping an eye on her and each other.

'Madame, we're going out; we're going to church,' said Claire.

They went to church, but not to the one where she had done her penance. Now she took her hands away briefly, and looked up. Oh, that brick-red colour, that colour which becomes so strangely clear and bitter just as the sun is setting. The tower rose upwards through the domed clouds, the edge of the sun that hadn't yet drowned, and the sea stretched out as lifelessly as an etching plate; the tower of the red monastery church, overshadowing all else, at times dissolving into a yellowy-red mist, the mist emanating from blast furnaces and smithies nestling down in the valleys; but it emerges again, rising up from the mists, more recognizable every time, more lovable, more painful when seen from so far away.

But a little lizard crawled out of the massive wall and, as insignificant as a beetle, it looked at first as if it might soon disappear into one of the thousands of cracks; but look: it started growing, its tail grew longer, was drawn up towards the spire, kept on spreading out sideways until its cold shell covered the whole wall. Its nasty, thin little head got closer and closer to the ground, and she slowly slumped forward, transfixed in a standing position down below, with her hands reaching up towards the spire atop the vanished tower. She wanted to yell out: gobble me up, you monster; but in her memory-dream, no words crossed her lips.

Then she was standing in Paul's room again, but this time she had her back turned defiantly towards the window; her back was completely cured, and light was dripping in through the Venetian blinds and clinking down on to the carpet. She knew he was watching her with every segment of his eyeballs, sucking her in, although he seemed to be lying there, half turned towards the wall and stroking the cruel tip of the bayonet.

'I'm going to have a baby,' she said, hooking her gaze on to that of somebody else in the far distance so as not to fall, 'I'm going to have a baby with a priest.'

111

He hadn't turned round to face her, he was still lying in the same position; but she could feel in her skin, which suddenly became hot, how he was thrusting himself upon her with his eyes, those eyes which were not crippled: they could scratch and bite, they could rip and claw, and they could shadow you, sharply and ruthlessly; wherever you were in the world.

Now the house was closed like a besieged fortress, but it was the house itself which was besieged; its walls seemed to be closing inwards bit by bit, the rooms became more cramped because the ceiling was also sinking and the floor rising, it became hard to breathe, the only way was to lie down with your chest as compressed as possible and gasp for air and love, like a beached fish.

And then there was the iguana business.

She was standing in Paul's room again, no, not standing: she was creeping, creeping painfully slowly over the fluffy carpet between his bed and the window, and the air was more stifling than ever and the Venetian blinds had all been repaired. She couldn't stand up, as the pressure of hatred and longing, sorrow, despair, cruelty that permeated the house immediately knocked you to the floor if you tried to stand up and bear it on your trembling shoulders. His eyes held his hands on the back of her neck, but she couldn't meet their gaze for they were always looking elsewhere, apparently unconcerned about her but always following her around the house, wherever she went. His voice, which had been shrill and old-mannish for so long, had acquired an apparently evasive tone, gentle, warm, the timbre of a melancholy cello. But in that tone was a trace of acerbity which called forth a special sort of despair in order to comprehend it properly, a particular posture;

you could only appreciate properly its warm cruelty on all fours with your hips sagging and your forehead buried deep in the grass of the carpet; it drove wedges into you which stayed, stayed there and swelled up. 'Can you feel the iguana,' he whispered, 'can you feel the iguana growing inside your body? Soon its skin will harden, its long tail will get even longer, its eyes will start protruding and there'll be no eyelids; its stiff, callous stare will take root inside you, eating you away. Can you see its skull forming? Soon it will be as long as it's going to be, its snout will have no warm lips, but it will press hard and cold against your membranes, trying to force its way out.'

Oh, she lay there on the floor of Paul's dark room for days on end, panting, on the fluffy mat between his bed and the window, and felt the iguana growing inside her, felt its skin hardening, its long tail growing even longer, its lidless eyes protruding more and more, its stare stiff and callous inside her, eating her away. She felt its skull forming, growing as big as it was going to be, and its snout devoid of warm lips pressed hard against her membranes, trying to force its way out.

'The iguana,' she screamed after the birth, 'I don't want to see it, spare me that.' They brought the baby in to her, held her down and yelled into her ear that the baby was normal, that the baby looked like all other babies, that it didn't have the skin of an iguana, nor could it only crawl on its belly. But she refused to believe it. Sometimes the door opened suddenly and somebody held up a newly born baby to the light.

'It's not mine,' she would shout. 'You've swapped it for somebody else's. Mine's an iguana.'

They were afraid she might do the child an injury if they gave it to her, so they let her be alone in her room.

All she could remember clearly from that time was that suddenly there was a smell of birch leaves, she could hear heavy carts clattering up the street, the sun was more fierce and dazzling than ever before, and without her realizing it, she was lifted into summer. It was so quiet in the house, but sometimes there was the sound of baking trays falling down in the kitchen and Claire would come up the stairs, heavier and more out of breath for every day that passed. But one afternoon, she had a dream which revealed to her that this silence contained something unknown, it was like a space surrounding a sound she must have been aware of for some time, but the film around it had only burst in her dream. There was a child crying somewhere in the house, shrill and hungry, complaining, then gradually falling asleep; she was lifted straight up into summer as if on a wave, delivered at last, restored to health at last, and she let the light and warmth embrace her. Her pain disappeared and she was at peace once more, the swell from her bad dreams rolled over the horizon and disappeared. Good God, she thought, iguanas don't scream.

Even so, she was still a little afraid when they wheeled in the pram with the sleeping child, and she bent slowly over it ready to close her eyes in a flash and sink back once more into her agony. But the child lay there peacefully, its lips were thin, thin, and the blanket covering it heaved gently from its steady breathing; it was not a pretty child, it was too pale and its forehead was depressed in an unusual way, but it was certainly not an iguana.

And so her life slowly got under way once more. She didn't go to Paul's room any more. They could often hear him thumping away on his headboard until the whole house shook; he'd recovered his old-mannish voice and pestered the black serving girl who was looking after him now with threats and invectives until one day she ran screaming out of his room and out of the house, explaining she was terrified when the old man tried to kill her with the bayonet.

The boy grew and grew, she hardly left him alone for a single moment, as if she were afraid something might happen to him, a rapid, brutal transition which would overturn her dreams and secret hopes in a flash. She had to be near him all the time, and when he'd gone to sleep in the evenings and she could hear Paul thumping away upstairs in his room, she would bend over him in the light from a table lamp and scrutinize every line, every new shadow and wrinkle in his face; but precisely because she was constantly examining him for fear of some sudden change, she failed to notice the gradual hardening of his features which started to take place when he was two. She didn't see how his lips gradually stiffened, how his skin grew taut around his jaw and his eyes slowly turned to ice in their sockets, how his eyelids acquired a sharp edge and seemed to be about to split.

Then she fell ill and lay in her room for several days, delirious; everything disappeared behind a green curtain, she tore frenziedly at its shiny folds, behind which so many voices were laughing, warning, threatening and commanding; but in vain. An alarming shadow, long forgotten, was dancing over the curtain; at first she couldn't make out its shape because of the shadow's size, but then she drew back in terror and fell down through years of horror. Shaking, half out of her mind with despair, she jumped up in the middle of the night, and raced through all the rooms until she came to

115

the boy; the old nanny woke up and tried to prevent her, but she'd already seen it all: the little shrunken face of an old man, finished with life almost before it had started living, marked by all kinds of experiences, already tired of everything before it had experienced anything. With an agonized scream which woke the child up, she ripped back the covers and stared at the tiny, deformed body and suddenly realized the awful truth: the newly awakened child didn't cry, its cold eyes were unaffected by anything that happened, and nothing would ever get through to it; the cold breath of an iguana soul wafted up towards her, and sent her screaming from the room.

Now she was in Paul's room again and it was an afternoon in autumn, leaves were lying on the window sill and the room was suffused with the acerbic smell of decay. She was walking to and fro between the bed and the window, and every time she turned, she stood still for an eternity in an attempt to entice him out of his destructive mood; she could feel he was watching her, but she was no longer singed by his looks, she had iguana-like armour plating which excluded fire and cold, nothing affected her and her armour was growing inwards.

'How's your iguana?' he inquired at last, caressing his bayonet all the while, 'I haven't heard it crawling around for ages.'

She went over to the door, and when she opened it she could see the boy sitting on a stool by the big bookcase; he was seven, couldn't read, was too old to start talking, too old to take pleasure in anything. He was taking books out one at a time and leafing through them as if to give his fingers something to do. He didn't even pause to look at the pictures, simply dropped each book on the floor beside him when he grew tired of it, and when he'd gone through a whole row, he just slouched on the stool, his arms dangling, hopelessly weary, his back hunched, knees wide apart, his cold eyes staring through a filter of hopelessness.

'The iguana's doing fine,' she said, closing the door. 'If you give me some money, I'll take him away for a holiday and then come back to you, without him, or not at all.'

And so they set off. Oh, how she suffered when everybody stared at them in railway carriages, dining rooms, ships' lounges and customs posts. She could see them glancing quickly at the boy's body before politely looking away and professing interest in something else; but their looks clung to the boy like burns, he was covered in malevolent eyes, which stuck to his face like postage stamps, and when she washed him every night it seemed to her the water was full of hostile eyes which stayed behind in the bowl like a disgusting scum.

Oh, how she hated him when they were travelling in the constant company of strangers. With the cruel aim of torturing both herself and him, she would take him firmly by the arm and point out demonstratively all the notable buildings they passed, strange animals in the zoos of several cities, which would fill any other child with terrified delight, or peculiar racial types scuttling about in some of the ports; but the boy's cold stare never varied, nor did his gesture of hopeless disinterest with his right hand, and people who noticed her efforts were rewarded by her furtive laughter, and turned away with a smile.

But when she was alone with him, she noticed to her painful surprise that she loved him. When he fell asleep at night, she would spread the sheet over his face, fumble for his hand, caress it and kiss it; indeed, she frequently didn't sleep at all, and in the devout confusion which often sets in after an all-night vigil, she got it into her head that a change, violent and comprehensive, must have taken place in the boy during the night: his old-mannish features had slipped away and been replaced by a new, child-like face still full of restlessness and expectations. Gently and with extreme care, she would uncover the boy's head; but no miracle had taken place under the blankets. Then her frustration made her flushed and she would go out on deck, on to the platform, into the hotel corridor, or wherever, and try to cool down, try to wriggle away from the temptation which always tingled in her finger-ends on such occasions. Oh, how she longed for some preposterous occurrence, some fantastic experience which would engulf them like a heavy sea, some hideous animal which would appear and force that tightly closed mouth to open up, those frozen eyes to crumble around an ice-hole of honourable horror, that lifeless body to shake with pain and despair.

They'd travelled far into the Orient and her money was running out, but now there was nothing else that mattered except this search for the animal, the occurrence and the horror. And then came the storm as they were on their way from Ronton. All of them were thrown below decks, shuffled together like playing cards, and their qualities seemed to change places and wander about from one to another. With a mighty effort she tore herself away from the confusion of terrified passengers and staggered over the heaving floor to where the boy and the captain's dog were lying at the bottom of the staircase. They were huddled up together, each of their backs pointing outwards like shields, and through the mist of her seasickness and the soft membrane of her fear she could see how the convulsions shuddering through both bodies were identical, as if they were coming from the same body.

Ah, she thought, now he's shaking at last, and she felt new hope. With trembling hands, she turned him over on to his back in the hope of seeing his face distorted by human fear. Then she collapsed on to the floor in desperation and was forced over towards the bulkhead, unable to defend herself against everything bearing down upon her. Oh, his eyes were as cold as an iguana's when they turned to look at her, what he was feeling was the fear of an animal. The iguana had sought out the dog, and the dog the iguana, the animal the animal.

When the ship ran aground, the bulkhead was split open and the saloon filled rapidly with water; half-drowned and almost blinded, they all waded towards the staircase. Someone was pushed by someone else and fell back into the water, gurgling and twisting as he sank, and the ship rolled slowly over under the water, in the direction of the hole. No one saw what had happened, they were too busy fighting for their own lives on the narrow staircase leading up on deck, lashing out with feet, elbows and knees. Her knuckles were sore where she'd punched the boy on the chin, and at this moment, standing there on the staircase, that was the only thing she could feel. When they emerged on deck, the storm swooped down on them, masts snapped off and bounced over the rail, the men working on the lifeboats were repeatedly bowled over by giant green waves surging over them aft, and suddenly the cage with the cook's parrot was caught up and whirled around in circles on the foredeck before being washed cruelly overboard. The lifeboat dropped from the

119

davits at breakneck speed and avoided being smashed against the starboard hull, but then rolled over and disappeared for no apparent reason. The cook's white hat was whisked around in a series of endless circles on the deck without having the sense to sink, and the next she knew she was falling into this devil's brew, grabbing at the cook's hat, before everything disappeared as if she'd been given an anaesthetic.

The whole of her life had consisted of waking up after bad dreams, short periods of good health after long illnesses, brief moments of bitter clarity after endless anaesthetics. She hadn't woken up yet, but something inside her was awake and preparing by means of far-reaching treachery for everything that was going to happen next. There was that high wall of unconsciousness stretching from the very floor up to the highest point of the ceiling, and you know everything is hopeless, that this wall is the most cruel of all walls as well as the most silent, the only wall in the world that can keep a secret – and yet you have that nagging, silent awareness of something happening on the other side, where there's the sound of voices, as yet unknown but eventually identifiable, and other noises, and then that thudding, that loud thudding that so uncannily familiar knocking – oh, if only the wall would collapse.

She's still not sure if she's awake in fact. As slowly as a mountain tarn opening up to greet the morning, she gradually comes round, warmth presses up against her limbs, she fumbles for something to hide under but can't find anything as yet and although she already knows the awful truth, she turns her aching head towards the cliffs and is even so paralysed by the sight; the whole of her cliff is covered in large, brown iguanas, motionless in the heat, but new ones are arriving all the time, their bodies smacking hard against the stones. She suddenly senses they are all staring at her, she can feel the whole cliff sliding towards her with its dreadful cargo, and once again she slips back in through the protective swing doors of her unconsciousness.

The next time it's night, a fire's burning close by and she's covered by warm cloth; someone is lying beside her and seems to be asleep. Someone else is walking towards her across the sand. He stops, bends down over her and pushes food into her mouth, gives her something to drink; she swallows eagerly and licks her benefactor's hand when he's finished.

And then all those dawns, with the thudding of the iguanas piercing all over her body, those iguana mornings, days, sunsets, dusks, evenings and nights. Over and over again, she found herself contracting like a muscle, and would sit motionless, waiting, by the fire, unable to feel anything, think anything, say anything. She wanted to mourn the dead boy, but could only grope around the glass roof of her apathy without finding the way in to her sorrow. She wanted to regret what had happened, but something inside her was not functioning; she was numb and dumb. Well, what could she do about it?

Then she killed the iguana. That day at sunset, watched by all the other castaways, she wandered up the cliff path towards the plateau, found the stone lying in the grass; the iguana emerged from the gloom, was overturned and crushed. Why did she do it, why did she kill the iguana? Well, in the first place, she had no idea. It wasn't a plan worked out long in advance and carried out suddenly and brutally; when she set out up the cliff path, she wasn't clear about anything, but something

121

was nagging her in the back of her mind, sharp and stimulating – but what?

But when she was led down from the scene on the captain's arm, she could feel this new mellowness inside her, this relaxed feeling of liberation from what had gone before. I must know what it feels like to kill an iguana, she thought, I must know that so I can say: I've never done it before, I've never turned a reptile over on its back and found the vulnerable spot on its belly to hit with a stone. In that case, the boy was not an iguana, in that case he was a human being in spite of everything; that's not what it felt like when I punched him, it was much cleaner, just that brief soreness in my knuckles and then it was all over.

Her sorrow closed in on her, that sweet sorrow which absorbs everything, consumes everything with the same voracious lust – evil intents and impudent desires, love and hatred; how marvellous it is just to let oneself sink down and hope to re-emerge whole again when everything is done, when regret has been satisfied and *angst* has faded away. But even sorrow is treacherous, divers are at work in its depths and thrust their long spades into one's mud; the memories one has allowed to gush forth like tears, innocent and with no apparent relevance, are suddenly linked to form a chain as steadfast as iron, and nothing can be done about its ruthless, stifling logic. The staircase rising steeply from the saloon to the deck keeps coming back, the handrails on each side with large, brass knobs at top and bottom, and its iron-shod steps resounding to the flurry of footsteps. The dog is always bounding up and down the staircase by the captain's side, and the boy is sitting in its shadow; the boy is always just sitting there, his chin resting on his hands, oblivious of the sea: the swordfish have nothing to say to him. Then the lamps start swaying in the storm, swinging wildly on their hooks, and suddenly there's a wide crack in the saloon wall, and water comes pouring in. How could she stay there to the very end, although the water level was rising rapidly and the list was making it more and more difficult to force one's way to the staircase? She stood there on the first step with water almost up to her knees, and the boy came wading towards her, and tried to get past her; she let him get five steps up before running past him, and then that punch which sent him hurtling backwards into the water below, and it was all over so quickly, she hardly realized what was happening herself. But suddenly the staircase is empty and long and steep and silent; the image of the empty staircase with water rising swiftly up it pursues her deep down into her sorrow, and then she understands that something has to happen to her on account of that empty staircase. Why did she hit him, why did she let him die? If it really was the iguana, the detested iguana, can she mourn now, can she let herself sink down into voluptuousness? But if she has killed the one she is mourning, the knife edge must be turned upon her; then it was a beloved human being who fell down that staircase, killed by her own hand.

She opens her eyes now and sees the horizon quivering over where the sun has set, with just a few tardy streaks glinting red over the sea and in the English girl's hair. Then she feels that despair rising inside her like a pillar, and to prevent herself from being split open, so that her own head is not pierced, she stands up and rushes up the cliff path, everyone watching her as usual, and hastens through the grass where the light of sunset is still gleaming like dew on a few blades. Then

123

she sees the lizard lying there, apparently asleep or making its painfully slow way to somewhere or other. Then she sinks to her knees and, with her ulcered lips, kisses the iguana's slowly softening skin, the old hypocrite.

The Obedience of Twilight

When twilight fell, Boy Larus, the airman, liked to stand on the highest cliff; only the breeze penetrated that far, and the spot was concealed by undergrowth which was just turning deep blue as silence engulfed one in wave after massive wave. The wound in his groin was getting worse every day, he could feel a nagging shooting pain all the time, as if there were two small animals with sharp teeth, each one gnawing away at one of his testicles and working its way further and further in by the hour. He ran his hand carefully over the wounds, but the sensitivity of his fingers which had always embarrassed him, and yet of which he was quite proud in private, had been spoilt by the grinding sand, the hard rocks and the corrosive sea-water; all he could feel were a few lifeless calluses, and that couldn't be right. When he crept away to an inaccessible spot and had a look at the wounds, what impressed him was the way they seemed to be alive, eating away voraciously at his flesh. He'd hurried back as fast as he could to the camp, all the time aware of how the little animals were triumphantly exploiting his weakness. When he got back, he asked Miss Hardlock in a whisper for a length of cloth.

'I have some wounds that require to be bandaged,' he said in halting English, 'some rather bad wounds that I have acquired.'

'Oh,' she'd replied, 'can I be of help?' – and then, when she noticed his embarrassment and his reluctance to say any more: 'How much to you need?'

'Oh, not much,' he'd assured her, and then disappeared into the grass with his piece of cloth. Of course, it hadn't helped; his wounds were not open wounds after all, and although they did make him feel a little warmer, the bandages fell down his leg as soon as he started moving at all strenuously, and in general they were a nuisance.

The exertions involved in climbing affected him badly, and his condition seemed to deteriorate rapidly. He didn't dare look at the wounds any more as, when he let his hand venture anywhere near his testicles, he was horrified to discover how quickly they were getting bigger. The temptation to look at them was enormous, plucking away at his fingers, and at times he had to search frantically for something to do, spend ridiculous amounts of energy doing things that didn't need doing at all, just so as not to give way. Apart from that, it wasn't too bad during the day when everybody else's eyes, everybody else's attention prevented him from giving way to his innermost desires; but when it started getting dark and no one could keep an eye on him any longer, it became appallingly difficult.

Of course, you could point out that it wasn't possible to see the wounds when it was dark, at least not as clearly as in daylight. At most, all he could make out would be a few dark shadows, much darker than the skin of his thighs, standing up slightly in relief. But the fact is that while twilight on this island lasts only for a brief second, it's nevertheless long enough for anyone who's waiting apprehensively for the opportunity to have a look at two wounds. It's characterized by an unusually sharp light, a light which is certainly condemned to death and is squeezed out of existence by the darkness, but even so its sharpness is awesome; it's like a flash of green lightning, lasting a little longer than the time it takes an ordinary flash of lightning to penetrate the world, and for that lengthy moment, it demands that all secrets be exposed to its ruthless gaze.

In order to avoid being tormented by this sweet temptation – sweet yes: it was precisely that strange feeling of painful enjoyment, of persistently agonizing, dirty satisfaction, which worried him most – he'd rush off with some excuse or other: he was looking for an unusual stone, he wanted to see a particular star which was invisible from their part of the beach, or something of the sort; well, rush off is relative, since as the wounds were getting deeper and deeper and at the same time bigger and bigger, it naturally became increasingly difficult to walk. It was extremely hard to go uphill, especially when it was a steep slope, but he chose that difficult and exhausting path even so, because once he'd got as far as the little plateau of bare rock about the same size as a skating rink in the middle of the island, high above everything else, he lost all trace of desire to expose his wounds and caress them eagerly with his gaze. He felt as if he were standing in the middle of a stage, in the cruel glare of spotlights and watched by naked eyes shackling his movements, binding him fast to normal respectability, preventing him from exposing himself in such a dreadful way.

The birds were soaring beneath him, their large wings like reflectors casting the green light upwards as sky and sea merged into one, and the wrecked ship lay slumped over its reef. The big searchlight was still there on deck, looking like a doubled-up human being; we've all learnt to conceal our wounds, from ourselves and from everybody else, to show nothing of our pain, to keep ourselves under control until something gives way and we're bowled over with devilish speed. Everyone has heard about the Spartan boy, with the stolen foxcub under his tunic, who allowed the animal to eat its way through his chest rather than confess. That was very courageous, and we're all expected to be Spartan boys, we're all expected to let our wounds grow until they cover us entirely and no one can whisper to his neighbour and say: look, he's concealing something, but he's doing it well; it's admirable, the way he lets his wounds grow till they cover his entire body, without bothering any of us others with his problems. Not until it's all too late, if you can talk of a thing getting too late when it was too late right from the very start, only then is anyone else allowed to know, and nothing can be done about it, of course, because the wound we carry instead of skin always grows inwards, gnawing its way all the time into a tender kernel which will also turn into a vast wound, and the kernel inside that kernel, and that kernel's kernel, and all the kernels that all the kernels have inside them, and all the kernels all of us bear inside us will turn into wounds, but we're not allowed to show any sign of it until the immense wound we're carrying bursts open and we fall down like a disgusting piece of flesh cut off the end of a giant's finger, and we roll over and break open and pus flows in all directions. Then we've kept control of ourselves for long enough, and if we're ruthless now, then it's the first time after all, for someone shouted to us as we clambered into the aeroplane: Right lads, Boy, Esper, Loel, Grenn, when you start dropping your bombs bear in mind the houses round the power station are close together so if you hit one of them, the fire will spread rapidly to all the others and light up the power station making things more effective from a bombing point of view, and the wound that I, Boy, was carrying around inside me nodded assent, because it was an obedient wound and it no doubt thought obedience is good for wounds, for a man who just does as he's told and is faithful to the task he was forced to marry himself to because that year everybody with amputated limbs had to be married off to people who hadn't yet had amputations, and so a man who just does as he's told feels the Spartan boy panting through the ages with blood pouring from his thin chest.

Maybe he was an ordinary pimply little boy, a bit like you were yourself when you always carried peanut shells around with you in your pockets and dropped them wherever you went, in doorways and on landings, and of course he would have a Greek profile but his shoulders might be thin even so, his back hunched, and he might well have had freckles as he stood there before the stern gentlemen with the fox inside his tunic, accused of having stolen it, and determined to die rather than let a confession or a cry of pain pass his lips. He might have just been eating, nuts maybe, or porridge if they had that in those days, and he might have had a crust of dry milk or perhaps even honey on his upper lip as he pressed it stubbornly against his teeth with the help of his lower lip. The stern gentlemen in their togas, no, it was the Romans who wore them, they mightn't have been taking it all that seriously even though they were pretending otherwise, because who could care less about a foxcub and there must have been lots more foxcubs besides this one in ancient Sparta; maybe they were just teasing the boy, pretending to be twice as strict as they really felt like being, and after a few minutes of uncompromising sternness they would have burst out into guffaws and everything would have been relaxed and the boy would have been allowed to run out into the sunshine, and they would have shouted after him that he shouldn't take everything so damned seriously, only that crowd in Athens were as silly as that, where laws about cruelty to animals and all that silly nonsense spoilt all the fun.

But before they got round to that, that business of letting him go again, the fox trapped in his tunic was scratching its way deeper and deeper into the boy's chest, and the blood would have been pouring out under his tunic and if he wasn't wearing a long coat or an ankle-length cloak, it would soon have started running down his thighs and down his legs and at any rate some of the men accusing him would have seen it and shouted: Look, the boy's bleeding! We'd better help him! Or maybe they would have just let him go on bleeding, because such things do happen after all, and Loel who was in charge of the machine gun got hit in his arm, it must have split his artery because he turned white almost straight away and slumped forward and there was nothing anybody could do; the battle had started and the enemy shells were coming up in waves from below and suddenly they were screaming vertically past us and streaks of flame were flashing by and up above there was a roaring sound as if a gun carrier was running away out of control and something big and black that looked as though it was going to gobble up the whole earth seemed to be sliding along just over our left wing and it couldn't stop itself before it hit the dam beside the power station and in the glow from eight blazing houses you could hear through all the noise from God knows how many different kinds of guns how the burning plane was gobbled up by silence and then first a thin, black angry spurt of smoke and then just a big white cloud that engulfed everything.

While all this was going on, Loel had probably died, it would be silly to deny that, and he'd been dead for quite a long time when they lifted him out at the airfield in Berling and took him without more ado to the abandoned garage that served as a mortuary; but you might well say this was war after all, and the Spartan boy could no doubt have been saved, because come to that, what kind of a fox was it that didn't start yelping when it was being suffocated under that tunic, could it have been a Spartan fox that thought to itself: If I can just keep quiet for five minutes and instead rip open the boy's chest so that he collapses and dies through loss of blood, I'll go down in history, I'll be a fox that they read about in schoolbooks for hundreds of years to come, a really important fox that'll be of enormous significance for philosophers and for human thought in general, and in that case it's worth my while to keep quite for five minutes, because normal foxes just start yelping and the fox that I, Boy Larus, had under my shirt when I was eight and wanted to be famous, he made one hell of a row and everybody in the kitchen started staring at me and my Auntie Anna who was operating the separator let go of the handle so suddenly that I remember the warning bell that goes off when you're not pumping hard enough started ringing and she ripped open my shirt and pulled out the foxcub and I only had a few small tears in my vest and I got a box on the ears and had to go to bed without anything to eat even though I was only doing my best to be courageous.

But the wound inside me was no less big for all that, Mum, will you have a look at my wound, but when she'd unfastened my vest and rolled down my socks, my skin was unbroken and there was no sign of blood, no sign of any abscess or swelling or red patches. Over and over again I was exposed as a liar, and eventually: being obedient was to keep calm and feel the wound growing, to keep the pain bottled up, not to let anybody else and in the end not even myself know how the wound was spreading, spreading to more and more new parts of the body, and before long the inflammation was necessary in order for me to keep on living and living meant obeying and obeying meant never wanting anything, obeying meant receiving and passing on whatever couldn't be kept and letting whatever couldn't be passed on stay and form new wounds, obeying meant keeping quiet how sister Betsy was treated by Mum's lover, obeying meant standing with the rest of the class by an open grave and singing: 'All hail the glittering memory of our nation's valiant son, His name will live in glory for the famous deeds he's done', though everybody knew that what he'd done was to embezzle his firm's pension fund and money collected for a new hospital and anything else he could lay his hands on, and then obeying meant –

No, Loel would probably have died anyway, even if I had gone against orders; but what about Brosius? Well, who knows? It was so idiotic when there were only two people in the marker trench, it was so idiotic of Brosius to say he would climb up to the target and stick a three-mark stamp over the first hit, because even before he'd got above the protecting mound on his way up, a ricochet slit his neck open. He was still alive, rolling over and over on the ground as if he were having a wrestling match, but you couldn't just run and fetch help because they were shooting and when they suddenly stopped the only sound to be heard, and heard it certainly was, and how, so shattering and so horrible that he thought his ears would burst, that was the noise coming from Brosius' dying body as he lay there wriggling in the dust like a maggot, rolling over and over, over and over again, and when the shooting stopped there was somebody yelling down the telephone: Mark! Naturally, he tried to shout and interrupt him: But, but . . . Mark! And he slammed the receiver down, and he tried to ring back but the telephone only worked in one direction and of course it would have been possible to jump up and shout and tell them what had happened, but who could know whether they might start shooting again straight away and they'd drummed into us that we must never leave the trench until we'd been ordered to do so and besides: how could anybody know Brosius was in such a bad way when he was rolling over and over so violently, as that must mean he had strength left and it was only a little bit painful and when he just lay there without moving, well, that could mean that it wasn't hurting any more, it was only a short time after all, and the orders said we had to mark, and there was probably blood on the bat when he marked, just on the handle, they couldn't see it from the firing line, but it was on his hands and Brosius was lying on his stomach, all quiet, and if there'd been time to bend over him and see how he was, well, but then they were off again, the whole row, and all twelve targets were riddled at the same time and bits of paper floated down into the trench and the smell of acrid powder came wafting over and up towards the woods, and it seemed as if the shooting would never end, the telephone was silent and dead and when somebody came over late in the afternoon to relieve him and asked how long Brosius had been dead, he said: Oh, about four hours.

And nobody could believe this perverse indifference, this lack of respect for death, nobody could understand how terrified he'd been and how he'd dashed up and down the marker trench, dragging with him the blood-stained bat and his own pitiful despair and his own terrible regret and his own harsh cowardice, which he'd had imprinted on his mind 'because that's how it's got to be' and because thou shalt obey thy mother and thy father, and all other mothers and fathers all over the world, all commands and superiors, all officials and laws and rules and regulations and native chieftains and policemen and everything which is big and strong and healthy and has muscles, a rib cage, and authority to fall back on. He sat in jail working out one defence speech after another, and this would be the authorities' downfall because now if never before it had been proved how inhuman and how cruel, how deadly cruel, literally, the authorities were when they forced him to stay put and mark while his comrade was bleeding to death, but in court he cut a sorry figure and couldn't understand at all why everybody maintained it would have been so easy to shout when he'd had that telephone command: Hallo, there's been an accident, you must stop the shooting for a minute, and nobody seemed to understand he couldn't do that because it's strictly forbidden to reveal your wounds to anybody else or to yourself. The hypocrites just sat there in their gilded masks and accused him of this and that and the other although they knew full well they'd have done just the same in his place!

But they never were in his place, that was the strange thing about it: he was always the one it happened to, nobody else got in the kind of ridiculous situation he did, he was always getting into the most absurd conflicts and then everyone would say he'd acted in such a stupid way, maybe he was born unlucky because they couldn't say of anybody else in the regiment, indeed, probably not in any other regiment in the world, and probably nowhere else in the world full stop, that because he was so frightened of making a mistake and even more frightened of being disobedient that he would call out the guard when the most insignificant person came into view in the distance, for instance, or that he would give his superiors quite different and of course much more important titles than they actually had. No, he wasn't born unlucky, and once he'd got over the worst, when he'd managed to discipline his urge to obey, and loyalty encircled his inner kernel like a nutshell, everything grew better and easier to bear, and he threw himself into all the tasks assigned to him with commendable enthusiasm.

He can still remember very clearly that parachute that needed testing, it required fifty-eight stages from when you put it on to when you actually jumped, and he knew them all so perfectly, more perfectly than anyone else, and he counted the seconds mechanically as he approached the door where they were leaping out one after another with their arms spread out and then there was that time when he was on a commuter tram, maybe it was hot or maybe the sliding door was open for some reason or other, anyway, there he was pressed tightly against the wall and in front of him stood a man with a rucksack looking very much like a parachute, and the man moved quickly to one side and disappeared from view and suddenly Boy was in an aeroplane, he started counting to himself and closed his eyes as usual as he staggered the few paces to the door and he grabbed the frame to give himself a thrust outwards and he'd already let go and was just about to jump when somebody grasped him hard by the shoulder and dragged him violently back in again. It was a most embarrassing situation, nobody would believe him if he said he thought he was in an aeroplane, because how could you possibly confuse an aeroplane with a tram, everybody asks. This man just tried to commit suicide, says the tubby little man who'd saved him, inflating himself with his own splendid performance, but I managed to grab him at the last moment, and all the passengers stand up and stare at him in disapproval, and their lips curl in silent contempt as if to say: You go off and commit suicide if you want to, young fellow, but not while we're here, we don't want any blood and we don't want to give evidence or any of the other unpleasantnesses that go with such an occurrence – and poor Boy had to get off at the next stop.

That's the way it is with disobedience, it can so easily turn the tables on you, it's so practical for everybody else but very rarely for you, it forces you to do the most outrageous things, and then you get into a fix and you can't blame somebody else because nobody will believe you anyway. How on earth could you get such a daft idea into your head, they ask with a sneer. I was only obeying orders, you reply without sneering, just obeying orders. But that's impossible, they say, there aren't any orders like that, and if there aren't any such orders, who were you obeying, God or the devil or some other devil? After that really witty punch line they start guffawing and take no notice of any assurances you give which are a waste of time in any case. They don't see the wound that's starting to spread all over you, the wound that starts just under your collar, leaves your head and your bare hands free but apart from that spreads all over your body.

Boy Larus wandered around in the dusk on the stony plateau the size of a skating rink to which he had to flee with his groin wounds in order to avoid the temptation of looking at them, enjoying them, tasting the agonizing pain they provided. Meanwhile, the great flash of twilight that was hurled through the world singed away the little island where six human beings were being tortured together, by their hunger, their thirst, their sorrow, their paralysis. Nights came and went, days came and went, but hunger, thirst, sorrow and paralysis came back refreshed every morning; he saw hopes born, bitter furrows growing deeper, beards growing longer and more brutal, bodies becoming dirtier and smellier, hair growing shaggier and wilder, faces slowly but steadily shrinking as hardships increased, clothes hanging looser and being shredded bit by bit by the island's sharp edges, backs growing more rounded and submissive, eyes more defiant and crazed from lack of sleep and lack of hope, skins rougher, more sunburnt and covered more and more in nasty spots, feet growing more blood-stained and more careless about where they trod, words becoming fewer and more blood-stained and more careless about where they trod, arms thinner and ever more helpless, elbows more pointed and pitiful, skin stretching over hip-bones, kneecaps, ribs, collar-bones, elbows, finger-joints, knuckles, nasal bones, temples, frontal bones, jaws, cheek-bones, vertebrae, shin-bones, thigh-bones, wrists, pelvises and crania – but even so he felt he was in another world, like a man lost in a menagerie: maybe he won't find his way out before dusk falls, but sooner or later the caretaker will turn up; he raced around between the locked cages, hoping they were locked at least, and searched in vain for the exit while the lion roared and heavy snakes rattled behind their glass screens, monkeys howled frenziedly, relentlessly, shrilly, and a solitary tiger raged somewhere in the darkness. Indeed, he was always backing off from the wild animals staring at him from his companions' eyes, from their faces and bodies. There seemed to be no barriers holding them back, no wounds too shameful to display, their ruthlessness terrified him so much he felt like screaming, so that he too could feel this wild urge to tear off his clothes and bellow: look, I've also got wounds that hurt, spreading all over me, sinking into me, driving me mad with agony. Look at them with your greedy eyes, feel them with your greedy hands, kiss them with your greedy lips.

Oh, how scared he was of them, and how comforting it was to feel the green flash and its surging heat sweep them out of this world, from this wonderful world of shattered hopes, disciplined coolness, and vacuous freedom from problems. He walked over to the mound, which looked as if it might have been made by human hand as a bulwark, so regular was its height over the rock, so carefully was it thought out as a protection for someone afraid of a rear attack, a surprise attack and any other kind of treachery. It ran round a third of his plateau and had red streaks like no other stones on the whole island. On top of it were mysterious black hollows looking like some strange form of box; he tried to work out what could have been pressed into the rock only to be squashed just as everything stiffened up. He took a little stone and knocked inside the boxes, but nowhere was the stone as hard as it was here, and all he could do was produce a few shallow little scratches. Then he ran his fingers slowly over the contours, closed his eyes and tried to shut out everything except his fingers, to force his senses through the hard outer shell and find out what there was living inside there, to try and hear the music that must be trapped inside, still being sung even after millions of years in captivity.

But he himself was dead, his fingers were so insensitive, their skin felt like sandpaper, and his ear could hear nothing, apart from the soughing of the wind as it drifted along the autostrada of the dusk.

Oh, those fingers of his, they used to be so long and sensitive. You'll see, my dear, you'll be a musician when you grow up, said all too many people; to be sure, he had become quite an artist on the machine gun and had the longest fingers in the whole company. There was a certain tune in the aeroplane, no, not in the aeroplane but in the air round about it, which reminded him of a melody he'd once heard at a funeral, and it came just when they had to bank and gain height at the same time. Now his ears weren't much good either. He kneeled down and stroked the stone, listening for the captive voice even though he knew how pointless it was.

Then he came to with a start, for something was moving fast just below him, something was on its way up to him, something indescribably horrible, something that wanted to leap on top of him and bite off all these membranes anchoring him to life. He looked up, but it was only the smoke from the fire down below which had changed direction, the green dusk had acquired long, black shadows sailing through it, darkness was seeping in from all sides and the dazzling white smoke wavered gently and floated slowly up towards him in wisps. He looked down at the camp, the grass and the

139

tall bushes were in the way; the ship was slumped as usual over the reef, however, and the strange green light was still dallying in the undamaged portholes, the funnel was leaning over the bridge and seemed to be involved in intimate conversation with the mast, which was leaning backwards, broad-chested and as yet unbowed, a solid countryman sniffing the morning weather with hands in pockets, and the cook's hat had got caught on a wire and was fluttering backwards and forwards as if looking for a head to settle on. The water was still shimmering slightly but obviously sensitive to the falling darkness, and he thought he could see something floating towards him; he was suddenly scared and tried to close his eyes, but they refused to obey. Something drifted slowly forwards about a hundred yards to stern: was that white patch a human being, or a part of a human being slowly surfacing on an undercurrent?

Oh, how terrified they all were at the thought of the moment when the lost souls would return and be washed up on to their beach, bringing with them all the recriminations of the dead faced with those who had been saved at their expense: what would happen then? The sea never reclaimed its dead, it wasn't like throwing a stone out to sea in the knowledge that it would sink and never be heard of again; you couldn't just throw dead bodies back where they came from, the way back would be barred, and you couldn't escape the stinking accusations in the shallows off the beach, that threat, that eternal reminder of your own imminent death.

Then the white object swung slowly round in a series of circles and was lit up brilliantly and briefly as the green light died away, and he could see it was a white bird drifting into land with the tide. Then there were those steps he was frantically trying to defend himself against, but there they were even so; it wasn't just the smoke tickling his nose, it was heavy footsteps crunching in the grass, beating through the undergrowth, padding over the hard rock, pausing for a moment as if in doubt. He crept back behind the bulwark, desperately trying to protect himself from this new threat, but after what seemed an eternity of agonizing waiting, they continued up towards him, apparently hesitant, but never in doubt about their goal. And all the things he'd tried to run away from by leaving the camp and the six people on the beach and everything they symbolized in the way of executioners and nagging certainties and constant doubts about himself and all the rest of it leapt over the bulwark and stabbed him viciously in the back of the neck till he lay gasping, outstretched on the naked rock, himself more naked than ever, and of course Loel's hands were more attractive than his and everybody made fun of him because he was so sensitive, his ears were always burning and always seemed to be trembling in some secret draught and then he said the last night, that last night before it all happened, and they were all pulling his leg as friends do because he couldn't stop brushing his teeth, no matter what was happening or what was going to happen: I have to brush my teeth, just think if I dream of my fiancée and I'm going to kiss her; and then when he lay slumped behind his machine gun and the life was draining out of him and maybe, or maybe not, but maybe something could have been done if only somebody had been as brave as people after-wards suggested he should have been, but he was dead when they got back to the airfield and two or three of them lifted him out, he was so still and his lips had parted and showed his lovely white teeth which weren't really as white as you might have expected.

141

Then there was this obedience business, was it really possible as people said to be brave at the same time as you tried to obey all the orders you were given, all instructions and company orders and tables dealing in all aspects of life, because the fact is that if you don't obey you don't dare to live properly, it was so ridiculously easy to make a mistake every time you tried to do something off your own bat and so you didn't dare to do anything people might think was idiotic, the fact is that right from the start you'd learnt how necessary it was to have doubts about yourself and rely on somebody who was right, who knew more than you did and could tell you and would tell you what to do and if anybody had killed Loel, it wasn't him, if Preses who was Loel's best friend shouted that Boy killed Loel, that wasn't fair and Boy had the right to cry as he did do in fact, and to roll around on the mess carpet with pain surging through his body in a series of convulsions.

And he himself, he'd loved Loel so much, liked Loel so much for his sensitivity, a sensitivity Loel dared to display, and which Boy also had but never dared to display, and that last night before it all happened, and everybody was pulling Loel's leg because as always, no matter what had happened and no matter what might happen, Loel had said with that innocent sincerity of his that was always so frank and so sincere: I must brush my teeth in case I dream about my fiancée and have to kiss her, she's so particular about things like that, and later when they lifted him out of the aeroplane and everything inside Boy was so numb and silent, he'd noticed Loel's teeth weren't as white as he'd always thought, but all yellow like in people who smoke a lot, and in the midst of his indifference he'd felt a noticeable pang of satisfaction.

Yet, the footsteps were getting closer, the stranger took hold of the top of the bulwark and then that wheezing which suddenly wafted over him and when he accepted he'd been found out and looked up, the captain put his other hand on the bulwark and wheezed again after the strain of it all. He pulled himself up with great difficulty, he'd picked a particularly difficult place to climb over in fact, and he sat astride the bulwark for a moment with his shiny jackboot on the right side; he had about him a little of the twilight which was almost over as it was squeezed more and more by the darkness, he had a little of that pale green light on half his forehead, his deep-set eyes, his cheek covered in stubble and on one side of his neck a vein had swollen up and looked as if it might burst at the slightest provocation.

The captain dangled his boot on the plateau, kicking slowly as he'd got plenty of time, and in a way designed to calm Boy Larus's nerves. Boy rose to his feet in confusion and suddenly felt the wounds in his groin flare up but before he had time to show any pain the fear that had just shot through him disappeared and he turned to the captain, calm and without giving anything away, and said, 'Aha, the captain's also taking a look at the world I see.'

And he looked round, round the plateau, out over the dark grass and the sea which was still streaked with a few narrow, painfully extended, deep green stripes, and the sky looming darkly over the sea, threatening to suffocate it, as if it were the whole world, and a few stars twinkling here and there like little red fireflies in the night over the black rushes.

'Larus,' said the captain, still kicking away at the rocky ground, the iron clinking regularly if somewhat nonchalantly against the stones, 'Larus, you're keeping something back from us.'

'But captain, I can assure you, please let me assure you . . .'

'I didn't want to say anything before. I thought: well, we've all got our own little ways, perhaps one can't expect everybody to submit themselves to the organization, although I've always been absolutely convinced that an efficient organization demands the submission of all concerned, everybody must do his bit. So, I've been tolerant, I've told myself there may perhaps be something in his tale about a stone he's looking for, perhaps it's an innocent enough hobby that no one can begrudge him, although I must say, Mr Larus, that the situation is extremely worrying. Indeed, I have to say I've been turning a blind eye on your tendency to go your own way.'

Boy Larus looked down on the man balancing on his bulwark, his own bulwark, which he'd discovered with his own eyes. He was tall, but not so tall that you'd remember him for his tallness; his body was thickset on the whole and his specific weight seemed to be quite considerable, his shoulders could have been borrowed from a marble statue, so brutal and so well formed and so cold; and then that face, used to giving commands but with a constant hint of worry from the corners of his mouth and down towards his chin and the same tendency around his eyebrows and that line running from the root of his nose before losing its way in the network of lines around his mouth. But none of this was what he feared most, those haggard faces which had conceded defeat to hunger and allowed all previously hidden secrets to seep through. Already he felt drawn to him by a remarkable feeling of sympathy, no, not all that remarkable because the only person he might possibly still be able to tolerate had come to seek him

144

out, a person who may well have had wounds of his own but kept them hidden, a person he would be glad to obey, the only person who still wanted him to obey, the person who could still rescue him.

'We're both military men,' said the captain; it was almost completely dark now, and the iguanas down below were rattling their way into their sleeping quarters. 'We're both used to discipline, and we know what it means. Please, do sit down: we're going to have a little talk.'

Boy Larus sat down on the bulwark; it was uncomfortable, but he didn't dare sit in any other way. He was pleased at having been rescued, proud of the opportunity to obey this man who was still kicking his jackboot on his plateau. He knew just how well tended this boot was, how he always felt every time he polished it with grass and sand and leaves with what admirable care the makers must have constructed it, it was as well made as a city hall with rooms for all imaginable occasions, as harmoniously conjoined as a musical instrument, and yet so hard and brutal in a completely natural way, like a beast of prey.

'Come a bit closer,' said the captain, moving closer himself. 'I remember once in Verdisse, we'd set up camp on a hill near a church, and started a fire near the churchyard wall, just a little fire, made of leaves and a few branches, nothing much to warm yourself by, but it made a cosy glow and the plains around Verdisse are so damned lonely. We felt as if we were all on our own, not just in Verdisse but in the whole world; it was autumn, and it was dark, and I had that fire made so that we wouldn't feel so damned lonely.'

Boy Larus listened respectfully to the prattle about the fire, that fire at Verdisse which must have been a remarkable fire since the captain said so, but he was only showing respectful interest; the last strips of twilight were now breaking up, just a few faint glows could be seen on the swirling sea which sounded deeper now as if a lid had been placed over it and one was straining one's ears to hear the sound under that lid. And everything was cleaner and better now, the two little animals in his loins could gnaw away to their hearts' content now, he was no longer tempted to eye them voluptuously and feel the the same ruthless, primitive, animal-like expression of abandonment in his features like several of his companions, no, not companions: fellow-survivors.

More and more stars emerged into the conquering night, unsure whether they should stay there or fade away again; he stroked the hollows in the bulwark and everything was calm and silent; he tried in vain to pick up the hidden melody under the stone, but he was startled by a low but nevertheless crystal clear signal which made him feel uncomfortable. He was not sure at first where it was coming from and started tapping the bulwark nervously with his knuckles in a state of extreme uncertainty. Then he fell silent and started listening intently to the captain, and noticed immediately the new tone that had crept into his voice, affecting his speech as if a jammer had started interfering with a radio station and almost obliterated the normal programme and making it irrelevant: the main point was now the jammer. He was still going on about the fire at Verdisse, how as the night wore on they had taken the blankets from the horses and burnt them, and scraped the bark off a maple to keep the fire going, and plucked grass from off the hill, taken oats from the horses and cotton waste from the mechanics to keep it alive.

146

When Boy Larus made as if to stroke the hollow between him and the captain, he suddenly felt his hand burning from below and pulled it back quickly as if he'd touched a red-hot stove.

Then suddenly, the captain stopped talking about the fire, broke off in the middle of a sentence and said, quickly and rather nonchalantly, 'You're keeping something back from us, Larus. You're keeping something back from me. Why do you come up here every night?'

'Captain, don't make me talk about that, it's too difficult.'

'My friend, we're both soldiers, aren't we? As we're both soldiers in the same army, we shouldn't have any secrets from each other.'

He suddenly swung his canvas leg over the bulwark and sank down on to the plateau at Boy's feet.

'Captain,' said Boy, and everything was closing in on him, he felt he had to obey before something even worse happened. 'Captain, if you have a wound, if you have a . . . if you have a . . .'

'Come on, out with it my friend, there's no need to be frightened of me.'

'Well, if you have a wound, if you have a wound somewhere on your body, a big wound you feel is just getting bigger and bigger, what is best in a case like this: to keep it secret or to find a confidant you can show it to and get advice and help?'

'To find a confidant.'

'But captain, if there's nothing you can do about it, if you yourself are well aware the wound can never be healed no matter what, what's the point of showing it to a close friend?'

'Oh, there are always good reasons. You can never be sure about wounds. The worst-looking ones can be easy to cure if you get the right treatment; other types of wound that seem minor, not much more than a bit of inflammation in fact, can be the worst kind and just spread inwards.'

'In my case both types apply,' said Boy. 'They look awful, it's really a question of two wounds which both look equally awful, and both of them are growing inwards.'

The captain lay back on the rock and started kicking the bulwark, not loudly, but regularly and unnervingly. Then he raised his head and rested it on his hand.

'Where are they?'

This tone, this jammer breaking in and provoking resistance.

'Captain,' said Boy, 'I can't tell you that, I can't tell you that, captain.'

A few periods of eternity ensued; there was a smell of smoke again, acrid and irritating, and a group of birds swooped down over the plateau, their wings beating urgently, round and round, as if they were on an exercise. The captain rolled over on to his side and pounded on the rock with the palm of his hand.

'Which squadron did you belong to, Larus?'

'Seventeenth west, based at Weston, CO: Colonel Tolov.'

'You were moved when war broke out, weren't you?'

'No, not straight away. We were in Weston for a year and a half; guarding convoys was our main duty.'

'But you eventually moved to a base on one of the islands out here, didn't you?'

'Yes, in the end twelve per cent of the original squadron was moved there; to an island called Brondona in fact. It looks like a horseshoe on the map, and the aerodrome was surrounded by both arms of the horse-shoe. It was a pretty efficient harbour, come to that, protected by long, high breakwaters.'

'What were you doing there, then?'

'Reconnaissance. There were rumours of a fleet assembling in the channels around Ronton, but as usual there was lots of smoke and little fire. We didn't do much good to tell you the truth, just a couple of sorties every week, and the rest of the time it was gymnastics and fencing, eating and games.'

'Who was your commander on Brondona?'

'Captain Simmon, captain.'

'When were you attacked then?'

'It was at dawn, the twelfth of January this year.'

'Was it just at dawn and not during the night?'

'No captain, just at dawn. They came out of the mists and bombed the station, and part of the fleet that had closed in during the night sailed into the harbour.'

'The attack came as a complete surprise?'

'Yes, absolutely. There was a bit of resistance when they landed, but that was overcome more or less straight away.'

'You were all taken prisoner, then?'

'Yes, more or less everybody apart from eight of us who were killed in the bombing, three who were shot during the landings, and Captain Simmon and a lieutenant called Osp who committed suicide in the HQ bunker.'

'And then you escaped. Yes, you've told me about that before. You found a sailing boat to take you to Ronton, and caught this boat to get you to the seventeenth squadron on Rivinos. Is that right?'

'Yes, captain.'

'Yes, as I say, you told me all this the very first day,

and everything fits in with what you say. Everything fits in so incredibly well, it all fits in so well it sounds as if you've learnt it all off by heart so that you can give all the right answers in convincing fashion if anybody should be so cheeky as to ask.'

'What do you mean, captain?'

'Well, I mean there's something about all this that doesn't make sense.'

'What do you mean, captain?'

He suddenly felt in dire need of support and slid down from the bulwark, leaning hard against it with his back. He pressed his back hard, hard against the stone and tried to sink into it, but was rejected coldly. He was so extremely hot inside, but felt cold even so.

'Well,' said the captain, sitting up and blowing out air as if he were smoking, 'when I started thinking about this business, there was something that just didn't fit in. I remembered a certain picture I'd seen in a certain newspaper when we sailed from Ronton, with several emaciated prisoners from the camp you say you were stationed at. They'd stolen a sailing boat and landed on an island north of Ronton called Bellos. There was nothing remarkable about them at first glance, they were considerably thinner than you are, but that needn't be very significant. But if you held the paper steady and looked really closely at them, there was something special about them you noticed, and quite rightly the article commented on it: they were all wearing enemy uniform – and why? Well, quite simply because the prisoners' own uniforms had been burnt, in accordance with the old tradition of trying to squeeze out of them the last dregs of resistance. Now you are wearing a uniform with the flashes of the seventeenth squadron. Unfortunately I don't have the newspaper

with me here, I expect it got left behind on the boat –
but if –'

'Yes, captain,' said Boy, and everything collapsed:
himself, the plateau and the island and the world, and he
was consumed by dizziness, 'yes, I'm a deserter.'

The captain didn't need to stretch far in order to slap
Boy's face, three quick slaps like whiplashes, and he fell
back along the bulwark gasping as the sensuous darkness
swallowed him up, only to spit him out violently and
cruelly once more. The captain was leaning over him,
breathing heavily, and Boy noticed for the first time the
acrid smell of sweat emanating from his body and from
his words and his breath,

'Now I've got you,' he said. 'Now I've got you.' And
he added in a whisper, 'Show me your wounds, where
are your wounds, you must show me them now.'

'It's so dark, captain, can't we wait till it gets light? In
my groin, in my groin.'

He scrambled warily to his feet, gave the captain a
little push and flung himself over the bulwark and down
into the darkness and the silence. He slithered noisily
down the slope, it sounded as if the earth was opening
up beneath him, and landed at the bottom, then tried to
crawl away into the sheltering grass. But the captain
caught him and helped him to his feet.

'Be careful,' he said reproachfully, 'you shouldn't
waste your strength in silly ways like this.'

They walked into the grass together, and it closed
gently over their heads like a gigantic wave.

'I don't mean you any harm, I just want to have a look
at your wounds.'

Boy Larus tore himself violently away from him and
tried to escape, but one of those treacherous potholes
that were everywhere and which the iguanas often used

151

as a refuge at night caused him to fall, something screamed in acute pain and clattered away into the grass.

Boy Larus was so scared of the darkness and of that mysterious scream and of all that was happening to him, although it hadn't yet happened. 'They're my wounds,' he yelled, 'Leave me alone, get away from me. I know your type. I know what was going on in a certain library at the Brosto garrison shortly after midnight when the fire had gone out and the armchairs were pushed together in pairs and there was whispering and panting behind the locked doors. What do you want with my wounds? I can assure you, there's nothing to see, just two ordinary wounds. What do you want to do with them? Let me feel the pain myself, they're mine, mine, not yours, go and stroke your own wounds instead.'

'You should take this in a different way,' said the captain, kneeling down beside him in the grass. 'Don't get so excited, calm down a bit, there's nothing outrageous about what I want to do, and anyway: I can order you to do it, I can give you an order and you must obey.'

'Obey!' he whimpered. 'As if I haven't obeyed enough! Haven't I obeyed all of you, haven't I always done what I didn't want to do, what I found so horrible, things that hurt so much I wanted to die?'

'But you didn't die.'

'Everything people shouted at me, funny how they always shouted at me, never requested, I did everything people shouted at me I should do. You always said things were going wrong, everything was collapsing, the system won't work if you don't obey – and I obeyed all right and the system didn't collapse, but there was something inside me that did collapse. I got a wound –'

'It's not bleeding.'

'I got a wound that just grew and grew, but you didn't care about that when it still wasn't too late, you didn't demand to see it then, you didn't shout then that I should kindly show us all your wounds, please, we're all so interested in wounds, especially the kind that still haven't turned nasty. You just let it go on growing inside me and outside me and through me and round about me and I did everything you told me to do just so that I could forget about the wound under my clothes; I obeyed you every time, in everything.'

'That's why I can't understand why you haven't obeyed on this occasion,' said the captain, getting quickly to his feet and pulling him a little way through the grass, and it was so endlessly silent; stars seemed to be hanging from the swaying panicles and smoke was blowing in regular puffs over the grass and the rocks, but the faint splashing of someone wading along the beach perforated the silence. Everything was so late, and so excessively late, the thought that it hadn't always been like this rose like the red star above his head, just as high and remote, and then this wound spreading over his body like a carpet, covering everything, extending into him, covering everything, and if wounds could talk this one would have screamed out in despair: And now this, now this as well, but he was so much a wound that he hadn't even the strength to bite when the captain's hands started caressing him voluptuously.

The Longing of Evening

No, obviously, there was no evening on the island. After the brief, green twilight, night fell like a weary snake gliding down over its rock and everything became pitch black. Well, the stars could sometimes serve to guide anyone who really had to go for a walk, as they sent small, thin, fragile shafts of light falling almost like puffs of breath through space; unsure of themselves and seemingly unwilling to arrive at their destination, they emphasized the stubborn and bitter stringency of the darkness in its role as night, hopeless night, eternal night. For a while, you could get your bearings from sounds if you wished. Most iguanas had retired for the night, of course, and soon they could no longer be heard rasping their way through the rocks with their hard skins, but there must be some special strain of iguana here that felt most at home in the dark; no one knew what they looked like as none of them had ever come near the fire or even come down from their rocks. Nevertheless, as long as it was dark, from time to time you could hear loud and clear the hard slapping of tails, quick shuffles over stones and a strange jabbering sound like that made by birds, something you never heard by day; but the slapping was harder, the shuffling quicker, as if they were bigger, more ruthless and less indolent animals that had now come to life; or could it be that the uncertainties of night encouraged the ears of the castaways to magnify all noises, make everything more scary, stir up eddies of hidden desires and apparently dead fears in which the ego could rotate like an abandoned snail shell?

'Oh, my God, I'm so scared,' said the English girl, 'you must understand how scared I am of night. Jimmie, surely you can understand that it shouldn't be like this, why couldn't everything be quite different? You must realize how scared I am of everything that happens here, and what has happened, and what is soon going to happen. I'd thought I could help you, you must know yourself how unhappy you looked when we first met. I'd really have liked to – no I wouldn't, because I was shy, and frightened as well, really frightened. I knew straight away who you were, and I couldn't very well have known how dangerous it was to know and let other people know, I mean, I thought the whole time all the others knew as well and I just assumed it was all an innocent masquerade that could end at any minute. Obviously I got frightened and sorry and worried when I saw how you looked when I gave away your secret. It was just that I wanted to talk to you, but you must surely realize that when I knew who you were and had sort of known you such a long time, it would have been so awfully difficult to talk to you if I couldn't talk to you and laugh with you in your real identity rather than the one they had down on the passenger list.

'You think I'm silly, sitting here telling you all this when it's dark and we're as shipwrecked as it's possible to be and scared of the dark and hunger and iguanas and all the rest of it. I can see you think I'm extremely silly and I can understand I'll never get you to pull down the canvas from over your head as long as I'm sitting here. You're probably thinking she does go on and on, this young idiot who's been chasing me all the voyage and still can't leave me in peace even now when everything's gone wrong, I can hear you're saying that by your silence and the way you're not moving a muscle, but here I am still sitting here prattling. Oh yes, you're going to hear all sorts of things this evening, even if you are lying under your canvas with your fingers in your ears and think you can shut me out. You'll see that you can't in the long run and then you'll fold back the canvas and start talking to me about all the things that have been happening to the two of us and how important it all is, even though it does all seem so hopeless just now. But first we've got to agree about one thing, and that's that it's evening now; come on, tell me if you agree with me that it's evening now, and that it won't be night for a little while yet. You see, I think night is so horrible, it gets so dark and all sounds get so awfully loud and I don't want to have to beg you to help me endure it, 'cos I know you want to be left in peace, really I do, and you think what I'm saying and what I'm frightened of is just childish nonsense that doesn't affect you in the slightest, but because it means so much to me that it's evening now I only hope you'll help me to believe that it really is evening.

'You don't need to roll your canvas down and answer me, I'll be able to tell whether you want to help me or not even so, not that there's all that much I want helping with: just that you can make me believe there really is a period of evening before it gets night, and that you'll listen to me until the evening has passed and it's time for me to go to sleep as well. You don't want to look, and I can understand that I think, you think we're all awful because we can . . . no, I mustn't remind you of what's causing you so much trouble. I thought it was unfair, so cruel and horrible of you to send me away, and I didn't understand you at first. All I could understand was my desire to get even with you, my own anger and my own sorrow; I thought you were making fun of me behind my back the moment I'd left you, and what I really wanted to do was to throw myself . . . no, no, listen, I wouldn't have done that in fact. You see I'd had to learn right from the start never to show what I was thinking, not to show what I was feeling, and Daddy always said that was what you should be like, that's the way the world is, and so you have to behave like that if you want people to respect you. Poor Daddy, you'd never believe how much he suffered if people didn't respect him. All the others in the regiment had at least somebody who liked them, who'd embrace them and pat them on the back when they met; but Daddy always surrounded himself with a sort of glass cage that kept everybody at arm's length.

'Oh, if only he'd dared to show just what he was thinking and what he was feeling, just occasionally, then everything might have been different; but he was always so sure and so blind about all that business that it'd never have occurred to him to change his mind. And if only I'd been able to tell him what was wrong even so, 'cos I soon caught on, caught on to the fact that if you go around like that and never let anybody know what you're feeling or thinking, well, in the end you just can't feel or think any more. You sort of freeze over, you see, and before long there's simply nobody anywhere around you who's warm enough or even sufficiently interested in your frigidity to thaw you out. That's what was happening to me as well, but then something happened, or various things, well, really it was a series of evenings that were nights for years on end that saved me. Oh, I know you think that what I'm trying to tell you is a bit ridiculous 'cos for someone like you who's seen so much, I mean had so many really vivid experiences, well, what happens to me must seem incredibly uninteresting and insignificant and dull. But I'm going to tell you all about it even so, I feel as if I were full of steam and I'm going to burst any minute if I don't. Are you listening or have you got your fingers in your ears? Never mind, you see, nothing can stop me as long as the evening lasts.'

The English girl paused for a moment and stretched out in the warm sand listening to the water caressing the beach and everything else was quiet apart from the muttering from the fire and as if she wanted to open herself up to the fire and the water and the evening, she flung aside the heavy cloth she had round her and lay naked and thoughtful in the warm darkness. With her hands that were still soft, she fondled her tightly stretched skin, stretched more tightly than ever around her hips and her forehead and her knees and the ice that had lain hidden in the horizon of her body melted rapidly. Oh, your hands, she whispered, your hands at last, keep on caressing me all evening.

Then she heard footsteps on the cliff, someone was hurrying down and stopped abruptly on meeting someone else.

'This can't go on,' she heard someone say, as if from the depths of a well, 'it can't go on like this any longer, we've got to do something. We've either got to get rid of him, that'd be the surest and safest way. And . . .'

But she heard no more. Either the pair of them must have been whisked away into the sky, raised up like chimneys into the night, or she herself must have sunk down into the depths with lightning speed, the voices grew vague and floated like shadows through her consciousness. It suddenly occurred to her there was something very urgent, there was something very urgent she'd almost forgotten about and she came to with a start, lying there in the sand and the coldness, the coldest chill of all flowed into her hands and she felt as stiff as glass and couldn't even pull the blanket over her again, over her body that felt so brutally cold. Hands, long thin hands with no wrists but with thick veins sticking out on the underneath came creeping towards her over the sand, radiating cold, and crept all over her, slowly, slowly. They were crawling on fingers which dug sharp claws of ice into her flesh and she wasn't even shivering, for she was a block of ice herself. But all the time, like a frozen lake remembering the summer thanks to a tiny current still flowing deep down, she remembered that there was something urgent, something that had to be done before it was too late. Then one of the hands creeping over her breast suddenly gave up, it couldn't go on, and the nails digging into her dug in even further and the hand just lay there with its spiky fingers sunk into her body. Deep down inside was a tiny muscle, a sensitive string, and when the nail on the weary hand's forefinger rubbed against it, the string started singing, a sharp, high, dreadful note with sharp edges, and it swung around inside her like the pendulum of a clock gone mad. It ripped her open from within and blood started running through her body, all of it rushing to the same place, all of it rushing to the same source, and she grew heavy and hot just there and the pendulum

159

slowed down and the note sank back into its source and little bubbles rose from the bottom.

'Evening's over and it's getting dark,' she whispered or perhaps shouted. 'We must hurry, I must hurry up and speak, you must hurry up and listen now.'

Some shadows flitted by, vague shadows with hard voices on the waterline.

'This is no good,' said one of the shadows before it disappeared into the darkness. 'Everybody must see that we can't go on like this. He's been here long enough now.'

'No, we've got to do it, and preferably as soon as possible,' yelled the other one in a hoarse voice. 'Not least for her sake.'

Both of them had disappeared as quickly as if they'd passed through a swing door into the darkness. Oh, she couldn't afford to wait until it swung round again and some stranger came towards her.

'Now listen to me again,' she shouted or whispered. 'Somebody's been running around shouting and quietened everything down, but now you can listen to me again. You must listen because I've been longing for you to do that. I've been longing for that all my life, longing for you to hear me, but up to now there's always been something getting in the way, like that mountain at home when we used to shout on a summer's night and wait for the echo, or the croquet lawn where Daddy used to keep watch and make sure nobody cheated. We'll have no cheating here, he used to say, banging his mallet against his boot, anybody who cheats at games is a bad person, yes, a very bad person. But you should have heard how he said that: I can't imitate him now, but Nicky could, my only sister. She used to drag me into the arbour after every game, pick up a branch and knock it against her heel as she imitated Daddy. He'd retired by then, and every morning he used to go out and inspect the croquet lawn as if it were a battlefield, measure the distance between the hoops to see if anybody had moved them during the night, dry them off with a rag if it had been raining, and rub them until they shone. He'd lie down and look to make sure all the lines that were supposed to be straight really were straight, and that no obstacles had been placed on the lawn under cover of darkness.

' "Do you think he's all there?" Nicky used to say. She was two years older than me and pretty disrespectful already. She disgusted me actually, and used to chew gum from morning till night. She liked to hop between the two windows in our room, and suddenly fling herself on the floor and pretend our bed-ends were croquet hoops.

' "Hey, this one's out of line. Come over here and bring your mallet, and we'll put this right. Disgraceful, this is, it's absolutely awful. How can you play an honest game in these circumstances? Anybody who doesn't play an honest game is a bad person." '

'Then she used to roll under the bed we both slept in and pull down the red cover so that she couldn't be seen. She'd lie there in her red grotto, you see, and I'd have to go and fetch tea and biscuits and wait outside and pretend I was a eunuch. One day Daddy must have heard us 'cos he shouted through the window that we should go out at once and play croquet, but I shouted back that I couldn't because I was Nicky's eunuch. I could see how furious he was, and he hurled his mallet on to the ground and more or less ran towards the house. Then I got scared and crawled under the bed as well and flung my arms around the two years that Nicky was

161

older than me and sobbed: "I'm so frightened. Daddy's coming and he's going to beat me. What is a eunuch when it's at home?"

We could hear his boots thundering down the corridor, there were lots of big nail-heads in the floor and they always made a loud noise when Daddy trod on them. The door was flung open and he stood for a moment in silence on the threshold, breathing angrily, like hounds do when they come back after a hunt. I crept deeper into Nicky's two years, but there was no place for my heart which kept on pounding away, and I grew sweaty and sticky and in the end Nicky pushed me away from her. Then Daddy slammed the door behind him and stood there threateningly and invisible somewhere in the room. It was like when you hear a snake slithering through the undergrowth somewhere but you can't see it. I was trembling, and Nicky did nothing to console me. Then he walked slowly over to the bed, and although he was walking so softly and slowly, the floor shook underneath him. Then I tried to hide in Nicky one last time, I spread her long hair over my face because I didn't want him to see my eyes, but she shook her head angrily so that her hair fell back in place, and held me away from her. "Beware, the elephant's coming," she whispered in my ear; it was all right for her, she hadn't done anything after all.

'Then Daddy flung the cover to one side; he'd known I was there all the time, but instead of coming straight up to me, he'd been playing soldiers, he always played soldiers: first recce, then attack. He always knew everything, of course, and the trouble with him was that he could never pretend he didn't. I was eleven now and had had a difficult childhood; I thought so then and I still thought so afterwards, but it does often happen that

162

somebody who's really had a hard time and suffered unjustly as a child gets so depraved by it all that when the time comes to look back on it, he decides it must have been a marvellous childhood if it made such a marvellous man of him. That's not how it was with me, though: I was very scared when I was little, and I remember well how the slightest little thing, in fact those little things more than anything else, practically scared me to death sometimes.

'I was very frightened of little animals, you know, the sort you find under stones or old croquet mallets that have been left outside for weeks on end and got yellow grass underneath them. Big animals like eagles, St Bernards or bulls, couldn't frighten me; but God, I was scared stiff of little ones, I daren't go into the kitchen for weeks and could hardly eat anything just because a nasty little insect, no bigger than an ant, had crawled out from a crack in the sink surround when I went to the kitchen one night for a glass of water. It was quite late and all the others had gone to bed and the night train was going past outside, and just as I was going to turn the tap on, this horrible little insect came creeping out from under the copper surround and under the chopping board. I was so frightened, so awfully frightened, I thought I would faint and I ran out in panic and then stiffened up out of the same panic, jelly at first, then something much harder and firm. I imagined in horror what terrible things might happen if I so much as brushed against the chopping board with my fingernail, and though I knew how stupid and idiotic it was to think like that, I got it into my head that the creepy-crawly was breeding thousands and thousands more under the chopping board and before long, it would be lifted up on their grey backs, and in an endless procession they'd march over to the edge of the work surface, using the chopping board as a bridge to cross over on to the statue of me standing stock-still on the kitchen floor and then crawl in under my pyjamas and cover the whole of my body with their stinking bodies (they had to stink as well!) and in the end I'd suffocate and die with none of Daddy's dignity.

'I realized in the end the thing to do was to keep staring hard at the chopping board to make sure nothing of the sort happened, and I fixed my gaze so firmly on that chopping board covered in bits of onion that my eyes started burning and I had to close them just for a second and as soon as I blinked I was aware of how awful the consequences of my slip-up would be.

'Well, I thought I was going to die. I didn't dare look any more, but I thought I could hear the chopping board being slowly lifted up and starting to move. I was beyond help now, I could feel it, beyond help – and I screamed. Daddy came rushing down the corridor, he must have been sitting up reading his usual topographical handbook 'cos his boots clanked on the nail heads as usual.

' "What do you want?" he shouted; not: What have you done, what's the matter, have you hurt yourself? If you screamed, you must want something, he couldn't imagine any other possible reason.

' "It's the animal, Daddy," I yelled, "the animal under the chopping board."

'I wanted to hug him and get support and warmth, but he drew back, lifted up the chopping board and squashed the little beetle against the work surface. Then I thought I was going to die, I thought I was going to throw up all my insides, 'cos he picked up the yucky remains between his finger and thumb and held it up so close to my face I thought I could smell its acrid fumes prickling in my nose.

' "You mean this?" he inquired contemptuously: he was always contemptuous with subordinates when he wasn't giving them orders.

'You should have seen me running through that silent house, chased by horrible tentacles, acrid smells, sticky signals from little insects, the kind that always huddle under small, flat stones, in the joints of old chairs that have been standing out in the rain, in the seams of old military overcoats, in the window-frames in the summer-house, in the holes where the croquet hoops have been taken away as autumn sets in, in tennis racquets that have been up in the attic for the winter, in your handkerchief when you just put it down for a moment on a bathing beach, in old newspapers that haven't been thrown away yet, under the thwarts of leaky rowing boats, in the cracked putty in old windows – all of them just waiting for some human to display a moment of weakness, just one second when they all shut their eyes, so that they can swarm out in their millions and spread out all over the world suffocating all other signs of life.

'It was horrible, and in fact those little insects were the only thing that beat me when Daddy came and lifted me out from under the bed and sat me down with a thump and shouted: What did you say you were playing? Eunuchs, Daddy, I said, I was Nicky's eunuch. Then do you know, he took two big paces backwards, as if he were going to take a measurement, and gave me a series of quick looks like electric shocks.

' "Just you say that word one more time," he said threateningly. And I said "eunuch" one more time because I wanted to know what it meant.

'Then he gave me such a thwack on my cheek that I'd have fallen over if the bed hadn't been in the way.

' "Just you say it one more time," he said triumphantly, not believing I would ever dare to do so.

' "Eunuch, Daddy," I said. I still had no idea what was going on.

'Then he thwacked me on my other cheek so hard the bed disappeared in a shower of stars and I fell over. As I lay there, trying to find my way back into the room, I heard him shouting in the far distance, "Come on out, Nicky. Did you teach Draga that word?"

' "No, Daddy," I heard her saying from the roof of a well, so cheeky and wide-eyed you'd have to be a soldier not to realize she was lying. "I've never heard that word before."

'Then he shouted for Mrs Muehlhouse, and she came rushing in and picked me up, breathing onions all over me, and dragged me off to the bathroom.

'Daddy had said I should be shut up in disgrace until I said I was sorry. She put me down on the floor, put the light on and locked the door as quickly as she could, so that I couldn't get a look into her eyes and see that she was really ashamed of herself. There I was, you see, thinking I wanted to stay in that bathroom for ever and ever and never come out, never ever, because everything was so unfair. I found a comb and combed my long hair over my face, so hard and wild and defiant I dared not even look at it in the mirror. I made a couple of little cracks so I could see through, and hoped I would look like Clara Bow when I grew up.

'But that was when I remembered the little insects that lived in the bathroom wall. Milli always used to show me them when she bathed me. What a life, she would say, what a miserable existence. They were little, hunched-up grey insects that could fly a couple of inches at a time when you touched them with your finger, but generally they just sat there on the wall like little bits of hardened dirt. I just can't tell you how horrible it was when they tried to fly. There are kinds of butterfly that look so like rats when they spread their wings out that you have to keep thinking: butterfly, butterfly, in order not to feel sick; and there are all kinds of insects that move through the air with a sort of mechanical jerkiness you just can't imagine is natural; but there isn't a single bird or insect or beetle that flew in as horrible a way as these did, 'cos you could see all the time they were creeping really, that somehow or other they'd been given a pair of dirty little wings by mistake, and they could use them to help them up or down a wall, but not in the air, not when it came to flying.

'I sat down on the edge of the bath, and all of a sudden, are you with me, everything started spinning round, and I could feel the walls slowly creeping in on me, just as slowly as Daddy had walked when he approached the bed a few minutes previously. They gave off a piercing, painful smell, and although I didn't dare look at them for fear of falling, I knew they'd changed colour, they weren't green any longer, they were grey, grey because they were covered all over from floor to ceiling in a layer of these little flying insects. The room was getting smaller and smaller, and when a few drops of water dropped from the ceiling and into my hair, I thought I was finished and I started screaming, I just screamed and screamed until the boots started clumping up the staircase.

' "What do you want?" shouted Daddy through the

locked door. "Are you going to say you're sorry at long last?"

'I'd do anything to get out of this prison, no price was too high to pay.

' "Yes," I yelled, so scared I thought I was going to die, "Oh, yes, Daddy, I'm sorry, I'm sorry Daddy."

'There was only an inch left before I suffocated to death, so there were still sacrifices to be made.

' "Promise me you'll never say that word again!"

' "Yes, Daddy," I shouted. "Never, never again." I couldn't even remember what word he was talking about.

'Then I was lying under the bed in mine and Nicky's room, without crying, as cold and lifeless as a log floating in a lake. All I had strength to do was to give Nicky a kick, the little hypocrite, when she came to console me.

' "And he's supposed to be a soldier," she said scornfully. She'd heard Uncle Bennie (Mummy's brother, who did exist once upon a time, but now he only emerged as God and King) use words like that about Daddy when he was reprimanded for borrowing too much money from the gardener in order to go gambling; and she pinched my bottom gently but I just kicked at her till she went away giggling. I just lay there, you know, like I'm lying here now with you, on my back, my heels pressed down on to the ground with my toes pointing straight up, and my hands pressed so tightly against my breasts they must have left a red mark afterwards, and I was staring up at the stars, I was pretending the bottom of the bed was the sky you see, and nothing hurt any more, and nothing felt nice either, but down inside me was a scream that was still hidden like an unknown fish under the mud at the bottom of a little lake, but then: look how it's working away, digging with its nose, slowly forcing its way up through the green light at the bottom, then it swishes its tail and shoots up to the surface, and eeeeh . . . and I screamed under the bed and nobody heard me even so, everybody was down on the croquet lawn, and only seconds earlier I'd heard the regular, dull thuds of the mallets, maybe somebody was standing in front of one of the hoops, leaning on his mallet: Did you hear that fox yelping over there in the park? Nobody heard me, and you could say: Who would understand why I screamed? That I screamed because nobody came to keep me warm, nobody came and unbuttoned his coat and let my head nestle up against his chest, nobody came and bent over me so that I could stroke his head and caress it, nobody came and saw that I could feel cold even though it was so warm inside the house and so warm outside as well during the day. They just laughed away on the croquet lawn, in a dignified manner, of course, maybe they were laughing at one of Daddy's jokes which always ended up with a command: Laugh now, one, two, three.

'I sneaked up to the window and saw the newly varnished croquet balls gleaming in the wet grass, and the six players – Daddy, Nicky, Mrs Muehlhouse, Uncle Richard the old major and his two grown-up daughters, known to Nicky as the Giraffes – wending their way among the hoops like partners in some complicated formation dance. Daddy was at their head, and he kept turning round with a stern expression on his face, checking on how they were behaving and barking out advice they all pretended to follow with a smile, while their hands were in fact trembling with suppressed irritation. Kate, my giggling grown-up cousin who had to bend down in order to pat me on the head, had forgotten to fasten the belt of her pink dress, and it hung down behind her like a tail, switching and swinging in ridiculous fashion every time she hit a ball.

'Oh, I was so high up and could see everything and everything was so silly that I burst out laughing and then I suddenly started crying because I thought they'd locked me up in the house and I felt so cooped up inside myself and so much excluded from everybody's heart that I wriggled over the floor like a worm, back under the bed, and stayed there until it was evening and Mrs Muehlhouse picked me up and examined me under the light as if I'd been ill in some awful and mysterious way.

'Oh, many times over the years I would lie there all alone under the bed, waiting for someone to come and pick me up and put me down carefully as if I'd been some nasty little animal that made their hands dirty as long as they were in contact with it. She's stubborn, this little girl, people would say as they passed through the rooms, damned stubborn she is. And they were right: I was stubborn; I'd built up a saga all around me that I could creep into every night and I could defy the whole world from there. It was a saga about evening, about the longing of evening, and it was a long and stubborn saga. I would creep into it as if it were an incredibly big, blue shell, and right up at the top was a big, warm star. And every night Daddy would stand in the doorway of mine and Nicky's room and say in that metallic voice of his: Time to go to sleep now, girls, it's night now; and I would pull my shell over me and the most marvellous things would happen.

Sometimes, just imagine, the red star would come loose and fall slowly down towards me, and sometimes it would turn into a stallion's eye, and the horse would start growing from it, with its neck and mane and hooves and lovely big tongue that it used to lick me with, all over my body as I lay naked so that it wouldn't wet my pyjamas; but other times the evening star was a lamp on the top floor of a tall building, and the man said Hurry up as he helped me over the blue street full of red buses and flowering plants, hurry on up while your Mummy is still alive. And so I'd run like mad and I could hear a loud screeching noise behind me and I realized he'd been run over by one of the buses, but I hadn't time to turn round 'cos the lift was just leaving. We flew up past all the storeys, and one after another the passengers would disappear through a hole in the floor, leaving behind big white rings of saliva that I'd try and keep clear of in my horror. But the lift just kept on rising, faster and faster, and it started rocking like a rowing boat and suddenly I saw somebody trying to force his way up through the hole, several long fingers were crawling in through the crack in the floor and at first I thought they were snakes and so I ran at them and jumped on them, only then they started squealing and when I looked down I could see they were fingers in fact and the littled screams were coming out from under their nails. Then they disappeared all of a sudden, and when I opened the lid over the hole I could see Daddy falling down the lift shaft, but slowly, very slowly and gently like they do in slow-motion films, and it all looked so ridiculous I started laughing so much I nearly fell out through the hole.

'Daddy's face was bright red, he was so furious, and he was trying in vain to fall a bit faster so he could catch up with his boots that were falling about three feet below him, but it was no good and the boots just wiggled annoyingly backwards and forwards. I must

171

have done a good job on his fingers, though, 'cos they'd broken off his hand and were falling in a bunch a couple of feet above Daddy's head, and the area between his head and the fingers was full of wobbly spots of blood.

'Then all at once the speed of fall increased, not gradually, but with horrific suddenness and I'm convinced the fingers and the blood caught up with Daddy before the drum roll sounded, that drum roll they always have just before a trapeze artist launches himself into space. Anyway, the lift stopped now and I didn't stop to listen to the crash, but leapt over the nasty saliva and found myself in the blue room, as high as a church nave, bathed in the blue light of evening. Draga, my own little girl, come on through to me, shouted Mummy from the next room, and I popped through an oval in the wall into this equally big, blue room, but there was nobody there, and I had to pass through a never-ending series of blue rooms, and Mummy's voice got louder and louder, and suddenly there I was in the hall I'd seen from the road outside. It was also empty, but I could still hear the echo of Mummy's voice, and in the big Gothic window was a lamp with my red star in it, and then the lamp called to me: Draga, I'm your mother, said the lamp, and the pink shade fluttered and suddenly I felt so cold I started shivering and I ripped open my dress and clutched the burning lamp tightly against my breast.

'Then it started growing and it became heavy and warm and we fell over together and lay on the floor and the lamp was still growing, and it grew arms and legs and wrapped itself round me and it was so warm and nice and my eyelids were so heavy I just couldn't see anything. But then the star fell out of the lamp and it slid over my breast, oh so lovely and warm, and down towards my stomach and then back again. Then all of a

172

sudden, I seemed to have swallowed it, I could feel it floating through my guts like a red-hot bullet, through my stomach, and finally it came to rest between my legs and the light from it must have been so strong it shone out from the whole of my body when I got to my feet, but then the lamp had gone and I felt very strong and almost weightless, and the light followed me wherever I went.

'I went over and lit up a solitary organ made of dark-stained wood right at the back of the room, sat down on the stool and played a pretty little tune that rose up like smoke into the blue evening, but I had to stop because the music was making me cry so much. Then Mummy said from inside me: Draga, my own little girl, now I'm inside you; and I replied: Yes, Mummy, now you're with me, and I felt so warm all over, but warmest of all between my legs where the star still was.

'Then I suddenly thought about Daddy and I said: Mummy, I feel so sorry. I threw Daddy down the lift shaft. That's nothing to be sorry about, replied Mummy, he's up here as well. And she directed my gaze at a window, and there was a statue of Daddy just on the point of jumping out with his boots and his sword-belt and a croquet mallet in one hand. Mummy, I said, can I push Daddy down into the street? Yes, my child, said Mummy, that won't matter, there are so many of him.

'Then I ran over to the window and opened it and I could see some children down below stop with their fruit baskets in their hands and point up at me, I expect they thought it was a bid odd to see a luminous girl. Then I gave the statue a hefty shove and it started falling, and first it fell about halfway down like a statue, but then it suddenly came alive and started waving its arms about, and when it hit the roof of the bus it seemed to have turned back into a statue again. The red bus didn't stop as I'd expected it to do, but it just carried on calmly to the crossroads. When the crowds had dispersed, it looked as if someone had been having fun smashing flowerpots underneath my window, and a few men in bowler hats were waving excitedly on the pavement beside the pile of bits, and I realized it must be all that was left of Daddy. Then one of the gentlemen waved down a concrete lorry, one of those with a container spinning round and round on top of it, and the driver jumped out and all four of them helped to throw the bits in through a gap in the mixer. The lorry set off again and one of the men in a bowler jumped up on the running board and waved like mad with a red hand-kerchief, shouting to everybody to get out of the way, and with its horn sounding non-stop and the man in the bowler hat clinging to the side like a miniature devil, the lorry disappeared from view. Then the star started burning and I grew warm and heavy and fell over on to the floor and I was so happy at the thought that I need never get up again. We lay there, Mummy and I, as if we were on the bottom of a little blue sea, and I whispered: Mummy, you'll stay with me now, won't you? You'll stay for a really long time, won't you? Oh yes, said Mummy, all evening. I'll stay all evening.

'And the evenings got longer and longer, and sometimes I couldn't get to sleep until dawn. My dear child, Mrs Muehlhouse said, and I gave a start because no one but Mummy had the right to call me "My dear child". But the people sitting in the lounge or walking through the rooms always said: She's stubborn, that one is, and they were right: I noticed how my shell was getting harder and harder for every evening that passed,

174

while deep down I was getting softer and softer, and I could see I had to have a hard shell as my inside was so terribly soft, but nobody else could see that and that was why I was so keen to keep everything that might possibly scratch it, knock it or stroke it with rough hands at a distance. With well-bred nonchalance I accepted everybody's advice, took part in all the games people forced on to me, and behaved impeccably on the croquet lawn where on one occasion the jolly little general's wife nearly made Daddy burst with anger when she actually kicked her ball through the double hoop, and when he told her off she just laughed and waved her mallet in his face so that he just had to smile in order to be polite, although his lips were tightly set and his ears red with fury; but later that evening I heard whispering coming from the arbour: My little buffalo, my little buffalo, and I was possessed by a curious indifference and peered between the branches, and saw her lying full length on the wooden bench with her head on Daddy's knee, playing with his free hand.

'That evening I jumped straight out of the lift and ran through all the blue rooms and with an urgency which startled me hurled the statue of Daddy down from the mantelpiece. And do you know what I did next? Mummy, I shouted in triumph when I heard the crash in the street down below, now you can . . .

'Not yet,' the English girl went on, worried, 'not yet, do you hear me, it's still evening you see,' but someone was standing in the darkness behind her, tapping something hard with his knuckles. Silently, she rolled a little closer to the boxer before whispering bitterly, 'Now listen to me, Jimmie, I'm the one you should listen to and as long as you do it's still evening.'

But whoever it was standing in the darkness behind

her sat down in the sand now, still tapping away, and she could hear the others creeping up, slowly, slowly through the grating sand.

'Then there was a time when the star got smaller and smaller, it lost some of its heat, and it wasn't as bright as it used to be, either. When Daddy turned the light out, I used to burrow down into the pillow in desperation, and try to pull the shell over my head; but I felt so hollow and washed out, I just couldn't keep up any more. Sometimes my tall cousin, one of the Giraffes, used to come out by car from town to pay us a visit, with her big, green parasol and her daughter Vivian. When Vivian and I were alone in the garden, I used to pick her up and whisper in her stupid ear: It's your mummy, Vivian, it's Mummy, and when we were alone in the lounge I used to lay her down beside me on the sofa and unbutton my dress and try and pull her head to my breast, but she used to kick and bite and my cousin would come running from wherever she was in the house. Mummy, Draga isn't my mummy, is she? the silly thing would shout, and one evening I was listening outside a half-open door and heard the Giraffe say: I don't like the way Draga plays around with Vivian, it seems really perverse.

'Later on, when we were sitting round the tea-table in the drawing room and I was as stiff and cold as if someone had driven a frosty pole right through me, I suddenly broke right through all the conversation with my enormous chilliness. Daddy, I said, Daddy, what does "perverse" mean? Straight away, he turned just as red as I thought he would and bit through a sugar lump in frustration, while his hand just chewed and chewed away at the edge of the table; but Uncle Bennie, who'd lost twenty pounds on the horses that day, explained to me as loudly as he could. Now I'm going to give you a really good hiding, said Daddy that evening when we were on our own, and he did, and then the evenings started coming back again.

'For a while, Nicky was out nearly every night, and if anyone asked where she was, I had to say something or other she'd told me to, I've forgotten what it was. I hated her, because I had a vague idea as to why she used to be so flushed when she crept into our room in the mornings, and I loathed the way she would lie and tell me she'd been running the last bit in order to get back home in time – when it was five o'clock in the morning. But one evening I sneaked out myself and stood trembling on the steps, but no one had heard me, and on the road near the dead oak tree was the young man waiting for me; he'd asked Nicky to tell me he'd be there waiting for me by the old oak tree at ten o'clock every night for a week, and if I didn't come out and meet him one of those nights, a leaky rowing boat with him in it would sink in the middle of the lake and we'd be fishing him out on our stretch of shore a couple of weeks later. I went to the old oak tree just because I wanted to be polite, I went because I didn't want a potential suicide to do anything rash, and when I came up to him I said: Well what do you want?

'Then he grabbed me hard by the arm and marched me backwards and forwards in the woods for a whole hour, and I was freezing cold as I only had a thin dress on, I'd intended going straight back in again you see, and the dew started settling on us and all you could hear was a cuckoo saying something or other on the other side of the lake, but I'd had my evening ruined and wanted to yell out in protest, but every time we turned, his grip tightened and I realized it was a clenched tongue that was being punished. Then he suddenly burst out: Are you cold? and when I said I was he seemed to think he'd conquered me at last and dragged me half-running through the woods.

'I could see the sky all white through the trees and I was horrified at the thought of it being so late, but as we came to the edge of the trees I could see a big tent in a little clearing. I thought at first it was a circus, but I could tell from the stale smell that hit you as you went in, and the long, silent pews and the ugly little altar on the podium that it was some kind of evangelical church marquee, abandoned by both God and man. A stove was crackling away on the podium not far from the altar, and we walked hand in hand down the aisle towards it. Are you still cold? he asked when we'd come up on to the podium and found ourselves at a complete dead end. No, I said, and he thought I was giving in and he put his arms on my shoulders like a dog and we fell down together.

'I lay still on my back and could feel the heat from the stove creeping all over me, and the roof of the tent was rippling like the surface of a lake, and then all of a sudden I seemed to realize what he intended to do to me, and it was all so horrible I wanted to throw up, and I raised myself on to one elbow and started kicking him till he yelled out in pain.

' "That's not what I want," I screamed, and it seemed as if somebody else had put those words into my inexperienced lips, "that's not what I want."

' "What do you want, then?" he spat out scornfully as he staggered back towards the stove.

' "I just want to be warm," I said, "I want to get really warm, and I've got a star there that'd burn you if you tried."

178

'Then he started banging the stove doors and smoke billowed out and started us off coughing. He tried to keep me there by pretending to be suffering badly and spluttering and moaning away, but I ran through the church as fast as I could and managed to duck and avoid the lump of firewood that knocked a chip out of one of the pews instead.

'It was only when I'd got home and snuggled down under the covers I realized not how scared I was, but how much it had all hurt. I started crying, but not in the usual convulsive way at all, the tears just flowed out as easily as if there was somebody else crying inside me, and it was just as incredibly easy to scream afterwards: I just opened my mouth and Mummy or whoever it was did all the screaming inside me.

'One evening Mrs Muehlhouse forced me to go with her to the tent church for a service, and among the people gathered around the entrance was a tall, grey-haired man with drooping eyelids, with his arm round a youth of about my age. The pastor and his son, whispered Mrs Muehlhouse respectfully, and then I recognized him, then I recognized the boy: it was the one who'd threatened to drown himself on my account, the one who'd flung me on to the floor between the altar and the stove.

'Later on, when we were sitting there and I was feeling numb because of all the bodies giving witness and overflowing with worship and warmth, somebody, I can't remember who, but somebody went up to the podium with me and I found myself standing there singing, singing all on my own some song or other I didn't know in a voice I didn't recognize. The pastor and his family were sitting on a little bench right at the front, and while I was singing I heard the pastor's fat wife say: Somebody should shut her up, somebody ought to shut her up, but the pastor said: Why, it's lovely.

'Then the song was finished, but I didn't realize that until there was a long silence afterwards and it was Mrs Muehlhouse with her white face and her raised eyebrows who made me come to. Then I went down on my knees at the side of the altar and the rich, mellifluous voice inside me said: Sinner, sinner, sinner . . . who's sitting on the bench with the white chip in it, who threw a lump of firewood at me when everything had gone wrong for him?

' "There," I whispered, pointing at the pew where the pastor and his family were sitting. "There, just look at him blushing and turning pale, first one then the other, and see how he'd love to run out of the tent in shame and fear, look at him, all you who have lifted up your hearts, look at the pastor's son: he's the one who threw me down one night between the altar and the stove, and tried to rape me."

'Suddenly, there was nothing but silence, the kind of silence you get between lightning and thunder, and once again I was raised up to the cruel surface of reality and I looked at the pastor's son who had turned as pale as a sheet – and something horrible must have happened: I didn't recognize him at all, there wasn't the slightest similarity between him and the boy who claimed he wanted me, oh, it was all so awful, and when I suddenly saw Mrs Muehlhouse's red face below me, all swollen with embarrassment, and with the abnormal urgency of a suicide I just opened myself up to the scream within me, I gave myself up like a beast on heat to the scream within me, I dissolved myself in deadly acids, I dived straight down with wide-open eyes into the octopus and was pulled to the floor on the podium, as the scream was so heavy I just couldn't carry it in a standing position.

'Afterwards, they told me they'd had to carry me all the way home, screaming like crazy, and it must have been ages before anything happened to me apart from a white flagpole constantly being taken down and then raised up again in front of my eyes. When they thought I was fit enough again, they sent me off on this voyage together with a stout lady who never said a word and who's lying in bed ill in Ronton just now, waiting for us to come back; when she gets hold of your wrist, it feels as if you have handcuffs on.

'But I was rescued from her – and Jimmie, I met you, I heard the captain telling somebody who you were 'cos I didn't recognize you even though I said I did to get you on my side, I was surrounded by enemies you see, everybody was keeping watch on me, everybody except you. I thought: he's the one who can give you warmth, he can keep evenings going on for ages, he can give you back the warm body you lost and I know you'd like to do that, Jimmie, I can feel it in the heat of that star that's come back again, Jimmie, shall I fold back the canvas and kiss your throat? You have a little red mark just under your adam's apple and that's where I want to kiss you; or shall I stroke your arms and hands and give your muscles little bites, I think they'll taste like rhubarb; or shall I undress you and give you my warm star so that it can keep both of us warm, 'cos I need to be warm, Jimmie. I do so long for warmth and evening. I need to be so warm, so warm, Jimmie.'

But the drumming behind her became more and more unbearable, and now somebody was beating the sand with a stick, hard and nastily.

'Leave me alone!' she cried, flinging herself backwards

181

in fury; but they didn't leave her alone. The four shadows in the sand, crouching round some invisible camp fire, came closer and closer, one step at a time, like pawns surrounding a king. Oh, they knew everything, they had octopus arms and eagle eyes and the venom of a snake and the agility of a puma, and she was useless against their combined strength and there was nothing she could do: just give in, once again, dive down into the octopus, bare breasts for the eagle's beak, take off her shoes for the snake and embrace the puma – and then the scream:

'You think I don't know, don't you? You're probably thinking: there she is, the fool, prattling on and on without having the slightest idea, it's just incredible, it's not normal, it's horrible; but you see, you're all wrong. Oh yes, I know he's dead, I know he's been lying here dead all day, and you say: how can anybody be in love with a dead man, how can anybody talk to a dead man like that, how can anybody want to caress him? But look: why do you think I loved him, why do you think I dared to love him? Because he was so strong, so healthy, so full of power and strength? No! No! Because he was ill and weak, because his wounds had started stinking, because he was a cripple, because I never needed to think: he'll want to have me tonight, he'll come and force himself into me in his hut or in the bushes and he'll pour out his rugged manliness all over me, he'll come and force my legs apart, with a plank if needs be, and he'll hurt me as much as he needs to do in order to satisfy his desires and his vanity, he'll slobber all over my face and convince himself I love him as a result, he'll shower me with nasty words and think they turn me on; oh no, how could I love anybody I'd be afraid of getting all that from? – But a dead man, a dead body that's stopped longing for such horrid embraces, what's purer than a dead man, what's more worth loving than a dead or dying man, because you can confess everything to a dead body that's still got its living consistency, and yet you can still retain your innocence; is there anything you can love more passionately and more painfully than someone who's just died and who can no longer lure out of you in all kinds of dirty ways the impure undercurrents of your emotions? Oh, to be loved in return, that's what I was always so afraid of, I was always afraid of being loved in return, I was always seeking warmth, but only I could provide that in my love of the defenceless, those who were not strong enough to force their own cruel, ugly love on to me. So take him away from me now, bury him, and put sand and stones over him, but don't forget to do what I can see your eyes brimming over with desire to do to me. Fling yourselves on to me and force your way into me, look, I'm defenceless, I don't even have a star between my legs as I've always boasted of having, press me down into the sand and let my hatred inflame you even more, really turn you on, so that your performance gets more and more frenzied. Poor little thing who's short on love, you all think, she's not worth anything better than being raped, than being forced into making love, in the name of justice, amen. Get on to her then. Roll me over – no, you won't need a plank, you won't even need to use your fists, I shan't defend myself, I just don't need to defend myself any more, a dead woman doesn't need to defend herself, a dead woman who's lost everything already, or gained everything, so there.'

And the four shadows soon pounce on her, the beach is suddenly a very lively place, it's as if herds of all kinds of animals come charging out, wolves, bison, hyenas, tigers, and all their heavy bodies make the beach shake and each animal that flits past her showers her with the acrid perfume of wolves or tigers or lions and then the smoke from a stove in a white tent wrapping itself gently and as soft as cotton wool like bandages round her limbs until she almost chokes – and then those flagpoles, those white flagpoles, those eternal flagpoles being lowered and raised and lowered and raised with a fluttering pennant from a thin, thin scream.

The Fires of Night

Now the fire is flickering brightly on the beach. The tide is sliding gently in over the sand, and the fire is reflected in the water. But the night has many fires. In Verdisse, the camp fire burned until dawn, the horses shivered in their nakedness, and a giant had slung a necklace of fire over the plain. Then, the stallions snorted loudly just before the explosion came. But the night has many fires. Petrol over the bodies, frozen stiff and breaking like twigs, and then the fires sinking slowly through the ice, leaving behind eighteen graves in Lake Tibirsik when morning came. But the night has many fires. Lying alone and freezing in the heat before the open fire, where all the apples have already burnt to a cinder, and hearing somebody coming downstairs and a whiplash dragging along behind on the stairs like a rat's tail, then the pain in your back a quarter of an hour too early and then the fire flaring up in response to the drama. But the night has many fires. See the fire smouldering in someone's eyes, feel the heat radiating from a body that wants more fires but for its own part only wants to be extinguished the whole of the long night, and then extinguished more and more, all the time just covered in ashes, then only ashes. But the night has many fires. Lying stretched out under a canvas sheet and feeling how hot your fingertips become, feeling the heat running through your fingers and into your hands and into your arms and into your shoulders and down through your trunk, down through your legs, into your feet, into your toes, and knowing all the time, always knowing above all else that the only way of getting rid of this pain is to cool yourself down through contact with someone else's skin, someone else's body, someone else's arms, hands. And fighting with yourself as with the devil, fighting with your own limbs, struggling with your own fingers, resisting with all your strength and still not winning, because in the end you get so hot, you'd burn up if you didn't let your fingers have their own way.

And then those hands, those hands that are always so hot, sneak out on to the canvas and slide over towards the person sleeping by your side. He's fast asleep, the glow of the fire is breathing in Boy Larus's motionless face, his eyelids are closed yet alert, and his hand is clenching and unclenching on the canvas. There's a little way to go yet, the heat is getting worse and worse, it's as if your skin were burning but not being used up, and that's the worst thing of all: that you just can't burn up once and for all and put the whole business behind you at last, and then that hand clenching for the last time and slapping your wrist while that look, filled with the deepest scorn imaginable, digs into your face like a needle, your unprotected face. Boy Larus hasn't got up, he's still lying there as usual hunched painfully in a posture made up of equal parts of fear and contempt, exactly the same as usual, but in that case how come the captain now sees him creeping towards him like a snake, his tongue has suddenly grown longer than all the others and is shooting out from between his teeth lightning-fast, but before his feet are covered in the patterned skin he gives Tom Solider a big kick, as if to wake him up, to warn him of a very real danger.

'Oh, if only you'd been on your own, you're so cowardly when you're alone,' whispers the captain to the snake but the snake just keeps on creeping nearer and nearer, its head swaying slyly and wearily from side to side, and Boy Larus's eyes are set deep, deep down inside it, as motionless as glass beads.

'If only I'd had an awl,' says the captain, 'a long, cobbler's awl, you'd have been hopelessly beaten,' but the snake just keeps on coming and there's nowhere to run away to, there has never been anywhere to run away to: just wait for the whip, the strike, the bite, the blow – and suddenly the snake's head falls on him like an axe, its little scales glittering in the firelight, and the bite-wound, always equally horrific, must be gaping like a mouth just above your knee.

All is lost, and he knows that when he starts running, but he runs even so until the poison turns his knee into a stone which first aches and then becomes as heavy as lead and doesn't hurt any more. He's pulled down by it and lies there on his back like a beaten iguana while the transformation takes possession of him and everything happens as it usually does. There is a shattering kind of solitude which can change the whole world into one big field or rather, one flat surface; you can see everywhere and yet at the same time you can't possibly see everywhere, it's a stretch of metal gleaming like a ball-bearing without any trace of a soft patch, not a single hollow to hide in, not a single hole to crawl down into. This surface gives off a shiny, oily light but it is also lit up by a cruelly sharp radiance from above, coming from some motionless heavenly body, a huge sphere made of the same cool, oily metal as the one you're attached to yourself, sweating this light through its milliards of pores. On this surface of your solitude, there are no shadows either; you can't raise your hand or your arm for instance and try and hide behind the shadows they cast, the light just keeps on pouring all over you, and moreover, it's not possible to move either, you're stuck to the spot, not by some unseen rope or bond you can tear away or chew to pieces; the remarkable thing, the key to it all, perhaps you might even say the meaning of your situation is precisely the fact that you can't do anything about it, and you just lie there with your back pressed against the hard surface like a drawing pin sticking to a magnet, and all the time, light keeps on pouring down over you, and suddenly, the whole of space starts singing out of solitude.

You're alone in space, cast out like a raft at sea, exposed to it like a dartboard to its darts, and you can no longer run away from your destiny and anything can happen. You can expect eagles or hawks to swoop down from the stars and cast themselves over you in a frenzy, because you're the only thing in the whole world that's soft, something a beak can sink into, something a talon can dig into; you can expect meteors or whatever to slit open your bare breast, naked in the face of eternity; but the only thing that happens is that space starts singing, space starts singing out of solitude. 'The only thing' – but no, it's more than just 'only', it's pretty horrible.

The odd song, you think you could no doubt put up with the odd song; but that's not how it is: you can't put up with it, you just have to. 'Space', that silly little concept you like playing around with when you're out walking through the reeds and the trees, in parks or refrigeration plants, or sitting in your rocking chair watching the sky flickering over the top of the lilac hedge; space, the little lake where idyllic cloud boats glide along before the wind; space as it seems to be when you're still in the little hole on earth where you were born, grew up, were ill-treated or ill-treated others and where you're going to die any minute – that space is just a lie for anyone who has experienced properly this enormous, all-consuming, embittered solitude, stuck on to a shiny metal field and with nothing around you and above you but the most gigantic, the loneliest of all wildernesses, the whole of space, the true extent of which you never dared think about while you were living in your hole on earth: it's like a bottomless well, and you lean further and further out in the hope of seeing water, of seeing something tangible instead of just this terrifying emptiness, and in the end you lean so far out, you fall, and then you fall and fall and fall for the whole of your life without experiencing anything but this endless falling and you die while you're still falling and although you haven't come to any sign of a bottom you're annihilated while you're still falling and gobbled up by the darkness after your pitiful failed effort at filling it with meaning, the meaning that comes from looking for a bottom.

But even so, you don't realize how huge this space is by falling or lying there stuck to the ground like that, feeling the pressure against your chest; it's only when space starts singing you begin to grasp what you've had no idea about before, and you catch on with such shattering certainty that you'd burst like a balloon if only you could. But when you're lying there stuck so hopelessly to the magnet, there's nothing you can do

about it: all you can do is listen, you can't even raise
your hands and stick your fingers in your ears, and in
any case: that wouldn't help either because when space
is singing out of solitude, you're changed into a big,
tense, listening ear and if you don't want to hear
anything you'd need a meteor to stick into it, or a
heavenly body might do, a star perhaps. As for the song
– oh, it's so beautiful and yet terrible, it's the most
beautiful thing there is and yet the most horrible thing
there is. If only you could be killed by it, but all you can
do is lie there alive and let the song flow through you
like water through a turbine, and it will always be like
that, you feel space will always echo with solitude and
you yourself, a vulnerable ear, will lie there outstretched over a heartless, naked surface listening to a
cruelly beautiful song made even more cruel by the lack
of echoes, atmospheric turbulence and earache.

But somehow or other: you must have been cured of
this solitude, or just simply fallen asleep; you wake up in
your hole on earth and see the usual little glimpse of
eternity smiling through between the roller blind and
the bed-end.

So, you're not alone any more, then, you think, all
right, the awkward adventure, the desperate episode is
over – and life goes on, a little bit less solitary all the
time; but in fact it's not over, it's only just beginning.
You sit in your room or you go out of your room, it
doesn't matter which, and you meet people or you don't
see a soul, it makes no difference, you talk to your wall
or you don't say a word to your wall, you write a letter
or you just buy a stamp, you set off on a journey or you
just buy a ticket, you go out dancing or you just go to the
dance hall, you do something or you don't do anything,
you let things go or you don't miss a trick; it makes no

difference, no difference at all: you'll always feel this glass wall separating you from everybody else even so, this hard pane of glass you always carry around with you and look through and are seen through and which you brought back with you from your journey through space. You're as isolated as a fever patient, and that's only right: you've got a higher fever than most people; you could also say: you're as isolated as a condemned man, and that's also right: you're more fit to die than anybody else.

You're alone now as well, but in a worse way than you were before; space isn't singing out of solitude, space isn't singing at all: it's raining or snowing or it's windy – but so what? You're alone in a dirty way, in a miserly way, an unaesthetic way – and when there isn't any way out in any case (if ceasing to feel alone is in fact a way out), don't be surprised that you long to be back in that huge space with its devilish but sublime music, its heartless but hygienic solitude, its absolute freedom from any kind of life, that's true, but at the same time an absolute freedom from any necessity to seek company, to open doors where no doors exist, to smile when you feel like crying, to caress when you feel like scratching, to look for friends when you have learnt that the world is full of enemies.

You long for moments of absolute self-effacement, of the most brutal and sublime solitude with as much intensity as you can muster, with all the fire of your dreams; you have become a party to a dangerous secret, you have been initiated into the use of a dangerous poison called solitude, and like a drug addict you now divide your life into two periods: intoxication and recovery. But what should you do when you're in your hole on earth? Should you try and acquire close friends?

– No, because you're afraid, and probably rightly so, that having a close friend, even if 'close' is as relative as you like, will put you in an awkward position from the outset, for your chances of being flung out into wide, cold space will be all the fewer. You should keep people at arm's length, then – and come to that, the glass pane or the membrane surrounding you is of considerable help. Should you get yourself a mistress? – Yes, but only so that when a suitable moment comes, you can terrify her with your coldness, get her to hate you, to push you away from her with the coldest of hands, give you a push full of hatred which flings you head over heels into space, that was just what you wanted – thank you very much! Or join the social whirl, perhaps, mixing with sympathizers and people of like mind, and letting yourself be bitten by the snakes slithering around the salons and claiming they admire you, respect you, etc. Or why not expose yourself to the contempt of the whole world, to the anger of the whole world, how you do it is irrelevant, and the result is irrelevant come to that as long as it can drive you into a state of absolute solitude, if only it can make you hear once again how space is singing out of solitude.

As he says to her one night, their last night in fact: the train is leaving the next morning with the three thousand volunteers and he's still quite a young man: 'We're a special kind of person, we solitary ones, we're a race on our own. We really ought to be marked in some special way so that everybody can tell straight away and say to themselves: ah, he's one of those solitary types, I'd better leave him alone in case he infects me, he's got big wounds under his clothes, like all of them have.'

He stands there in front of the mirror in the hall made

brown from all the smoke, where all the inherited dark furniture from the smoking room is, looking into a young face, tense with excitement, criss-crossed with small furrows caused by the despair he's already lived through, his eyes are shining and slightly bloodshot after the whisky, his chin displays a souvenir of a careless blow from an axe when he was a boy, a white scar sliding down towards his neck; it's not a handsome face, but it's quite an honest one, it tells surprisingly few lies for a face, and he thinks: I don't need a sign, you can tell by looking at me even so. But he covers the scar with his scarf and continues talking to her while looking in the mirror and arranging his scarf, because he wants to leave shortly.

'We could have a sign, as I said, a little patch sewn on to our chests, a patch with a big letter L, L for Lonely, Loner, Lonesome and all the other compounds beginning with lone- ; just one sign, note, not two, not six, not a hundred. When we go out to war as volunteers, we could . . .'

'Ernst,' says his wife, in that gentle tone of voice you reserve for when you're feeling desperate and want a particular person, but only him, to know you are, 'thank you so much for torturing me so splendidly. I'll remember it always. But Ernst, don't go just yet – what on earth will you do with yourself all night? Your train doesn't go until six.'

His rucksack is already packed and ready by the front door, ready to take off at any moment, a big, heavy bird that's finally got tired of waddling around on land. He looks first at his rucksack, then at his wife, and then back again, and he pictures to himself those long, miserable streets lined with bare poplars all round the station, and thinks about how he'll wander around aimlessly, chain-smoking and watching the butts drown in puddles, whistling snatches of melodies as they come into his head, being accosted by dubious types who think he's looking for company, feeling cold and all alone but still not managing to get that lovely feeling of solitude.

'All right,' he says reluctantly, slowly loosening his scarf and examining his scar yet again, stroking it, 'all right, I suppose I might as well stay a bit longer – but don't get any ideas.'

'But my dear Ernst,' she says, going and lying down on the bed, 'I stopped getting ideas ages ago.'

When he comes in to her, she's naked under her dressing gown and, thanks to a carefully staged coincidence, she lets him notice. But he just pulls up a chair to the side of the bed and sits down and looks at the little painting over the bureau, one of those things people inherit: a few cats are playing with a ball on a patchwork quilt. The frame is cracked in four different places, and he thinks how he could have mended it were it not for all that solitude that got in the way. But there's a corner he's not looking at and he knows it's empty: all there is there is a few crumpled bills, but until last Friday there used to be a desk there, and then it was sold all of a sudden. What's the use of a desk when you don't write any more, when you've exposed the whole business, the whole works, and there's a war on not far away, and you don't need a desk when you're there.

'But darling,' she says, tugging away at his arm even though he doesn't lie down beside her, 'surely you weren't going to go away without saying goodbye, I mean, that's the least one might have expected, don't you think?'

'Why?' he asks, turning to look at the empty corner

194

so that he can really feel the pain inside him. 'Why? Why should that be the least you might have expected? I thought nobody expected anything of me any more. There's nothing to be expected from here any more, oh no, we've closed down for today, we've closed down for the night, we've closed down for every day and every night for as long as there are days and nights. Can't you see I'm hollow, I'm squeezed out, I'm like a fish that's just been caught and bashed against a stone and it bursts and all its juices come spurting out. There's only *one* thing I live for now, and that's nobody's business. I'm going, yes, OK, but not because I have any special desire to go clambering around in those mountains everybody's on about so much, or to start fighting with bayonets in all those tunnels. I've no desire at all to do anything. But you see, solitary types like me are important for wars. We say to ourselves: hey, here's an unusually distinguished way of committing suicide. Here's a chance to die while still observing all the respectable rules, and you might even get a medal to hang on your tombstone as well: this is a death that might satisfy both your vanity and your death wish – what more could you ask for?'

The woman just lies there on the bed, calmly and quietly, and he can sit down beside her without her flinging herself on top of him.

'You see, we don't care about which side we're on or anything like that. It's all the same to us, nothing matters as far as we're concerned, and the generals would be horrified if only they knew how many empty shadows they had in their army, how many who'd go over to the other side without any hesitation if only they knew they'd stand a better chance of being lonely in a definitive sort of way over there.'

'Good God,' she says softly; but before she knows what's happening, she'd dug her nails into his thighs and is screaming at the top of her voice: 'For God's sake, just go away, can't you? Go away, get to hell out of here, I never want to see you again, just leave me alone with all the debts and this rotten life and the boy in hospital. You couldn't care less that everybody's going on about you and calling you a ruthless bastard who's running away from everything without so much as a word of explanation, not a single word, a ruthless . . .'

She screams herself naked and writhes about like a patient in a high fever, and her throat is positively foaming with all the curses.

'Just think, I might even have taken you seriously,' he says, slapping her lightly on the throat and mouth until she quietens down, 'if your anger hadn't reeked so much of sex!' He fastens her dressing gown for her as if he were most offended, and before he gets up and leaves, he takes one last, long look at the empty corner. He thinks he can see a shadow sneaking out of it and giving him a contemptuous nod as it passes him on the way out; a whole procession of shadows, in fact, some of them pacing backwards and forwards between the desk and the bed and representing the young dramatist Ernst Wilson, chewing over some lines that never got properly written, and the shadows rolling about on the floor by the wall look remarkably like the not entirely untalented young poet Ernst W. Wilson just three weeks ago. What's gone wrong? What kind of a tornado is it that's devastated this existence that seemed to be on its way to success?

His wife has stopped screaming, true, and now she's crying instead; but you can't take into account everybody in the world who starts crying, and now he really is leaving: he closes the door behind him and can hear her crying, but it's too late to worry about that now. No, he doesn't even feel that little pang which so often tries in vain to warn people when they've done something bad. The rucksack is standing there in the hall, ready to fly, and he lets it do just that: you can let a rucksack do whatever it likes, a rucksack doesn't cry, a rucksack doesn't spoil things by shouting when you want to hear space singing, you can say what you like to a rucksack, it doesn't care whether you're cold or warm; and they go off together the rucksack and Ernst W. Wilson, and wander along lots of the long, asphalted streets, all shiny with rain and loneliness, and all the time he is aware that something has happened for the last time, it's as if he's been stricken by some incurable disease, or maybe incurable healthiness, it all boils down to the same thing in fact.

Already as he leans against a poplar tree and closes his eyes and lets the wind and the rain flow over him, he can see the desolate track leading straight into solitude, a broad track, like a railway without rails, a heavy track pressed down into the earth, whimpering, with flames rising up from it, and somebody is lying crushed between the wheels but the wheels just go on turning, heavy, implacable, stabbing down into the mud with their cogs, water seeps slowly up into the horses' hoofmarks, smoke rises from the sand as the track passes through deserts, the snow screeches shrilly as it progresses over wintry routes, many lie down wheezing and think they're drowning and just as they die, they dream the track is a log floating past them and all they need to do is to grab hold of it and they'll be saved, and they do grab hold of it with their fingers, but then new wheels come along the same track and crush their fingers without any hint of mercy and then Ernst W. Wilson appears, sweat pouring off him, and he's half-running in order to keep up, and he stands on the odd liver or kidney or stomach, there isn't much time you see and they're all dying anyway and they're lying in such a way that you just have to stand on them if you're going to get past – and of course you do want to get past, you want to follow that track as far as it goes, to the point where it suddenly leaves this wicked earth and leaps out like a rainbow into space, the space that's singing out of solitude.

One after another, cigarette ends sizzle and die on the asphalt that's slowly getting lighter, but the track just keeps on going, on and on; it's a good track to follow, a straight track, a track full of hatred and curses and he's never going to leave it, he's going to love this track with all the hatred and all the love he can muster and trample on anybody who tries to spoil it, who tries to debase it with the stink of their rotting corpses, and with sweat pouring off him he'll run along it through crunching snow, through dusty sand, through sticky mud, through fields flowing with blood, and he'll be a private, then a corporal and a sergeant and a lieutenant and a captain – and the track will never desert him. He'll be faithful to his track. He'll be faithful to his solitude and unfaithful to everything else.

And just before dawn, when he and the girl go up to her room in a damp little riverside house, she flings herself straight down on to the bed in the alcove and he says to her harshly, 'Don't get any ideas.'

And she replies, 'You don't get any ideas in this job. But aren't you going to take off your rucksack?'

Feeling better, he takes off his rucksack and sits down on the edge of the bed and he notices she's naked underneath, but the way she shows it is less brazen than when his wife did it.

'You've got undressed for nothing,' he says. 'I just want to have a little chat for a while, just a chat.'

'Go on then,' she says, closing her eyes.

'Why are you closing your eyes?'

'I've no desire to see you naked.'

'Have you ever felt really lonely?'

'You're never lonely in this job.'

'Oh,' he says, and wanders off although his body stays on the bed for a while and his nose can smell all the men – the sweat, sandwiches and whisky – who have cashed in their despair in the alcove, 'Oh, I've felt so lonely, so lonely and so happy.'

And he goes on to recall all the sublime moments of solitude when everything has sunk out of existence, people, needs and thoughts, and only that fearful music was left to flood his being. A little boy is left behind in the grass, very high grass; he can't walk properly yet, and they've just seen a long, black grass snake wriggling under a tuft of grass and all the other children have raced back to the house screaming, but they've forgotten about him, because you can't run as fast as you'd like to if you're dragging along a little boy who still can't walk properly because he's been ill, they've just left him behind with his fear, his extreme terror of the black snake. He's just about to start crying and already he can see the house and the long, soft grass through a surging haze of tears, but then the rain starts falling, violent and brutal rain that hammers away with its fists on all the roofs and swishes down into the grass and the abandoned boy is soaked to the skin straight away. There's a dull rumbling behind the house and suddenly the thunderstorm approaches, lightning crawls over the roof and rain comes pouring down the path and swirls about at his feet, the grass hangs down like hair when you've just been swimming and then, all of a sudden, he realizes he's not afraid, not the slightest bit afraid any more, he's so alone, so abandoned by everybody, but it feels good to be alone, good to be abandoned. All there is in the whole world apart from himself is this wet grass, the rain, and the thunderstorm; there's nobody left to pull his hair, to force him to chew his food even though everything he's ever eaten in all his life is rising up into his throat, the lightning doesn't have any whips and the grass doesn't have any nails and the rain doesn't have any harsh voices – and that's why he starts screaming like a thing possessed and kicks and struggles like the very devil when somebody suddenly remembers about him once it's stopped raining and runs out to fetch him in.

And then another time his piggy bank is lying in pieces on the sideboard like a shattered dream, and he's stolen money from himself so that he can buy a little atlas showing all the countries where he can be alone, and his father, a chauffeur for the upper classes, beats him into solitude with a little whip. How delighted he is when he suddenly realizes he can get away from everything and everybody with the aid of a little whip, and he's in a state of ecstasy as the lashes cut into him; and then he remembers all the times when he does what seem to be the strangest things, the most disgusting deeds, the cruelest acts, just so that somebody will beat him into another world, that everybody will hate him into that sweet solitude. The time comes when he's too old for that sort of thing, but he takes secret delight in discovering all the possibilities opened up by self-torture: you can take your protective membrane with

you and move among people who are all laughing and
with no effort at all turn their laughter into arrows that
tear your heart open; or you can be desperate for sex but
just as desperate for deprivation and on midsummer eve
you can stroll about the big public parks where
everybody's making love all over the place in the grass,
and take bitter delight in feeling your heart fill up with
tears; there's so much you can do when you're that age,
when you're sixteen, seventeen, eighteen, nineteen,
twenty, and every day God gives you can discover even
more things.

You can discover contempt, for instance: oh how
lovely it is, how delightful, to recall some twisted
memory of laughter distorted by contempt, thousands
of red lips, all of them curled in disgust, and to be
launched by them into the solitude of space. There's
that time when the middle-aged stoker on the little
coaster he worked on as an ordinary seaman when he
was still at school invites him into his cabin and seduces
him after making him feel disgusted by all the nasty
smells women have and all the diseases they spread and
getting him to drink a few glasses of whisky, and what
takes place is so surprising that he doesn't get round to
putting up any resistance, it's so incredibly novel, it's as
if some animal he's never seen before has suddenly
revealed itself to him and rendered him helpless through
surprise and fear; but afterwards, when he goes back
over the deck in the dark and down into the dormitory,
he feels so dirty, he wants to jump overboard and drown
himself in order to get clean. And all the ones playing
cards and all the ones writing letters turn to look at him
at exactly the same time as he comes down the ladder.

'How did you get on with Christian, then?' one of
them shouts.

'I hope you were really nice to him,' another one bellows.

'It's about time you got yourself a boyfriend,' yells a third. But nobody hits him, nobody laughs, and in the end everybody's face is stiff with contempt, and he's infectious, and everybody else has gone into quarantine. He just stands there with his arms dangling and feels their contempt seeping into his blood, and then he realizes with a feeling of enormous happiness that he couldn't care less, it's just good that people feel contempt for him, perhaps the best thing that could possibly happen, and he has no problems at all when he goes back again up the ladder after one of them shouts, 'Clear off, you've no business round here! Go back to Christian, you can sleep in his cabin from now on! There's plenty of room for you as well in his bed.'

And so he stays in Christian's cabin for the rest of the trip because that makes him lonelier than ever and you can get used to anything and there are ways of lying like a desert island miles away from anywhere: true, it can be plundered and pillaged, but when the plunderers and pillagers have gone away the water is still lapping around its shores and it's still just as remote as it ever was, as long as nobody builds a bridge to it.

But he's brought back to school, and time passes and heals all wounds and a romantic teacher tricks him into believing there's such a thing as sublimation, you can sublimate your urges, you can get away from all your bad experiences by experiencing all your actions on an inner plain. He leaves school and starts work in a solicitor's office, works as a language teacher, gets married early and becomes a father and hasn't felt any urge to travel out into the world of solitude for ages, because somebody has told him the only possible way of doing things is the normal way, and all you can do is to laugh in the right place and cry in the right place and conform to all the conventions and only go against them on an inner plain, the popular inner plain; you want to be happy after all, and happiness means being ruthless with yourself and considerate towards everybody else, and then again: time itself has bidden farewell to all freebooters of the soul.

He sits on the girl's bed as the hairy dawn creeps animal-like over the window-pane, and diagonally opposite the house is a bridge and when the two halves of the bridge start to open all the sand in the tramlines slides down like white beams and dives into the water.

'Hey,' he says to the girl, grabbing her by the shoulder for she's fallen asleep, 'you should have seen me marching backwards and forwards along that triangle between the table, the bed and the window, trying to condense my solitude and to believe that I was the greatest because I'd been the most solitary of all, and all the time being aware of how impotent I was, understanding all that poetry business, which was a waste of time in fact because nobody was interested, and knowing full well that whatever went on between me and my desk was just a pitiful case of opting out. Sometimes I nearly choked, and managed to save myself at the last minute by throwing myself to the ground and ripping my clothes off; I felt I was being got at, and I screamed at my wife: Why are you getting at me? I'm not your judge, she said. No, you're my executioner, I yelled. I don't have a chopper, she yelled back. No, but I do, I screamed back at her – and so it went on: our confrontations went on for ever and ever without end, like an escalator, and I was choking more and more and not getting anywhere on any front. But one evening a

couple of weeks ago when I was all on my own – she'd
left me, just for the time being, as usual – I suddenly
overturned the table and stood it in front of me like a
barricade, because I was convinced somebody had just
come into the room with the aim of attacking me, biting
me to pieces, crunching me between his teeth, and it
was as if I'd just been bashed violently on the back of the
head: the room disappeared, erased from my consciousness by a giant with a rubber, and I was consumed
by a dazzling light and then I was lying once again on
the shiny surface in the midst of space, and everything
was so boundlessly silent at first, and then there was a
whining sound as if a drop of water had let go and had
suddenly started falling at tremendous speed through
eternity, and then there was that invisible rain that
always came before the song started – and then space
would start singing and I could see myself like an ear,
just growing and growing out of the ground, and once
when I woke up my room was just the same as it always
was but I was sweating because of the singing and I
didn't realize that I would never again be able to run
away from my solitude, least of all by using artificial
methods like poetry, and all the past homed in on my
scent and flung itself upon me and I got the strange
feeling that I was a woman and a man at the same time
and I got dressed up in my wife's clothes and I got drunk
and I masturbated and suddenly I found I had something
to do up in the attic. Nobody saw me going, but when I
got to the attic door I found I'd forgotten the key, and I
could hear a noise on the stairs and when I leaned over
the rail I could see a mass of black figures, among them
my wife, on their way upstairs. I curled up into a ball on
the attic stairs in the hope that no one would notice me,
but, needless to say, somebody grabbed me by the

shoulder and rolled me over. Why, Ernst, somebody shouted, and I ran into my room but they came racing after me. I looked round the room in a panic and was shattered to see that the disorder everything was in was a woman's disorder, a slightly confused disorder, not the spiky, brutal disorder a man creates. I pushed my desk into the corner and crouched behind it so that I could defend myself.

'What do you know about solitude?' I yelled at them, 'What do you know about the great solitude of space? You don't know what it's like when space starts singing out of solitude. You may have read poems about it, you may have heard something about it in Gothic novels – but that's about all.'

'But,' I screeched in a voice that rose up as wild as a stallion, for the executioner within me had grasped the axe outside me and chopped off my normal, decent self, 'what is the whole of literature compared with a single suicide? What is life but an unsuccessful suicide attempt? What's the point of decency in life compared with the decency of death?'

'But now it's all over and done with,' he says to the girl, who has fallen asleep again. 'I've sold out, and there's only one way out now.' And he wakes her up cruelly and stuffs a banknote into her ear.

'I didn't hear a word you said,' she says, yawning, 'but thanks all the same.' He's already hoisted the rucksack on to his shoulders and is on his way to the station.

And the track slices its way through the deserts, it glows blood-red in the sunsets and he runs through it and his sweat and his blood spurt out of him like a fountain, and he curses the track as well as loving the track, and it's covered in pure white snow which crunches under his feet and under the wheels, and rib-cages of animals and humans stick up like white spikes out of the track, and in the rivers the skeletons of ancient, wrecked ships all look the same; occasionally, fires flare up alongside the track and sometimes he feels fires burning within him, but the best he can do is to keep going with the only hope he has left now that all the others have gone bankrupt: that the track will dare to make the final leap into solitude, that gigantic solitude where solitude itself sings, and the best thing to do is to sacrifice everything, to be faithful to your solitude and unfaithful to everything else, and maybe the track will pass over Boy Larus at an acute angle, or maybe one of the other survivors, and press down on to his rib-cage, or somebody else's, because there is always a hope, the only great hope left: the hope that the final leap will be from that very rib-cage, that very heart.

THE STRUGGLE OVER THE LION

Such a little volcano for such a big fire

1

He must have suddenly acquired the vacant look of a murderer or a drunk, because everybody starts staring at him, leaning forward over the empty water keg, or so he thinks, and their movements betray both menace and fear. Somebody has woken them up by screaming, and the shock at being so rudely awakened is still flitting about their faces. Worried stiff, he moves a few steps to one side so that the sun won't expose him even more. The captain slowly turns his hip to the right, towards him, and his clenched fist hovers just below it, as if he had a revolver at the ready underneath his rags.

That was stupid of me, thinks Lucas Egmont, that was really stupid of me. Why didn't I think of my gormless face which gives away everything I've done and everything I will ever do: I might just as well shout out what I've done at the top of my voice, and then it wouldn't feel so awful, so damned creepy. It feels as if my face were covered in crawling ants, and I can't lift a finger to shift them, because nobody's supposed to know they're there.

Now the captain bends over towards him at a ridiculous angle, and his hand is trembling as if he were on the point of going for his revolver. They don't surround him straight away, they just come closer, menacing, and yet at the same time as cowed as a lion in a circus, and he thinks that if only he had a whip he could get them to lie down in the sand and come creeping up to him with their heads scraping into it – then just one lash of the whip: and they'd be licking the sand from his feet. It's the fear inside him that's dreaming.

But the fear inside all of them is dreaming, it's just about the last day they have to live, and they all know that in a ridiculous, sub-conscious sort of way; just as an old horse knows it's destined for the slaughterhouse when a little bow-legged fellow smelling of blood comes up to its stable one afternoon and puts a different bridle on it, and he's hopeless when it comes to taking it out and he leads it out on to the road without even letting it have a drink from the butt by the well and then he sets off in the wrong direction, the wrong direction altogether; or a cow that stands outside a stall all evening, mooing her head off, and she can smell death oozing out of the doors even though she's been out at pasture all day long and shouldn't know anything at all, although the heifer that was slaughtered around noon in the stall that day is already hanging up in the shed with swarms of flies crawling all over its stomach.

'Who screamed? Who was is that screamed?'

It's the captain talking, and he cocks his invisible revolver, and they all remember the scream that started waves rippling over a mill-pond, made a deep hole that would last forever in a mirror, a hole their lives could drain away through. If a human being is like a white bath-tub which it always is when you're a child, and when you're really little it gets filled with fresh, clean water for you to play around in, lukewarm at first, but later it gets hotter and hotter, water fit for actions, thoughts, feelings to bathe in, water condemned to stop being clean but maybe it doesn't have to become all that dirty, water that's destined to be emptied out when the bather hasn't the strength to wash off any more dirt – if a human being's a bath-tub like that, then there'll be a point in his life when the plug is suddenly pulled out by some unseen hand, and all the water, cool now, full of dirt and purity, flows out of him and the gurgling of death as it pours down the drain first fills him with horror, and then with resignation, and in the end he just longs for the same unknown hand that pulled out the plug to come with a brush and scrub away the rim of dirt from the sides of the bath. But with a pitiful sort of whimper, the last drops of dirty water are sucked down into the black hole and the tub becomes silent and empty, the bath-tub is dead and darkness falls over the bathroom. A key is turned in the lock from the outside, and the bathroom is closed once and for all: there'll be nobody else taking a bath in this bathroom.

They remember the scream – but who screamed? They can hear the roar of the breakers – but where does it come from? They're scared already – but why? They walk slowly back up the beach, towards the cliff, and a cluster of iguanas that have evidently been lying there watching them turn back slowly and defiantly and shuffle up towards the grass. Then they stop and hesitate, and the smell of the corpse under the canvas sheet wafts over to them in broad waves of velvet and threatens to choke them. They're filled with death, they're like vases that have been standing for so long in an empty room that both the flowers and the water have gone musty.

The scream hovers over their heads, it has the

211

ruthless shadow of a gallows, and the weaker their memory of what it sounded like, the more tangible it becomes. The scream gets hotter and hotter, and they all start sweating; the scream turns into this shadow, and they all shiver with the cold like dogs; the scream is in the way the iguanas move and in the lazy rustling sound from the plateau and the scream is hiding under a canvas sheet, which is held down on to the sand by stones so that it won't suddenly rise up and reveal what nobody wants to see.

And what's all this about the water keg?

2

There's nothing you can do about it: you take a glass and empty it, or you take an evil deed from the pile of undone deeds and carry it out – and all at once, you look different. As far as you're concerned, it's something you can put up with. You yourself are not too worried about what you've done, but it's as if there were muscles in your face which like playing at being your conscience.

A few brisk winds have got up, and just for a moment blown away the sticky sweet smell of death out into the lagoon, so that it's easier to talk again.

'It must have been one of us who did it,' says the captain. 'The water can't have run out of its own accord like this.'

As he speaks, sweat comes crawling over his face. Big, grey beads of sweat, sweat that looks scared. They all move closer to each other, as if they could avoid death that way. The captain hardly has room to swing his revolver hand round, even. They have their backs turned towards the beach, and they're facing the cliffs, as if they were expecting to be gunned down from behind.

'No, somebody must have done it.' Boy Larus echoes his words, but his voice is so uncertain that everyone apart from Lucas Egmont glances up at him and his eyes shy away like a horse, because no innocent person can look as innocent as a guilty man.

It's his temples, his cheek-bones and profile that give the game away. It's always been the same, thinks Lucas Egmont, the tiniest glass of wine and everybody can tell just by looking at me that I've been on the booze. I could hit a fish on a stone and afterwards look like a double murderer. It's too late now of course – God knows I've got used to the idea of dying! – it's too late now, but I should have always carried a mask to hide behind.

They haven't noticed anything yet, though; they're more scared of the dead boxer than of the dead water keg. Tim Solider was the one who'd come up with the idea of the stones. We must do something to stop the canvas from blowing away, he'd said the previous night when he was pacing up and down restlessly between the fire and the rambling English girl; something that'll keep the smell in until we can bury him.

Tim Solider is very scared of the smell, more scared of the smell than of anything else. He once had an aunt who lived on her own in an attic room, and she used to say until the day she died that you should go to a funeral or a house where somebody's just died, and take note of how you can smell the corpse, because just before you die you'll notice a similar smell coming from your own body and you'll lock yourself in and scrub yourself down, but nothing helps, there's nothing more you can do.

Bunched tightly together, like a winning football team leaving the pitch, they walk up the cliffs and the morning is as clear as a peach although the air is terribly difficult to breathe. They stop, panting, after almost every other step and pretend to look round, to gaze out to sea, to peer at the clouds in the sky or the peaceful horizon; but it's all a put-on act, for no one must hear that you're out of breath, no one must know that you're bleeding, and when you cry, it must always be hidden by a smile. Oh yes, everything's a put-on act: hardly any of them knows what the sea or the sky looks like this morning, because if they do look out to sea, all they can make out is an oblong bundle, half-covered by a canvas sheet, tossing in the waves, and an unpleasantly familiar keg rolling slowly in towards land, and the whole of the sky is obscured by the dead body and the empty water keg.

Oh, how they hate him. Imagine being so isolated, and still being so betrayed. It feels like having been set down in the desert, with no hope of rescue – and then even being robbed of the salvation offered by the empty water keg. They hate him, but the ashes of fear are raining down all the time, and as they climb up towards the plateau, where the smell can't reach because its wings are too heavy, the dead body is slowly covered by those ashes, and soon there's nothing left but an inadequate outline of his memory – and then when they stop to get their breath, the whole beach is filled by a gigantic water keg, and they start back slightly in surprise, and now they're even less keen to look at one another than before; but when they hastily turn their backs on the beach, they imagine they can still see that same, nasty tank falling slowly over in the grass and reluctantly disappearing, for fear is a cunning beacon which isn't satisfied with useless symbols when there are so many useful ones.

In their eagerness to get away from the corpse they've got as far as the first bushes and it's there, on the steep, shiny cliff, its green furrows glistening in the sunlight, that the first explosion occurs. Tim Solider is standing like a negro with his arms dangling, and staring at the mysterious bushes which still frighten him just as much as they did at the start, he's just parted some branches and peered into the green darkness, and then with a sudden start, as if he'd unexpectedly caught sight of a snake in the woods, he jerks back his hand – and at that very moment of terror, the captain pounces on him, almost like a tiger. His heavy body crashes into Tim Solider's with potentially cruel force and they fall over more or less straight away, locked closely together, and Tim Solider's back smacks into the rock with a sickening, dull thud. Perhaps he's broken something, or something's been crushed: he just lies there at first and ignores the way the captain is pounding away non-stop at his chest with his clenched fists.

There follows a brief moment of silence as the captain, sure of his superiority, stops punching; the whole world falls silent save for the panting of the two men. Someone has stifled the pain of the sea, the wind has suddenly dropped, and not even the iguanas clatter over the stones, although on the cliff face just below the two combatants, two large iguanas are lying motionless, evidently watching them.

Lucas Egmont is the first to notice their potential menace. The iguanas on the island have short, wiry, immobile eyelids which have had many thousand years in which to shrink; behind those permanently open curtains, their eyes always seem as though they are crouching ready to jump, but they also have lazy bodies which, thanks to congenital idleness, always hold the leap in check. But the two iguanas lying motionless in wait just below the captain and Tim Solider seem suddenly to have lost their iguana-souls, and intense fury is almost threatening to burst their shells. They're lying so very, very still, but that's just the fateful gathering of strength before an enormous leap.

Then he notices the thin brown liquid trickling down the rock and sees how the iguanas let it pass between them, their bodies tensed and threatening, and then it all falls into place. He gropes around for an arm to catch on to, but fails to find one as he is standing all alone. He wants to shout a warning, but can't as the captain is bending over Tim Solider's face and screaming, 'You did it, you bastard. You're the one who emptied out the water, you're the one who unscrewed the tap and let it all run out of the keg. You're the one who tried to trick us saying you'd found some food, you're the one who brought us a box of glass beads and said: Here you are ladies and gentlemen, I've brought some food for you. Oh, don't think I don't know how much you hate us, just because you're inferior to us, because you were put into the world in order to serve people. And so you thought you'd murder us, because let's face it, from the moment you emptied that water keg you became a murderer, my friend. When you murdered us, you thought: now we'll see who's strongest, who's going to live longest! Ha ha, I'll laugh at them when they're writhing in agony, and when I start writhing in agony I'll still go on laughing. Oh yes, I know what you were thinking all right, but you were wrong, you mark my words, because when we start getting thirsty, when we start getting visions of wells and streams and springs, you won't be alive any more. You won't be alive any more the moment we start getting thirsty. We'll all be out of our minds with fear and thirst and we'll shout: Where's the murderer? and somebody will reply: There he is, he's marching up and down on the hill up there, and then we'll all chase him till he drops and we'll leap on him with all the strength our fury gives us, and if anybody tries to protest about what we're doing, we'll say: It's only a murderer, it's only a murderer getting his well-deserved punishment.'

Oh, how scared he feels while he's yelling and screaming, how full of morning air he fills his lungs as he forces out his fear so that it spatters all over the man lying underneath him, but the man underneath him has plenty of fear of his own, and he wriggles and writhes as he tries to get out of the grasp of the squashed iguana. An iguana you have squashed between your back and a rock after a violent fall is surely not something you should be afraid of, but even so he can feel the dead iguana's body swelling up beneath him until eventually the whole of his is resting on it and the cold rises up around his hips like a wave of death and then when he manages to turn his head and sees the thin brown trail containing the iguana's life-blood trickling down the cliff he opens his mouth wide and shrieks in a frenzy, 'The iguanas! Watch out for the iguanas!'

But everybody except Lucas Egmont thinks he's trying to get away with what he's done, and trembling with an excess of obedience and an excess of fear, Boy Larus goes up to him and bends over him and spits straight in his face. At the same time, the captain sits up so that he's astride Tim Solider's knees and that's what saves him for the time being. The iguanas have been slowly and apparently nonchalantly getting closer and suddenly they attack, their heavy bodies leap forwards as if borne by a flash of lightning, and side by side but on each side of the brown trickle they crash into Tim Solider's chest in sickening unison. They bite straight through his thin shirt and into his flesh, and hang on limply like rats as the blood oozes up around their armoured snouts. All his blood seems to be flowing down to his wound and his face turns quite yellow as it does on a corpse and when Lucas Egmont kneels down beside him, his eyes have crept back into their horror and the nails on one of his hands are scratching and scratching away at the rock till they bend backwards.

The iguanas are completely passive again, but the leap is still trembling in their bodies and in their treacherous eyes, and when Lucas Egmont gropes around over Tim Solider's chest he can feel the creatures trembling inside their shells, lying there like time bombs, incredibly sensitive to every pressure. As he draws back his arm he can feel from the silence just how lonely he is in the world, and when he glances quickly round without letting the iguanas out of his sight even so, all four of them are standing quite closely together, at the mid-point between his fear and his hatred.

'Come and help me,' he shouts. 'We must get them off him before he bleeds to death.'

But no one budges an inch. They just stand there irresolutely, like the chief mourners by a graveside after the final oration. Boy Larus makes a symbolic move as if preparing to jump, but is easily stopped by the captain's foot.

Then Lucas Egmont crouches down beside Tim Solider, takes hold of his hand and pushes it in front of him like a shield over the red battlefield of his chest, and as he watches the limp, insensitive hand sliding forwards slowly towards its goal, it occurs to him with the suddenness of a flash of lightning how shatteringly familiar it all is. This hand is a hand he's seen in his dreams, time and time again he's hidden behind the big, yellow hand as its fingers drag it in fits and starts over the red dress, and behind it there have always been animals, hidden but dauntingly present, silent but bellowing out their silence, motionless but burrowing their way into his breast. So everything important and shocking in one's life is just a re-run of one's nightmares, everything that happens has happened so many times before; how often has one been forced to suffer the same, familiar pain?

But while the hand is still on its way towards the invisible iguana snouts and the unconscious man starts shivering as he's on the point of regaining consciousness, Lucas Egmont hears the patter of tiny, tiny feet on the rocks behind him. Someone has stepped outside the magic circle, and he shudders as the female footsteps come nearer and nearer, and when they're as near as they can get he can feel how the animal he's trying to forget has imbued the footsteps with its supple caution – and then comes the scream:

'Leave them alone,' she yells. 'Leave them alone,' yells Madame, and even while she's screaming she bends right down and strokes the iguanas – and they don't react at all. Then she raises her arm like a victory pennant and goes on talking, calmer, more rationally, not quite so loudly now she's found her Jesus, ready to let himself be bitten by her iguanas, ready to be killed reluctantly in her stead.

'Leave them alone,' says the woman who's overcome her fear by letting it bite someone else, 'leave them alone. It's too late anyway. Let him take his punishment, it's no more than he deserves after all, it's no more than a murderer deserves, after all.'

He can hear the patter of her feet as she walks away, but it doesn't sound like an animal any more, not now when she no longer needs to be afraid. But now something is happening to Lucas Egmont: so far everything that has happened since that incident with the water keg has been just as real or just as unreal as a dream; in your dreams, you can feel scared and sweat can be pouring off you, but in some vague way you feel that it's all a charade, and because all the time, somewhere back there beyond all the smoke and cloud, you can just about make out the curtain that'll fall when you simply can't go on any longer, when you can't become any more frightened than you already are without bursting, precisely because of all that, the fear of dreams and the guilty conscience of dreams are never definitive, there's always a clear dividing line between death and the extremes of suffering – but in real life there's a line beyond which balancing acts are no longer possible, a line beyond which you lose all vestiges of earthly peace, innocence and happiness, and that's the line between dreams and extreme awareness: you're living in the world of dreams, you're breathing the air of dreams, but at the same time you're cruelly aware that the dream's over this time, and reality is more real than ever, and the terror of your dream has escaped from its dark cage and in the brightest of bright daylight it's wrapping its snake-like body round your neck.

Suddenly, then, Lucas Egmont emerges from his long dream of thirst, and it's in that dream everything has been happening: it's in that dream he has returned to a skilfully disguised childhood, it's in that dream the big fish with its long sword has momentarily pierced the surface of the bay and transformed the tiny lagoon into an ocean of terror, it's in that dream Lucas Egmont has emptied the drinking water, their last hope, into the sand, and it's in that dream he has watched nonchalantly as the five survivors possessed by the fear of death have hunted down the guilty man, nonchalant because it was all so unreal, because everything that happened was merely the only possible continuation of a bad dream – and hence his plunge into wakefulness is so horrific, he suddenly goes all stiff and can feel the sun, can feel the sun for the first time, cutting into his neck like a knife, and how the air is forcing its way into him and pummelling his lungs, and the stones are starting to get hot and burning his skin, and the acrid smell from the bleeding man on the cliff suddenly sets him panting in disgust – and then all the screams from all the terrified people on the island are vibrating in his ears, and the agonizing spotlights of reality are drenching his whole being with their steely beams.

But worse of all is the blood, the blood that has brought him to his senses, and suddenly Tim Solider's hand is sticky and red and the lukewarm liquid is suddenly crawling beneath his own hesitant fingers like a toad – and he's overcome by utter helplessness, swamped by an unstoppable surging sea of terror, and it takes possession of him and all the pointless things he has done on the island come charging towards him like bulls, and they gore him with their horns and trample him with their hooves and the ocean of terror hasn't a single island of forgiveness. Sacrifice everything and die, it roars to all the miserable creatures wallowing in their own degradation and gradually realizing just how pitiful they are, sacrifice everything and die – and the pitiful wretch sacrifices everything and dies or survives according to his strength. Oh, you paradoxical hero! Oh, what wretched bravery!

Lucas Egmont must have been born lucky, because almost without trying he manages to stick his fingers into the mouth of the lower of the iguanas and then he prises its jaws open with a violent heave which almost severs his hand from his wrist, and just look: the iguana falls away, bleeding from its mouth, and thuds on to the rock and he sets upon it with all the strength his terror gives him and he whips it over on its back and kicks it in the belly till it slides away down the face of the cliff and crashes on to the rocks on the beach below. When he spins round, trembling all over from a mixture of effort and fear, to meet the new danger, Tim Solider is alone with his wounds, but a narrow reddish-black line wends its way over the rock and into a giant bush. A strangely bitter smell of decay is wafted by the breeze from the undergrowth, as if some dead body were lying in ambush there. A cold shudder runs down his spine.

They're still on their own; the other four, the captain and Boy Larus, Madame and the English girl are all clambering slowly down to the beach where the fire is unwinding its never-ending string of smoke. Lucas Egmont tears strips off his shirt and presses some of them into the wounds. The cloth quickly turns dark red, and he lifts Tim Solider on to his shoulder and starts to carry him down the cliff face as a red wave of blood flows up into Tim's face like a flame, and he starts whimpering like an animal as he crawls back into consciousness.

Then the English girl screams. She's flung herself into the shallows near the dead boxer and is coating her hair with sand in a series of hysterical gestures.

222

'Why did you have to kill him? You murdered him, that's what you did! You just come here and I'll . . .'
But for the moment they all keep a respectful distance.

3

Eventually, they gather around her in a circle, or rather: a semi-circle. Tim Solider joins in as well; he's groggy but he's regained consciousness, the bleeding has stopped, he's very weak but he walks stiffly, straight as a ramrod, a skeleton of terror holding him together. He's afraid they'll gang up on him again and if he falls asleep, use that as an excuse to kill him. That's why he hardly dares look down at the sand: it seems to have eyes sucking him down towards them, his knees are buckling, a dull feeling of weariness is taking possession of him and anyone who likes could overpower him. Instead, he's constantly looking round, scrutinizing them all one after the other just as a chess player scrutinizes his opponent's pieces as he fights to keep them at bay. They keep their distance because they respect his wounds, because one ought to have more respect for a dying man than a living one; but Tim thinks it's his fierce glare that's holding them off, and the moment they overstep a certain mark, the moment they come one inch too close, his arms start twitching and his hands clench to form fists.

He's still dazed following the attack and he thinks they hate him because they were all passengers and since he's the only one of the crew to survive, he's taken on the captain's responsibility for the catastrophe. He's not even sure any more which one of them flung him to the ground, his last recollections are completely over-shadowed by the giant iguanas as they hurtle down upon him like thunderbolts and burrow down deep into his agony. Nor can he remember who rescued him. He thinks they all deserted him and he managed to drag himself down the cliff face all by himself only to collapse with exhaustion on the beach, and he's just grateful they didn't take advantage of the situation in order to get rid of him.

They approach the screaming girl cautiously from three directions: from up the beach and from out of the water on either side of her. It's as if they're carrying a bird-trapper's net between them in order to capture her screams and they're all taking the same short, stealthy steps, no matter whether they're edging out into the water or tip-toeing over the sand. And all the time the screams are pouring out of her, without a pause, as if all her dams had suddenly burst and all her pent-up screams were cascading forth in one rush. Now and then a word tumbles out like a scrap of bark tossing about in the raging torrent, but before anyone can catch its meaning, it's been dragged down by the eddies and disappeared. She's lying on her stomach in the water and her head is smothered in wet sand and as they get nearer she starts crawling out of the water like an iguana, with her breast and stomach pressed hard against the sand. Her screams subside into a shrill whimpering and then she's just sobbing loudly and steadily as she starts taking away the stones holding down the canvas sheet over the boxer's dead body.

But she doesn't manage to see him: as many as there's room for fling themselves upon her and drag her away towards the fire, she's kicking and screaming – oh, those screams are so horrible they all want to start screaming

– and the sand and the water come showering all round her and cool them all down, for the heat is starting now and steam is rising from the boxer's canvas and the reek of his death spreads slowly over them like a parachute. Then she breaks loose and runs stark naked into the water up to her waist and Lucas Egmont wants to shout and warn her about the big, dangerous fish at the bottom of the lagoon, but then she stops and turns slowly to face them and they can see her white body glistening through the water like white marble through a torrent of green rain. She stands there motionless, looking down at her feet, two small white fish sleeping belly-up on the bottom, and just for a moment the whole world stands still. Behind her silent head lies the calm ocean, a single, eternal wave arches its way over the horizon only to be swallowed up swiftly by the silence of the sea and it seems to one of them as if she's leaning back against the thin line of the horizon, so beautiful is the backward curve of her body.

Then she raises her arms out of the water and rubs off the sand, muttering half-aloud, 'Let him come to me, let him come to me . . .'

But they don't let him go to her, no matter how entreatingly she pleads. They stand guard round the dead man, their fingers turning white from the painful strain of holding back a scream. They glance quickly round, sizing each other up and down as the hot sweat starts trickling down their bodies, and everything grows harder to bear for the ones that aren't in the water: the heat is now suspended over their heads like a heavy, heavy extra-cranium and their pulse suddenly starts running wild, it's like being locked in a sauna with the heat getting more and more intense until in the end you're crawling around on the floor, moaning, and begging for the most absurd of rescues: please let the earth open up beneath us so the sauna collapses and we can get away from this fiendish heat.

Oh, if only the English girl would start screaming again, if only there would be some violent explosion which would get them out of this awful predicament – but all that happens is that the girl cups her hands and quietly proceeds to pour water over her breasts and all the time she keeps on repeating in a nagging monotone, 'Let him come to me, let him come to me.'

Then she stops pouring and comes a few paces closer and suddenly she starts dancing in the water, at times her body is completely submerged and they can see her legs pedalling away with short, painful movements while her arms rise and fall like the skirts of a jellyfish and then her dazzling shoulders leap up and she soars high over the horizon before sinking back down into the greenness like a silken sheet. It's a dance of desire, a dance of desire which would hate to be satisfied, a desire for oblivion.

Then Madame finds the English girl's cloth on the sands and she flings it over her shoulder and she runs away from the stench, the heat, the men whose horrible smell of manhood she has only just become aware of; she's shaking with shame and bitterness, having just realized how horribly naked she herself has become thanks to the naked girl's obscene dance: the mad girl is exposing both of them to the lustful stares from the beach – and Madame grabs hold of her by the shoulder and stops her in mid-leap. They glare at each other like two people confronting each other on the lonely rope between terror and hatred and there's nothing for it but for one of them to fall. Madame shields her with the

226

cloth as they approach the beach and then she says disdainfully, 'Are you on your way to your lover now? Is this how he wants you?'

The English girl punches her right between the eyes with her hard knuckles, and as she butts Madame in the back and tries to bite her, she yells at her, 'You killed him, that's what you did. Don't think I don't know. Just wait till it gets dark, just wait till it gets dark.'

'Is he dead? Is your lover dead?' asks Madame in mild surprise, holding her at arm's length. 'That can't be true, my dear.'

And she lifts the girl's hand and lets it glide over the three angry red bites on her shoulder. And the hand is surprised and then the hand is filled with hatred and one of those standing on the beach feels painfully moved by the gesture of ice-cold fury described by the hand as it slumps down to her hip.

4

As they don't have any spades nor anything else they can dig with and moreover the sand is too hard for their nails to cope with, they have to carry out the burial by fetching wet sand from the bottom of the lagoon and spreading it over the dead body. They work for a large part of the hottest period around noon and make no attempt to hurry, except at first when the stench is so awful, but then they bury their terror, with the kind of calm, sweeping, convincing gestures you make when you're frightened, under four layers of wet sand which soon hardens in the heat. They dig away with their hands quite close to the shore but at different places along the beach and all the time the burial is taking place they hardly ever look at one another. Sometimes they arrive at the corpse simultaneously and then they get down on their knees side by side and their hands touch as, full of devotion, they spread the new, soft sand over the old, hard surface.

But no matter how much sand they carry under the hot midday sun, they cannot bury their fear along with the corpse. Even if they had a whole desert, the vast Sahara Desert or one of Mongolia's deserts, they may not have had enough sand. One of them wishes they had a train, a little train with lots of deep wagons, like the train that used to run from the claypit to the brickworks back home when he was so little that everything was an animal and the train was the biggest animal he'd ever seen. If only they'd had that train and the wagons heaped up with sand! He could have run from one wagon to the next with the biggest spade the parish had to offer and emptied them just as they were clanking past a boxer lying dead by the side of the track.

Another of them is walking in the desert. The sun is blazing down from a sky as empty and relentless as the white of an eye. Nothing but sand all around, all the sand in the world is spread round about him and he is the shifting centre in this ocean of sand, for no matter where he goes, the centre goes with him. There's no end and no beginning, no up and no down, no forward and no backward. The world's clock has stopped and God is busy with a *lit de parade* on some other planet far, far away. The sun has also stood still, and now it's going to burn away until it melts: that's the challenge it's taken on. And everywhere, nothing but sand. You've stripped naked and lain down on your back in the sand, and the sand is millions, milliards of little animals that have been asleep for ages but if the sun blazes down as fiendishly as this for just a few more hours – no, there's no such thing as time! – as few hundred paces forwards and backwards and round and in a square until they wake up and they're raving when they wake up and all they want to do is to grab hold of this swine who has disturbed their sleep – 'and in order to reach the sun they climb up on me, the lonely wanderer in the desert, but then eventually when they realize they're wasting their time they'll turn their fury on me and creep into all my grottoes, over the bridge of my tongue, into the sewers of my nose, through the mineshafts of my ears, and into my eyes, the things I'd like to have preserved till last so that in the least false moment of annihilation I could establish that all my hopes of salvation were just as naïve as I'd always thought, and they'd bore their tiny little holes into the middle of my pupils and then trickle in through them, curious about the marvels they were bound to find behind such beautiful membranes – but God only knows how disappointed they'll be, oh, how disappointed they'll be'.

But of course, like all the rest, the man walking through the desert is just as keen as all the rest on preserving his fragile life and is prepared to sacrifice anything, even his life, in order to preserve it. He wants to create a shadow, a big, deep shadow like the one cast by the chestnut trees of summer, and armed with that shadow he'll traverse as much of the desert as anybody manages to traverse in a normal life, and he'll bend under the shadow like an all-too-small cross – let's face it, there are pitiful little crosses that bend under the people carrying them – in the vain hope that the shadow it casts will be so soothing, the slumbering creature of

the desert will not be wakened unto life until he himself
has passed away, since 'if anything, I regard it as a basic
human right, perhaps the most basic human right, to
choose the manner in which one dies. In a way, I think it
was more humane in the old days when some people at
least could be executed by the sword. As for me, I'd like
to be crucified, crucified in a desert like this one,
provided the cross could cast enough of a shadow, cold
enough to keep the animals of the sand in check until I'd
managed to die. But somebody will say you can't
crucify an innocent man, assuming you can talk about
abstract concepts like a crucifixion when there are so
many concrete alternatives, and I reckon it's obvious
you can't, but it all depends on the fact that my attitude
to innocence is quite different from that of lots of other
people's.

'I think that being innocent means that either you
haven't been born, or you're dead, and once anybody
has got as far as agreeing with that, I'd probably be
prepared to admit there are many kinds of guilt: a sort
of guilt that's more innocent than most, and a sort of
guilt that's more burdened with guilt than any other,
guilt positively dripping with guilt, and guilt which
merely drips. Many people can't see that, they can't
understand that, they'll never have the faintest idea of
what it's all about, they'll just go to sleep by the fire and
they'll have forgotten all about it by the time they wake
up and are overcome by the heat and all they can yearn
for is a shapely woman, a juicy orange, a glass of sweet
wine, a better class of toothbrush, or nothing at all.

'But for me, wandering through the sands of the
desert, always having been wandering through the
sands of the desert, and at last aware of the fact that I
shall die in the sands of the desert, all that is no longer

hard to understand; but it's true that it's only just recently even I've begun to catch on, once upon a time I too had a fire to sleep by – I was lying when I claimed I'd always been wandering through the desert, that's something which must have happened to me quite recently, in fact – but the difference between me and lots of the others was that when I woke up, I was so cold I was shivering and my teeth were chattering and I hadn't the slightest yearning for any of the usual things, the things you ought to be yearning for if you're normal. But as I lay there freezing and agonizing, I kept thinking after a while that I too had a yearning, that even I wanted something, just like all the others, but at that time I was so frightened of not being normal that I never dared to put it into words – but now that I'm finally wandering through the desert and nobody but me can hear my confused words, I can say it however many times I like.

'I yearned for the deepest feeling of peace there is, a peace that passeth all normal understanding, not the peace of the tranquil creek, not the peace of the fishing rod, not the peace of the bank after closing time, not the peace of the cellar when the rest of the house is asleep, no, a peace which can only be found in innocent solitude, the peace of a lonely man who hasn't forsaken anyone in order to be lonely, a lonely man who stands apart from all contexts of blood and suffering without anyone being able to pin any responsibility for that on him. And maybe I was aware even then that there was one place on earth, that there was a desert somewhere or other where that kind of peace is possible, or rather that there's a place in that desert, not a banal oasis, oh no, on the contrary: a place which is sandier, hotter, more unbearable than any other in this sandy, hot and already inherently unbearable desert, and if I haven't yet found that place, I'm still wandering around looking for it and if I don't find it even though I think I've got down and stuck my nose into every hollow there is among the sand dunes – well, gentlemen, in that case I would beg to be crucified, in that case I'm guiltier than anyone else, guiltier not because I've acted more unjustly than anyone else, but because my self-reproach, my feelings of guilt and my part in so much suffering had a higher temperature than those of anyone else.

'Being guilty is feeling guilt, not the result of crimes committed; being innocent is being happy and joyful and not letting one's peace and contentment be affected by all the terrible things that happen and take place. In my view, therefore, the judicial system has gone off course when they execute the less guilty instead of the more guilty, execute the criminals instead of those who feel they are bearing the guilt of the whole world in their hearts. It's like executing children for things they've done in the dark because they were so unaccustomed to the darkness, they couldn't understand how their bodies functioned in it. No, as the only criminals are those who feel that they've committed criminal acts, the judicial system responsible for tracking down and passing sentence on criminals could be abolished and replaced by a judicial system which executes those who deserve it, since after a while there's nothing a guilt-laden person desires more than to be allowed to die, to be allowed to die because of his guilt and that of the world, and he hasn't the slightest doubt, nor the slightest fear of death, for as there's nothing more to hope for, as he's plumbed the very depths of the world, he can beg the judicial system to grant him his sentence of death – and no head will ever bow down before the guillotine more gracefully than his, no woman has ever felt her most precious necklace caress her neck with more ecstatic tenderness than he feels as the rope settles around his neck.

'Myself, I want a cross. I'll take the storeman with me to the warehouse and pick out the most attractive one, I might choose one made of chestnut, because I've always liked the deep gentle shade of the chestnut, or maybe one made of poplar, since there was a tall poplar in one of the back yards where we used to live and I loved that tree as if it had been the only piece of greenery in the whole world, but there is *one* tree I don't want and that's the one which creaks like a gallows when the wind blows, and I'll ask the storeman what kind of a tree it is because I don't want a cross that creaks like a gallows when it's a crucifixion I've asked for. I don't want any help with the nails and I don't want any help with carrying it, I want to be my own executioner right to the very last and if there is one thing I want at the very end it's that the shadow cast by my cross is so big and so deep that the animals of the sand don't wake up until it's all over.'

But the sun is always devising new games for anyone who wanders through the sands of the desert. Sometimes it puts a blow-pipe to its lips and amuses itself by spurting glowing lava into your bone marrow till you collapse and wriggle on the sand like a snake. No, like a worm, like a maggot, you can feel the angler's brutal finger and then suddenly he sticks the hook into your belly and he can't have heard you screaming because the hook just goes further and further in and it's hot and it's glowing red hot and it hurts especially much when it goes on up through your throat and one of the barbs has got stuck there and is struggling desperately to break

233

loose because the hook has to keep on going, right up into your head, it's just longing to bathe in your brain, it's probably been lying on its side in a box at the ironmonger's thinking of nothing else but the prospect of bathing in some human being's brain. But then comes the most brutal twist of all, it feels as if your legs are being ripped off – and nothing is too incredible, too horrible, too impossible to endure; of course, your legs have in fact been ripped off, let's face it, you can't expect to be left alone no matter how long you are and the angler can use your legs next time, and all of a sudden there you are in the sand, you struggle, you wriggle around as much as you can, but you can't do all that much about it, you ought to have practised wriggling more often while you still had the chance, but in the end you give up because there's no point and you just let yourself sink down and the sand closes in over you like flames and you keep on sinking further and further: your heart has to go under, your neck has to go under, the whole of your head has to go under and then you go deeper and deeper down, deeper towards the ultimate horror, the hottest fire – and you just wish you still had your legs left so that you could feel your way, so that it would have taken a little bit longer between the first touch and the terrible knowledge which suddenly flares up in you about what's lying there hidden under twenty-five feet of sand. But as things are, as things are your nerve ends hit him straight away and your scream comes all of a horrifying sudden – oh, if only there were another three feet to go, just another three feet of bone, flesh and sinew to cope with that first horrific contact, you evil devil of an angler, do you realize what you're doing! – and you scream and scream and suddenly of course you're full of sand like a sack.

Sand everywhere, sand sand sand, the sand is darkness and light, the whole of your head is full of sand now that everything else has trickled out, sand is rattling away in your intestines and your stupid stomach is doing its best to digest it all, but even so the sand doesn't help you to get away from your terror, get away from the horrific awareness of what that devilish angler let his bait rest on. Shudder after shudder of terror stutters through your sandself and they follow the twists and turns of the hook as faithfully as anyone could ask. It's so horrible, perhaps the most horrific thing of all, to hit directly against a dead body with your nerve ends – you want to explode, you want to be blown to pieces, but sand is so merciless in that it can't explode no matter how hot and agitated it gets, no matter how wildly and how long you scream at it that it really must get a grip on itself and blow itself into the skies, but sand is so scornful and so unreceptive to flattery or warnings, and just to show you what it can do twenty-five feet under the surface, if it is that deep, it creeps close up to you and starts tickling you for all it's worth, and you can't even laugh.

Then at last comes the signal from up above, there's a slight tug on the hook, and you do all you can to make sure you don't come loose from it, oh you dear little hook, your sand thinks, don't abandon me now. And the hook doesn't abandon you, you're pulled up, relentlessly up, and you bless the hook for being so strong. But then you're suddenly hit by that horrific moment when you realize you're not alone, that you're not the only one on the way up, that the booty the angler had been hoping for so much is also on its way up, clinging fast to your nerve ends as if on to a rope and the dead man won't let go even though you start wriggling more and more violently and your nerves don't snap even though you wish they would with all the heat of your sand. And then daylight at last, daylight at last, you're not wriggling any more, you just hang limply while the sand runs out of you without anything else coming in to replace it apart from pain. Your legs are lying in the sand underneath you and they must be dead, they're not moving in any case but your feet are clamped fast into the sand, possibly out of despair and because they're longing for a trunk.

Then the horrific thing that's followed you up comes loose and the angler laughs so much he sprays you with red-hot saliva and he kicks it and it responds with a dull clang – and before your eyes fall down into the sand, weary from having seen so much pain, you manage to make out that it's a water keg, quite a big, green water keg, there's nothing else to say about it, but perhaps there must have been something wrong with it even so because suddenly the angler kicks into shape a big hole in the sand and he pushes the water keg into it until it disappears, yelling and screaming all the while. And what happens next is just that the sun swells up like a red-hot toad and finally explodes and turns into balloons, millions, perhaps even milliards of balloons, all of them glowing just as terrifyingly red-hot as they sink slowly down over your desert and merely increase the heat of the earth and you're just glad that you don't have legs any more to feel the heat with, and the balloons come nearer and nearer and suddenly there's an enormous crush as all the millions and milliards of them are just as keen as the next one to fall into your eyes – and all at once, in a single singeing stabbing moment they all join up with their heat and the whole desert trembles and the angler falls into his hole and the water keg goes up in smoke and your eyelids quake till they shatter in the horrific cascade of blinding light and all-consuming heat which is now pouring over the earth and over you yourself.

And when Madame and the English girl return from their secret excursion to the inland part of the island and one of the three men sitting in the shadow of the cliff, their hands and arms covered in dried grey sand, suddenly remembers how full of hatred a hand was as it moved down against a hip, they stop in surprise at the sight of the two low sandhills that have appeared on the beach.

'He got a decent burial, nobody can deny that,' says Tim Solider, and he's forgotten all about keeping his distance now that so many horrible things are behind them.

'He passed away from us so quickly,' says the captain, anybody would think he'd got sunstroke, he'd stopped walking over to the boxer, and all the sand he carried he just flung over the emptied water keg, it was as if he were even less able to bear the sight of that than of the dead body. He worked like a slave to get it covered up and in the end he was crawling on all fours between the tank and the water with sand in his hands, and when we tried to help him up he squirmed like a snake and kept yelling that we ought to let him go because he was just as dead as we were, he just yelled. Anybody would think he was the one who'd done it, nobody knows any more, knows nothing, knows nothing about that.

Then Madame goes up to Lucas Egmont who's lying outstretched like a gravestone on the grave over the water keg and his body is all limp when she tries to lift him up.

'We ought to try and get him into the shade at least,' she says. It's just then she notices the white rock, and she lets him slump back on to the sand and wades out into the water and bends down and strokes it, for under the sand they have carried away to make the graves is a shimmering white rock, but none of them had noticed. 'You must have been blind,' she says, brushing the sand off it, 'you must have been blind as bats.'

She's no idea how blind they are.

5

The white rock is quite different from what they had first thought. They imagine it starts at the spot where Madame discovered it and then runs out towards the middle of the lagoon, covered with a thin layer of sand; but when they scrape away the sand with their weary hands, they find it takes off in a quite different and unexpected direction, and suddenly they're all possessed by a powerful, compulsive desire to uncover the whole of the white rock, and to persuade it to reveal its white secrets. Indeed, they're all so keen to get to work that they kneel down in the water and start digging away the sand with urgent movements of the hands.

It's already less hot than it was and the water in the lagoon is motionless. There's a slight breeze higher up and they can hear the panicles of the grass rustling, a single iguana is falling from one stone to another, and although the sea is so near it sounds as though it's in the far distance, swishing like an invisible waterfall from a point beyond the horizon. The closest noise is Lucas Egmont's voice as he talks in his sleep. They've put him in the shade next to the cliff, and he's still asleep, lying on his stomach, and convinced he's on the water keg's grave; from time to time he says, quite clearly: I want to be crucified, and he seems to be groaning with happiness. There are five of them kneeling in the water, digging, and they're working so doggedly, so self-sufficiently, as if what's lying hidden under the coarse sand is the soul of the world, the solution to the riddle of earthly suffering, and they've forgotten about everything else apart from this warm, shallow water and this sand which is still hot when it fills their cupped hands, and the white rock whose whiteness grows more and more dazzling the closer to land its nakedness shines upon them.

And they've forgotten everything else, in fact: little mouse, says the grey cat of fear, little mouse, go and run around in the grass for a while, forget my mouth, forget my claws, let the sharp, white teeth hovering over you be swallowed up by the twilight. Little mouse, dear little mouse, let me stop torturing you for five minutes or twelve minutes or two hours or three days, run as far as you have time for, run as far as you can manage, run as far as you dare! Run through the clear night whose brightest stars are my eyes, they'll light you up for as long as you deserve, run through the dewy morning and don't worry about who's forcing the grass apart just behind you, run through the long, sunny day and seek oblivion in my merciful shadow which is following you all day long, just as faithfully as your own! And never complain about the loyalty of fear, little mouse, but do so occasionally about your own disloyalty whose only excuse is that it won't last any longer than I let it.

They're working away now lustily and energetically, as if they were digging a canal leading to their rescue; they've stopped using their hands as they're not efficient enough, the rock goes down deeper the closer it gets to land, and the captain is scooping sand with his jackboot while Boy Larus and Tim Solider are using their canvas shoes, which means they have two tools each and in order to make the work go more quickly – needless to say they hope the rock will prove to be endless and they'll still be working away stubbornly when the liberator comes with his teeth and claws – the women's job is to empty the filled receptacles in the deeper water beyond the far tip of the rock, and a circular membrane of sand rests like a blind eye on the placid surface of the lagoon and this eye is the only happy eye on the whole island. They can't see the shadowy ruins of the stranded ship which has sunk to the bottom of the lagoon, nor the graves on the beach over two hopes which no one had expected anything of and which are therefore mourned all the more deeply, nor the fire which is slowly going out because no one has felt cold for such a long time, nor the images of terror which keep on flitting like bats across their field of vision, images of what each of them fears most grinning scornfully down at them even though they persist in gazing down at the sand and the water.

Suddenly the rock rises up quite steeply, just at the point where land and water meet, and at the same time it gets thinner and shoots off almost at right angles and about three feet across, towards the cliff; it's only a few inches into the sand now, so shallow that everyone's surprised they haven't stumbled over it at some time during the few days they've been on the island. The women come up from out of the water and stand behind the men and gaze down on their naked backs, burnt brown by the sun and glistening as hard as an iguana skin, and the men's hands are working like pistons as they brush away the sand which is steaming in the heat, and the rock emerges more dazzlingly white and clearer and smoother and more polished than ever, like a woman's back.

But as mercilessly as any destiny you like, the rock heads straight for the buried water keg and they hesitate just for a second, although you couldn't notice any change in their mechanical movements, before opening up the grave. The sand is hard packed and steam is rising just a little from its dampness and then they can feel the keg under their fingers and they roll it to one side with an enormous heave until it comes to a halt splishing and splashing in the shallow water at the edge of the beach. After just a few more seconds they've removed all trace of Lucas Egmont's work and they've barely finished when they realize it was all in vain as the rock suddenly comes to an end, quite pointlessly, like when you check one movement in order to make another one which is just as pointless; it's grown tired of creeping any further up the beach, maybe it thought the island was too awful for a little white rock to rest on but then it couldn't be bothered to crawl back again as the bottom of the sea wasn't much better either.

It's an awful moment when the rock comes to an end: they've been ejected from a horrific existence, with no hope of rescue, it's true, but obscured by forgetfulness, and thrust into a horrific existence with no hope of rescue where the only certainty is pointed awareness; and as they kneel there with their necks bent over the opened grave, their backs reflect their terrified indecision in so comical and so frightening a fashion that the women observing them from above first want to roar with laughter and then scream in fear.

Cover your backs up, we don't need mirrors any more is what Madame wants to shout to them, cover yourselves with sand, cover yourselves with ashes and clothes and let's see your terror in your hard faces instead, it's much purer there, it won't frighten us there so much, not any more, we won't need to see how awful we look when we can't control ourselves any longer, when we've spread ourselves to prepare for the first bit of terror that comes our way; but just then the English girl grabs hold of her arm just above her elbow, so hard it turns white, and with her free hand, the same hand that's been stiff with hatred for three hours now, she points quickly at one of the backs on the beach and Madame notices straight away the little red teeth marks on its right shoulder-blade, and she glances up at the English girl and sees how clearly her mouth remembers its bite of hatred and her tongue the taste of blood from the previous night, and from this mouth and this hand which drops down to her hip once more she can see what is soon going to happen, the inevitable that can't be prevented just as you can't stop an avalanche by standing in its way, and he's burnt by their gaze and turns his head round quickly and spits a glance over his shoulder and straight away he's just as hideously aware of it, for when he turns his head back again and looks down at the sand, his shoulder is trembling something awful.

Then they don't really know what to do: they all walk down to the water's edge and roll the keg out into deeper water and let it fill up slowly and when they roll it back over the rock it makes a dull, heavy clanging noise and it's only when they get it back to the little crown that they realize fully how sadistic they're being towards themselves. Oh, how will they be able to open the tap and let the water rinse away the last grains of sand from the rock without remembering those marvellous moments of blissful coolness when a handful of water trickled down their throats and then continued to spread coolness through all the canals of their bodies? Then someone shuts his eyes and quickly as an axeman he turns on the tap so that the water starts cascading down the rock, making it still whiter, making it sparkle like a jewel of salt and mother of pearl – but the thirstiest of them all, who was still hoping desperately that the last drop of drinking water which might have still been there at the bottom of the keg could possibly be still there on the rock, flings himself down headlong and starts licking the rock and he licks it all from top to bottom until he vomits from all the salt and starts crying, starts crying salt tears which he can't drink either. And he's terribly ashamed when he gets up again and with a gesture of simulated defiance kicks the empty keg over the beach, down the rock, and before it starts floating it clanks away so piercingly and frighteningly that Lucas Egmont wakes up and sits up with a start – and immediately realizes what's happening.

'What are you doing with my water keg?' he yells, 'Why have you dug up my water keg, how dare you!'

They stare at him with the empty, ruthless gaze of a statue, and he casts down his eyes.

'Why did you do it?' says Madame, though like the rest of them she knows it doesn't matter any more, 'why did you pour away our water?'

Then he remembers his dream and then he remembers all the moments of guilty horror when all the world's prosecutors marched up to him in order to make him answer for everything that happened through no fault of his own, and bitterly furious and offended at being accused of such a petty matter he first looks round and then starts yelling once more: 'What about the fire, then ? Why did you let the fire go out? And the food! Why did you eat the food? What's the use of water without food? And what's the use of food and water if there's no boat to take us away from here? And what's the use of a boat coming to rescue us if we don't want to be rescued, if we're all refugees who have come to the only no man's land where we belong!'

After a while somebody says, 'Have a look at this rock we've found.'

And everybody stands looking at the sparkling white rock and it's much less hot again, the sun is setting extremely slowly but they can sense that it's falling slowly down towards the tongue of the horizon; slowly and just as frighteningly pointless as the truth, the sea is moving in on the island in hundred-yard breakers, and, howling lazily, the wind rises and falls between the sea and the sky on that extremely beautiful day in May in the southern, northern, eastern or western hemisphere. Oh, how indifferent fear and death are to our geographical situation.

Then Lucas Egmont says, 'What do we want a rock for? What are we supposed to do with a rock? Is it a rock we need? For God's sake!'

But perhaps it is.

6

Yes, what does anybody want a rock for? Can anybody say what you're supposed to do with a little white rock about nine square yards in size, and with half of it under water come to that? Is there anything more pointless than a little rock, in fact, that you can't bore holes in and then blow up and extract some meaning from, some sensible meaning?

They've sat down round it on the sand and they're thinking and pondering, sitting there quietly and feeling for one horrific moment God's or somebody else's hand swishing through the silence of the bathroom and taking out the plug from the bottom of the bathtub and the sucking feeling as their life begins to run away is like a punctured artery somewhere in their bodies. But it was only a test after all, the plug is back firmly in place and the hand is as motionless as a fly on the ceiling – and look! The cat of fear has once again let its little mouse go, and constantly shaded by its enormous shadow, they're all running away through the grass of the world. Little mouse, the cat whispers disdainfully, little mouse, don't forsake me.

They sit thinking about all the little white rocks they've come across during their lives, but there aren't many of them, there's been a distinct shortage of white rocks in their lives, and the English girl doesn't even remember the white cliffs of Dover because she's so busy thinking about that other business.

'Back home,' says Tim Solider after all too long a silence, and the bits of rag that have grown into his iguana bites are flapping in the breeze, they're stinking already, 'in the square back home there was a statue the same colour as this rock and we used to call it the ghost, because it was so white. Especially in the moonlight it looked as though it was luminous, quite luminous. It seemed as if somebody had given it a coat of phosphorus, but they hadn't.'

'We can't very well make a statue out of this rock,' says the captain morosely, brushing the sand off his jackboot, 'and even if we could, what'd be the point, it would be a waste of effort here where nobody will ever see it.'

'You're forgetting the birds, captain, and the iguanas,' says Lucas Egmont, who's suddenly got such a burning desire to burst out laughing, he'd really like to lie outstretched on the ground, all alone with the sun and the cloud, and just roar with laughter, make fun of the ridiculous lunacy which makes six people already condemned to death, six people who have already got used to the hard padding of the electric chair, six people who have already got a thin, sharp line straight across the back of their necks because they've so often felt the axe tickling them, negotiating over a rock, worrying about how a useless bit of rock flung out at random somewhere or other in the world should be used. Pointless indeed, so pointless, so disgustingly pointless – but as he sits there looking down at the rock, he notices how the silence has suddenly become loaded with hostility, and all at once he realizes he's hurt all of them by what he's said, and he glances cautiously at them all in turn without letting go of his eyes and he realizes from the seriousness creeping into their expressions that the rock is a sacrament as far as some of them are concerned, the only firm foundation, the only fixed point in this world that's rotating so madly. Peter – the rock. Maybe it's Peter who's turned into a rock and is offering his back to them as a firm foundation.

'Would it really be as pointless as all that to make a statue?' he says, therefore. 'We could draw lots to decide who would be the model and then make one, always assuming of course that we had the chisels and sledge hammers and drills and crowbars necessary to enable us to break off a big enough piece, and it might only be enough for a bust come to that, assuming there's a sculptor among us.'

'It would be meaningless in any case,' says the captain, 'since nobody would ever come here no matter what. There's no point in leaving a statue for the birds and the iguanas, as you just said.'

An icy silence ensues, freezing the air round about them, and their thoughts hang like stiff clouds of smoke from their mouths, even though it's at least eighty in the shade, and snares of hoar-frost tighten round everyone's neck – but there's an unspoken word, an as yet unformulated truth or lie which could redeem them all, at least for a few moments. And Lucas Egmont has a completely new experience: without being the slightest bit interested, not even for a moment, since he doesn't need to feel thirsty just now, in the kind of salvation which needs a rock in order to be realized, indeed, without being especially interested for a single moment in salvation in any shape or form, since he's convinced or at any rate posits that the only thing which could make a human being seek a way out of the jungle that is this world is total, clearly acknowledged awareness that no salvation is possible on the grounds that a jungle is a jungle is a brutal jungle, that is, without having any sympathy at all for the hunger or salvation shining forth from the eyes of several others here present, he suddenly feels an irresistible desire to express the blessed opinion which everyone except the captain – that man with his perverted ideas about solitude – is longing to hear, he wants to be a medium, an anti-spiritualist medium, and suddenly he discovers the enemy that is his and everyone else's. He leans over towards the captain and glares short-sightedly, and anyone who can't detect the animosity in this gaze must have been blind for a hundred years, it's like staring at an old suit of armour where four hundred years of solitude stare at you from under the rusty visor, while the memories of the knight's hate-filled eyes during the battle are still glinting in the eye-slits.

Oh, captain, he thinks, what an old suit of armour you are, what an old, empty suit of armour. All your life you've been going around like a suit of armour without a knight. Someone wanted to stroke your brow and you said: One moment, I'll just lower my visor; someone wanted to feel your heart beating, and you replied scornfully: you'll need a sword for that, and someone fetched a sword and thrust it through you and it just came out of the back-plate without doing you any harm at all, well, maybe it would rain in through the hole, but that's not much of a risk as rain doesn't often fall horizontally when all's said and done. You couldn't bleed because suits of armour have some trouble in doing that and you were proud of it and you were happy to be an empty suit of armour, since empty suits of armour have such a good time: they're lonely and they'll always be so, and in their solitude empty suits of armour can hear all the singing inside them and round about them. Old hunting horns are tooting away, and the ancient cries of falconers, long since forgotten, are once more echoing through the air and suddenly the whole suit of armour is filled with the noises that used to be heard in the days when the armour was alive, in the days when the armour was full of life, of flesh that could bleed, of limbs that could writhe in agony, of rattles and screams of terror, and the shrieks and the old noises rise and fall through the empty suit of armour and there is such a marvellous singing and vibrating inside it. It has no heart, you see, it can only feel vibrations as if they were wonderfully beautiful music, and it misses out completely on all the *angst* in them, the fear of death and the hatred of life: there's nothing more stupid than the solitude of an empty suit of armour.

But above all it's through your severe eyeslits, captain, that we can see you're proud of being an empty suit of armour; an empty suit of armour can't be afraid, for instance, it can wander through any forest you like without being worried, without being afraid that a snake might wriggle up through the heather and wrap itself around its leg. You think it's an advantage, an enormous advantage not to be able to feel afraid, and in your emptiness you are laughing away at all the many people who are terrified at the prospect of dying of hunger, dying of thirst, dying of loneliness, dying of paralysis, dying of wounds, but if you pause and think about it then maybe it's not as much of an advantage as you think. Your lack of fear isn't in fact due to your store of courage, but rather to your inability to feel anything at all, to your not being able to feel anything because you haven't had anything to feel with for the last four hundred years, and your memories of the time when the armour was bristling with life just fill you with ridicule and sterile defiance.

That's why it's right to say to you what someone once said to somebody else: I say unto you, the man who fears not life shall not love life, the man who does not harbour fear, neither shall he harbour courage, the man who fears not death shall not be enabled to die with dignity, the man who fears not himself, neither shall he love another. But let's not talk about that, captain, you can't be opened up with words, you can only be opened up with a tin opener or a five-inch nail, and when you have been opened up, people will only wonder why they bothered.

Perhaps the suit of armour heard what he's been thinking, for suddenly the captain looks him in the eye, thrusts his gaze into Lucas Egmont's eye like a lance and breaks it and leaves it sticking there and suddenly they're united by a warm current of animosity. Lucas Egmont would like to sit close up to him and clutch his arm and his hands and thank him for giving him his animosity. After all, it's so comforting to know one has a steadfast enemy in this vacillating world. And eventually, the next minute or in an hour's time or some time before darkness falls, they'll face up to each other and they both feel that strange feeling of dull gratitude and fear that grips you just before a terrible confrontation.

But it was a medium he wanted to be, an anti-spiritualist medium for all the others, for the salvation-seekers who still didn't know where their enemy was, and that's why he wanted to defeat the captain first, really flatten him, on behalf of the others.

There's a while to go yet before dusk, and far away to the west clouds are being sprayed in through a hole in the horizon like puffs of steam. Somebody suddenly gets the idea it's the smoke from a steam ship cruising towards the island, and gazes at the spot where the black funnel will first appear like a periscope, but the clouds just keep on rising and turn into mountains and then even bigger mountains and all hope is dashed.

'I don't believe it's as meaningless as you think, captain,' says Lucas Egmont. 'You say it's pointless to make that statue just because nobody will see it when it's ready, always assuming of course we really could make a statute, but I can't believe it would be as pointless as that, even if the situation is so awful that no boat will ever go past and be attracted to the island by the wreck. The way you think, the way you argue, anybody who's alone would never be able to act at all just because he knows that nobody else in the world will ever get to know about it, and so anybody who's alone ought to be completely paralysed and think he might just as well put an end to such a meaningless existence.'

'That's exactly what I do think,' said the captain, with a hint of hostility, 'that's my way of looking at it exactly. Life is completely meaningless for a solitary person, in fact, and he would die, might just as well die as you put it, if it weren't for one thing, if he didn't have one thing to live for, namely: his solitude. It's in order to be able to make the most of that solitude he chooses to stay here for a while and carry out all the meaningless acts life demands of him. Great and formless meaninglessness, that's the price of a ticket to solitude.'

'But in that case,' counters Lucas Egmont, 'I don't see why you object so much to the meaningless nature of the statue. To dedicate a statue to solitude is surely no more pointless than, for instance, opening a gate even though there are so many gates open already, or building a road to add to the many unnecessary ones that exist already.'

'For the solitary person,' replies the captain, pulling off his boot with a sigh and placing it on his knee, 'for the solitary person there's only one kind of permissible meaninglessness, and that's the kind of meaningless acts which help him to achieve his solitude, and there are many impermissible, indeed forbidden meaningless acts, and the most meaningless of all these meaningless acts are of course the ones which take him back to any kind of threatening, all-consuming, inexhaustible fellowship.'

'But there's something there which doesn't hold water,' Lucas Egmont points out. 'You maintain that everything we do in this life is meaningless, but on the other hand you claim that in so far as you're a solitary, life actually has a meaning, and that is, solitude for its own sake. But solitude which can be compared with a blissful existence in a combined snake pit and concert hall, this state doesn't just take possession of you for no reason, it's no good just lying down in a basement and waiting for it to come over you from out of the darkness; oh no, the most craved-for demands the most positive action on your part, demands that you should play a positive role in what you called the meaninglessness of the world – but that's where I think you make a big, terminological error. In so far as they assure you of the meaning of life, unshakeable solitude, it can't really be true that these actions are as meaningless as all that, not for you that is; in fact they're on the contrary very important and meaningful actions, and it seems to me what you should be drawing distinctions between is not meaningless and very meaningless actions, but meaningful and meaningless actions. Although you're so keen to deny it, therefore, there are meaningful actions even for you, just as in my view there are others for whom there are meaningful actions in life, even if life itself is meaningless. Of course, no doubt there's nothing here which is meaningful in itself, or we'd never be able to forgive life; but everything we do and everything we have done is surely meaningful for ourselves, for our own feelings of fear, for our own feelings of guilt. Hence action, ridiculous, meaningless, paradoxical action, is so full of meaning, so weighed down with responsibility even for the many of us who are longing for fellowship but wandering around as isolated as heavenly bodies in space which is growing more barren for every pulse-beat that passes. That's why one has to carve one's bit out of the world's meaninglessness and confess before one puts the knife between one's teeth for good: I believe in the meaningless nature of the whole, but the unintentional meaningful nature of the part.

'And since we've got a rock,' he goes on, and they all stand up and look down at this white rock, this white, virginal back which has become so endlessly white by dint of having spent a few hundred thousand years waiting for the sun, 'since we've got a rock, it's pointless not to use it, but extremely pointless to do anything with it. There can be no question of a statue, of course, as, apart from anything else, we don't have the necessary tools; but we should be able to do something else. You can carve things into a rock, for instance. There are white rocks that, with a bit of effort, you can scratch black or green lines on to if you use sharp enough stones.'

'What should we carve into it?' asked the captain caustically. 'That there were seven of us to start with, but that one of us died more or less straight away because we thought he smelt so awful, we couldn't bear to do anything about his illness and get him on his feet – a little arrow pointing to his grave – and that somebody else murdered us by means of emptying our drinking water, and that a third one served us up with glass beads when we were at our hungriest, saying, here you are, eat these.'

Then Tim Solider gives a yell and he runs at the captain with his hands clenched pathetically over his iguana wounds like the heroes in old melodramas.

'Shut your gob, will you! Shut up!'

He stands opposite him, panting, and his wounds suddenly start bleeding and two little streams trickle slowly down towards his navel where they join and pause briefly and, throwing caution to the winds, he hurls himself violently at the captain, but of course he falls to the ground, falls right on to the rock, knees first. The captain helps him up and Tim is so weak again he hasn't the strength to do anything but hold on to the hated hands stretched out towards him.

Then the captain whips round with a nastily powerful movement, the brutal turn of a soldier, and faces Lucas Egmont and the visor falls open in the empty suit of armour but the hatred sparkles forth through the narrow eye-holes like the beams from a lighthouse and as he stands there with his back-plates glittering with hostile solitude and the copper shield at his chest beautifully curved by its longing for a lance, he says so firmly and decisively that everyone can tell he's made up his mind long beforehand, perhaps even before they found the rock, perhaps even before the catastrophe took place, perhaps even as he was trembling at the very start of his solitude: 'We'll carve a lion.'

'A lion?' says Lucas Egmont. 'Who can remember what a lion looks like? It'd be better to do an iguana.'

But Madame remembers what a lion looks like. There's a tree swaying in the breeze over the lion cage at Bretano's zoo and an escaped monkey's sitting in the tree, trembling with cold and despair; people bring a long ladder and she points up at the brown monkey and says to the boy that monkeys are dangerous, especially ones that have escaped; they can swing down out of the tree and split your head open before you know where you are; but the boy isn't scared, he just looks as uncomprehending as usual, just as bereft of humanity, and in despair she drags him over to the lions' cage. Look, she whispers, look at the lions, you can't believe how dangerous they are, look how soft their paws are so they can slink around, you can't hear a sound, you might think they're the nicest animals in the world – and then suddenly there's a terrifying growl and a roar of anger as they fling themselves at the bars, do you see how thick they are, you only need to annoy them the slightest little bit and they hurl themselves at you and try and tear you to bits. Just stick your arm in through the bars, and you'll see, that's it, further, a lot further. But nothing happens, nothing at all, except that the biggest lion lies down in the middle of the cage and meets her wild eyes with its bleak gaze. Look at me, she says then to the boy and he pulls his arm slowly back, look at me; and she wants to scream when she sees his eyes, no lion can call them to life, no hungry, roaring lion can touch his soul. Does it ever happen, she says excitedly to the keeper as he climbs down the ladder with the trembling monkey clutched tightly to his chest, does it ever happen that a lion tries to escape? Never happens, answers the keeper like an echo, never happens. Like an echo.

Then the captain holds his jackboot up in the air so that everybody can see its shiny leather and he taps it with his hand just above the heel and when they all get near enough they can see the big lion emblem burnt into the leather.

'There we can see what a lion looks like,' he says. 'Is there any animal with such a simple outline as a lion?'

'It would be just as good to take an iguana,' maintains Lucas Egmont, 'iguanas are also very easy. There's one lying just down there: we could bring it here, remove its skin, and just press it into the rock.'

'I think the lion's better,' says the captain, 'and there's something special about this particular lion even though it's just a simple trademark lion. If you look really closely' – and everybody looks really closely, but they don't notice at first even so – 'you'll see the lion isn't sitting on the ground or in the air; the lion's sitting on a human being, on a freshly killed human being, and you can see from his stiff outline how surprised he is suddenly not to be alive any more. I've sat round many a camp fire and never ceased to be astonished at this trademark, at this painfully honest trademark, the lion's vibrating solitude after slaying his last enemy, the only one to bar his way to solitude.'

'Captain,' Lucas Egmont suddenly shouts out, 'you surely don't mean we should also include that detail on your sadistic trademark. It's quite enough with just a lion.'

'Oh, it's not difficult in the least, I can assure you of that, there's hardly anything easier to draw than a freshly killed human being. There's more of a firm outline than ever before, a monumental simplicity and clarity of contour which has always pleased and surprised me, and it's often made me feel pain when I think that all that beauty, that delicious purity will soon be lost forever without having been captured by the hand of an artist. Therefore I have to say I felt extremely attracted to this trademark, no matter how sadistic you might think I am, and of course we shall have this man on the rock as well, since that's what gives the picture its meaning, it interprets our situation so absolutely splendidly. Of course, there aren't any lions on this island, if there were we'd certainly have heard them before now; but what there is here, for instance, is a silence, a silence so hideously ancient that every little tiny hole in it, even a hole as tiny as the one we've made during the four or five days we've been here, is such a terrible deed that once the perpetrators grasp the full extent of what they've done, they have no choice but to be horrified and try to obliterate all trace of their crime by taking the fastest possible steps to deprive themselves of any possibility of disturbing this silence in future, and in the end the silence weighs down upon our breasts with all the weight of its lion's body, alone at last, alone again at long last – and everybody who comes here and finds the rock is bound to think: what courage, what heroic courage, accepting one's solitude voluntarily and without the slightest quiver, by baring one's breast to the claws of the lion!'

Then Lucas Egmont cries out in desperation, 'Is there anyone else who wants to commit suicide? Anybody else who wants to carve a dead body under the lion?'

'I don't know,' says Boy Larus.

'I don't know,' says Madame.

'I don't know,' says the English girl.

'I don't know,' says Tim Solider.

'In that case,' says the captain, 'I suggest we all go for a stroll round the island, and meanwhile think about what we want to do. We can assemble here again at dusk.'

But as they are on their way up the cliff, several of them turn and gaze down for quite a while at the beach with its graves, one of them desecrated and one not yet desecrated, its footmarks suggesting madmen have been dancing along the water line, its little grey hollow where a fire once burned, the battered ship leaning right down over the lagoon as if to drink, the ocean as blue and indifferent as the sky and the silence, and the tall strand of smoke from the vessel of their longing, which has engraved itself deep and indelible into the sky, a chink in the door to eternity; they stand there gazing for such a long time before continuing on their way up to the grass and the solitude, as if they would never return.

7

There's a point in a person's life which exists so as not to be intruded upon. It's like a little, blue mountain peak which, bluer and sharper than the darkness, shoots up out of the darkness, and an invisible lighthouse which only operates occasionally during your lifetime and then for the shortest of times flings out a serpentine beam of dazzling light into the night, illuminating it for one dizzy second – just one second, but that's enough. The darkness itself seems to be cloven by a terrible wall of light and you're drawn implacably towards it like a moth and then suddenly it's all over: the light goes out, but it's still burning on your retina and with eyes burning with light, you grope your way forward to a particular spot whose existence you've only suspected before, ready for anything, ready to come up against both salvation and destruction, the whole truth or the whole lie. And fumbling through the darkness but with deep wounds of light, you fling your arms around that little mountain peak, that fortress of ruthlessness, where everything hounded, cast aside, silenced clings on like a leech, and you become nothing more than a giant leech sucked hard against the mountain, while everything you believed was prescribed bites on to the nipples of your terror. Nothing is prescribed, nothing can be prescribed: not a thought, not an action, not a word; that's the terrible thing about living as you do, without fear in a darkness which you think is definitive but which is really just a respite before the lighthouse flares up. Just think how much you wish you'd been blind, so that you could have been spared this final light as well, this light which is so terrible because its ruthless edge cuts through even the most tightly shut of eyelids – and as you end up lying there in the night clamped to your blue stone and being breastfed by all the forgotten horrors, you'd scream if you weren't the leech you are: why only now, why didn't I come this way before, why didn't I take the strokes I needed to swim into range of this invisible lighthouse? I knew all the time where it was and how the little mountain peak lay in wait, crouching like an animal, enticing with its claws and its leeches which only grew more savage the more time passed by. I've known about this for a long time, but I relied on flight as being the most crafty deceit of all; but as I was running away I was constantly aware of certain signposts whose enamel had been chipped away by flying stones, of certain snakeskins which had been nailed fast to the road by heavy vehicles, of certain glowworms crushed by some mad fury and piled up by the roadside, and hence knew I was getting closer and closer to the horrors. Then suddenly it was too late: one is transfixed by the violent shaft of light and in the darkness is a blue vortex which knows no mercy.

There's something in the very air which rouses her and she awakes with a start and looks round quickly and suspiciously – but she's alone. There are still rustling sounds in the thickets and the grass: someone is slinking or running in towards the middle of the island, but after a while it's probably just the wind through the tops of the grass. Even so, she stays there for a while yet, her gaze flitting like a grieving dog backwards and forwards along the thin strip of sand, punctuated by steep cliffs. She's stood here before and gazed down at the beach, but it's always been different, always been alive, and never has it been so narrow. It looks as if the water has started to rise slowly, slowly but absolutely inevitably, determined to creep up the island and lick off all the dryness, all the desert dryness the water is thirsting for. But then her gaze is stopped short at the burnt-out fire and the dead, singed hollow is just as far from the water's edge as ever it was and a remarkable, a strange blue deepening of the air, a tall, narrow shadow pointing straight up into the sky above the fireplace still reminds her of the smoke that once was the stuff that hopes were built on, and the acrid smell of unwillingly burning wood still tickles her face when she closes her eyes. She could wake up after dreaming about a burning house with pale faces darting about behind the window panes cracked by the heat, without ever wanting to save them; but she borrowed a pair of binoculars from the chief fire officer and saw they were in fact balloons with faces painted on to them, jerking about on their strings in an effort to break loose, but they always burst with a loud bang and she would wake up from the crackling sounds in the fire. Good God, is it the fire that makes the beach so horribly deserted, so horribly dead?

The graves are also there, the water keg is bobbing securely against the beach, and there are the lines she made in the sand, the sharply outlined furrows in the sand she used to flee to when she wanted to be alone.

Then, at that very moment, her gaze wrenches itself away from her will and makes a mad leap out into the water, a leap throbbing with fear and despair. It races through the water, setting spray flying, then launches into a fast crawl across the lagoon and suddenly is about to dive underneath a floating object when the white thing flings itself at the bold swimmer and blinds it, first with pain and then with mad terror, then with overwhelming relief.

It's not the boy who has been thrown over the reef by the waves and is now drifting closer and closer to the shore, it's something else, something quite different, and her gaze returns to the white rock in a calm, smooth breast-stroke. The sun gradually turns red with poppies, and she remembers the lion, and is just about to turn and head for the grass and start thinking about such an easy problem and then return as the sun dips sizzling into the sea and all is well, when all of a sudden her gaze leaps up the cliff and something forgotten, something long since forgotten but lying crushed far below hurls itself upon her gaze, and it's bleeding when she drags it away and runs along the red curve of the rocky path and the high high bushes close over her and she suddenly notices the smell as it slips a disgusting hood over her head, but she doesn't stop even so, she has no time to stop.

She's surprised at being so alone; the world is emptied of all voices and suddenly the world is emptied of all sound. Dripping from all her wounds, she falls down in the grass but even then she doesn't want to stop, she kicks all around her in desperation but feels she's only sinking deeper and deeper down into the still-hot earth, the hard earth which is no longer alive, having been stunned by the sun and killed by the grass. There she lies, silent and still, listening to the silence; but she

261

daren't, can't listen for long for fear her eardrums will be burst by this highly charged silence.

And the smell is still after her, creeping like a caterpillar down the long grass stems, and at first, almost without any fear at all, she tastes it and tries to recall this smell. It's the sort of smell you might find in a cellar, it's a smell which requires you to go down many flights of stairs with a bunch of keys rattling from your finger, then you open a door, many doors, the last of them heavy monsters of doors you have to heave against with your shoulder before they slide open, creaking and squealing. This is a smell for the dark, for cellars, or for some other dark places. It needs a lamp, an insignificant flashlamp projecting its frightened glances into every corner of the darkness and only succeeding in making the darkness even more frightening and the smell even more mysterious. It's a smell for felt soles, the sort you take long strides with when you're running around in wet grass so that the damp won't go through them and because you're frightened of snakes. It's a smell that has to be overcome by stealth, a smell you must hurl yourself at and fight with for a while, bite, and fling your arms round to crush it. It's a smell that requires you to go right into the cellar and put the flashight down on the floor so that it just surrounds itself with a little hazy circle of light which doesn't even reach as far up as the dripping stone ceiling. Then there are things to be shifted out of the way: firewood, heavy crates with the lids nailed down, keeping mum about what's in them, odds and ends of fishing tackle with wet seaweed still clinging to them, lots of cracked croquet balls, sacks, empty but tightly knotted sacks of coarse material that rattles – sand, maybe? – when you move them, the odd axe gone rusty because it's been left out in

262

the rain and nobody's bothered about it, and perhaps the misshapen skeleton of an old iron cot which still seems to tremble when you lift it up in the air, tremble because it belonged to a child that recently died of tuberculosis. You pile all these things up behind you to make a barrier and it's so high you can hardly imagine there's a light behind it and as you stand there enclosed by four walls of darkness and a ceiling of darkness and a floor of darkness you suddenly realize there's a smell of fear as well, a smell that makes you search all over the cellar for a pickaxe, shaking all the time, and when you find one you start bashing away at the floor behind the barricade, carefully at first so that only cracks appear in the concrete, but then more and more violently, increasingly afraid of all kinds of things: of the people in the house waking up and failing to understand what it's all about, of finding that looking for the smell under the cellar floor is a waste of time, or that the outcome is as awful as you're already imagining it will be.

But it's only when she's groping her way through the grass again, almost closing her eyes because of her desire to be able to go past the thing that's waiting for her, only when she stumbles against the dead iguana does she realize what a cruel fate lies in store for her. She goes down on her knees beside the stinking iguana and at first she wants to yell out: that's not it, that's not my iguana, somebody else has killed this one: but the outline of the stone in the rotten green mass still retains its horrific sharpness, and her lips are burning with the memory of kissing the iguana's skin and the sound, the horrible wet, sticky sound of the stone embedding itself in its belly starts vibrating devilishly slowly in the air round about her and the fatal stone's heavy fall down on to the rocks on the beach suddenly starts echoing and

263

the echo darts piercingly from one wall to another throughout the room that's the world and forces her down closer and closer to the iguana – oh, how she struggles to protect her mouth!

And then she's running again, for she's come up again despite everything, it's even possible to emerge from this, and as she runs, she's rubbing her lips all the time with the back of her hand, but her lips are just as dry and chapped as always and there are no bits of rotting iguana stuck to them. Feeling calmer, she slows down, but the smell catches up with her again, screws itself on to her, is intimate with her, presses itself against her face like an anaesthetist's mask. She forces herself to think clearly and calmly, to make a decision which won't drive her into a state of lamentable panic. After having walked for quite a way through the grass, walking calmly and with strides as confident as one can manage when one's scared, after having gone in a particular direction and with all her senses on edge to ensure that she doesn't deviate from this safe route and come to a part of the island that's unfamiliar to her as yet, after having noticed the smell gradually dispersing and wafting away and just hanging on in the grass around her like a dim memory, she stops and wraps her arms round the grass in front of her and pulls it down over her. Then, hidden by the grass, she gets undressed and lies down stark naked beneath it. It's so dark down there, a reddening haze is crawling along the ground and she realizes it can't be long to sunset, she can see the white rock glistening with solitude when she closes her eyes, and she keeps them closed for a long time and allows herself to be soothed by the stifling warmth rising up from the ground. It's so nice to be naked in the grass, and sleep comes creeping up on her, all she has to do is to reach out for it and pull it towards her. The moment before she falls asleep, she has a dim recollection of the lion and the white rock, but it's so far away, so pointlessly far away, that she just lets it sink out of sight. What are you supposed to do with a white rock when you can forget everything even so?

She doesn't sleep for long, however. In actual fact, she starts waking up straight away. It's a dream she dreams and wakes up from, and there is a big, fiery yellow carpet with a green border and she's walking slowly over it down an endless corridor. She's been placed somewhere in the middle of the corridor and isn't allowed to turn round and see how far she is from the end and now she's walking very fast and she's glad the carpet is muffling her rapid footsteps. A vast number of doors open out on to the corridor, all of them with frosted glass in their upper half, and it strikes her that none of them is thrust open by scurrying people, nor is there a sound to be heard behind any of them and even so she feels she is far from being alone. She stops outside one of these doors and examines it through her shoe. It's funny: there's a hole in her shoe sole, quite a big hole, but instead of having it resoled someone has put a piece of glass in the hole, a powerful magnifying glass, and she's examining the door through it. Nothing at all escapes her attention, she notices fingerprints on the yellow handle and she takes out her handkerchief and rubs them away; the glass panel in the door has cobwebs in the corners, and she blows them away with a careful puff. Then she notices something quite new about the door: it has a name plate, an enamel name plate in line with the handle. But the plate is caked in thick dirt which can only be scraped away with sharp

265

nails. She dreams she's scraping letters out of the dirt, and then she drops her shoe in surprise and it shatters with a loud crack even though it did fall on the carpet, and it's that noise she wakes up from.

There's somebody standing in the grass beside her, swaying back and forth on the soles of his feet; it's a man and he has his back turned towards her and he's whistling softly, as if to a dog. Without looking round, he throws a little twig over his shoulder and it falls quite close to her and after a while he throws the next bit of the newly broken twig in the same direction. He's waiting for somebody, and is indulging in pointless activities to pass the time. She's looking at him from such an unusual angle and is so nervous that she doesn't recognize him at first, but all of a sudden he pulls off his shirt and rubs his bare back with it and the shiny little red wound on his right shoulder blade immediately gives him away.

It's grown redder and angrier since she saw it last, or maybe it's just the slowly encroaching twilight that makes it glow something awful, she thinks it looks like a little cruel, greedy and sensuous mouth busy trying to bite its way further and further into his body. Then he stops whistling, then he stops breaking off twigs, then he stops rubbing himself with his shirt, he drags it quickly back on over his head and then stands still and in silence as he waits for the person who's now approaching.

Someone is running through the grass and panting hard, and all at once the English girl is standing so close to her that Madame could grab hold of her ankle, pull her over to her through the grass and beg her to refrain, plead with her to have mercy on the doomed man, indeed, even cling on to her so that nothing could happen.

But everything has to happen, there are courses of events one just can't interfere with because they're so devilishly logical, so inaccessible to one's efforts, that it suddenly seems meaningless for anybody to exist at all with free will, human reason and all the attributes people go on about so much.

They meet more or less at her feet, and the man leans forward towards the English girl and clutches her to himself with a ruthlessly quick movement. They stand there in silence for a minute or so, and it looks as though they are pressed tightly against each other in a clinch, but from behind it's easy to see from the girl's tense body that she's drawing back, that she hates and is disgusted by this contact, one of her shoulders is trembling with fear and reluctance, but the man who is resting his chin on her other shoulder doesn't notice a thing. He's gazing into the grass behind her with a cold smile of triumph and suddenly he lets go of her and swings her round as if he were her trainer and he grabs tight hold of her trembling shoulder and wants to drag her away with him. Then she tears herself loose and falls down on her knees so close to Madame that she's sure she's been detected – but it's something much worse.

'Somebody's killed an iguana,' she says, pointing down at the ground with a piece of grass.

'Come on, it stinks something awful, we can't hang around here, we can't put up with this smell,' says the man impatiently, pulling her to her feet, and she says it's cruel and horrible and that one of them must have done it because this thing has been killed in such a human way, and then they disappear into the dusk of the grass and the silence of the grass, and Madame is all alone

267

with everything she's been running away from. And everything's so horrible: she only needs to stretch out her hand and the iguana is lying there, sticky and stinking, just waiting for her hand, and she tears up clumps of grass and rubs her hand clean but that's not good enough, the horrible stench clings on to her more firmly than ever, and on the plate she'd been scraping in her dream was the word iguana, although she'd forgotten that until now,

She has no choice but to flee. She tries to hold her breath but in the end she has to gulp in air and the air is full of the stench of a dead iguana. She runs up towards the highest peak on the island, thinking the wind up there would surely blow away all the unpleasantness in the air, but the higher she gets, the more oppressive it all is. As she's clambering up, she has to keep stopping and breathing in deeply and her lungs are full to bursting with the horrible stuff.

But high up at the top of a narrow little hill that looks like a shrunken volcano and drops down to an unfamiliar beach with little white rocks glittering in the sand, stained pale pink in the sunset, the air is pure at last, bitter and thin but pure. She kneels down on the brink of the precipice and watches the empty ocean stretching its shivering, glowing sheet over the darkness of the depths, and everything is forgotten. She is alone on her cliff and nothing can reach her, so high is she now. It occurs to her she could be mistress of the world: it's so easy, all you need is to be alone on a higher peak than anyone else.

Then she thinks she can see an iguana creeping along among the stones on the beach far below; it's a little iguana and its scaly skin is gleaming and it's crawling very slowly, as if it had been injured or was frightened of something behind a stone. Madame leans forward as far as she dares and spits down at the iguana, but she misses.

I'm not scared any longer, she thinks, iguanas are nothing to be afraid of. They only bite men who are lying on the ground, and you can fight them, kick them down the cliff if they come too close.

But just as she's about to spit again, she sees the big iguana crouching behind a burning stone by the water's edge, and she thinks she should shout to the little one to look out, to run away as quick as it can, but her tongue has stiffened inside her mouth and there isn't a single loose stone up here she can throw down at the lurking danger. And the little iguana is so comical in its attempts to escape death, it suddenly changes direction and heads straight for the stone where its enemy is waiting, and it's crawling much faster now. Oh, if only she could throw herself down and save it, but of course, it's all too late. Without making a single move of its head to ensure that death isn't lying in wait behind the nearest stone, it crawls past the burning rock and the big iguana jumps out at the little one and hurls it against a stone so hard that its armour-like skin bursts open and as it slithers down the stone twitching with pain and death, the big iguana burrows mercilessly into the little one's belly and all the time the big one's tail is smashing into the stone on either side of a gap between two rocks like a vicious whip. It's a horrible noise which drowns everything else, drowns her heartbeats, drowns her agitated, squeaky breathing, drowns the sea and the whistling wind. But then all is silent and the big iguana, superior in every languid movement, clambers lazily up on a dazzlingly white rock, desecrating it with the death of the little iguana. It lies there motionless on the rock and the sun gleams warmly on its horrible snout, and in the shadows below the little one is still gaping in surprise with its belly, and the echo of its tail whipping the stones seems to be echoing still, loud and terrible.

No, it was a different noise, it is a different noise, it's something sharp and distinct coming from just behind her, but as yet she'd rather not turn round and face it.

The lion, she crouches there thinking in desperation, still on her knees, which lion should I choose, the lion which . . .

. . . but suddenly she's walking down a long staircase, glittering in the bright light from the ceiling above, and the stairs rise towards her with their newly polished copper edges and the yellow bannister rail which she clings on to with both hands is hot and shaking, as if it might explode at any moment. Everything's bubbling away beneath her, tables are being overturned and there's creaking and clanking as chairs are crushed to bits against the walls. Her legs and thighs have turned to iron as, in the grip of some ruthless fear, she struggles towards a green rectangle, the beckoning rectangle of the door opening above her – but then suddenly the staircase has become an escalator and the water grasps hold of her ankles and calves with a short, piercing giggle and she sinks down and sinks into the sticky, offensively warm water, it clings to her hips, it clutches at her breasts, it twists itself round her neck and pours into her mouth, callously and with a shrill sucking sound, and into her ears, and her eyes – and now the whole of her has sunk below the surface of her fear . . .

She turns round very quickly, she almost flings herself round and stands up at the same time, as if to scare somebody with her agitation. But the iguanas are not easily scared, the hundred, the thousand, the tens of

270

thousands of iguanas that are spread over the whole of the cliff behind her, and the gap between their snouts and the cliff edge starts shrinking and the space she has in which to work out her salvation is getting narrower and it doesn't tremble under their armour-plated skins when she stamps her foot on the rock. They just keep on crawling closer and closer, and the sun which is about to set glistens on a gigantic carpet of iguanas, a rolling carpet without a beginning and soon to be without an end and already she's being stifled by the choking stench these million or so iguanas are thrusting towards her. She's stopped stamping, she's gone down on her knees again with her face bravely confronting the mass of iguanas, accepting whatever comes. She can't run away from these iguanas that are already dead, she can't run over the top of their armour plating as she would over a spiky carpet: she'd be overcome by the stench and fall and they'd be on her in a flash; she can't fight them: once roused they'd just surge forward and squash her under their horrific, stinking weight. The silence is unbearable as they creep towards her, all the cracks from their twitching tales have been silenced, the soft scratching sound from their scaly skins scraping against each other is the only, the last sound of her life.

Then she screams, then she flings herself down before the iguanas and screams as she tries to scratch wounds into the rock, in vain of course, with her nails: 'The lion, the lion, I must go to the lion! Let me through, do you hear, I have to get past!'

But the iguanas make no response, they just keep on crawling closer and closer and the ledge is now so narrow that she can't even lie there with her arms outstretched, as if she were swimming; she has to pull back the arm she's stretched out towards the iguanas

271

and roll over closer to the precipice so that her other arm is already hanging down over the sharp edge, and roll even closer and with a desperate thrust, with enormous strength born of fear, roll closer still, roll over with clenched eyelids and bleeding fingers and a hunched body that has already accepted all the horrors of the fall and she rolls over the edge and as she falls, eyes closed and with all her senses numb from terror, she can't even see that the cliff she's falling from is just as empty as it always was, glittering emptily in the sunset which no longer follows her as the shadows close in.

8

I must keep my face nice and friendly, my hands must be calm and amorous and full of longing, she thinks, and then my body mustn't tremble, and I must sound calm and my voice must be sufficiently keen for him not to suspect anything. He might fling his arms round me and hug me into his sweat, and if he does I mustn't vomit, not yet, but I must pretend I'm enjoying it, as if there's nothing I'd like better than him hugging me close, so very close.

Just then he walks past the bush where she's hiding and she calls to him softly so as not to frighten him and cautiously takes hold of his arm. When he turns to face her and dives into the green, stifling shade under the bush there's a glint of fear in his eyes and she can see the tension in his face, and his hesitant movements as he approaches her tells her how suspicious he still is.

You're so scared, she thinks, but she half-closes her eyes so that they won't radiate triumph and give her away, you're so scared, you're sweating with fear, your shirt is damp and stained, everything about you stinks of fear.

Someone walks past just then, next to the bush where they're hiding, and she pulls him quickly towards her and gently places her hand over his mouth and with a surge of pleasure she feels his tongue tickling her skin. They stand there for a minute or so, hugging tightly, both of them pretending to listen to the rustling noise as whoever it is walks quickly away through the grass; but in fact, they're just listening to each other. She can hear his hot breath hissing past her ear, he's swaying backwards and forwards on his feet and making the leaves rustle, and with a strange feeling of excitement she can feel his heart beating hard, hard between her breasts. Then she suddenly lets go of him and takes her hand away from his mouth as she kisses him quickly just under his eyes and then the cloth falls away from her and she presses her naked body forcefully against his. With a shudder, she feels his horrible hot hands stroke her back with eager caresses, he leans back and lets her rest on his quivering body and he bites on to her mouth like a leech and his crazy hands have intertwined behind her shoulder blades. Just as they're about to fall, however, she braces herself and whispers vehemently, 'No, not now, wait, wait, you must wait, you must wait a minute, just a minute.'

A little branch has come between them and she takes hold of the branch and tickles his naked chest with it until he's smiling again, and with her other hand she caresses his back tenderly until she finds the little hollow made by the bite and her lips remember it and they grow agitated as well and when she bends over the branch and bites his lip he just thinks she wants to be

273

kissed and he strokes her with both hands in the most disgusting way.

'When,' he whispers at the same time, and there's a heavy veil over his eyes, as on a drunk, 'when shall we meet?'

Carefully, so as not to annoy him, she removes his clammy hands from her body and returns them to their owner.

'Just as the sun's setting,' she says, 'the moment the sun sets, I'll meet you in the grass below that plateau where you usually go in the evenings.'

Then he's back again with his wet mouth and suddenly he's sucking away at one of her breasts, but she controls herself, she keeps control until he lets go of her and disappears into the high grass with a knowing, intimate wink. Then she punches the little branch with her clenched fist, punches and punches at the bush until she falls flat on her face with the effort, and lies panting on her stomach in the deep shadow of the bush.

Maybe she dozes off for a while in the suffocating closeness under the big bush, or maybe she just glides away from reality for a moment, for suddenly the pain in her back returns, it's a stabbing pain which cuts into her like a knife, a knife being thrust in and pulled out by some inexhaustible hand. Now, as then, she wriggles about in an attempt to get away from it, but there's no respite, she can't get away from anything at all, she has to go through it all again.

It's a hot jungle and a green haze filters through the quivering roof of the treetops, tall grass and trembling parasols of leaves on slender flagpoles. It's a wet jungle, and where she's slinking along its floor with tortuous steps there are stinking green pools, covered with green membranes that heave but don't burst as creatures move underneath. She's hot and sweaty in a more unpleasant way than ever before, a shameful sort of sticky heat wraps itself round her body like a wet bathing costume, and in order to be rid of it she flings off all her clothes, screws them up into a rough bundle and hurls them into a serpentine bush, which lets them sink down whispering through its hairy branches. But nothing is any better even though she is naked, the jungle has a fever and she herself is enclosed by the jungle's fever; the trees themselves are feverish, their crowns whistling in the wind and balancing on shaking, sweaty trunks; poison is dripping from the parasols, falling down in sizzling drops to the ground, and the ground itself is feverish, hot, evil-smelling vapours are rising from it and the dirty pools with their green membranes are the ground's wounds.

Oh, she's so frightened of hurting herself, of cutting herself on something, and her blood spurting out in a green spray until the wound is suddenly covered by one of those green heaving membranes. She throws herself down before one of the ponds and wallows in her heat, then she breaks a little twig from a bush and, frightened but nevertheless convinced it's the only thing to do, she pokes a hole in the skin over the pond and watches in horror as it slowly grows bigger and bigger and an animal or at any rate some living creature wriggles its way under the membrane towards the hole. And she wants to drop everything and run, drop everything: dignity, reason, and every trace of courage and every trace of protection from her fear, and to race pell mell into the redeeming maw of the jungle, but she's incapable of moving, she can't even raise her eyes and look away, she has just to lie there outstretched by the pond and watch the animal she's aroused by poking a hole in its prison come closer and closer and suddenly, suddenly its head emerges unseeing and slowly from the water and wriggles its way forward over the membrane, its body comes pouring out of the water, yard by yard, there's no end to it, and spreads itself over the whole of the membrane, strong enough to bear it all, and at first the snake just lies there motionless, at first the red snake just lies there with its eyeless head not moving at all, as if surprised by all the new sensations it's come up against: the sudden dryness, the heat which is so different, and the noises that have lost all their muffled quality and are now piercingly shrill.

They lie there quite still, she and the snake, and she can't move and wouldn't want to do so for fear the snake would realize she existed and perhaps chase after her or make some other of the jungle's inhabitants aware of her existence.

The hot, damp ground suddenly starts shaking beneath her and the sound of a terrifyingly shrill trumpet cuts through time. The snake grows nervous and its long body starts shivering slightly while its eyeless head, with no place for any eyes even, rears up as if listening. There's a sound of snapping twigs and dry grass breaking quite close by, and suddenly the elephant trumpets again, she turns to look and sees the elephant has come to a halt among a clump of parasols and its red tusks gleam ominously, its mighty body is still trembling with a desire to crush everything in range, its little eyes are glinting evilly in their little sockets, and suddenly it raises its trunk and squirts its thick, red, evil-smelling jet straight into her eyes.

While she's still blinded, she hears the elephant departing, crashing through the jungle quite close by her, and a little tree falls over right across her back and

276

wounds her superficially with its sharp trunk, and the hissing animal gets further and further away and its trumpeting rides off through the jungle with it, while she's trying to rub her eyes clean, and she feels weak and scared as what has happened dawns on her. Then at last she can see again, and the first thing she wants to do is to find some grass so that she can dry her red hands and get rid of all the elephant's fluid, but it's only when she throws all caution to the wind and sits up with a start and looks down in horror at her body that she realizes the whole of her is this same, poisonous red colour, her skin has disappeared and her blood has acquired a thin, blood-coloured membrane to replace it. Carefully, she feels her body, frightened this membrane will suddenly burst, and she feels hotter than ever and more ashamed than ever, something dirty has happened to her, something which means she's suddenly got problems when it comes to staying alive.

Then all of a sudden, with a stab of surprise, she notices how the light of the jungle itself has changed colour, it's not green any more, like a shower of blood, radiantly red, it pours in through the roof of the jungle and the earth and all the leaves and the branches and the parasol poles are the same colour as she is. A few fiery red birds parachute down from some tree or other, shrieking shrilly and urgently to each other all the time, pecking at the air with their beaks; a large animal, armadillo-like, is hanging asleep on a branch swaying dangerously high above her head: sooner or later it might break, and the animal come crashing straight down on top of her. But even so, she's not as frightened as she was shortly before; she's taken on the colour of the jungle, and she thinks she's entitled to the protection of the jungle, and so she lies down calmly on her back beside the pond, its red water is glimmering under the body of the snake and she's no longer as frightened of the snake as she was, since now she's so like him, and as it glides towards her over the red, shuddering membrane, she doesn't scream, nor does she offer to fend him off.

He trickles up her leg like stiffened water, and the contact she's dreading is not all that awful but tender, ticklish, and she even caresses the snake with her red fingers and feels how similar they are, both of them are blood held together by some silly little membrane, and the snake makes her feel warm, the snake generates heat, not unlike her own but more intensive, more stupefying, not so shameful because he's so strong. And she gazes straight up into the red roof of the jungle where butterflies as big as swallows and with burning wings are fluttering around, living lianas that aren't snakes squirm from branch to branch, giant chameleons thrust out their tongues and butterflies get caught by one wing which then comes loose and they float down through the red air, fluttering pitifully with their only wing, and when they hit the ground they crawl away like maggots; but she can see other animals hanging down motionless from the network of branches that forms the roof, she can see their eyes gleaming like diamonds in a grotto, and suddenly they let go and swoop down, their glittering claws outstretched, they're like big, big cats, sixty feet they fall, down to the ground, and they thud down with a dull thump and she can hear them hissing like cats as they struggle with the animal they've leapt upon and soon everything falls silent, all the time the glittering one-winged butterflies keep on stuttering down through the hot air – the drama is cruel yet stimulating, nice, her body is warmed up by all the things happening above her and around her and now the snake is lying between her legs, heavy and warm and motionless – but suddenly he bursts into life and before she can move a muscle to prevent him, he creeps inside her with all his terrifying length.

She wants to scream and fight and curse, but it's all too late and she has no choice but to go along with it – but then comes the pain in her back which drives her mad, the snake's head forces its way along the inside of the thin membrane covering her back, and he stretches out and stretches out into eternity, and soon he'll snap and she hopes he'll snap as soon as possible, if only this devilish pain would abate, if only this horrible dirt filling her existence would drain away together with her own defiled blood. But the pain only gets worse, and suddenly the armadillo launches itself out of the tree and swoops down towards her in a shower of blood, and with a scream, or maybe she only whispered a scream, she wakes up under the bush where she's been lying, but she feels no relief on discovering it was all a dream, she only feels the violent heat of a throbbing hatred rising inside her in waves, and as she drapes herself in her cloth once more and slowly gets to her feet, she keeps on whispering with her hot lips, bursting with desire, to somebody or other, 'Give me strength, oh, give me strength to do it.'

9

He hides on the plateau until dusk falls, crouching behind the natural barricade and listening, or rather trying to forget to listen to all the things moving in the grass and on the rocks down below. Although it's not especially hot, although the wind is blowing with the irregular breathing of a feverish patient, his head is sweating as never before. He lies quite still so as not to provoke his body, he unbuttons his clothes and lets the wind breathe directly on to his skin, but it's no good: he still can't break free from his sweat. With an agonizing feeling of disgust, he feels his pores opening quite independently of his will and shedding their dirty tears, and he grows painfully aware of the smell, the smell from his sweaty body. Every time he breathes in, he can feel the nasty, acrid smell surging into his nose and filling the whole of his head with its brutal weight. And everything is clinging to him: his stinking trousers, his open shirt, his clumsy shoes, and his hair – for the first time in his life he can feel his hair pressing against his forehead, sucking on to his skin like a cold, slimy marine creature that attaches itself to you while you're swimming, and then just won't let go, seems to fuse into your forehead in the sunshine, and is impossible to get rid of until you go for another swim.

In order to have something to think about, and to make sure none of the things he's afraid of can creep up on him from behind, he starts thinking about his hair, how he's always had, or at least for twenty-five years or more has had ash-blond hair of varying thickness and size; all kinds of things have happened, he's lost lots of things and many of them have never been found, he's voluntarily disposed of other things but then, unfortunately, found them again; but there's one thing he's never lost nor disposed of once and for all: his hair. You could say he's been loyal to his hair even if he has been disloyal to quite a lot of other things. He strokes his own hair like a mother, but he doesn't burst out crying even though he knows he's going to die, he's discovered how much salvation there is in being very sentimental, in stroking oneself, in being aglow with peace even though there might be an awful long time left to live.

The thing about hair, he thinks to himself, is that hair is really a part of your life, perhaps a more important part of your life than you often think, and every time you have it cut, you die, an important part of yourself is cut off, and although you survive you're more dead than you were before your haircut even so; the innocent barber is in fact a little executioner, an amputator who's always doing you one of the last favours. And if that's how it really is with hair – and why shouldn't it be when there are so many other things that are similar? – then the same thing applies to our nails. Without a second thought and without reproaching ourselves in the least, we cut our nails even though they may be just as much of our life as so much else, such as our eyes, such as our actions that we're so proud of, such as the thoughts we're even prouder of churning out, although in fact they're no more remarkable than our nails growing, or our hair.

He's lying face down and his sweat is making big stains on the rock, but he pretends not to notice and maybe he doesn't in fact. He runs his fingertips over the ragged horizons of his nails, and all the time he keeps his eyes shut and tries to think of his life as a big nail, a giant's nail on an otherwise insignificant creature. It's trimmed occasionally by a pair of scissors or a file, or it's not trimmed at all and allowed to grow, big and shapeless and with lumps of black dirt under the rim, and eventually it grows so long it breaks off as a result of some careless movement – *finis*, that's it, curtains, this marvellous life no more than a dirty fingernail flushed

281

down the lavatory – or it's trimmed too much, every day the cruel scissors crawl along its edges and gnaw and gnaw away till the nail would cry out if only it could. Other nails are as well trimmed as hedges, and polished until they shine, and they squirm with self-satisfaction as soon as the hand they're growing on moves, just as if they were completely independent of the hand's movements, just as if the hand were their most obedient servant.

Boy Larus, lying there on the rock and dripping with sweat, just as accommodating torwards his cowardice as he's always been, closes his eyes so tightly, the shadows are imprinted into his retina, and he knows that the tighter he can close them, the clearer his own position in the universe will be to him; his own adventure is revealed in all its happy glow. Suddenly he sees the hand before him, the hand his life is clinging to like a nail, a severely trimmed nail on a hard hand, perhaps the world's hardest hand, a hand much too accustomed to handling fire and red-hot iron to have any gentleness left when the time comes for a manicure. Then, he just grabs the first pair of shears he can find and cuts loose on the nail so that it doubles up in pain and splits right down to the root.

Maybe I should have had a different hand, thinks Boy Larus, maybe things would have been a bit better if my nail had been attached to another finger on another hand, but you can't choose your hands – and who knows what I might have ended up with instead, perhaps an executioner's hand, a thick-skinned scoundrel who trims his nails with his axe after every execution. Then I'd have been caked with congealed blood and all the time, all my life been longing for the executioner to miss just once, and cut off the whole of his finger.

It's amazing what metaphors cowardice can dream up for us. He rolls over slowly on to his back, calm just for a moment, and in a state of deep satisfaction he opens his eyes. The heavens loom high above him, blue with many flashes of cloud; he stretches out an arm and grasps hold of the wall and listens to the grass down below, no trace of anxiety, and it's rustling away with no sign of fear. The world is bright and cheerful, the man who's lying there is soon going to die and he knows it, but it's in the dim distance, and he's not particularly frightened because there's no other way out after all, once everything's come to an end, once all possibilities of living in peace have been eliminated, and everything's so simple, so horribly simple: a nail's going to be clipped right off, pulled out by the roots even, because its owner's grown tired of it – and so what, what's so remarkable about nails being trimmed, things that happen every day without anybody thinking twice about it?

He lies there as if anchored to the rock, and lets the sun – for the last time, maybe, he thinks, and the whole of his body glows in sympathy with the bold way he dares to think of it like that – lets the sun blaze down straight into his face, it's still hot and the refined profile he's always been so careful about, the way one's careful about a rare china dish, sticks out from his face like a red-hot ember. He's just lying there peacefully and at one with the world, and his past life isn't flashing past his eyes like they say it does for people condemned to death, for all our friends who are dying. He's not thinking of anything in particular, he feels perfectly contented, really contented because he deludes himself into thinking he's accepted everything, knows all the rules now and isn't going to be put out by anything; he knows about hunger, thirst, sudden weariness, gradual fading away, and all that. He thinks he's accepted everything, but in fact he's accepted nothing at all, all he's done is find some new prop in some new experience, it's like a mountain spring and he plunges the straw of his fear into it and sucks and sucks till he chokes and bursts internally – and everything is as pointless as it was always destined to be.

But nevertheless, he's had a new experience which almost fills him with ecstasy because it's so incredibly unexpected, because he'd never realized before he was capable of any such thing.

It was that night the English girl was screaming something awful. To start with, she scared everybody stiff with her confused babbling, going up first to one and then the other and begging for quinine for some patient or other with malaria who might just be saveable, or she asked where the boxer had disappeared to, wondered whether he'd just gone for a walk or whether he'd found some boat and left in it, in which case it would be pretty tactless of him because he'd promised faithfully to take her with him in that case, after all, they all knew how close she was to the boxer – oh yes, they all knew that, and that's why they daren't yell at her to cut it out for God's sake, as the boxer had presumably died during the night and they'd only noticed the next morning when it was time to share out the water and there was a different sort of smell coming from under the canvas, not quite so dirty but no less horrible, and there were no more groans of pain to be heard, although they'd all been listening for them with a tiny, tiny bit of hope. Somebody lifted the canvas quickly, and then let it fall again even more quickly – the English girl had been present then, and it was obvious from her face that she'd caught on, even though she tried later to hide all that behind an attitude of defiant, convulsive lunacy.

And this chaotic day was followed by a horrific night, and the darker it became and the quieter it grew on the island and over the endless ocean around them, the more suspicious they were that her madness was really play-acting. They all sat round the fire then, huddled more closely together than ever before, more scared than ever before as well, because this hadn't been some impersonal storm that no one can do anything about anyway, or some raging floodwater you can't possibly beg for mercy, oh no, what made it so awful was that it was something that could happen to any of them at any moment, could affect any one of them without a moment's warning, and take hold of any of them who were still normal and hurl them into the most terrible solitude: as lonely as a man lost in the depths of a forest filled with ghosts – oh, why couldn't he just be a gnarled trunk?

They could hear her mumbling away in the distance, sometimes monotonous and rambling, sometimes as clear as a bell, and that made them even more frightened because it could be the first stages of a scream, a scream so terrible it would never cease being hurled backwards and forwards over the island like an eternal echo. It was so dark round about them now, even though the fire was crackling, but it was so good to feel their faces were mercifully hidden when this is how it was going to be no matter what. It was so good because you always notice these things first from people's faces: the English girl had suddenly acquired a

285

frown, a remarkable line running from one of her eyes and right up to the base of her hair, looking like a mark of extreme surprise, and her mouth was pursed without her knowing it: several times while all this was going on, she tried to open it and say something, but her lips just wouldn't obey, and when she eventually mastered them, she didn't seem to know what she was saying. And now they were all so grateful for the shadows cast by the firelight, because they didn't need to fear that outstretched, ruthless index finger aimed shakily straight at them and backed up by that terrifying pupil screaming at them all: There you are, you look just like her!

All the time Boy Larus had been frightened, but irritated as well, irritated because no one was taking the initiative, because the captain didn't say what ought to be said so that they could intervene and restrain her, and when the captain eventually put his decision to them he more or less started shaking with joy and, filled with determination and ready to obey no matter how unpleasant things became, he strode out into the darkness alongside the captain with a smile on his face, and he had a strange feeling of how marvellous it would be to rub up against him briefly and he enjoyed the sensation of the warm sand tickling the soles of his feet. Boy Larus and the captain walked past quite close to her several times, talking all the while in an attempt to rouse her aggression so that during the unpleasantness that followed they could tell her the whole truth. But it seemed impossible to attract her attention, and as they were having trouble in putting up with the horrible smell, the captain decided they should approach her one at a time, at intervals, and try to irritate her in various ways.

But all of them came back depressed after having failed, and her voice grew increasingly shrill and in the darkness they could hear the scream creeping up over the sand like a big, black animal that would suddenly strike at their throats and somebody said the best thing to do might be to leave her alone until she fell asleep from the strain of keeping herself so terribly tense in tune with her mourning; but Boy Larus didn't dare abandon the idea that something might be done, and hence he kept on walking backwards and forwards in the shallows behind her with the warm water lapping lusciously around his ankles, and occasionally he would stop just behind her and dig in the sand with his toes evidently without her noticing. Words just tumbled out of her in a confused torrent, and the more frightened he became, the further he went out into the water until it came up as far as his knees, and then he stopped with his feet buried comfortably under the sand and stared towards the shore, at the silent group huddled around the fire and the two motionless bundles straight in front of him, one of them silent and the other prattling, one dead and the other alive, and it dawned on him that no one could see him standing there in the darkness and he felt so protected from everything that was frightening and dangerous, he'd fled to the safest place in the whole world.

It was then he suddenly realized the English girl was lying naked in the sand, having cast aside the cloth she normally wrapped round herself so carefully, and her body was glistening like a rock of marble through the darkness, glowing in the sand; her breasts and all the other contours of her body were gleaming with unusual intensity, it seemed that hot, glowing, slender chains were trembling in a frenzy all over her body – and he suddenly realized with a start that he was standing on the beach very close to her: he must have wandered out of the water in a trance and now he'd been brought to his senses by his burning desire throbbing away inside him and filling him with burning pus.

Then somebody over by the fire moved so suddenly that he couldn't fling himself down beside her for fear that somebody might be approaching. Instead, he withdrew hesitantly towards the fire, and the captain rose quickly to his feet and came to meet him, and slowly and quietly they sneaked up on the naked girl. They stopped a yard or so short of her motionless head and listened vaguely to her ramblings as they gulped in the flow from her outstretched body.

Then Boy Larus let his discipline slip and he grabbed the captain by the arm.

'Somebody ought to,' he said excitedly, 'somebody ought to.'

'I forbid you to do it,' said the captain sharply, and turned on heel so suddenly the sand screamed, and he marched back to the fire with swaggering, brutal strides.

Boy Larus waded slowly out into the water, and just for a moment he felt a stab of cold in his burning boil; but once he was back with the water swirling round his knees, everything was just as it had been before. He was facing the lagoon, and outlined against a little reef of stars on the bottom of the sky he could see a blurred detail of the ship's outline, but then all he could see was a little white rock shining forth from out of the water, and, all eager, he leant forward to grasp it, and the water that crept up his thighs and his stomach was so burning hot, he had to forget all about the rock and instead turn and walk towards land – and there it was, that thing lying on the sand, and he was drawn towards it but even so he might never have gone down on his knees and pressed first his hands and then his arms and then all of himself up against her if she hadn't asked for it, if she hadn't yelled at him to rape her.

It was then he ripped off his clothes, it was then he became so hot, no water in the world could have cooled him down, and no ban, not even the most scarifying, could have stopped him: always, he'd only been able to perform his best with the sort of girls that could overcome his weakness by flinging all the words you shouldn't say into his face as he pressed himself against them. He can't have known anything about how he hurled himself upon her and just what happened at the beginning, but he came to his senses a little when it was all over and he was panting as he pressed his lips against her hot, white ear and found his mouth filling with sand, and then he came round a little bit more when she twisted violently and with a thrust which only made him feel all the more delirious she bit his shoulder blade, and as she struggled to throw him off, and succeeded because he had no strength left to resist, he was more or less wide awake again and waded out into the water to rinse the rest of his heat away.

When he eventually returned to the fire, they were all sitting there as before, but not huddling in quite so much terror, and when he listened he realized the girl was silent now and he just wondered whether they knew everything, or part of it, or nothing at all. And then he realized that he didn't care, that it didn't matter what anybody thought or knew, all he could feel was the sense of jubilation, jubilation over finally having defied an instruction that something was prohibited, having disobeyed an order, having discovered for the first time how his own will operated, having seen that one can do whatever one likes, and that it's just marvellous to do it.

But for the first few hours, indeed, for a large part of that first day, he was still so paralysed with sheer joy that he automatically responded to the captain's whistles, but just occasionally it would dawn on him and he'd recall his incredible experience, rather like a new graduate the first day after the ceremony occasionally glances at the diploma hanging on his bedroom wall and, with a pang of joy, thinks to himself: wow, I'm a BA!

And there they are sitting around the white rock, when suddenly he remembers: Of course, I have a will of my own, I can do whatever I like on this island, I don't need to carve anything into this bit of stone; and so, shortly before dusk, he leaves the English girl and all the time he's thinking he won't go back, that nobody can make him go back if he doesn't want to. And so a little bit closer to sunset he's lying on his plateau and imagining himself as a badly treated nail that's soon going to be trimmed once and for all, but he's not afraid of that, he thinks. The image is so perfect and he's so proud of being able at last to do whatever he wants, and to think whatever he wants about anything he wants to think about.

He stands up and the world is stained red by the sunset, but the rock beneath him has a wet outline from his sweat; he doesn't want to think about that, though, he hears somebody approaching through the grass, and he climbs back over the parapet. It's about now I ought to be back there again, he thinks, that I ought to be standing down there on the beach listening to those idiots babbling away, but what do they want with a lion? Why bother about a lion when you can have sexual intercourse?

When he starts clambering down the hillside, however, he can feel a stabbing pain in a little bite on his right shoulder-blade, and he rubs it aimlessly with the index finger of his left hand, and thinks it's probably just a pimple after all.

10

They leave Madame to her fate, then, without having seen her lying there in the grass, and the iguana they've both seen and smelt, they're walking closely intertwined and Boy Larus is slightly taller than the English girl and he beats down the grass in front of them in triumph. They suddenly come upon a biggish hollow in the grass and so as not to remember what it was like when the captain caught up with him that time, he guides her to one side so that they only pass through untouched grass and all the time he thinks he's the one who's leading her, taking her to a quiet, hidden place where they can lie down together: the illusion of free will has so benumbed his mind that he thinks everything's happening because he wants it to.

But in fact it's the English girl who's leading them both to a certain place she has in mind, a quiet, undisturbed place that people rarely go to. Sometimes, she glances up at him when he's not looking and sees her reflection in his contented smile and if she hadn't made up her mind what she was going to do, she'd scream and run away from him because it's all so disgusting, the stench of his body, the musty dampness he presses into her cloth when he clasps her tightly, the fear of failure, although he's not yet aware of it, restricting his muscles and making his tender movements so horribly brutal.

She blesses the moment they arrive at the cliffs which fall steeply down to the beach at this point. There are two big rocks leaning towards each other in an embrace, and between them is a crevice, wide enough to let a big person pass through; it's the same crevice Tim Solider climbed down when he was chasing the box of his dreams; but there are no birds there now, the whole of the flat ground they're standing on and all the ledges on the cliff face are speckled with bird lime, and in the sunset it looks as if the rock is criss-crossed with red veins, as if the cliff face is bleeding.

He lets go of her because he's uncertain now, he hadn't expected anywhere so bare and inaccessible, and everything here is naked, everything so ruthlessly obvious when there's no darkness to hide in, no tall grass to give protection, and he's afraid his weakness will trickle all over his face and expose him, and in near-panic, he wraps his arms round her and presses her tightly to him in desperation.

'Shall we go into the grass instead?' he whispers, whispers because he's afraid his voice will tremble if he speaks out loud. 'This place is no good.'

A wave of sweat and dirty animal warmth breaks over her and she struggles to wriggle free, struggles, but struggles gently so that he won't have the slightest suspicion. She caresses her way free from his embrace, takes hold of him under his chin and raises it towards the red light and sees that all he wants to do still is to throw her down, bite her, and make animal love to her.

'Just a little while,' she says, 'we'll just stay here a little while. Then we can go into the grass and we can roll around together and you can bite me while it's all happening.'

And she notices with satisfaction how provoking little words can excite him, she doesn't need a whip to keep him there, all she needs is a few hot little words.

She grips him gently by his damp shoulder and pulls him down and they sit side by side on the cliff and watch tips of the rocks apparently burning away in the red, gradually fading light.

'What's it like, doing it with me?' she suddenly asks. 'You see, I'm so inexperienced, I don't know anything about it, maybe you noticed it was my first time.'

He bursts out laughing, and for that laugh alone she'd have done what she's going to do anyway, for nothing else but that.

'Don't worry about that,' he says, slapping her hard on the back. 'Don't you worry yourself about that. I gave myself a good wash afterwards.'

Her fingers suddenly became so full of desire to strangle him, but she has to control herself a bit longer, he's so much stronger than she is after all, and he'd only get even more excited and fling himself on top of her and yell: You're hot stuff! like he did that other time. Oh, he just lay there full of power and desire and translated her hatred into love.

'Why did you bite me?' she asks, stroking the hard membranes of his lips, 'why did you bite me so hard?'

He bursts out laughing again and fumbles awkwardly after her fingers.

'Why did you bite me, come to that?' he asks. 'You weren't exactly ice-cold yourself, you got your teeth stuck into me all right. You don't realize you're doing that sort of thing, you see, you just do it because you're feeling so wild. You did just the same, but you didn't know that, did you?'

And he grows more eager and he starts pawing her body and damp, cold hands start jumping like toads over her thighs.

'Once,' he whispers animatedly into her hair, 'once I had a bit of skirt who bit my ear, nearly bit my ear right off in fact, when we were doing it. You can feel the scar if you put your fingers just here.'

Nothing is too horrible to happen, nothing is so disgusting that it can't happen to her. He grabs tight hold of her wrist and her fingers throb with pain as she feels the bow-shaped scar on the inside of his ear.

'Can you feel it?' he whispers, and she can hear how excited he is at the memory of it all and she lets her hand fall.

Then she asks straight away, so that her silence won't alarm him, how it all happened, how they came to the boil together like that, as she can't remember much of what has happened since the boxer died, there's just a big white vacuum between then and now, and of course he delights in telling her all about it, with broad, boastful gestures, and that's exactly what she'd expected. And as he's telling the story, he remembers his great discovery, how she helped him to recover his will, and he feels he must mention that as well, and indeed stress it because it can help him achieve the right degree of superiority.

'And so the captain said,' he concludes, placing her poor head between his legs, 'and so the captain said: I forbid you to do that, I forbid it in the strongest possible terms; but later, when it had happened anyway, he said that since I'd done it even so, we can take it like men.'

Men, she thinks, men. Blowflies more like it. Men.

Blowflies. They crawl from one thing to another with all their filth and spread their wings and, the next time they meet, boast about how terrific it was to defile this or that bit of cleanliness.

Someone goes past in the grass quite close by, and they both sit up with a start for their separate reasons; but no one appears, and soon all is quiet again.

Now it's so dark that everything that's supposed to happen should happen, the stones are still glistening and when he looks into her eyes he can see a little red gleam and for the sake of that red gleam he thrusts himself upon her with his mouth and bites her lips hard.

'Your eyes looked so bright and enticing,' he says afterwards as she lies curled up in his arms, quivering with pain.

She strokes his hair which is cold and damp and sticky and clings to his skull like a thick, thick skin, and she whispers, 'Darling, before we go into the grass, can I ask you to do something for me?'

'Ask me whatever you like.'

'But I don't know if I dare, it sounds so odd.'

'Go on, say it.'

'Well,' she says, trembling a bit, but he just thinks it's because she can hardly wait to get into the grass, 'it all happened so quickly last night and I knew so little about it, I knew so little about my body and I knew nothing at all about yours. Can I, perhaps, can I see what you look like naked?'

He gives a whistle as he gets up and she'll make him pay for that whistle when the time comes, and for the horrible, disgusting way he flings his clothes off.

Then she cuddles up close to him and guides him very carefully to the edge of the crevice. They both look down and the sea is glittering red as if it were full of sunken lighthouses. He's standing right on the edge with just his feet clinging hard but unwillingly to the hard stone and gazing down at the beach thirty yards below and the gap is suddenly filled with soft dusk and all the sharp edges of the cliff are smoothed away and for a giddy moment he can feel the water sucking its way in between the rocks. Then she says slowly from just behind him, breathing heavily into his right shoulder, 'Just wait here a moment while I go into the grass. Stand just like that, don't hold on to anything with your hands, just relax, relax, that's right.'

It grows so silent and in the silence he thinks over her words, spoken like a photographer, and then, when it's too late, he remembers what she was like on the beach during the day, her looks and movements when she discovered what had happened to her during the night, but by then, all of a sudden, the little push has launched him out into space and he doesn't know if he's falling like a trimmed nail or like a hero, a lion hurls its roaring memory towards him and perhaps he remembers a tone of voice, the one that said: 'Why this last act of disobedience, Boy Larus?'

But it's too late.

11

He's been walking slowly at first, but suddenly he's in a hurry and he starts running up the cliff path, without really knowing why. Lucas Egmont, who's right at the front, feels the tug of a hand on his arm and when he turns quickly, a little bit afraid, he finds Tim Solider standing panting behind him, staring at the wounds in his chest, and then he looks down at the cliff and notices the trail of blood left by an iguana retreating into a bush and when he looks up again, he's smiling for the first time since he landed on the island.

'I see there's a bit of your shirt missing,' he says to Lucas Egmont. 'Thanks.'

Then he follows the trail into the bushes, but when he gets into the thick, almost impenetrable undergrowth, he regrets having given way to a temporary whim and emerges again into the grass without having tried to find and kill the iguana that attacked him. Just as he plunges into the grass, he can hear soft, animated voices coming from a nearby bush and withdraws rapidly so as not to disturb them. He follows the jagged line of undergrowth and eventually comes to a sheltered little corner between a steep cliff and a thick clump of bushes, but when he looks up he sees a whole crevice full of motionless iguanas, perhaps asleep. He feels a pain in his chest, but even so he sits down under the cliff: he's never been the frightened type, never been afraid of people who might want to hit him, injure him; he's only been afraid of his own body when it has suddenly disintegrated into its pitiful constituent parts before his terrified eyes, when his legs haven't been able to move because he's seen an illustration in a textbook about the way leg muscles are constructed.

He's not strong at all now, of course. His face is quite hollow with hunger and he can't carry any significant burdens, especially after his latest loss of blood, but then there's nothing to carry; however, despite all his weakness he doesn't feel as awful as that time when he thought he'd found a food chest but it turned out to be nothing more than a box of glass beads, a heavy, useless box on which he threw away all he had left of his old strength so that he could carry it back to his comrades in distress. It felt so awful on that occasion because he was alone, he felt rejected by everybody, and when his hunger really started and he couldn't resist it any longer, he was so happy to be rejected because in that case he wouldn't need to share anything he found with any of the others, he didn't need to feel solidarity — but nevertheless, solidarity forced itself upon him; it wasn't possible to be as solitary as he'd thought, and when he'd calmed down, he realized it was a good thing, that in fact it was the best proof there was that he was still functioning like a real, living person, that when anybody has ever been really under pressure, solidarity is as essential as food and water. You can't survive without others, it's as simple as that, and hence solidarity isn't in fact a trait of character; but there are moments when you feel lonely and abandoned by everybody, and if on such occasions people don't just think that even an outcast has his pride but instead display solidarity in a given situation when they might just as well have displayed contempt and malevolence instead, then solidarity is the only proof there is that you aren't an iguana, a creature that simply lets its skin grow when everybody turns against it.

Of course, that business with the glass beads was a terrible shock for him. He'd gambled everything on that possibility, sacrificed several nights' dreams, sacrificed several days' terror, and finally struggled hard with himself over how to divide it all up – and the result of his great efforts was simply: Madame's shrill laughter, the mistrust of the others, and then all the rancorous expressions. In a flash, his world had collapsed round about him, he lay there buried beneath a house of cards, a heap of illusions, and didn't dare to move in case the whole world came tumbling down.

What was the point of it all, what was the point of all the sacrifices, what was the point of all the courage, what was the use of all the good deeds if they only led to a ridiculous result? The boundless immorality of existence was suddenly crystal clear to him. Life was like running around in a gigantic labyrinth, one of those they have for children at certain sophisticated fairgrounds: in the middle was the pearl glittering so temptingly on its stone, and as a young man, you'd run into it rosy-cheeked and certain in the trust you placed in the honesty of the labyrinth, and you'd run round and round for the first few circuits in the happy certainty that you'd soon reach the centre. And so it went on, all your life through: you just kept on running, still convinced about life's goodwill towards all those people scurrying around eagerly; and only when it was far too late did you notice that the route you were following only seemed to be leading towards the middle. In fact, the builder had made several routes; and only one of them leads to the pearl, and hence it's blind coincidence and not all-seeing justice guiding the destinies of the runners, and only when it's too late to turn back, if at all, do you realize that what you've been devoting all your strength to only had a certain value in terms of effort, but could never lead to a practical result. In such circumstances, it should be no surprise or dismay to anybody if the more clear-sighted contestants break away and miss out a few circuits in order to find a short-cut to the centre. Call that immoral if you like, call it criminal behaviour if you must, but you should bear in mind that a human being's immorality can never hope to compete with the well-oiled, perfectly functioning criminality of the world order. On the one hand a rapidly flaring despair which takes on rather less than balanced forms, on the other hand a conscious immorality, gleaming coldly like nickel, proud of its coldness and its shininess.

Thanks to that terrible failure with the box of glass beads, he found himself more of an outcast than ever; he kept well out of everybody's way, and was careful to ensure that no one would have any cause for complaint against him. He tended the fire as if it had been a sick little child in need of constant care, and as long as there was still water slopping around in the keg, he dug it deeper and deeper down in the sand every day, so as to keep it cool. But he didn't do it out of a feeling of solidarity: on the contrary, he was keeping his solidarity on ice. What drove him to act as he did was the effort of a servant to conceal failure, just as obvious a reaction as sweating when suffering from *angst*.

But then came the morning when the water keg was empty and the sand underneath it soaking wet. He realized straight away that everyone would suspect him, and knotted his face to protect himself from all the heavyweight stares hurling themselves at it to tear it to pieces. The captain's attack was not as unexpected as that of the iguanas, for when he eventually came round and found himself on the beach with bits of cloth stuck in the big wounds, the giant lizard bites were all he could remember and he didn't spend much time wondering about how he'd got down there again, he just assumed casually he'd managed to find his own way and then fallen and nobody had helped him; but then, who would dream of assisting a glass bead catcher and a water thief?

However, soon afterwards when they were burying

the boxer and he was getting tired out from the least bit of effort, he started wondering about what had actually happened, and then the merest glance at the steep cliff convinced him how impossible it must have been for a solitary, badly wounded person to drag himself down such a precipice without falling. Somebody must have helped him, and he looked around to try and find out who. It couldn't have been either of the missing women: in the first place, they wouldn't have had the strength, and moreover, they always radiated that half-unconscious bitter coolness women often surround themselves with as a protection in case of attack. The captain was out of the question, of course, as this was a question of life and death and not some chivalrous parlour game. Actually, he was surprised the captain hadn't just thrown him straight over the cliff after the iguanas had bitten him. Boy Larus was much too loyal to the captain and wouldn't dare do anything he might have wished to do for his own sake but knew was against the captain's wishes.

That left Lucas Egmont, the Lucas Egmont nobody knew anything about, who maybe had something to hide or just looked as though he did – there are secretive faces just as surely as there are open faces. And as he was looking for him, he noticed the bits of cloth stuck in his wounds; of course, he'd seen them lots of times during the course of that hot day, but he hadn't thought about what they looked like or where they'd come from. Now, for the first time, he noticed the details. He felt them and discovered they were bits of fine, soft material, better quality than he'd ever felt before, and before they'd been stained by the dirt on the island and his own blood, they had been white, and part of a white shirt.

They were all stripped to the waist as they worked, but he walked over to the shadow of the cliff where their clothes were lying, and could see straight away that Lucas Egmont's shirt was the one in question. He stroked the soft, white cloth briefly in gratitude, but also because it felt so nice and cool against his skin, and when he went back to the grave, possibly intending to embrace his saviour, he saw him crawling up the beach with staring eyes and quivering lips, his hands full of wet sand which he used to cover up the empty water keg.

It was such an amazing sight, he just stood there, his arms dangling, and watched; and the other two had also stopped working and were staring at him, but Lucas seemed oblivious to the lunacy of what he was doing and kept on crawling with a patience that was almost intolerable to watch, backwards and forwards between the keg and the water, carving a little canal in the sand with his knees.

All of a sudden, it dawned on Tim Solider what the others hadn't yet realized: Lucas Egmont was the one who'd emptied the water keg, and Tim first grew hot with rage and wanted to run up to him and thrust his head under the water, again and again, till it no longer had the strength to raise itself any more, but then the heat of of the sun suddenly became so terrible that it wasn't possible to stick to a single resolve and he walked mechanically back to the water's edge below the boxer's grave and started carrying sand again, but his head was swimming. For a while, he actually felt sorry for Lucas Egmont: he wasn't an especially tall man at the best of times, more or less normal, but now as he crawled over the sand he seemed to be so hideously shrunken that Tim was tempted to leave the boxer to his fate and instead help to bury the water keg.

But then came his thirst and rubbed away like pepper and ginger against his guts and intestines and stomach and throat, his mouth and his dry, chapped lips hated Lucas Egmont with the greatest hatred in the world, or on the island, at least. But afternoon arrived and brought with it cooling shadows and quenched all hatred except just one and when they were sitting around the white rock and the captain was taunting him and hurting him with his biting superiority, he found once again he was in league with Lucas Egmont, he was the one Lucas Egmont was defending in his long speech, they were his thoughts Lucas Egmont was presenting to the audience, whether or not they were listening, gathered around the rock, and suddenly he felt the same overwhelming gratitude he'd just felt at the burial.

'Solidarity,' he thought, 'solidarity from a water thief, but solidarity even so, the only time anybody has offered me any here on the island. I mustn't reject it, because it's the only solidarity in the world, because it's the only sign provided so far by the world order that there may be cracks in its compact injustice.'

Now he's lying in the angle between the cliff and the undergrowth, thinking about Lucas Egmont's lion, a solitary lion. Oh, he doesn't need to wait until sunset before choosing sides, it's all clear to him already and he can start fighting straight away; he feels glad, para-doxically glad, because when all's said and done he's going to die at any moment, of his wounds, of hunger, of thirst, or of what at the moment is the worst of all, his bites. But he's glad because despite the late hour, he's been given an opportunity to show his solidarity with something, with an idea, with a fellow human being, with a symbol. He's glad because a life without water, a life without food, a life without cinemas and banana skins, chewing gum and church bells, can still give somebody who wants it a chance to defend himself against the indifferent criminality of the world.

Only symbolic? So what, what isn't symbolic? Aren't all our achievements, even if we are struggling in a world where there are millions of human relationships and where we have the destinies of millions in our fingertips, aren't all our achievements so pitiful even so, that the struggle we put up for them would be meaningless if we didn't acknowledge the symbolic significance of the struggle, the significance of the struggle as a struggle? Would it be possible to do anything at all, to perform a single deed, when the practical achievements are as puny as they are, if we didn't acknowledge symbols as practical realities?

Suddenly he can't bear to sit still any longer; he has holes in his chest but he thinks he can feel his life throbbing stronger than ever behind those two rust-coloured rags stuck there like corks in a big blood tank. He's weak, but in a stimulating way, rather like after a late-night party when you're on your way home and all the thoughts that have to be thought and still haven't been thought come surging in over you and you're almost stifled by your own weary vitality. He walks quite quickly through the grass, forces his way through a few clumps of bushes, feels the hard shells of several iguanas under his feet but has no time to worry about them. When he reaches the cliff there's still some time to go before sunset and he settles down to watch the clouds spreading out over the stranded horizon in large clusters, looking like the smoke from cannons firing a salute. He finds a stone up there as well, a narrow, wedge-shaped hard stone which might be useful if you want to carve something into a white rock. He takes it with him, as well as some branches he'd broken off on a previous occasion but left up here on the cliff, but when he gets down he suddenly remembers there's no fire burning anyway, and with an impatient gesture he throws the branches out into the water without paying much attention to where they go. He puts the stone on the rock and then stands gazing out over the lagoon, thinking about the shape of a lion. Then he suddenly feels a prick in his right ear, it's as if a little flash of lightning had struck home there and he turns round with the speed of a bird of prey and he sees the bird bobbing up and down like a big float where it's drifted in to the edge of the beach.

He's paralysed by the sight at first, he wants to laugh and to cry, and his face is actually contorted by a couple of sobs, but then he stiffens and looks round cautiously as he tiptoes towards the dead bird, as if he were afraid it would fly off and leave him all alone with his hunger, his desperate hunger which is spreading its flames and burning through all the ceilings and all the floors of his intentions and expectations. And then he races forward and jabs his fingers into the stinking bird and, holding it pressed tightly to his trumpeting chest, he gallops away over the beach, afraid all the time that someone will prevent him, shout at him to stop and share it. He slithers over the slippery ridge that marks the end of their strip of beach, and as he jumps on the shiny stones where little green animals with suckers as mouths are clinging and burst with a sploshy crack when he treads on them, as he stumbles over the uneven surface of this beach, he bursts out crying, violent, shuddering sobs which force out the blood from the wounds in his chest, and he's not crying with joy, not with joy at having at last found something to satisfy his hunger, no, he's crying with sorrow and hatred of himself because he hadn't been any stronger than that, and it's mainly from desperation he takes a bite out of the bird, from desperation rather than hunger, and suddenly he has a mouth full of feathers and he spits them out and then his mouth is full of loose, rotten meat and he vomits, lying face down on the slippery stones. And he vomits and vomits but that's not enough, he feels like a sewer and he must have water, lots and lots of pure water to rinse all this horrible stuff out of his system, and so he lifts up his miserable, shaking body as best as he can and crawls out into the water. But just here the bottom suddenly drops vertically and he can't move at all to save himself as he sinks and he's probably too disgusted by himself to want to even try and defend himself from the ocean which pours in through his mouth and chokes him. And he sinks and sinks as far as he can go and right to the very end he has rotten bird in his mouth.

12

The lion, king of the jungle. When Lucas Egmont is alone, he wanders around aimlessly through the grass and thinks thoughts about the lion. For someone like him from a northern country, it was always so exciting when, as a child, he heard the lion described as the king of the jungle, for there weren't any lions in his country and, in the poor area where he lived, a boy went to the circus just once and when he got back home a few lads from the street took him out into the courtyard and beat him up with skipping ropes in among the dustbins because he had a father rich enough to take him to a circus. It was offensive somehow that the lion, the lion from so far away, should be the king of the jungle; it was as if a Negro king in Africa had suddenly declared himself to be the king of some northern country and all anybody could do was to accept it because that's what it said in the school books.

Why is the lion king of the jungle, wonders Lucas Egmont as he wanders about in the grass, slashing at the long stalks. Why not the elephant, why not the python, why not man? Is it because the lion is stronger than all other animals, cleverer or bigger? No, it's probably not because the lion is all that remarkable an animal in fact, but it's got its status, been given its status because it's the best symbol for regality anybody can think of. The actual concept of a lion is so unusually attractive to the essential part of our ego which deals with symbols, which lives in the world of symbols, which we despise precisely because it isn't real, just as if there were anything especially honourable in being real, in being faithful to your reality, when there are so many unrealities it's much more important to be faithful to.

He kneels down in the grass and catches a little yellow butterfly with little red blotches on its wings, and as he holds it in his hand one of its wings suddenly drops off and turns into a clear drop of liquid which runs slowly down his clenched lifeline. He's never seen a butterfly like this before, and he pokes at it carefully with his nail, but even the slightest touch is obviously too much because it suddenly melts away and turns into a grey lump and when he blows at it, it wafts away like ash.

Is a struggle of this nature defensible at all, he wonders, and he can still feel the tickling sensation in his

307

hand from the drop of butterfly, and see the cloud of ash drifting down into the grass. Does it really make sense to give up any vestige of a struggle to survive, and instead to devote ourselves to squabbling about the shape of a lion? But if we were to keep on living, if we tried catching fish or digging a well that could supply us with water, if we devoted all our efforts to living for a few more hours, wouldn't that also be a symbolic act, a symbol for survival, not our own personal survival which doesn't matter a fig to us potential suicides, but a symbol for the survival of the human race, which doesn't worry us all that much either, but which our imagination, our talent for finding symbols, is so tempted to occupy itself with? Aren't all actions symbolic in fact, is there such a thing as a meaningless action? And you could also ask: is there such a thing as a meaningful action, or are there just symbolic actions? Aren't our actions, no matter how mad or how meaningless they might seem to a neutral observer, full of meaning when we have a specific symbolic intention when we perform them? When we tie a piece of string round the nearest oak tree and try to pull it down, it's just as meaningful an action as demolishing a house or hanging oneself in an attic, because all of them symbolize the meaninglessness of all human effort. Those summers when I was able to accompany a well-to-do family to an archipelago, there were always a few islands enveloped in a shimmering blue haze, and we never visited them because those islands symbolized for us the meaning of life, the shimmering, secret meaning of life, and it was so nice to have it constantly before our eyes whenever we gazed out to sea, the meaningless sea; and the butterfly you have in your hand and poke at until it falls to pieces wouldn't mean anything in itself –

for what's the significance of a drop of some sort of fluid and a little cloud of ash? – it wouldn't mean anything at all if it didn't symbolize the depravity of poking around, of poking too closely at the truth of the world.

He crouches in the grass, listening. There are plenty of voices and footsteps all round him, and he suddenly thinks of all the lions that have suddenly been born on the island and are trampling down the grass with their heavy paws. He's so curious about, and at the same time afraid of the others' decisions: it will be difficult for him to give way if the captain's lion turns out the winner, not for his own sake, as he likes to think the whole business doesn't mean anything to him, but for the others whose reality he's tried to identify himself with, having realized how terribly difficult they found it to formulate their opposition to the captain. He thinks it's their thoughts he's going round thinking, just as if you could think a single thought or express a single opinion without having to accept responsibility for it yourself, and he gets quite a shock when he suddenly finds he's come to the edge of the grass where there's a terrible smell of something dead which he nevertheless can't see, but he does see Boy Larus and the English girl with their bodies closely intertwined beside a cliff reflecting the red sunset. They sit up with a start when they hear him coming, and move apart, but he stands absolutely still, to fool them, and before long Boy Larus pulls her towards him again and he wants to run up to them and shout at them and ask what they think they're doing, kissing and cuddling has to wait when there's so much else at stake, there's a lion which is so much more important than any particular mouth, he's really upset, the identifier, that they have failed to justify his trust, but in the end he hasn't the heart to spoil their happiness and he glides away like a pike in the reeds.

Lots of people have left trails behind them in the grass now, and he follows a winding path into the undergrowth and notices for the first time how oddly shaped the bushes are, it's as if he'd never really seen them before, they'd only flitted past his eyes, looking green and prickly. As there is still a while to go before sunset, he has a good look at a big bush with bulging leaves and hairy branches. He tugs playfully at the bush's hair in an attempt to pull some out, but it doesn't budge at all. Then his fingers suddenly brush up against a little pouch hanging down from one of the branches above, and when he looks more closely he sees the whole bush is full of green pouches, miniature pumpkins, and when he plucks a few he notices a splashing sound from inside them. He thinks at first he's misheard, but when he holds one to his ear, he discovers it's full of some sort of liquid. He carefully breaks it in two and produces two halves, each of them filled with a clear liquid looking like water, and all at once he becomes so agonizingly aware of his thirst, and he has a sudden urge to throw the halves away and to run off so as not to be tempted any more, but instead he raises one half of the pouch towards his lips.

There's a violent rustling noise in a nearby bush and somebody comes rushing out and Lucas Egmont realizes he's been watched all the time.

'Be careful, Mr Egmont,' yells the captain, 'don't drink that whatever you do! That innocent-looking little green thing contains one of the most dangerous poisons there is. In some places in the islands, the natives dip their poisoned darts in it to make them really effective.'

310

Then Lucas Egmont's hands start shaking and the grass and the bushes flow out and are elongated like shadows in disturbed water, but the captain grabs him reassuringly by the wrists and although Lucas is thinking desperately about the lion, it's quite a while before he can keep his hands still. The captain pulls another fruit from the bush, however, and opens it, and they both go into a clump of undergrowth by the rock and the captain leans over the rock and places the two halves on the gleaming stone and then withdraws into hiding once more.

After a while, a big iguana comes crawling from near the edge of the cliff and they can see immediately it has caught sight of the two halves but, possibly because it's conscious of how terribly dangerous they are, it doesn't dare to go any nearer. It goes round and round them, but the circles get smaller and smaller and suddenly there it is, lapping up the contents of first one and then, after a moment's hesitation, the other as well. Then the iguana plays around with the empty shells for a while before suddenly leaping up into the air with a horrific growling noise, and Lucas Egmont thinks it's still playing but it's dead and stiff by the time it hits the ground.

The captain kicks the iguana casually over the edge of the cliff and they hear it hit the sand with a dull thud and when they eventually get down there themselves there are just three dead bodies waiting for them in silence and emptiness, two iguanas and one human. The captain puts his hand protectively on Lucas's wrist and smiles at him so intimately that Lucas can't help but realize what the captain expects of him in return for having saved his life.

One can put up with false friends, Lucas thinks to

311

himself as he draws back his hand, but God protect us from false enemies whose animosity you can't count on.

13

Oh yes, there are three dead bodies waiting for them, but no living person and the dead boxer is waiting for them more than ever. They don't notice at first, but when they kneel down by the white rock and start examining the stone Tim Solider had found for them, they hear an all too familiar sound: it's a piece of canvas flapping in the breeze, and they're both quite shocked when they see the boxer lying there, just as he was before they buried him, with only a piece of canvas over his body. Somebody has scraped away all the sand and the beach is churned up by feet that seemed to be in a very great hurry, and they think they can follow the trail, the light footsteps leading away over the sand.

But before they take up the chase, they go up to the boxer, cautiously, as though they're afraid he might suddenly get up and reveal his terrible secrets. They kneel down beside him and are almost bowled over by the stench, but he's hidden from their view: he's not only covered by a sheet of canvas, he's also wrapped in a piece of thick, grey cloth, the English girl's cloth.

They follow her trail the length of the lagoon. She's been uncertain about the precise route she should take, sometimes running out into the water as far as the point where the bottom suddenly falls away and it gets very deep, at other times she has splashed along in the shallows, or moved quite a way inland. Then the beach comes to an end, however, and a submerged rock runs out into the lagoon that peters out a bit further ahead and the girl has skirted round that before striking out at right-angles inland; it's all stone now, and hard to keep track of her, but occasionally she's strayed out into the mud and perhaps sunk down over her ankles before withrawing to the stones once more. The captain suddenly kneels down, and without a word points at a large rock a little way out in the water. There's a little red stain on it, fresh blood, still not congealed. Then there are more or less similar red marks on lots of stones leading to a low cliff that drops steeply down to the deep water below, some fifty yards beyond the end of the lagoon.

Lucas Egmont gets down on his stomach and shuffles his way to the edge of the precipice and shields his eyes with his hand so that he can see down into the water. It's all green for a long way down, but then he suspects the green gives way to something white shimmering through the water. But he can't make out any clear outline, the white patch just spreads and contracts, it could be a white rock or it could be a girl's corpse or it could be an optical illusion. It could be nothing more startling than an optical illusion. He throws a little stone at it, and watches it whirling round as it sinks before slowly coming to rest right in the middle of the white thing, like a frog on a cushion. But the next moment everything has disappeared, something has been edging its way along the bottom and stirring up the mud, and no matter how much he strains his eyes, he can't see anything, nothing at all of the white, just some kind of ray floating up and down between the bottom and the surface like an underwater lift.

When they get back to the beach, an enormous flock of birds takes off from some stones only a few hundred yards from where they are. The birds rise in complete silence, and when their curiosity drives them forward to investigate, they see a little white bundle bobbing against the rocks where the water occasionally surges in and tries to snatch it away.

'They're eating their own kind,' says the captain, kicking at a rock in scornful disgust, 'just like us.'

When they then sit down on either side of the white rock, they notice how the birds are hovering directly above them, more or less motionless, their gigantic wings outstretched.

But Lucas Egmont isn't really thinking about the unpleasant birds, he's thinking about all kinds of other things; he realizes straight away that none of the others will ever come back, because none of this was anything to do with them, because they weren't talking the same language, because they weren't talking any language at all, because they were just living for their unarticulated needs and had to be exploded when they suddenly discovered their needs could no longer be satisfied and they could no longer control their explosions. He has over-estimated their interest in opposing the immovable injustice of the world, their interest in the apparently meaningless action which is going to shake the world, their understanding of a man's essential task: to say at least half the truth about the whole lie that is the world. He's been identifying with them, not with them as they were but as what he thought they ought to be, and therefore, he acknowledges, therefore he must accept the awful responsibility of the identifier, the terrible burden; he must be like one of these people he's been identifying with. Hence he doesn't pay too much attention to the captain's obvious aim of frightening him when he suddenly raises his hands heavenwards and exclaims, 'Just look at those birds, Mr Egmont, those beautiful birds up there over our heads! How silent they are as they wait to have a go at our necks!'

14

Dusk is settling over the beach and over the sea and the water has almost ceased glittering. The wind gusts from time to time and there is a creaking from the masts of the ship, but apart from that, everything is more or less silent. One or other of them occasionally picks up a stone, throws it up in the air and catches it again, or drops it on to the rock, or one of them scratches a line on the rock but then stops because the other is staring at him so mercilessly.

In the end, the captain says, 'Well, it'll soon be dark, and if we're going to get started today we'd better get going as soon as possible, and we've got to know where we stand because it will be obvious even from the very first lines whether the lion is going to symbolize solitude or some kind of togetherness. I'm not at all clear about how you envisage the whole thing. You're talking about a solitary lion, right, but how is a lion that's so alone going to be able to symbolize anything other than solitude, a particular kind of solitude, not total solitude, as opposed to my lion with it's foot on the dead body?'

Lucas Egmont responds to that as follows:

'In the first place, it wasn't my suggestion from the start that we should choose a lion, but when that was what was agreed, it seemed to me the image of the lion you were proposing was quite unacceptable. Unacceptable because it celebrates cruelty, the cruelty of anyone who, voluntarily and with eyes wide open, embraces solitude, kills off anything that is weak and fragile, anything that needs togetherness, so that eventually all that will survive will be cruel, solitary creatures, the kind who love solitude as the only thing they can comprehend. A solitary lion, on the other hand, sitting there without trampling anyone underfoot, is something completely different. I won't go as far as to suggest it represents togetherness, but it does demonstrate calm strength, the whole personality, the harmony which might be rent asunder at any moment by the roar of a wild beast. Terror and harmony in the same character, you see, that's my lion. Personally, I'd have preferred to take a snake as a symbol. It's easier to carve into a rock, and it also says more about the horror that suddenly surges through your veins like a blood clot when it gets dark and your enemies find it so much easier to hide both themselves and their intentions.'

'I'm sticking to my lion,' says the captain. 'Good God, what do you know about solitude? What do you know about the loneliness one feels in an attic after the roof has blown off and sailed away like a pair of swan's wings? What do you know about the boundless solitude of the world, it's greater than anyone dares to imagine, apart from a few ecstatic moments when there's nothing you can do about them, but even so, you can feel it in every nerve-end.'

'I don't think anybody can take any account of your kind of solitude,' says Lucas Egmont. 'You enjoy it. As far as you're concerned, it's the greatest pleasure the world has to offer, instead of the greatest injustice. You're never alone in fact, you always carry your solitude around with you, you have your head stuck in it as though it were a big bag, and when you want to

316

experience yourself, because that's what you're doing when you say you're experiencing solitude, like a masturbator, when you want to experience yourself, all you do is pull the bag further down over your head till you almost choke and there's nothing you like more than choking. Just remember that.'

'It's not true that I enjoy it,' says the captain, 'but you must understand that the only way I can bear the enormous solitude that so often affects me is to accept it as a gift, as a welcome delight; and that's also why I think the little loneliness, the thing that X or Y feels when the mood strikes him, is much more dangerous to the health of the world than mine. Only the strongest of men can bear a solitude like mine. You need the right kind of ear-drums for a start, strong ear-drums that can put up with the terrible weight pressing down on them when space suddenly starts singing of solitude.'

'Have you really heard that song you talk about?'

'Oh yes, of course, quite a lot of us have heard it. And you!'

'Yes.'

'I can teach you to hear it if you like. It's quite easy, you see; of course, it's hardest the first time, but after a while you learn how to do it and it only needs a certain kind of thing to happen, feelings of aversion radiating towards you, contempt, hatred, and suddenly there you are, in this, the clearest of all spaces.'

The captain has gone over to Lucas Egmont's side, and now he sits down beside him and lifts up his hand and strokes it over his own as if it were a bow. Lucas glances at him and sees his face is covered in sweat, covered in crawling sweat.

'Are you so afraid,' he says contemptuously, taking

317

his arm away, 'are you so afraid of being alone? Can't your ear-drums cope any longer?'

'I'm not afraid,' answers the captain vehemently, 'I'm not afraid of being alone.'

Then he suddenly falls silent and stares down at the sand, and fear starts shaping his face skilfully, replacing his dimples with terror lines and the furrows get deeper and deeper. He picks up the stone and starts tapping it on the rock, making big black holes in the silence.

'What would you do if I left you?' asks Lucas Egmont. 'It would be so easy for me to run away after all, I could run up into the grass and hide there as long as you like and not reply no matter how much you shouted to me, not reply even when you started crying and sobbing out my name.'

'I wouldn't go looking for you,' says the captain curtly, 'I'd just take this stone and carve a lion, the lion that's on the back of my boot with a dead human underneath it, and then when I'd done that I'd lie down beside the rock and slowly glide into the ultimate solitude and my ear-drums would burst and my heart would stand still, but that wouldn't matter because I'd never have been able to penetrate any further into solitude than that anyway.'

'Would you take that frightened face of yours with you as well?' asks Lucas Egmont. 'Do you think that would burst as well, or that it would keep its fear even when your space started singing?

'Do you think I don't understand,' he goes on passionately when the captain looks the other way, 'do you think I don't understand all this perfectly well, understand why you've come and sat down beside me now, hoping to infect me with your solitude? It's because you've noticed we're suddenly on our own, that all the others have disappeared into the sunset and will never come back. They simply weren't interested in what we were planning to do, in all that lion business; not even your pretty little underling Boy Larus obeyed you on this occasion: just before I came down I saw him cuddling the English girl on a cliff up there. Now you're so frightened I'll go away as well that you're trying to keep me here by making me just as sick as you are, by infecting me with the same terrible illness as you have. Of course it's true you've been alone before, as you say, but as you're realizing, that was something quite different: you've always had unlimited access to other people, you've always known you would wake up out of your drugged sleep into a normal environment containing just as much solitude as you needed in order to become fully conscious again. But here, you don't dare to dive down into your great solitude because you never know what things are going to look like when you come back again. By then, here could be an even greater solitude than any of those others you've experienced during the whole of your life hitherto, and you want to guard against that by taking me with you: but you won't succeed, and that's why you're miserable and bitter now, and don't dare to look me in the eye because I've told you the truth as it is. But you'd better watch out: I'm also infectious. I've also got a disease, but I'm not going to try and pass it on to you, because you'd certainly never understand how to bear that illness, because you'd just think it was a pleasure, like all the other illnesses you've ever had.'

'What kind of an illness is that, then?' asks the captain in a hollow voice, his face averted.

'It's the illness called guilt,' says Lucas Egmont. 'It's also a disease you can play around with like you do, you

319

can also turn it into a pleasure if you want to, it can also uplift you into the most extreme states of bliss. In any case, I can assure you it's a terrible experience to wake up with a throbbing head, without having been to a party the night before, suddenly to wake up and feel you haven't the strength to get up any more that day, that week, that year or that life; simply not have the strength, you see, because you're bearing all the guilt in the world like a pillar of copper on your forehead, and every attempt to get up will just mean you fall over and suffer terrible injuries and you want to avoid that. Ah well, you lie there for a few days until someone comes along and establishes that you're not ill at all, just too lazy to get up. Start dancing the Charleston, they tell you, and you'll be fine, all your joints will be perfect. And of course you want to be perfect, in your joints and everywhere else, but it's not long before you discover perfect doesn't mean what you thought it meant, not by any means. Oh no, being perfect means mainly turning a blind eye on the guilt of the world, it means dancing on the left-hand side of the dance floor when there's shooting and bloodshed going on over to the right. Well, obviously, you can get used to it after a while; I've got used to walking upright, for instance, as you can see, though it was a bit hard at first, that's true, with all your advisers crowding round and considering and thinking and passing opinions to the effect that it wasn't worth overdoing things. That it was best to have a rucksack with you when you went walking through forests and over moors. Of course, you were grateful for so much helpfulness, but it couldn't do much about that fault which you considered to be the biggest one in the world: that there were so few people helping each other to bear the guilt of the world, so few with a conscience that the burden they had to bear was almost intolerable. You see, the guilt of the world is something quite different from the world's solitude: there are so many of you sharing the world's solitude that there isn't all that much of it for each one of you to bear, just a reasonable burden for a man to put up with, if that; but when it comes to guilt, you're overloaded.'

'What was it you felt guilty about? What have you done, what crime have you been guilty of?'

'Ah, that's what's so paradoxical about it all, you see. I haven't done anything, or at least, I hadn't done anything – not then. I was completely innocent – and yet I felt guilty. I thought I was responsible for everything that happened, it was my fault that the slum where my parents still lived even after I'd rented a little room closer to the bank, that the slum was teeming with children suffering from consumption, it was my fault that so many old people died in poverty in hostels dotted all over the city, and I even felt stabs of guilt every time I saw a beggar or some poor soul with pock-marks all over his face. Of course, I tried to help, using all the means at my disposal in order to reduce my guilt, and I tried all the channels open to a citizen who wants to do something to assist the underprivileged, but I have to say I found all of them inadequate, and in some cases criminally inadequate. The charities disgusted me with their onanistic self-satisfaction, it was as if they had to look at themselves in a mirror after every good deed to check whether they'd acquired a new little wrinkle round their mouths advertising their kindness. The political parties spent far too much energy on peripheral questions, claimed they were transforming the whole of society, a transformation which would liberate the world from the injustices currently bearing down on

321

my forehead, in the long run: but that was just a cynical way of referring to a permanent postponement, that's what they really meant. Occasionally they took up some of the problems of the very poorest in their propaganda, and what really disgusted me most about the whole thing was the way the poverty of the world was used as advertising material for a political party, that a self-evident thing like reducing the number of children with tuberculosis became a publicity stunt for a party whose behaviour in other respects has to be regarded with suspicion and even contempt. No, for guilty people like us there was no organization, the distress of the world was being taken in hand by people who'd ceased to feel guilty, if they ever had felt guilty at all, because they lived under the illusion that they were doing such an awful lot to ease it. The biggest problem, it seemed to me, was that people were talking so much about ideas, that's what took up so much of their energy; but I think ideas are something for the nursery. You need ideas, of course, but you should play with them; ideas are the pretty little toys grown-ups play with. It seemed to me, contests concerning ideas were taking place at the wrong level altogether: instead of sitting round tables where the fate of the world is supposed to be decided with the ideas they cherished so unscrupulously and with such sadistic logic, they should have been gathering at tennis courts and playing tennis for their ideas, or in a big theatre where they could act out scenes with them, or in big, green meadows where they could chase after them in the sunshine with butterfly nets. There's nothing more dangerous than taking ideas seriously, and nothing more praiseworthy, in fact I'd go as far as to say it's the only praiseworthy thing in this life, than taking ideas for the playthings they are in fact. Here we are, you and me, sitting here playing, and there's nothing in the whole world more important than this lion, yours and mine. Symbol as symbol – there are no gradations in the world of symbols, everything is equally big or equally small, that's what's so splendid about it. What happened next? Well – I grew tired of not being able to do anything but feeling as if I could do everything; I was falling between two stools, and in that situation I made up my mind on one thing. I decided to acquire real guilt, guilt I could really accept on my own behalf, guilt I could describe as being my very own so that I was the one who should bear it and nobody else. And so I pulled off a pretty bold feat of embezzlement, and with substantial funds in my pockets I'd left the country on the very first day of my holiday and was well on my way to a life to be lived in relative freedom from guilt; but it all turned out rather differently from what I'd expected.'

He's been talking into the space beyond the cliff, oblivious of everything round about him, and now the captain takes advantage of his carelessness and hurls himself on top of him, and as he presses his back ruthlessly against the rock, he shrieks, 'Now you help me to carve my lion into the rock, we'll have no more of this nonsense, I've had enough of your stupid prattle. Why do you think I saved your life – so that you could get in my way? Don't you think I had a reason for stopping you drinking that devil's potion? The point was that you need at least two people to do a job like this, the work involved calls for two people, you might say. I can force you to help me because I'm stronger than you, oh yes, I can buy you because I've got pockets full of glass beads and that's the only currency we've got here on the island.'

The edge of the rock is cutting into his shoulder-blade like a knife, and although Lucas Egmont twists and turns, he can't break loose.

'Captain,' he whispers, 'you can't force me the way you say you can. You can beat me to death, but you can't force me to carve that lion of yours. You can even tie me up, but when I'm tied up you've got even less chance of making me do what I don't want to do. And in any case, I've no reason to be grateful to you for saving my life in the way you think.'

No, he has no reason at all to be grateful. This is a life and death struggle, and the question of gratitude is hardly the most important one. It's more important to know whether you are capable of killing someone who's saved your life. Maybe you can.

'This isn't fair play, captain,' he goes on, 'and it's not doing you any good. You're just wasting time and it's getting darker and darker. Before long we won't be able to distinguish the drawing on your boot any longer – you've got to remember we haven't got a fire any more. No, there's another way, a way that's fair play and is quickly settled, and what we do is to set each other tasks, difficult ones but not impossible, and whoever fails to perform what's asked of him has lost, and his lion is defeated.'

The captain releases him and sits down on the other side of the rock and keeps tapping away incessantly at the leg of his boot.

'We'll draw lots to decide who goes first,' says Lucas Egmont. 'Whoever gets the stone I have in one of my hands has lost.'

He holds out both his clenched fists and, after a little worried hesitation, the captain chooses his left hand and there's a stone in both of them and quickly and

324

unobtrusively he drops the little stone in his right hand on to his knee and then holds it out to demonstrate that it's empty.

The captain stands up and an anxious little smile flits round his mouth like a butterfly.

'Well, what have you got lined up for me, Egmont?' he asks, pretending to be unconcerned although he's shaking like a leaf.

'Swim across the lagoon,' says Lucas quickly so that his voice doesn't tremble.

'There and back?'

'Yes, there and back.'

'Fully dressed?'

'No, stripped to the waist.'

'With my trousers and boot on?'

'Yes.'

He pulls his shirt off and throws it to Lucas Egmont, and he's shivering although it's not in the least cold as he strides down the beach and then wades slowly out into the water. It's that green moment of twilight when the world is filled with intense light, the night sticks its tongue out of its black mouth, and how light it is all around it! The surface of the lagoon is like a silken cloth, and it rustles almost like silk as the captain wades through the water. He wades as far as he can before starting to swim, the water is almost up to his shoulders when he launches himself into his first stroke, and then his head is bobbing up and down in the water like a floating drum, and he dips his forehead into the water and there's just a thick tuft of black hair visible over the surface as he cuts a little black furrow into the green water. Then he starts accelerating, and his boot is splashing away almost over the surface, and when he's about halfway across the lagoon it happens. The fish

325

must have worked its way underneath him without warning, and all he can manage is a short, stifled shriek which doesn't ruffle the smooth surface of the lagoon in the slightest, but just for a moment it rips apart the air round about Lucas Egmont and he finds it hard to breathe for a short while. But then the captain's shredded body can't manage to float any more, his head disappears as quickly as a float after a bite, and all is calm and peaceful. The silken surface of the lagoon has been slightly rippled, that's the only glimpse one has of the world's wounds, but soon it reverts to its smooth, green, shiny ruthless self.

15

Now Lucas Egmont is all alone, more alone than he's ever been before, even more alone than he's been when among sympathetic people. He throws the captain's shirt out into the lagoon, but regrets that immediately and wades out to retrieve it and instead he spreads it out over the freezing cold dead body. Then he sits down for a while beside the white rock, fiddling with the stone, and suddenly it occurs to him that neither of them, neither the captain nor he himself, had brought that stone down the cliff. But somebody must have done so. It can't have been the English girl, who was definitely down here on the beach after everybody else had dispersed: she was too blinded by her double desire, for the dead Jimmie Baaz and the living Boy Larus, to have been capable of anything of the sort. It can't have been Boy Larus, either: he was too busy trying to make love to the English girl. There's been so sign of Madame, and she looked so strangely vacant from the moment she spat out all her fear at Tim Solider's face when he lay there, bitten by the iguanas. Tim Solider. It must have been Tim Solider. And he remembers that Tim Solider was the only one who seemed to be interested in the lion when they were sitting arguing round the rock earlier in the afternoon; and he picks up the stone and tries to find his footsteps in the sand, but of course, it's a hopeless task when there's such a confused mass of footprints running off in all directions over the beach. Then he suddenly notices something white shining through the dusk, it's not far from where the fire was and it's a bird's feather and then he remembers the flock of birds that is still circling over the beach, but less purposefully now that it's started to get dark. He throws the stone away in the direction of the cliffs, and with the feather in his hand he rushes over towards the dead bird which hasn't been sucked out into the open sea yet, but is still bouncing backwards and forwards between its rocks. Then he sees him more or less straight away. He's hanging at a strange angle, with his head pointing downwards and one foot just under the surface, trapped in a little crevice, and he's fallen forwards and broken his foot so that his body is hanging down vertically. He takes a firm hold of the foot and tries to prise it loose, but it's well and truly hooked and it's incredibly difficult to do anything about it. Eventually, he gives an enormous tug and it comes loose, but he hasn't reckoned with how fantastically heavy the body is, and he loses his grip and the corpse sinks so fast and so deep that he has no chance of grabbing it again.

It's still grass-green dusk when he makes his way back, and he's unhappy in quite a new way. There's nothing he can do about it, but there's a persistent little worry nagging away at first one corner and then

327

another of his confidence, and in the end he lies down by the dead fire and tries to work out what's what. He really can't find anything to console him, and after lying there for a while he gets up and goes back to the rock which is now gleaming like a magic charm in the darker twilight; and he's sure so much struggling can't have been in vain, there must have been some point, the point must be that he should finish off things, including what Tim Solider wanted to help him with: he must carve that lion, his own and Tim's lion, before it gets even darker. He searches for the stone and then he lies down beside the rock in a comfortable posture and he can hear from the sound of the sea and the flight of the birds and the walk of the iguanas how intimate night is preparing to make its entrance.

– and that's when the terrible thing happens. He's raring to go, he's holding the stone tightly in his hand, he's lying in the right position by the rock, and it's not too dark for him not to be able to make out every detail in his carving for some time yet, everything's as it should be and he's been fighting to overcome all doubt and all doubt has been overcome, and even so, a terrible thing like this can happen: all of a sudden, he can't remember what a lion looks like, and the captain's lion, the only model, is lying dead on the bottom of the dreadful lagoon.

Oh, how he struggles to remember: he rolls around in the sand, he lies still in the sand and closes his eyes and tries to set the stone tracing lovingly round a shadow he remembers from his childhood, a lion on a circus poster, a lion in a zoology textbook; he tries to draw in the sand but the result is so awful that he bites at the sand in fury till he has a mouth full of sand and is choking and coughing and, blinded by the sand, he staggers around the beach and bumps into the cliff, falls on his knees in the water, stumbles over the burnt-out fire, falls over the white rock, and for one horrible moment grabs hold of the dead body and when he realizes what it is he shrieks like a lunatic and swallows the sand and rushes up towards the cliff face and stands there with his back to it and gapes around in all directions with his wild, still half-blind eyes, as if trying to protect himself from the most awful thing of all.

That's when the lions appear. With swishing tails and manes scattering rain and sand, they come thundering down the beach and stand roaring in front of him. There's an enormous mass of lions, the whole beach is full of them, indeed, no doubt the whole island, for now he can hear the swishing tails and fluttering manes high above his head and he curls up until he's the most insignificant of nonentities and in fact they don't seem all that interested in him, they swing round in the sand in front of him and the dust rises like a cloud and blinds him completely, they leap out roaring into the water, showing no respect in their bellies for the sharp fish, and they snort like horses in the water and when they come back again they shake themselves so carelessly that he's soaked and then they suddenly come racing down from the cliff and jump over him and land with their horrific limbs so close to him that his whole mouth is filled with sand and he bends forward and vomits convulsively and his head is a roundabout of roaring, panting, snorting and bellowing from unfortunate animals on the island which have got into the most awful mess and as he lies there vomiting a dribbling lion stands astride him and growls with its upper lip curled threateningly and the stink from its dirty, predatory teeth envelopes him in a stifling cloud. If only they'd go away, if only they'd go away again, now he knows everything about lions and, with both eyes closed, he draws one lion after another in the air around him until his arm is bitten off, and actually he doesn't have his eyes closed although he thinks he has, it's just that he's blinded by the sand and by fear.

Suddenly everything is ghostly silent, and all at once he can see again although that's what he wants least just now, and what he's forced to see while his blood and life are running out of him through the hole where his bitten-off arm was is the most terrible thing in the whole world. One of the lions has been down to the bottom of the lagoon and sniffed out the drowned captain and now he's sitting quite still on the lion's back, blue in the face and with motionless, staring eyes and his hair sticking down over his forehead like a horn, and, painfully slowly, they're coming towards Lucas Egmont. Get down on your knees, whispers the dead mouth, and he kneels down and screams the second before the lion gives him that fatal blow on his head, 'You won, you were the winner, I give in.'

But suddenly the world seems to have been transformed, and he's reincarnated as a young male lion, bristling with life and eagerness; he races up the cliff and then leaps down again in death-defying abandon, whipping up the sand with his frenzied rutting dance; effortlessly and playfully he knocks down the young lioness which playfully bites him in return for his boldness, and as the stars explode and the roars of the lions rip him apart and he them, night falls and stifles everything in its narcotic embrace. Its mask settles over everyone and everything, and now comes deep, terrible, liberating sleep.

16

He wakes up and it's still night and a handful of distant stars are trying in vain to come closer. He stretches, and realizes from the darkness and the silence that he's at the bottom of the world. Indeed, Lucas Egmont is at the bottom of the world, because the fact is, you can't just keep on falling for ever; the ego has an endless succession of glass roofs, but under the lowest of them is a bottom, a haven for the seeker, for a seeker about whom they said he'd go far when he was little, but all he's done is sink, deeper and deeper – right to the bottom.

At the bottom of the world, it's big and hot and silent, but not so big and hot and silent that anybody who's fallen can't make himself at home and feel comfortable for the brief moment he's there. When you're at the bottom of the world, you can ask every question and think every thought without needing to be afraid of the unknown, giddying depths beneath you. The bottom of the world is free from fear in that it's the secure bottom for all fear, and free from fear in that anyone who's landed up there is already familiar with all kinds of fear: the fear of death, the fear of cramp, the fear of hunger, the fear of a cycling accident and a sharp scythe, the fear of falling and the fear of landing in the ditch, the fear of the market square and fear of the hearse and all the other fears that adorn the whole of the way from the bottom of the world to its surface. But the bottom of the world is also free from many other things: it's free from love and free from hatred and free from guilt and free from happiness, free from hope and free from disappointment, because on the way there the seeker has peeled off everything that adorned or disfigured him and now he's completely naked, more naked than ever before, he has neither the swimming trunks of doubt nor the bath-robe of hope to hide behind, but it's not too dark for him to contemplate himself and see what he looks like without any kind of disguise, without any mask, and on that basis he can fix his position in the world, even though he's already dead and, with closed eyes, can observe the place where the drowning happened.

What I want is to do what's right, he thinks, I want to do all I can to carry out the rightest of right actions. Everybody goes on about doing the right thing, they take it so seriously, they go on about the man who does the right thing, but how can anybody be so cruel as to overlook the man who tries to do the right thing but is interrupted at the wrong time? What about the character who gets cut off by a stammer or an epilectic fit with fatal consequences, or the bloke who just forgets something: he can't remember what a lion looks like while it's still light, and before it gets really dark the beach is suddenly filled with lions that demonstrate exactly what a lion looks like and while there's still a chance of doing the right thing, of carving the image of the lion into the white rock, one of those lions bites off the only arm that can perform the only right thing, and then all of a sudden he's in possession again of not only his arm but also the memory of what a lion looks like, but by that time it's so dark there's nothing to be done. Is there any salvation for him? Oh yes, there just has to be some form of salvation, if you can talk about salvation rather than foundering. Maybe neither of those are appropriate. Why should we succumb, come to that, and how should we go about succumbing if we don't believe in some punitive supreme being above all other supreme beings? But otherwise, of course, it would fit in with our immoral world order if it weren't sufficient to put up with your pleasures and your problems while you're alive, but even later as well. It would fit in just perfectly with the Justice envisaged by our world order, with her miserable expression, and the brutal iron mask superimposed on the face twisted by desire.

What a splendid idea, that we should be judged according to whether we do right or wrong! There are so few of our actions we have control over. Pure chance, which can be distinguished from pure justice only because as yet it hasn't got any bandages on, sets off and rounds off our actions; and what we can do and of course ought to do and indeed must do because of our conscience, whose very existence is so often queried, is to let ourselves be propelled in a particular direction, and how stubbornly we cling to that direction. But we know thanks to the most wide-open of all the world's wide-open eyes that, as often as not, the goal is an illusion, and the important thing is the direction, because that and that alone is what we have control over. And awareness, oh yes, awareness: the open eyes which fearlessly scrutinize their dangerous position must be the stars of our ego, our only compass, the compass which decides which direction we take, because if there is no compass, there can be no direction. But if I put my trust in the direction, I have to question statements about human wickedness, because within a direction which might well be splendid in itself, there can be tendencies for both good and evil.

Just as you could say man has a natural tendency

towards evil, you could also say man has a natural tendency towards good, an irresistible urge to be good which can sometimes land him in ridiculous situations. I, Lucas Egmont, have naturally had to face up to both what they call good and evil within me. Once I'd been out fishing, and had to catch the last train home, or else be faced with several miles' walk: I was late, and I could hear the train chugging down the valley. Then I came across some little children looking for some house or other, I could hear them as I ran past on the road, but I was in such a hurry I couldn't possibly think of stopping; but as I approached the station, my pangs of conscience rose up like swelling lumps in my chest and when I got to the platform just as the train was steaming in, my stupid sense of kindness forced me to retrace my steps and help them to find their way, but just as we were about to say goodbye, the boy said something innocent which made me see red and I boxed his ears and his nose started bleeding and he screamed as if he'd been stabbed, but I really enjoyed it because I'd managed to make up for my paradoxical kindness via my para-doxical wickedness. I don't want to go along with the distinction between good and evil actions or even that between right and wrong actions, but just that between controlled and uncontrolled actions, conscious and unconscious actions; and since the most important thing is to maintain the direction aiming at the final goal, or indeed the more or less invisible goal, that is in fact the main distinction between controlled and uncontrolled actions.

As we're not alone in the world, or at least, not as alone as we'd like to be, we have an obligation to keep our explosions under control, to let our unavoidable explosions of paradoxical wickedness or paradoxical goodness proceed in the approximate direction of the approximate goal. As far as the goal is concerned, it may not be so desperately important so pin it down with the same sadistic precision as the one with which the world order and pure chance form a fascinating partnership and pin down the human condition in time and space. Of course, we have to fight about both those concepts, and since the most important thing is the right direction aimed at the possibly false goal, we need to sharpen our awareness until it becomes as sharp as a sword-blade, and sharp as an arrow-head supplemented by the brutal strength of a drill. Then our conscience operates in our consciousness, which is after all just an idyllic description of our fear, for our fear reminds us constantly of the right direction, and if we stifle our fear, we also lose the opportunity of directing our thoughts in a particular direction and we give vent to a series of stupid private explosions, first here and then there, which give rise to the greatest possible damage and the least possible result. That's why we must keep our fear alive within us, like an ice-free harbour which can always help us to survive the winter. The bubbling undercurrent beneath the winter floods.

Until I found my direction, I was living like an irresponsible freelance dynamiter who could feel guilt but had no idea how to expiate it. I was like a live bomb which could go off at any time, and not even I understood how it worked or when it would explode, I was just floating around like a fleck of soot in a gutter. I embezzled money from the bank in a completely meaningless fashion, I landed on that boat at Ronton just as pointlessly, and I emptied our communal water supply driven by the ridiculous straw of the freelance dynamiter: being faithful to your little distress.

But it was only when we'd discovered the white rock and the struggle over the lion began that my real life started. Only then did I acquire a direction towards a goal that was incontestably attainable, but in the end it didn't matter because it's the struggle that counts and not the goal, and because it's the joy of the struggle and not the joy of the goal that prevents you from going under, for there is a 'going under', even if it's not something concrete: going under is to live unawares and die happy without having struggled to achieve a meaningless goal, going under is to die calmly and peacefully without having put up meaningless resistance to the great meaninglessness of the world, going under is to spread your explosions over the enormous firing range of chance, going under is to shout like Lucas Egmont did then: I shall be faithful to my thirst, but unfaithful to everything else; or like somebody else: I shall be faithful to my hunger, but unfaithful to everything else; or like a third person: I shall be faithful to my sex, but unfaithful to everything else; or like some other person: I shall be faithful to my obedience, but unfaithful to everything else; or like this one: I shall be faithful to my paralysis, but unfaithful to everything else; or that: I shall be faithful to my longing but unfaithful to everything else; or again: I shall be faithful to my grief, but unfaithful to everything else; or finally: I shall be faithful to my fear, but unfaithful to everything else.

No, the only possibility is to say: I shall be faithful to my direction and faithful to everything within it: my fear, my hunger, my thirst, my despair, my grief, my longing, my paralysis, my sex, my hatred, my death. Oh yes, within my direction I shall be so faithful to my death that without so much as a shudder, but in grateful diffidence towards the fact that I've been allowed to live, I shall be able to walk down the beach, wade slowly out into the water, and there –

17

And he walks down the beach and the sand is soft and warm and so far his toes wallow in it, full of longing, but now he's come to the firm, wet sand which cools his burning, naked soles like a drink. And he continues slowly into the water and feels its cool softness rising over his feet, burying his feet, burying his ankles, slowly rising like a cool and merciful breeze up his legs, his kneecaps hover on the surface before sinking and the water licks his loins like a soft, rough tongue, the soft, rough tongue of death. And the water rises over all his memories of all his cool moments and all his hot moments, over all the burning words whispered just at the moment when . . . And the water ripples gently up his stomach and moistens the thirsty little mouth of his navel and his rib cage, rising and falling, suddenly finds itself enclosed in a much bigger, a much softer cage, and the tiny tips of his nipples suck at the surface, then comes his neck with its elegant little hollow as if made for water to trickle into, and his Adam's apple which he doesn't need any more because all his screams have already been screamed gives in without protest to the desires of the lagoon, and already a little wave is lapping against his chin, it comes out of the darkness and rolls on into the darkness behind him, and his chin sinks and his mouth kisses the water and they are just as delightfully cool, it and his mouth, and suddenly he's swimming. His legs and his trunk and his shoulders and his head rise gently from the darkness of the bottom to the darkness of the surface and his arms become wings and his body glides silently like a boat with raised oars through the gentle water and his ear which is resting on the water line suddenly hears the slight splashing sound from the bottom far beneath him and his eye which is leaning out over the blind surface of the lagoon fancies it can see the rapid change from green light to black light down below and he glides forward a few more inches before it's all over, before he's ceased to exist, ceased to exist for everyone and everything apart from the water for a short while, but a memory lives on a little longer at a certain bank, among a few pale counter clerks, in a man he used to buy illegal cigarettes from, a girl with sweaty armpits but healthy teeth who used to come up to his room on Wednesdays and share his bed, among a few iguanas he had come across on an island, and perhaps as the sharpest memory of all in the sword of the fish whose tigerish shadow is just now roaring up towards him – and then: *finis*.

STIG DAGERMAN (1923–1954) was regarded as the most talented young writer of the Swedish postwar generation. He grew up on a small farm in Älvkarleby, Sweden, and moved to Stockholm at the age of eleven. He published his first novel, *The Snake,* at twenty-two, and by the time he was twenty-six he had published four novels, a collection of short stories, a considerable volume of journalism, and four full-length plays. This body of work catapulted him to the forefront of Swedish letters in the 1940s, with critics comparing him to William Faulkner, Franz Kafka, and Albert Camus. He died at the age of thirty-one.

J. M. G. LE CLÉZIO, a French writer and professor, was awarded the Nobel Prize in Literature in 2008.

LAURIE THOMPSON is an academic and translator living in Wales. He is former editor of the *Swedish Book Review,* and his many translations include works by Henning Mankell, Håkan Nesser, and Mikael Niemi.